POLLY HERON

The Surplus Girls

CORVUS

First published in paperback in Great Britain in 2020 by Corvus,
an imprint of Atlantic Books Ltd.

10 9 8 7 6 5 4 3 2 1

A CIP catalogue record for this book is available from the British
Library.

Paperback ISBN: 978 1 78649 967 7
E-book ISBN: 978 1 78649 968 4

Printed in Great Britain

Corvus
An imprint of Atlantic Books Ltd
Ormond House
26–27 Boswell Street
London
WC1N 3JZ

www.corvus-books.co.uk

To the memory of John Copas (1940–2017).
Tarantara! tarantara!

And to Ron and Celia Dorrington, dear friends,
best of neighbours and surrogate parents.

Chapter One

Manchester, January 1922

'THERE'S NO CALL for you to visit the pie shop with the others, Miss Layton.' Mr Butterfield's tone was casual, but the brief flicker in his hooded eyes was anything but indifferent and Belinda felt a dip of dismay in the pit of her stomach. 'I know Mrs Sloan won't have sent you out this morning without your midday snap.'

'I could do with a spot of fresh air.' Why had she run downstairs? Where were the others? She edged nearer the door. Better to wait outside in the mill-yard even on a bitter day like today than to be backed into a grubby corner by Butterfingers. Shifting her shoulders beneath her woollen shawl, she made a show of gazing at her bare hands. 'I've forgotten my gloves. I'll nip back up.'

'They're sticking out of your skirt-pocket.'

Drat. She tugged them out and put them on, pushing them down into the gaps between her fingers with as much care as if they were kid gloves that fitted like a second skin instead of having been knitted by Grandma Beattie from an old cardigan she had unravelled.

Mr Butterfield moved closer; she stepped towards the door. He frowned and smiled at the same time, a pretend-humorous expression that questioned her silly reaction to his perfectly normal behaviour. She reached for the door-knob; her woolly glove slithered round it. Mr Butterfield stretched out his hand. He wore gloves without fingertips; there was a line of dirt beneath each nail and the ends of the pointing finger and middle finger on his right hand were a dull tobacco-yellow. He was much taller than her five foot two.

His hand stopped in mid-air. 'I were only going to open the door for you since it appears to be stuck. Why?' There was a triumphant smirk about his lips, there and gone so swiftly it might never have existed. A bland smile replaced it. 'What did you think I was going to do?'

The others clattered down the wooden staircase. Belinda glanced their way and when she looked back, Mr Butterfield was a couple of yards away. Her knees felt watery with relief – but only for a moment. Annoyance flared. It was horrible having to put up with Butterfingers, but they had no choice. As one of the tattlers, he was important. If someone was off sick, he could offer a day's work to one of the desperate souls who lurked outside the gates from the crack of dawn every weekday morning; and if someone left the mill, he chose which weaver took their place and which moved into the vacant slot left behind. Eh, they were powerful men, the tattlers. And they were all men. There was no such thing as a woman-tattler. Not now the war was over and the women weren't needed any more.

'There you are.' Buxom and keen-eyed, Maggie was in the lead.

The knot of women drew Belinda in. Crossing the lobby with its depressing smell of floorboards and low pay, they burst into the mill-yard. The January morning – well, it was afternoon now, just turned – was only slightly less raw than it had been first thing and the wind, as they marched along the street, was sharp as a knife. Normally, Belinda preferred to wait outside the pie shop since she never bought anything, but today she sneaked indoors for warmth. A mixture of delicious aromas wrapped round her, setting her tummy rumbling:

pastry, mince-and-onions and the bacony, mustardy smell of devilled chicken puddings that would form a savoury treat for some lucky families later. Grandma Beattie's fish-paste barm cake suddenly seemed unappetising – oh, what a disloyal thing to think. Shame on you, Belinda Layton. Disloyal was the last thing she was. The past four years had proved that.

Her companions chose their handheld pies, selecting the cheaper ones, cheese-and-onion, curried vegetables, suet-and-veg. Coins chinked and the shop-owner and the copper-haired girl who worked with him handed white paper bags over the counter. Then everyone scurried back up the street and through the tall gates into the mill-yard. The banks of grimy windows made the mill an unwelcoming place.

Jostling good-naturedly to get out of the cold, they hurried upstairs to the canteen, which was a grand name for a long, draughty room. They were glad enough of the draughts on weekdays when the mill was working full tilt and the hot, humid atmosphere left everyone gasping for breath, but on Saturdays, especially winter Saturdays, the draughts nipped fiercely, no matter how much hot tea you supped to keep them at bay.

Steaming mugs were handed round, then everyone plonked themselves on the benches and tucked in.

'Didn't them devilled chicken puds smell heavenly?' said Annie.

A chorus of agreement was mumbled through mouths filled with pasties.

'I might get a couple to take round to Mum's...' Belinda began.

'No, you don't, lady.' Annie spoke so sharply that pastry crumbs flew out of her mouth. 'It's not your job to feed them kids. It's your dad's.'

'Leave her alone,' said Maggie. 'But don't forget, love,' she advised Belinda, 'it's because of you that your family had a good Christmas.'

'Not just because of me...'

3

'Yes, because of you.' Even though she was hard of hearing after her years in the mill, Maggie didn't speak unnaturally loudly the way a lot of the women did. 'You're the one what came here every Saturday for two months and saved all the money so yon young 'uns got more than a sugar mouse on Christmas morning and your mum got a capon with all the trimmings.'

Belinda shrugged. 'I wanted to.'

'I know, and now it's time to spend a few coppers on yourself.' Maggie gave her a look. 'That's what your Auntie Enid's expecting.'

Belinda warmed to the older woman. She owed Maggie a lot. It was Maggie who had helped Auntie Enid get her this job at the mill when she moved in with her and Grandma Beattie; and, a few weeks back, it was Maggie who talked Auntie Enid into letting her work the Saturdays leading up to Christmas. Auntie Enid and Grandma Beattie would never have allowed it if Maggie hadn't stuck her oar in. When Belinda had gone to live with them back in 1916, Auntie Enid had made promises to Mum, one of which had been no Saturday cleaning. That had seemed to matter to Mum more than anything, though it hadn't stopped her accepting the Christmas goodies that had come her way.

Maggie raised her eyebrows and Belinda laughed, giving in.

'Yes, Auntie Enid expects me to treat myself.'

'Come Monday morning, I'll want to know what you bought.'

'That's easy. I'd like material to make a new blouse.'

'I'm pleased to hear it, lass. What colour?'

A flush crept across her cheeks. 'I haven't decided.' Hadn't built up the courage, more like. She knew what she would like, but would she dare?

Maggie patted her hand, then left her alone. That was one of the good things about Maggie. She never pressed you. Or did she need to be pressed? Deep down, did she want to be? Oh, heck.

She finished her barm cake and helped wash up the mugs. It was time to line up for their wages. Saturday cleaning was paid separately to the weekly wage. You cleaned all morning; then, while you ate your snap, the tattler checked the work and got the wages ready.

Queuing with the others, Belinda edged towards the front as those ahead of her received theirs. Mr Butterfield sat behind a table that did duty as a desk, courtesy of an ink-pot and a wooden pen-tray with grooves for pens and pencils. A ledger was open in front of him, a tin cash-box beside it.

'Name?' As if he didn't know.

'Belinda Layton.'

'Make your mark here.'

He always said that – as if the workers couldn't write. She signed her name, though what she felt like doing was scoring an indelible black X across his forehead. Make your mark, indeed! But her annoyance was short-lived. It was impossible not to be thrilled by the prospect of receiving of a whole two shillings and elevenpence for a morning's work. Two and eleven! You got a higher rate for Saturday cleaning. For the forty-eight hours she gave the mill Monday to Friday as a two-loom worker, she expected to earn twenty-six bob a week, give or take, which was sixpence ha'penny an hour. But on Saturdays, everyone got an extra tuppence one farthing per hour. Some said this was for working on the weekend, others that it was danger-money for hand-brushing the turning wheels to sweep off the floss. Belinda didn't care. It was wonderful to have been able to give her family a better Christmas.

Mr Butterfield reached into the cash-box and counted coins into his palm. The other tattlers didn't do that. They counted it straight into your hand, but Mr Butterfield held it out on his palm, obliging each woman to take it from him.

She had taken off her glove. With woolly gloves on, you couldn't pick up coins without fumbling, especially not a heap of coins like that. Did he really have to give her so much copper? Mr Butterfield wasn't looking at her; he was writing in his ledger. She reached towards his extended hand, wanting to scoop up her bounty in one go, but his fingers clamped around hers, squeezing her flesh into the edges of the small change. Her breath hitched and she tried to pull away. For one moment – just for one moment, as if maybe it hadn't really happened – he held tighter. He looked up into her eyes.

'I'm sorry, Miss Layton. I believe I've given you the wrong amount.'

He dropped his pen and twisted her hand the other way up so the coins lay in her palm. With one hand, he held hers in place while his other fingers sifted through the coins, his fingertips brushing against her skin as he moved each coin, one by one, from the heel of her thumb to the base of her fingers. Almost of its own accord, her hand tried to jerk free, but he held on.

'Careful, Miss Layton. You don't want to send your hard-earned wages flying all over the floor. I wouldn't be able to reimburse you if you lost any... And thruppence makes two shillings... and thruppence, sixpence, sevenpence, eightpence, eightpence ha'penny, ninepence, ninepence ha'penny, nine-pence three farthings, tenpence, tenpence one farthing...two farthings... three farthings... elevenpence. Two shillings and elevenpence in total. No mistake after all.'

She wrenched her hand away, clutching the money, forcing herself to clutch it when she felt more like flinging it away because it was tainted. Her eyes filmed with tears. It wasn't the money that was tainted. It was her hand. Switching the coins to her other hand, she wiped the hand he had held across the side of her skirt, brushing past the rest of the queue as she marched out.

She didn't stop until she was in the mill-yard. Only then did she pull out her purse and thrust her wages inside, snapping it shut.

'You all right, love?' It was Annie, eyes narrowing as she fixed her gaze on Belinda's.

Take a breath and smile. 'I'm fine. Butterfingers grabbed my hand, that's all.'

'Could have been a lot worse.'

She felt stung. Was she meant to be grateful that Mr Butterfield had 'only' played with the palm of her hand? Distaste wriggled inside her, but there was no point in dwelling on it. They all knew what Butterfingers was like. Should she keep her gloves on next time? Or would that simply spin out the process, as her wool-encased fingers struggled to take the money?

There probably wouldn't be a next time. Auntie Enid had only agreed to her working Saturdays in November and December so as to give the Laytons a better Christmas. Today, the first Saturday of January, she had been allowed to work the extra four hours, thanks to Maggie's influence, so as to have something to spend on herself.

'Don't let on to your mum and dad about it,' Maggie had said, advice that made Belinda's throat thicken with shame, the more so because she knew it must be what Auntie Enid thought as well. Auntie Enid and Grandma Beattie were always polite about the Laytons, but what did they say behind Belinda's back?

'Off to fritter your ill-gotten gains, love?' It was Flo, one of the three-loomers. 'Lucky you, able to spend it on yourself. Some of us have no sooner got us mitts on it than it vanishes down the children's throats.'

'Better that than down your old man's throat in't pub,' said Maggie. 'You go and enjoy your money, love. I'll ask you on Monday, mind, what you bought.'

'I already told you: blouse material. You never know, if I spend all weekend making it, you won't need to ask. You'll see for yourself.'

'I hope not, lass. I hope it'll be too pretty to wear for work.'

She chewed her lip. Could she? Was it time? Oh, heck.

A spiteful breeze caught Belinda's breath and whipped across her cheeks as she swung round the corner by the newsagent's, nimbly skirting the sandwich-board with its wonky black capitals about poor Sir Ernest Shackleton. In the tightly packed square where the weekly market was under way, the cobbles were slippery. The earthy aroma of winter vegetables bounced out at her, merging with the mouth-watering smell of sausage-meat cooked in sage and the heavy, burnt sweetness of treacle toffee. Alongside the cries of the stallholders calling their wares was the scrape and clink of pieces of china and the whirr and spark of the knife-grinder's wheel. Better-off housewives had their own knife-sharpeners, so it was the less well-off who queued for his services, though not the poorest, who sharpened their knives against the corner of a brick wall.

She rounded the corner by the ironmongery stall, with its array of pots and pans hanging up and all those different-sized nails and screws in little cardboard boxes laid out on the trestle-table. The draper's was along this row.

'Belinda – Belinda Layton! I thought it was you.'

She felt a burst of pleasure at the sight of her old school-teacher, followed by a rush of concern. Miss Kirby had a pinched look about her. Well, didn't everyone these days? First the war, then the influenza, and Miss Kirby wasn't a young woman. Everyone was tired and in need of a pick-me-up. But this was the beginning of a new year. New year, new hope.

'How are you, Miss Kirby?'

'Fair to middling. I'm retired now. I was well past the age, though I'd gladly have carried on.'

'Why didn't you?'

'Oh, the usual reason these days. A returning soldier needed a teaching post. Anyway, I'm sorry: I shouldn't call you Belinda Layton, should I?' Her eyes swept over Belinda's apparel, black from head to foot. 'I did hear – oh, ages ago; several years ago – that you'd got engaged. You can't have been married long before... I'm sorry for your loss.'

Chill streamed up her nostrils and down her throat. Her lungs went cold, then hot. She released a quick breath. It appeared in front of her, a huff of white cloud, like a cat-sneeze. She had never worked out what to say at these moments. Fortunately they seldom happened these days. A devil in her head pointed out that since she hadn't seen Miss Kirby since she left school, she wasn't likely to bump into her again, so why correct the mistake? Why not be a widow just for a few minutes? After all, it was what she was, really and truly.

Except for not having Ben's ring on her finger; except for not having his name. Belinda Sloan. That was who she should have been.

But she didn't want to tell lies. With all the troubles in her parents' home, all the bickering and her brothers running wild, it was important to conduct herself correctly, not just to set a good example to the boys, but because it was the right thing to do. She was – it shamed her to think it, but she was – better than the Laytons. When Ben's mother and grandmother had taken her in, they had lifted her not just into a cleaner, more pleasant home, but also into a more ordered way of life. She would be grateful to them to her dying day.

So: no lies. Especially, she couldn't lie to Miss Kirby, who had been so good to her, who had tried hard on her behalf.

'I did get engaged, but he... he were killed before we could get wed.'

'I'm sorry to hear that.' Miss Kirby sighed, shaking her head. 'It was just that, seeing you in full black, I thought... Anyway, I'm sorry.'

Please don't say: You're young. You'll meet someone else.

Miss Kirby said, 'What a shame you didn't go to high school.'

Raw air swooped into her eyes as they widened in surprise.

'It's true,' said Miss Kirby. 'Without a husband to rely on, you'd be in a stronger position with some education behind you. Think of the job you could have got.'

She didn't know what to say. 'I'm well suited where I am.'

'And where is that?' It was an honest question, not a snide remark.

'I'm a mill-worker.'

Miss Kirby's lined features took on the blank politeness of resignation. And just like that, they were back on the brink of whatever it was that she had seen in Belinda when she was a child of ten; only it hadn't been resignation on Miss Kirby's face then. There had been anxious determination in the furrowed brow and the steady, quiet voice.

'Your Belinda's different. She's bright.'

Miss Kirby had actually come to their house – sometimes it was hard to remember that the Laytons had lived in a house back then; a modest two-up two-down that seemed like a palace compared to the squalid couple of rooms they were crammed into these days. Miss Kirby had come to plead for her star pupil to be granted this potentially life-changing opportunity.

'Let her sit the scholarship. Let her go to high school. She'll pass, I'm sure she will.'

Listening, crouched on the other side of the door, Belinda had felt a moment of glory. Her heart drummed in her chest and she felt more awake, more alert. But she had known permission wouldn't be granted and, truth be told, she wasn't disappointed, not really. She had gorged on Angela Brazil books in those days, but when faced by the dazzling possibility of rubbing shoulders with girls called Philippa and Katrine, who got up to larks and had private art lessons and were captains of tennis, she knew she would die a thousand deaths if she fetched up in a place like that. What, a back-street lass stopping on at school till fifteen? Alongside girls whose fathers were doctors and senior clerks and owners of the better class of shops? Not on your life. Or not on Dad's life, anyroad, and his was the word that counted.

'Nay, miss,' he had told Miss Kirby. 'Our Belinda's the eldest. I need her out working. She'll stop at the elementary school, go to work half-time when she's twelve and leave when she's thirteen, and that's flat.'

'If she goes to high school, she'll get a better job.' Miss Kirby had managed to say the words *and bring more money home* without uttering them out loud.

'No point,' said Dad. 'She'll only get herself engaged and get wed. That's what girls do.'

And he had been proved right, hadn't he? She and Ben had had an understanding when she was just fourteen and had been allowed to get engaged when she was fifteen.

'A mill-worker?' There was no scorn in Miss Kirby's voice, only kindness. That was worse, because it felt like pity. 'That's hard work.'

'It's regular.' If she hadn't been talking to her old teacher, she might have jerked her chin in open annoyance. 'Skilled an' all. I could work my way up to six looms if I stay.'

'That's the point, my dear. You've got to work. You're a surplus girl.'

'A what?'

'A surplus girl. That's what they're being called. With so many of our young men having lost their lives in the war, there's now a generation of girls with no men to marry them.'

She bridled. 'I'm not looking for another husband. Ben were the only boy for me.'

'I didn't mean to give offence. My point is that surplus girls face a lifetime of fending for themselves. What education, what training, do they have under their belts to equip them for that?'

'I've been trained.'

'You're being deliberately obtuse, my girl. Yes, one day you might run six looms. I'm not underestimating the skill that takes, but – oh, Belinda, with the right education, you could have been an office girl. You could have started as the office junior and by now you'd be adept at typewriting and filing and the correct layout of business letters. You could be training up your own office junior. Goodness, a clever girl like you could have learned to keep the books.'

'Anyroad, I'm at the mill.' She might not have greeted Miss Kirby so warmly had she known she was going to get a lecture.

'I know. It's no use fretting over what might have been.'

Belinda laughed and then smiled because the laugh might have sounded bitter and she didn't want to give the wrong impression. 'There's no might-have-been about an office job. That was never going to be. I knew Dad would never let me try for high school. The only might-have-been I care about—' She stopped, clawing in a deep breath to stop her chest caving in.

'I know,' Miss Kirby said softly. 'I'm sorry if I've upset you. I'd best let you get on. It was good to see you again.'

'You an' all, Miss Kirby.'

But instead of being glad to see the back of her old teacher, she felt a stab of guilt. This dear lady had done her best for her and didn't deserve to walk away thinking she was hurt.

'Wait a minute.' Belinda went after her. 'Would you like to help me choose blouse material?'

The light in Miss Kirby's face was reward enough. 'I'd be delighted, if you're sure.'

Bolts of fabric were laid out across the stall, with boxes of cotton-reels, ribbons and buttons at one end, and pin-cushions (fancy not making your own!) and sewing-boxes at the back. At one end of the stall was a pyramid of bolts of blacks and mauves, just as there had been for as long as Belinda could remember, though the pyramid had been significantly bulkier since the outbreak of war. Surely it must reduce in size now that the influenza epidemic was behind them. Surely.

'What sort of fabric are you looking for?' Miss Kirby asked.

She pretended not to notice the glance that swept over her all-consuming black. 'Well…'

'Will it be more black? I'm sorry, dear, but I have to ask if I'm to be of any assistance. How long ago were you bereaved? I assume your young man was taken by the influenza.'

She drew her shawl more tightly round herself. 'No, he was killed in France at the start of 1918. Four years ago this month.'

'Four years? And you're still in deepest black. You must have loved him very much.'

Oh, heck, now Miss Kirby thought she was some latter-day Queen Victoria type. Yes, she had loved Ben with all her heart, but… but… It wasn't that simple. She took off her gloves and ran her fingers over some of the materials, testing texture and drape.

'What are you looking for today?' Miss Kirby's voice was gentle.

Go on, say it. You've been thinking it for long enough. 'I've been wondering…' Oh, Auntie Enid and Grandma Beattie were going to kill her for this. 'Something in mauve, not an entire blouse, but with mauve trimmings.'

'You're going into half-mourning. Don't look so stricken. I can see this is hard for you.'

Aye, but not for the reason Miss Kirby imagined. Belinda felt a complete heel. In spite of the chilly afternoon, her flesh felt hot and prickly.

'What about a mauve collar and cuffs?' Miss Kirby dealt her a sharp, though not unkind, look. 'That's pretty material, isn't it? Your hand keeps going back to it, even though you're meant to be choosing mauve.'

'Oh – this. No, really, I...'

Oh, but it was heavenly. Her colour-starved soul yearned for it. Rose-pink cotton scattered with a pattern of tiny rosebuds in darker pink with green leaves. It would be perfect with her colouring, dark brown hair, blue eyes. Imagine wearing something pretty, something flattering, instead of endless black.

'I'll have some of that mauve,' she said briskly. 'As you say, collar and cuffs.'

'You might try lavender, my dear, if you'd like something... prettier.'

'I always feel sorry for lavender matched with black. Mauve looks like it can hold its own better.' She took a breath. 'I have a blouse pattern with panels in the front so you can have contrasting fabric, so I'll need mauve for that as well as the collar and cuffs.' There, she had said it. Never mind all her shilly-shallying.

Her purchase made, she felt torn between pleasure and panic.

'Thanks for your help, Miss Kirby.'

'A pleasure.'

Turning from the stall, they began to walk away, avoiding an old girl carrying a sagging bag made of sack-cloth. Without planning to, Belinda stopped dead.

'Wait.'

She returned to the stall, heart pumping. Mauve wasn't what she wanted. She had dreamed of colour. She was sick of black.

Her hand trailed across the pink. It was a deep pink, a serious pink, not pale, not too summery, and the pattern was small, not too frivolous. Was she wrong to want it? Want it?

She ached for it.

If it was bad of her to buy the mauve, what sort of person was she to want this?

But she didn't have to make it up immediately, did she? She could start with the mauve and give Auntie Enid and Grandma Beattie time to grow used to it; then, at a later date, she could suggest having a colour. Tension held her taut; her muscles felt sore. She tried to roll her shoulders inside her shawl without making it obvious.

'It would suit you with your dark hair and fair skin,' said Miss Kirby.

'That's what I thought.' Was she really going to do this? She had worn black for four years. Four whole years. Her fingers curled into fists, then straightened. She caught the stallholder's eye. 'How wide it is, please?'

Moments later, she had a second paper bag tucked under her shawl, but there was no time to think about what she had done, because from behind her came a yell followed by the clatter of running footsteps. She glanced round – oh no, not them. As they barged past, Miss Kirby staggered and Belinda was a second too late to save her from falling. Her parcels dropped to the cobbles as she bent to help Miss Kirby to her feet.

'Are you all right?'

'Yes, thank you, just shocked.'

Folk gathered round. The draper came from behind her stall.

'Are you hurt?' voices asked. 'Did you see them lads? I'd tan their hides if they were mine.'

Miss Kirby's face had lost its colour, but there was a glint in her eyes as she met Belinda's gaze. 'Was that who I think it was?'

Oh, heck.

Chapter Two

SHE HAD LIVED here once, in squalid Cromwell Street. Simply walking up the road was enough to set little spikes of fear jumping beneath Belinda's skin. What if everything went wrong and she ended up back here? Things did go wrong. She was living proof. Look at her, losing Ben. Life could be cruel.

Not that she was one to complain. She wasn't like her father.

She arrived outside the house the Laytons squeezed into along with three other families. Dad blamed the war for the way they had come down in the world, but the truth was they had lived here before it started. Belinda could remember the gradual slide that had happened while she was in elementary school: Dad losing his job and finding another, only it hadn't paid as well; then losing that job and the family taking another step down the ladder. The scrimping and saving; the first time she was sent to the grocer's to ask for cracked eggs. The first time there was meat on Dad's plate but not on the children's. The first time she lied to the rent-man about Mum not being in the house when really she was hiding under the kitchen table. The time she looked at the sour-smelling, gaunt-faced children who took turns to come to school because they shared clothes with their brothers and sisters, and instead of the usual sneering pity, she felt dread streaming through her: *what if we end up like that?*

Things had changed between Mum and Dad. There had always been arguments, but now there was constant carping and bickering. It hadn't all been bickering, though. There had been plenty of making up afterwards. Oh aye, Denby and Kathleen Layton, who had had just three children between 1901 and '06, fell for three boys in two years. Two years! Twenty-three months, to be exact.

Belinda had not long turned seven when Thad was born. She had been thrilled to have a baby to look after; but by the time Jacob came along twenty-three months later, with Mikey in between, she was sick of babies. As the oldest, and even more so because the second-oldest was a boy, she had become a nursemaid; and if she complained, Mum would give her a thick ear and set her to mop the floor or fill the coal-scuttle.

'It's how girls learn,' said Mum.

She had learned a great deal in the next few years.

The time came when the family did a moonlight flit and went to their new home. It had never felt like home. Two rooms in a house bulging with people, mould and bad temper, with smelly, sticky fly-paper dangling everywhere, covered with houseflies and bluebottles, a single stinking privy out the back, and if one person came home with a flea or if one person had diarrhoea...

How could somewhere you were ashamed of be home? If they had been a happy family struggling to get by but making the best of things, it might have been different, but not with Mum and Dad at it hammer and tongs because Dad had raided the housekeeping jar again, and Thad giving Mikey a good kicking in bed and swearing he had done it in his sleep, and the girls complaining bitterly about the lack of privacy on bath-night, and all of them digging their elbows into one another, not always by accident, because there wasn't enough room to swing a cat.

Please don't let me ever have to come back to live here.

The gate, its wood rotten at the bottom, lolled from one hinge, permanently wide open. From gate to doorstep was only a yard, but that would have been room for a tub or two of plants or herbs under the windows, if anybody could have been bothered. But no one could be bothered, the same way the front step hadn't been donkey-stoned in years. Mum had done it when they first moved in, but then she got fed up of being the only one and had stopped.

As she let herself into the narrow hallway, Belinda's skin tightened over her bones so as to have less surface area to feel unclean. Entering the kitchen-cum-sitting room, she pinned on a smile.

The room was damp: it always was, but it was worse in winter. The pulley-airer was full and there was a clothes-horse that was undoubtedly meant to be stationed round the fireplace, only Dad had shifted it and was now ensconced in their one armchair by the hearth, with half of the newspaper, while George, wearing the pullover Belinda had knitted him for Christmas, sat hunched over one end of the table, reading the other half and steadfastly ignoring Mum, who, eyes weary, mouth sullen, was using the rest of the table for ironing. They had had an ironing-board once upon a time, but it had had to go, one in a long line of things that had had to go, because Mum had needed a few bob and, anyroad, they didn't have room. Mum looked like she was bashing the clothes rather than pressing them: Sarah was going to get an earful when she showed her face. Ironing was her job, just as it had once been Belinda's.

Mikey crouched on the hearthrug at Dad's feet, bent over something he was constructing out of matchsticks. He would have to defend it with his life if he intended it to last longer than two minutes after Thad returned.

Had her smile slipped? She hitched it higher.

'It's only me.'

'Shut the door,' said Dad. 'You're letting the warm out.'

She draped her shawl over the back of a chair, depositing her paper bags by the door before taking the iron from Mum.

'Let me help.'

'That's our Sarah's job.'

'Then I'll help both of you. Where is she?'

'Lord knows. Not where she should be: here, seeing to the ironing. Lazy cat, leaving it to me.'

'She's not lazy. She puts in long hours cleaning that hotel and she's on her feet the whole time, either that or on her knees.'

'Trust you to stick up for her.'

There was no talking to Mum in this mood. Belinda took the cooling iron from Mum's hand and popped it onto the iron hob on the range to heat up again, picking up the hot one.

'Take the weight off your feet, Mum. I'll make us all a pot of tea in a minute.'

'About time someone did,' George said without looking up.

Mum heaved a dramatic put-upon sigh and grabbed the kettle.

'Saint flaming Kathleen,' Dad muttered. He crushed the newspaper into his lap. 'Let our Bel do it, for Pete's sake. She does little enough else for us.'

Belinda's mouth dropped open. Had he forgotten already? The capon, the presents, the tin of Mackintosh's Toffee de Luxe – de Luxe, mind – the crackers, the box of dates.

'Steady on, Dad,' said George.

'Oh – aye.' He had the grace to look shame-faced. No, he didn't. That sideways glance was sly. 'At the mill this morning, were you?'

'Yes, Dad.'

'Give us your money, then. It's not needed for Christmas now.'

Her heart lurched. Would he force her? 'Auntie Enid said I could keep it for myself.'

'Easy for her to say. She hasn't got family responsibilities.'

'Nay, leave her be, Denby.' Mum perked up, the washed-out drudge transformed into a straight-backed lionheart. 'She spent all her Saturday money to give us a good Christmas. The least we can do is let her keep this one week's. I don't suppose Mrs Sloan will let her do any more Saturdays.'

'No, she won't.' Belinda threw her a grateful look.

'Whose side are you on?' Dad demanded. 'I'm the one with mouths to feed. It's not as if Bel has a husband and children at home.'

She flinched. How could he hurl that at her?

'Oh aye,' Mum taunted, 'and you'd use her money to top up the housekeeping, would you? I weren't born yesterday. What you didn't waste over the bar, you'd lose on the horses.'

Dad roared to his feet, scattering sheets of newspaper, and then they were at it, him bellowing and Mum shrieking like a fishwife. Belinda's energy seeped out of her. An all-out row like this made her mind freeze.

The door crashed open and Thad burst in, followed awkwardly by Jacob, clutching a half-full sack, their arrival cramming the already crowded room still further. George stuffed his fingers in his ears and bent closer to the newspaper. Belinda stood the iron on its end on the trivet, keeping hold of the handle in case she got jostled.

Thad gave his parents a filthy look. 'Ruddy hell, another barney.'

Mum and Dad stopped rowing and turned angry faces on the newcomers.

'I want a word with you,' said Belinda. Did she sound like just another loud-mouthed Layton? But she couldn't let Thad get away with his behaviour in the market. With luck Jacob might see that Thad's wasn't the best lead to follow.

'Have you brought us owt this week?' Thad demanded.

Was that all she was to her family? The goose that laid the golden eggs? She stepped across to confront Thad. He might be taller than she was these days, but he was still a schoolboy in short trousers. Not for much longer, though. He would finish school the summer of next year.

'I was there in the market when you two came racing through like a pair of hooligans, barging past all and sundry. Do you know who that lady was that you knocked down?'

'We never knocked no one down.' Thad gave a cocky sneer.

'You jolly well did – and don't answer back. You knocked over Miss Kirby, that's who.'

'Oh, her,' said Thad. 'The stupid old bag shouldn't have got in our way.'

'Miss Kirby from school?' asked Mum.

Dad snorted. 'Interfering so-and-so, trying to tell me how to run my family.'

'That was years ago,' said Belinda. 'She's older now and she's retired – and these two ran hell for leather through the market, bowled her over and didn't stop.'

'Who cares?'

Turning on his heel, Thad shoved Jacob, but Jacob, unprepared for a quick exit, stumbled and the two of them got tangled up. Jacob lost his grip on the neck of the sack. It slipped from his grasp, hitting the floor with a smashing sound.

Everyone froze; then Dad's hand landed on Jacob's shoulder. Belinda dodged aside so as not to get clouted by accident: it wouldn't have been the first time.

'What's in here, then?' Dad flicked at the sack with his toe.

'N-nothing,' stammered Jacob.

He danced aside as Dad swooped on the sack, upending it and scattering pieces of china on the bare floorboards. There was a rectangular lid painted with ivy leaves, still in one piece but with a crack across the middle; and bits and pieces of what must be the matching dish.

Belinda went hot and cold. 'You've been thieving. No wonder you were running like that. You were running away.'

'Nah,' drawled Thad. 'It were payment – weren't it, Jake? We helped a stallholder and he gave us this to pay us.'

'Rubbish.' George stood up at last. 'Firstly, no stallholder ever gave a piece of china as payment; and secondly, when did you ever do anything to help anyone? You nicked it.'

Dad landed a sharp crack across the side of Thad's head followed by a hefty slap that Jacob didn't manage to dodge. He yelled and sank down the wall, crying, but Thad was made of sterner stuff. Nursing the side of his face, he jutted out his jaw defiantly.

'To think that any lads of mine...' Mum pressed her hand to her chest.

'And what good is that to us now?' Dad kicked at the pieces of china. 'I can't sell it in that state, can I? It's no damn use to me.'

'Dad!' Belinda exclaimed. 'You can't punish them for stealing and then complain you can't sell things on. What sort of example is that?'

'Don't you speak to me like that, telling me what's what under my own roof. Go and lay the law down with your precious Auntie Enid if you want to lecture somebody, but don't try it on with me. Is that clear?'

'Is that clear, our Bel?' added Thad in a soft sing-song.

How had that happened? Thad and Jacob had committed theft, but she was the one getting it in the neck. By, there were times when she felt that she, George and Sarah were one family and the young lads were quite another.

'I think I'd best go,' she said.

'She thinks she'd best go,' mocked Thad.

George gave him a clip round the ear. It should have come from Dad, but at least it had come from someone.

'You two boys can get lost an' all.' Dad flopped into the armchair. 'Don't come back till teatime.'

'Suits me,' said Thad, 'but before we go...'

He trampled on Mikey's matchstick construction. With an indignant yell, Mikey snatched at his ankle, yanked hard and brought him toppling down. With a series of mighty kicks, Thad jerked free, aiming a few kicks at Mikey's head. With a bellow, Dad was on his feet. He wasn't a big man, but he picked up his brawling sons and flung them into the hallway, with Jacob scrambling after them. He slammed the door, muttering darkly.

There was a heated silence. Belinda gathered up the folded ironing and took it into the bedroom, flicking aside the tatty old sheet that was strung across the room to give a semblance of privacy to the sleeping arrangements, Mum and Dad on one side, George and two younger boys in the other bed with the third lad sleeping on a mat on the floor on a rotation basis. Poor Sarah had to make do with a straw-filled mattress in the other room and no matter what shifts she worked in the hotel, she could never lie down to sleep when their kitchen-cum-sitting room was in use.

Belinda laid the ironed garments on Mum and Dad's bed, looking round as Mum followed her into the room.

'Thanks for sticking up for me against Dad. I'd have pretended I hadn't worked this morning if I'd known he was going to ask for my money.'

'That's all right, love. We both know he'd only waste it.' Mum edged closer. Her tongue flicked out and licked her lips. 'But you can let me have some, can't you? I only stopped him so you could give it to me.'

It was dark before Belinda reached home. Some folk made a show of shuddering when she said she lived near Stretford Cemetery, but that was just them being daft. Their cottage was

23

at the far end of a row down an unpaved lane, no more than a cinder path, and once you got halfway down, it wasn't even that, just a dirt-track that turned to slop after a few days of solid rain. The lane had no board at the top with a road name, but it was known locally as Grave Pit Lane. Everyone knew it as that. Ben's letters, addressed to *End Cottage, Grave Pit Lane, Stretford*, had all arrived.

The telegram had arrived.

As she approached End Cottage, Belinda's heart lifted at the welcome sight of the lamplight's soft glow behind the thin curtains. If you thought about it, the cottage was nowt special. It had low doorways and low ceilings, which had made Ben and his ma and his nan joke the first time she visited them there that it was a good job she was nobbut five foot two; and it had no indoor pipes, just a water pump out the back, and candles and oil-lamps instead of gas-light. The rooms were small and the upstairs floors sloped, so that if you hauled yourself out of bed before you were properly awake, you stumbled about like a drunken sailor.

So no, it was nowt special.

But at the same time, it was the best place in the world; even more so after a visit to Cromwell Street.

Chilled through, Belinda let herself in, gloved fingers fumbling with the catch, but being cold became a pleasure of sorts as the mingled smells of onion and ginger enveloped her. She knew what that meant: poor man's pudding, which was like toad-in-the-hole but with onions and potato instead of sausage, followed by ginger pudding and custard.

She hung up her shawl on the peg inside the door. The paper parcels with her pieces of fabric felt vaguely damp. She slid them onto the shelf where they kept the clothes brush. It wouldn't be tactful to come barging in with them. Say hello first. Take your time.

Coward.

Grandma Beattie looked over her shoulder from where she stood in front of the range. It was a colossal beast that ate up most of one wall and took an age to blacklead, but, properly tended, it kept the cottage toasty-warm in winter. A dumpy woman all in black, Grandma Beattie was of an age to wear a headdress at all times, even indoors, and her iron-grey hair had a modest covering of black lace – well, it wasn't really lace, just some fine black cotton that she had tatted in a loose pattern.

Belinda went to her, slipping an arm round her ample frame. 'Grandma Beattie, have I told you recently that you're an angel?'

'Get on with you. I knew you'd need summat hot inside you on a day like today.'

Auntie Enid smiled across from the cramped window-seat, where she was knitting scarves for the poor by the light of an oil-lamp. The Sloan household might not be well off, but never let it be said they didn't do their Christian duty. The scarf dangling from her needles was a rich royal blue, which, in the golden glow from the lamp, was jewel-coloured compared to Auntie Enid's black garb, the black crêpe on the over-mantle shelf and the black fabric draped around the treasured studio portrait of Ben.

'Don't put your shawl on the peg, love,' said Auntie Enid. 'Hang it over a chair by the range. It must be damp.'

Lifting a chair closer to the range, Belinda fetched her shawl. She glanced at the parcels. Now was the moment. She braced herself. They would be disappointed, of course they would. Hurt, even, and she didn't want to hurt them. She slid the parcel with the mauve into the folds of her shawl and returned to the range. All she had to do was produce the parcel and say, 'Look what I bought. I hope you don't mind, but…'

Grandma Beattie bent to open the oven door, sliding the dish inside, careful not to spill batter. Heat poured into the room.

'There.' She straightened up. 'Did you buy yourself summat, lovey?'

Playing for time, she draped her shawl over the chair, easing the parcel out of sight under it on the seat as craftily as any magician.

'You've been out all afternoon,' said Auntie Enid, 'and you're not the sort to spend all that time trailing round the shops. I expect you went round your mum's, didn't you?'

'Yes.' *And to the market. I bought—*

'I bet you gave your mum some money an' all,' said Grandma Beattie.

'Well, yes.' There was still time to own up. Still time to produce the parcel.

'There, we said she would, didn't we?' Grandma Beattie said in a pleased voice to Auntie Enid.

'Aye, we did. We knew you wouldn't get owt for yourself.' Setting aside her knitting, Auntie Enid rose, her thin face with its hollow cheeks and lined mouth softening into a smile. 'That's why we decided to give you this now.'

What? A gift? She couldn't produce her parcel now, not if she was about to receive something. But she could reveal it afterwards. Make a fuss of the gift, then half-laugh, perhaps blush, and say, 'Actually...'

Auntie Enid reached under her knitting bag. 'Here. This is for you.'

Belinda saw what it was and her hand faltered. A photograph of Ben, a copy of the studio portrait on the over-mantel shelf, but with a black crêpe sleeve over it with a window in the material to display the picture. Fastened to the top right-hand corner of the sleeve was a red paper poppy. Poppies had been sold in November to mark Armistice Day and she, Auntie Enid and Grandma Beattie had each bought one, weeping as they pinned them to one another's clothes. The heavy thud of her heart was surprisingly calm. Auntie Enid held out the photograph and she took it in both hands. Less chance of dropping it.

'It's his anniversary in a day or two,' said Auntie Enid. There was a catch in her voice. She sniffed and carried on. 'Four whole years. We were worried about giving it to you on the day itself in case it got too emotional.'

'But with you supposedly buying yourself summat nice today, and us knowing you wouldn't,' said Grandma Beattie, 'this seemed the perfect day.'

Belinda swallowed. This was a generous, heartfelt gesture and she loved them for thinking of it. Her very own picture of Ben: she would treasure it. Yet after what she had purchased today…

'We got the idea when it were the anniversary of burying the body of the unknown soldier a few weeks back,' said Auntie Enid, 'and that's your poppy sewn on there. They're going to sell poppies every year from now on so, after every Armistice Day, when you take yours off, you can sew it onto the photograph-sleeve. Look, I made it slightly large, so you can add your poppies to it. What d'you think?'

Her stomach knotted. She raised her fingers to her throat, inside which a painful thickness threatened to suffocate her.

'Oh, the poor love,' said Grandma Beattie. 'She can't speak. She's too upset.'

No, too guilty. What would they think if they knew that while they had been busy planning this sentimental surprise, she had been planning – what had Miss Kirby called it? – to go into half-mourning? And, worse, she had bought a pretty patterned cotton an' all.

'Put it by your bed,' said Auntie Enid.

'Ben's face will be the first thing you see every morning,' said Grandma Beattie, 'and the last you see at night.' She sighed, adoration of her handsome grandson in the lingering breath.

'I've moved your library books aside to make room,' said Auntie Enid. 'Up you go.'

Carrying the precious photograph in one hand, she picked up her shawl in the other, bending over the chair to scoop up her parcel. Aware of their gaze lovingly following her every move, she managed to remove her other parcel from the shelf. The stairs were steep and her foot caught in her trailing shawl. An image swooped through her mind: the photograph falling – glass smashing – parcels tumbling down the stairs, working themselves open in the process – a splash of mauve and patterned pink. She righted herself and hurried to her room, a tiny space that used to be Ben's until she moved in.

'I'll sleep downstairs when I'm home,' he had said, leaving the words *and when we're married, we'll get somewhere of us own* dangling in the air between them.

The bed she slept in was Ben's bed, the cupboard she used was his, as was the small table, waiting now for Ben's picture so that she could have it at her side as she slept and when she woke. Oh, Ben. Old sorrow washed through her, a strangely sombre feeling, a stillness.

That was the point, wasn't it? She, Auntie Enid and Grandma Beattie had… stopped when the telegram came. All they had wanted, all they had hoped and prayed for, was his safe return and when that had been denied them, they had clung together, supporting one another in their desolation.

But their grief had never moved on. Four years later, they were still in deepest black. Maybe that was how it was when your son or grandson died; maybe you never got over it. She could understand that. But she, Ben's fiancée, much as she had loved him, dear and special as he would be to her until her dying day, she… she…

She owed Auntie Enid and Grandma Beattie so much. When she and Ben had started walking out, they had naturally wanted to know about her background. She had been careful what she said, not wanting to be disloyal to her family, but had Ben spoken more freely behind her back? Anyroad, when they got engaged, his ma had gone round to Cromwell Street and offered to take her in.

'It'll be easier on you, less of a squeeze, and it'll give me and Ben's nan a chance to get to know her properly. It's different for you, with several children, but with Ben being our only one, we want to feel close to his future wife.'

She had made it sound like they would be doing her an enormous favour. Oh, how wonderful it had been to move into End Cottage. Truth to tell, it wasn't all that much bigger than the two rooms the Laytons lived in, but the quiet and the orderliness had bestowed on Belinda such a sense of well-being that she had no desire to be anywhere else. It was the first time in her life she had had a room to herself, and who cared how small and cramped it was? It was perfect.

'Ben calls me Ma and you can call me that once you're wed,' Auntie Enid said to her on her first day, 'but until then I'll be your Auntie Enid. He calls his nan Grandma. You can call her Grandma Beattie.'

Auntie Enid, with Maggie's help, had got her taken on at the mill, so she had been rescued not just from her old squalid home but also from her old job, which she had found more of a strain by the day. Living with Auntie Enid and Grandma Beattie had made her feel grown up. She wasn't taken for granted or put upon. They treated her with affection and respect, listening to what she said and placing value on her because she was their Ben's choice.

She trailed her fingertips down the photograph. The black crêpe sleeve was a bit roomy, ready for sewing on more poppies over the years. One day, her lovely Ben would be surrounded by red paper poppies, the only splash of colour in his women-folk's swathed-in-black world. There would never be anyone else for her, but surely it wasn't wrong – after four long years, surely it wasn't wrong – to feel something inside her unfurling and looking forward to the coming springtime?

She owed Auntie Enid and Grandma Beattie so much and they had her undying gratitude.

But was she grateful enough to stay in deepest mourning for the rest of her days?

Chapter Three

'TELL ME ABOUT the material you bought on Saturday,' said Maggie. 'I hope you found summat fetching.'

Belinda glanced round. What if anyone overheard? But that was unlikely with the fent room being so noisy, as it was the last chance for spoken conversation before they went to their looms and the clatter of the machinery drowned out all other sound and mee-mawing took over. Women hung up their shawls and put on their sacking fents to protect their clothes.

'You're all in black still,' said Maggie. 'You're too young to look like a crow.' She brightened. 'Don't tell me. You found yourself some reet pretty stuff that's too good to wear for work.'

Was your conscience housed inside your chest? That was where Belinda felt a pang. Her gaze went to Auntie Enid, in a group a few feet away. She spoke close to Maggie's ear.

'I know you mean well, Mags, but leave it for now, eh? Please.'

Maggie wasn't stupid. She too glanced in Auntie Enid's direction. 'I'll have a word. I know what it cost her to lose her lad – God knows, I lost two of my own – but she can't keep you in widow's weeds for ever and a day.'

'Please don't say owt, Maggie.'

'Suit yourself.'

Maggie concentrated on tying her fent round her waist and filling the spacious pocket with the scissors and whatnot that she needed. Belinda felt guilty all over again. Now she had snubbed Maggie as well as going behind Auntie Enid's back.

Maggie was in a nowty mood most of the morning, which the others, muttering when they stopped for their mid-morning brew, put down to her having been landed with a new girl to train. Wanting to make it up to the friend who had always been good to her, Belinda offered to spend part of dinner-time helping Colleen practise the weavers' knots that she had to be able to do in her sleep.

'Ta ever so,' said Colleen as they left the canteen together. She was a scrawny fifteen-year-old with caramel-coloured marks on her skin, as if her freckles had merged into blotches. 'I don't think Mrs Sumner is happy with me.'

'It's nowt personal, but time taken teaching you is time her looms work slower, so her pay will go down. That's why you must pay attention and pick it up quick. Don't feel bad about it. We all start out as tenters. I was Maggie's tenter once, and she was a tenter herself years ago.'

Colleen's face screwed up. 'D'you mind if I nip to the lavvy before we start?'

She dashed off. That was another lesson she would learn. You didn't use the lavatory if you could avoid it. Most women had developed cast-iron bladders so they could hang on all day without using the facilities provided by the mill.

Waiting for her, Belinda picked up some pieces of wool, found a couple of stools and perched on one. Might as well take the weight off her feet; there was precious little opportunity to sit down during the day. A hand reached from behind her. For half a second, her eyes saw what they expected to see – Colleen's hand – before they snapped into focus and she found a gloved hand with cutaway fingertips about to land on her arm. She tried to jump off the stool but she was too late. Mr Butterfield was standing behind her and he had her forearm. His body was close to hers, pressed against her back.

'There now, is that what you've come for?'

She was frozen, her insides solid with revulsion and shame. Then she wrenched herself free and swung round to face him, breathing hard. There was a bitter tang in her mouth. He had no business touching her; he had no right. Only Ben should ever have touched her, only her lovely Ben. She wanted to shout at him, but how could she? He was the tattler.

'That's not fair.' He smirked. 'Coming in here, looking for attention, then playing hard to get.'

'I'm not playing anything. I've come to help the new tenter.'

'Oh aye? That's what it's called these days, is it?'

A movement caught her eye. 'Colleen! Over here.'

'Ready?' asked Colleen. 'Oh – Mr Butterfield. I'm sorry, sir. I didn't see you.'

'I'll leave you to get on with it,' said Mr Butterfield. He dropped his voice. 'Any time you need a spot of attention, Miss Layton...'

Humiliation made her body want to collapse in on itself, but she forced herself to stand up straight, trapping the sobs in her throat as Mr Butterfield strode away.

'You could have warned me,' said Colleen. Oh no, had Colleen seen Butterfingers lay hands on her? 'About the lavvy: you could have said summat. It's horrible. It stinks and it leaks.'

'Here, park yourself.' Belinda resumed her position on the stool. 'I'll show you and then we'll do it together.'

It was the oddest feeling, watching her clever fingers tying the same knot over and over again, and listening to her voice, not to the words as such, but to the patient tone. It was like she was standing a yard or two away, an observer who wasn't involved. All the while, her body was objecting to what had happened. Goodness knows, he had only touched her arm, but he shouldn't even have done that. It wasn't right. It wasn't decent. She felt peeled and vulnerable.

Was it her own fault for coming in here on her own? He would say she had asked for it. He would say that if all she wanted was to teach young Colleen her knots, she could have done it in a corner of the canteen. Oh, heck, she hadn't encouraged him, had she?

No, she mustn't fall into the trap of blaming herself. He would like that. He would use it against her, but she wasn't at fault. He was the one who had done wrong.

Imagine working in a place where you didn't have to keep your distance from the boss.

You could have been an office girl.

'I've got it muddled again,' said Colleen. 'I'll never get it right.'

'Yes, you will. Watch me, then you do it, one step at a time.'

Soon Colleen was beaming, her sense of achievement shining from her eyes. 'Thanks ever so. I wish you were teaching me instead of Mrs Sumner.'

'Only the six-loomers do the training. I'm a long way off that.'

'You'll get there one day, I'm sure. I can't think of owt finer than that.'

Oh aye, very fine, all those years ahead of her, dodging Mr Butterfield's wandering hands. She hadn't been supposed to stop in the mill indefinitely. It was meant to have been a decent job to see her through until she got married and started a family.

'Once we're wed, we'll save all your wages and live off mine,' had been Ben's plan. 'That way, it won't come as a shock money-wise when you give up work and we'll have a nice little nest-egg behind us.'

And here she was, still at the mill and looking like she would be here all her life, losing her hearing and possibly suffering from bad teeth. It happened to some women after years of kissing the shuttle. Even now, every time she sucked the thread through, she felt a nasty prickle of awareness.

You could have been an office girl.

Stop it. It was far too late to think of such things.

Was it?

She was much too old. Miss Kirby had said she could have started as an office junior, which meant she would have been fifteen, just leaving high school, so she was way past the right age; and of course, she never went to high school. No one would look at her for an office post.

Besides, how could she possibly leave the job that she owed to Auntie Enid? Auntie Enid and Grandma Beattie had done everything for her. Her life was immeasurably better, thanks to them.

You could have been an office girl.

Stop it. No point thinking like that. Drat Miss Kirby for putting daft ideas in her head.

As they jolted and swayed their way home on the tram through the cold, dark evening in which a fine drizzle shone in the glow cast by the street-lamps, the man on the seat in front of Belinda and Auntie Enid was reading the *Manchester Evening News*. When he got to his feet, he dropped the paper on the seat.

'Excuse me.' Auntie Enid leaned forwards. 'You've dropped your newspaper.'

'I've finished with it. Have it, if you like.' And off he went.

'What a disgrace, walking off and leaving his rubbish behind.'

Belinda reached over the back of the seat and picked it up. 'We'll have it.'

Auntie Enid snorted. 'It'll be all about whether the miners are going to go on strike, like last year. You wait, people will be hoarding coal – them as can afford to.'

Would Thad and Jacob start lugging home stolen sacks of coal? When had her little brothers grown into brazen thieves? And judging by his performance on Saturday, Dad would probably shake them by the hand and send them out for more. That bonfire belonging to kids in the next street that Thad had set alight on the afternoon of last Bonfire Night seemed now less of a joke that had got out of hand and more of a deliberate act.

They got off the tram near Stretford Station and hurried, heads down against the drizzle, Belinda clasping the newspaper under her arm beneath her shawl. At the top of Grave Pit Lane, Grandma Beattie awaited them with a lamp.

'You shouldn't be out on a night like this,' Auntie Enid chided.

'It's nowt. I know what time you're due home. There's not a lot of point having a clock if you don't use it.'

Belinda wanted to hug her. Grandma Beattie was proud of their black marble clock with its enamel dial, that they had saved up for and bought second-hand from the pawnbroker. Auntie Enid claimed the shame of entering such an establishment had nearly killed her, and Belinda and Grandma Beattie had had to act as look-outs to make sure no one they knew came anywhere near, but it was the only way they could be sure of getting a second-hand clock that was reliable.

With Grandma Beattie lighting their way, they walked up the lane, confidently on the cinder path and then warily when they reached the dirt-track, which was sludgy underfoot. They held their skirts clear of the mud: the Sloan women didn't go in for the modern shorter hemlines.

Belinda threw open the cottage door, standing back to let the others in first. It made such a difference having Grandma Beattie coming home earlier. Until last year, the three of them had been out all day at the mill, but after they had done the sums repeatedly, they had decided that they could manage if Grandma Beattie gave up the mill and worked part time in one of the shops over the bridge. The few bob they had lost in income was more than made up for by knowing that Grandma

Beattie's life was less taxing and by Auntie Enid and Belinda's coming home to a meal on the table.

End Cottage smelled of beeswax and coal and Grandma Beattie's herby dumplings.

'It'll be on't table in five minutes,' said Grandma Beattie, allowing them just enough time to nip out the back to the earth-closet. Auntie Enid went first. After Belinda had had her turn, she used the trowel to scoop some powder out of the box and sprinkled a mixture of earth and ashes through the hole in the wooden seat into the pail underneath to smother the odour.

She made a dash for the cottage, where Grandma Beattie was ladling winter vegetable stew onto mismatched plates, making sure they each got a delicious doughy dumpling.

'Thank you, Mrs Sloan,' said Auntie Enid. 'This is most welcome after a long day.'

That was something Belinda had never quite come to terms with: the way Auntie Enid and Grandma Beattie called one another Mrs Sloan. They were in-laws, not mother and daughter, and even though they had shared a roof since the year dot, they still Mrs Sloan'd one another.

After the meal, Auntie Enid resumed her knitting and Grandma Beattie sat with her darning. Belinda laid the newspaper on the table and read out some articles. Grandma Beattie liked being read to. She hadn't had much education because of stopping at home to be little mother to her younger brothers and sisters after the death of her mother when she was seven; but she didn't seem to pay attention the way she usually did.

'The newspaper's all right, but, me, I prefer *Vera's Voice;* you know, stories and such like, and helpful things, like lying potatoes in hot water before you roast 'em and putting a bit of asbestos under the cake in the oven so the bottom doesn't burn.'

Presently Auntie Enid and Grandma Beattie started chatting, so Belinda read in silence. Turning a page, she found herself confronted by columns of advertisements for situations vacant. This time last week, she would have turned over without a second thought, but now...

'Anyone for cocoa?' asked Auntie Enid, starting to get up.

Seizing the corner of the page, Belinda began to turn over – just as the words *Office Junior Required* caught her eye. She couldn't risk Auntie Enid seeing. She turned the page, her heart beating quickly.

Why couldn't she stop to read the details? Why mustn't Auntie Enid see?

Because she had an itchy conscience, that's why.

No, she wasn't going to keep this a secret. If she was going to take an interest in the advertisement – and she was interested, after what Miss Kirby had said – she must do it openly. She already had one secret tucked away in her cupboard upstairs, and that was bad enough.

She turned back to the previous page, skimming it to find the words that had jumped out at her, which now, perversely, seemed determined to hide themselves.

'You know I mentioned bumping into my old teacher? She said I'd have suited office work.'

'Oh aye, looks down on mill-workers, does she?' said Auntie Enid.

'Not at all. In fact, she said how skilled you have to be, but—'

'But what, lass?' asked Grandma Beattie.

'There's a post advertised here in the paper for an office junior.' She marked the place with her finger. 'That's how you start off in office work.'

'She's turned your head and no mistake,' huffed Auntie Enid. 'Foolish creature, giving you ideas above your station.'

Belinda nearly gave in, but this was her chance to sway them. She looked Auntie Enid in the eye.

'Office work pays better than the mill. We could have a

better life. If I earned more, you could cut your hours in the shop, Grandma Beattie.'

'I'm not sure I'd want to,' said Grandma Beattie.

'Even so,' said Belinda, trying to sound as if it didn't matter much, 'if we had more money...'

'We're fine as we are,' said Auntie Enid. 'I don't know what you're thinking, letting that woman put fancy ideas in your head. You're more sensible than that.'

'Imagine being able to hoard a bit of coal,' said Belinda.

'That's no reason to turn your back on your proper place in life,' Auntie Enid retorted.

'If Dad had let me sit the scholarship, maybe office work would have been my proper place.'

A spasm of shock vibrated around the room. What had she said? It had almost sounded like... She rubbed the heel of her hand in circular movements against her chest, feeling cold even though the warmth of the range surrounded her. Auntie Enid and Grandma Beattie stared, not in recrimination, but in outright grief, faces strained.

'I'm sorry.' Her mouth was filled with sawdust. 'However that sounded... You know I would never, never...'

Auntie Enid's hand reached across to clasp Grandma Beattie's. They sniffed almost in unison, breathing out and nodding, riding the tide of emotion.

'If you'd been an office girl...' Auntie Enid started to say.

'If you're going to say I wouldn't have been suitable for Ben because he was a dustman, well... just don't say it. I loved him. He were the best thing that ever happened to me and all I wanted was to be his wife and look after him all us lives.'

'We know, love, we know,' said Grandma Beattie.

'I had a horrid, ratty job when I met him. I used to feel sick to my stomach on Sunday nights, knowing I'd have to get up and go there on Monday for another week. But you know what? I'd do that job every day for the rest of my life if only Ben could have come home safe. You said about my proper place, Auntie Enid. Well, my proper place was to be Ben's wife. That's what was meant to happen, but it didn't and...' Loneliness built up inside her, a physical ache beneath her ribs.

'Eh, you'd have been a good wife and mother.' Auntie Enid dashed away tears. 'Our Ben would have made a lovely dad.'

'He would that,' sighed Grandma Beattie. 'It should have been me what was took, not him, a young man with all his life before him. Better to get rid of an old biddy like me.'

The room was washed in sorrow, sharp-edged and urgent. The pull of their shared mourning was as powerful as it was familiar and Belinda was no match for it. Nor did she want to be. Ben had brought her together with these two and it was Ben that kept them together and always would.

There were more tears and memories, an exhausting mixture of unhurried, glowing nostalgia and flat, empty sadness. It was only when she got up to trim the wick, because the lamp-flame was starting to give off sooty smoke, and her arm brushed the newspaper, that she recalled how the conversation had started. She couldn't mention the advertisement again, not after they had all been so upset. Was the subject destined to fade away? Was that what she wanted? Filled with longing for Ben and cherishing the closeness she shared with his mother and grandmother, maybe it was.

But when Auntie Enid was stirring the milk for their cocoa and Belinda was tipping boiling water in the hot-water bottles and fastening the brown-glazed ceramic stopper in each one, Grandma Beattie brought the subject up.

'What about this office job in't paper? Never go to bed on an argument.'

'We didn't argue...' Belinda began.

'Yes, we did and I want it sorted.'

'It's all very well talking about how you earning more would make a difference,' Auntie Enid said, 'but you wouldn't start on good money. The office junior is at the bottom of the pile, like being a tenter.'

'Aye, and you're twenty,' added Grandma Beattie. 'That's old to know nowt at work. People would look down on you.'

'It would be worth it if I got a better job out of it.'

'I hate to say it, Mrs Sloan,' said Grandma Beattie, 'but we have to let her try. Otherwise she'll always wonder and she'll end up blaming us; either that or she'll do it anyroad without our permission.'

'I would never...' Belinda started to say, but had to stop because she needed time to work out whether it was true.

Fortunately, Auntie Enid spoke over her. 'It's your Miss Kirby's fault, putting ideas in your head and leaving us to deal with the mess.' To Grandma Beattie, she said, 'You'd best buy her a sheet of good paper and an envelope, then.'

'Thank you,' said Belinda.

'Nay,' said Grandma Beattie, 'save your thanks for when we dry your tears after you've been knocked back from getting above yourself.'

Belinda tried hard not to look excited when she came home to find a crisp sheet of paper and a matching envelope, already stamped, awaiting her on the dresser. She had been planning her letter all day in her head. After they had eaten their pressed tongue and cleared away, she made a point of letting Auntie Enid wind wool around her hands, so as not to look too eager to write the letter.

But at last she was free. She started by writing a rough copy.

Dear Sir, or should it be *Dear Sirs* since there were three surnames? Or *Dear Messrs Grace, Wardle and Grace?* Get the rest of the letter written and worry about that later. *I should like to be considered for the job* – no, *the position of office junior in your firm* – no, *in the firm of Grace, Wardle and*

Grace, which meant she couldn't address the letter to the three gentlemen by name, as it would sound odd to use their names again so soon. *I went to elementary school* – no, cross that out. *At school, my teacher wanted to put me in for the high school scholarship, but my father… my father* what?… *did not want me to stay on at school.* Not bad. New paragraph.

My teacher said I would suit office work and she explained about starting as an office junior. I am a quick – no, *an attentive learner and would work hard to give satisfaction.*

Was it long enough? Did it say all that needed saying? Was it – her heart executed a little flip – was it good enough to pass muster in the office of Grace, Wardle and Grace?

Early next morning, in their walk through the bone-chilling darkness to the tram-stop, she dropped her letter in the pillar-box. She wanted to pause before letting go of it, to savour the moment, but she mustn't vex Auntie Enid. If only Auntie Enid and Grandma Beattie understood how much this mattered to her.

Her heart might live in the past, but the rest of her was in the here and now. Surely it wasn't wrong to want to make the best of it?

Chapter Four

Patience padded downstairs, carrying her bedside lamp, its flex neatly coiled. At the foot of the stairs, she passed the ornately carved monk's bench and opened the cupboard under the stairs to place the lamp on the shelf. The cheerful clink of milk bottles on the step drew her glance to the front door, but she didn't open it. Bolting the front door last thing at night and unbolting it in the morning was Prudence's job, self-appointed many years ago, and Pa had never minded.

Darling Pa. Patience's heart trembled with sorrow. Pa had lived his life immersed in his scholarly books and papers, surfacing occasionally for a toasted tea-cake, and with no more than a vague and, if she was honest, peevish awareness of mundane matters like how full the coal-scuttle was and whether the butcher's bill had been paid.

'Good thing we called you Prudence, eh?' he had been saying to Prudence for as long as Patience could remember, whenever a pipe burst or a tile blew off the roof; and true to her name, Prudence would set about dealing with the problem with calm efficiency. Patience had longed as a little girl, and as an adult too, for Pa to say to her, 'Good thing we called you Patience,' but he never had, even though she had never been anything but patient when he chopped and changed his mind about roll-mop herrings or sardines, and when he let his cocoa get cold because he was reading and then blamed her because... well, because he just did.

So what if Pa had been querulous? At heart, he was gentle, with an old-fashioned gallantry, and that was what counted. Was it silly to imagine that his gentleness had permeated yesterday's funeral? For Prudence and Lawrence to be in the same room without arguing was unprecedented. Lawrence had always thrown his weight around, ever since they were children, and over the years he had become increasingly condescending towards her and Prudence. Because they weren't married? Probably. The world looked down on spinsters. But it wasn't just that. Lawrence had risen in the world. He was a successful businessman and Evelyn revelled in her role as his perfectly groomed wife.

Was yesterday's courtesy and forbearance a sign of things to come? How wonderful if Pa's death had brought them all together.

She got the fire going in their little breakfast room before Prudence could come downstairs and say it wasn't worth it, with them going out straight after breakfast. She opened the curtains in here and the kitchen, letting in the thin, grey winter morning, and filled the kettle in the scullery. There was ice on the inside of the scullery window. In the kitchen, she reached for her apron and put the kettle on the gas, glancing at the fire-place where she had laid a fire last night. She couldn't justify a kitchen fire, any more than she could a sitting room fire. The house would be freezing to come home to later on. Her bones creaked just thinking of it.

'Good morning, Patience.'

Prudence came in, carrying the milk bottles. They always had two pints on Thursday, because it was rice pudding day.

'Good morning, Prudence.'

They were both in their funeral garb again, as befitted the reading of the will. Patience's eyes fell on the oval cameo brooch at Prudence's thin throat. That showed how important today was. Prudence wasn't one for jewellery and while it was only right and proper that Pa should have presented her with Mother's brooch, her being the elder daughter, it was rather a waste as well. Had he seen fit to give it to Patience, it would have seen the light of day far more often.

Breakfast didn't take long without Pa wanting a second cup of tea. In any case, Prudence had one eye on the clock.

'...though why we have to trail all the way into town, I don't know,' she fumed, evidently finishing a thought.

'This Mr Wardle must be Lawrence's solicitor,' said Patience, ever the peacemaker. 'I suppose he automatically made arrangements with his own man instead of Pa's.'

'Automatically threw his weight around, you mean.'

So much for lasting forbearance.

They cleared away and Patience washed up, looking at her hands before she dried them. She got through lashings of hand lotion but, honestly, there was no disguising an ageing hand.

She put on her faithful wool overcoat, its tailored lines proclaiming its pre-war origins. Her wide-brimmed hat was pre-war too. Winding her scarf round her neck, she tucked it inside the front of her coat, checking her appearance in the mirror that hung between the front door and the deep alcove of the cloakroom.

Prudence produced a long, thin envelope and folded it into her ancient leather handbag.

'Pa's will. It's a good thing we've got it. I don't suppose Lawrence took that into account when he made the appointment with his Mr Wardle. For all he knows, the will could be lodged with Pa's solicitor.' She pressed her lips together. 'I've half a mind to leave it behind. That'd teach him.'

'Oh, Prudence.' Patience felt that horrid flutter that had upset her ever since childhood. She hated it when the other two did battle.

'Don't panic. I wouldn't stoop so low... however much Lawrence deserves it.'

Usually, when she walked along Market Street, Belinda enjoyed gazing in the shop windows, but today all she cared about was finding the turning into Rosemount Place. At last she found it, a quiet haven with what looked like a row of handsome houses, except that each one had a brass name-plate beside the gleaming black front door.

You could have been an office girl.

She was here. She was really here. She didn't know whether to be excited or frightened to death. She would lose a day's pay and if Auntie Enid and Grandma Beattie were right, it would be for nothing, but, give her her due, Auntie Enid had agreed to tell Mr Butterfield she was poorly. Without that, she couldn't have come.

She had arrived early, in her borrowed coat and hat, kindly loaned by Mrs Harrison from up Grave Pit Lane. Mrs Harrison was the rag-and-bone man's wife and the garments had been cast out by someone with, as Grandma Beattie roundly declared, more money than sense. Old they might be, but there was wear in them yet. Belinda felt smart and trim and, if it didn't sound stupid, business-like; and she must have looked the part because the gentleman who arrived just as she was anxiously checking the names on the brass plate, said courteously, 'After you.' She had a fleeting glimpse of a narrow face and a splendid overcoat with a fur collar as he ushered her up the steps. She didn't want to go inside this early but didn't feel she had a choice. She knocked on the door.

'It's unlocked. Go straight in,' said the gentleman.

At the same moment, the door was opened from within, sandwiching her between the tall, lean gentleman behind her and a grand frock-coated gentleman in front. He was bald on top but sported mutton-chop whiskers to make up for it.

'Mr Hesketh, sir. I saw you from the window. Come in, sir. A chilly morning.'

There was nothing like being overlooked, was there? Mr Mutton-Chop clearly recognised quality when he saw it, and the gentleman was quality and she wasn't. Simple as that. She slid aside.

'Morning, morning, Hathersage. How are you this fine morning?'

'Very well, thank you, sir. Mr Wardle asked me to show you upstairs immediately, if you'd care to follow me.'

The two of them disappeared up a handsome staircase with a dark-blue runner. The spacious hallway smelled of beeswax. Three wooden chairs stood to attention against the wall on the left. Over to the right, a door stood open. Belinda glanced in, trying to be casual. The office! Her gaze ran over a vast desk with an ornate tray with glass ink-bottles and a stamp-box laid neatly on top of it and glass-fronted bookcases standing behind. Next to the bookcases was a table with decanters and a water jug and glasses. There was even a rug on the floor.

She hovered near the front door beside the umbrella-stand. Mr Hathersage returned, pausing on the staircase, as if noticing her for the first time, before joining her in the hall.

'Good morning. May I be of assistance?' His tone was faultlessly polite but there was a flicker in his eyes that suggested she was in the wrong place.

'Good morning, sir. I'm here for an interview. My name is Belinda Layton.'

'Really?' Another flicker. 'You're older than I was expecting. You do realise we are seeking an office junior?'

'Yes, sir. If I could explain—'

He held up a hand. 'Wait for your interview, if you please. Kindly take a seat over there.' He indicated the wooden chairs. 'You're rather early, but never mind.'

Sitting on the chair felt like waiting outside the headmaster's office. Presently another girl arrived and then a lad, neither of them more than sixteen. The boy's suit had a certain middle-class smartness and the girl's coat boasted a velvet collar and cuffs. Belinda stopped feeling business-like. She felt dowdy in her borrowed togs. Was coming here a colossal mistake?

A young fellow with cheeks with the colour and texture of boiled ham appeared in the office doorway.

'Miss Ainsworth, please.'

The girl stood up, smoothing her coat, and went into the office. The young man shut the door. Belinda's heart beat as hard as if it were her interview. She sat up straighter, clutching her handbag on her lap, her fingers wrapped tightly around the handles. The boy placed his hands on his knees. His gloves were leather. Hers were knitted.

But this wasn't about being smartly turned out or middle class. Who was she trying to kid? Of course it was. Everything was about being smartly dressed and middle class.

No, it wasn't. That was why the scholarship existed – so poorer children had a chance of a better education. Ah, but she hadn't sat the scholarship, had she? A lot of poor children didn't because their families needed them to work.

You could have been an office girl.

Miss Kirby believed in her. She must focus on giving the best interview she could.

Miss Ainsworth was shown out of the office and, with polite goodbyes, left the building. The boy, Mr Unwin, was called in. More waiting. When he emerged again, Belinda stirred and was half-standing before the young clerk said, 'Mr Hathersage will be with you shortly,' and retreated. She sank down again, trying to look as if she hadn't got up in the first place.

The front door opened and a pair of middle-aged ladies walked in – sisters, obviously; both thin and pale, but one had a sharper face and keen eyes while the other, lacking the angles and planes of her sister's face, looked softer.

Mr Hathersage appeared by magic. 'Miss Hesketh and Miss Patience Hesketh? My name is Hathersage. Mr Wardle is expecting you. May I show you the way?'

Hesketh. Presumably they were connected to the lean-faced man from earlier, but whereas Mr Hesketh's bonhomie suggested roast beef dinners with whisky to follow beside a roaring fire, his relatives had an impoverished look and probably lived lives of good works and church flowers, getting by in reduced but infinitely respectable circumstances, poor old loves.

She pulled her gaze away. She mustn't be caught gawping. Surely it would be time for her interview when Mr Hathersage came back downstairs. Had she got what it took to work in a high-class place like this?

Mr Hathersage opened a door and Patience followed Prudence inside. The office was a large square, with a high ceiling and long sash-windows, its walls lined with row upon row of old books with identical spines. Pa would have loved it. There was an imposing desk twice the size of their kitchen table, with a smart desk-set complete with ink-bottles and pen-cradles, and a leather blotter, its blotting-paper pristine. Over by the fireplace, two button-upholstered armchairs, very gentlemen's club-looking, faced one another, each with a small circular table by its side. Just the right size for a brandy, which was a bizarre thing to think because Patience didn't know the first thing about brandy. Pa had been a port man and the most she had ever had was a sweet sherry.

Seated in the armchairs were Lawrence and a tubby gentleman, looking very comfortable in one another's company. The men politely came to their feet.

'Here they are at last,' Lawrence said jovially.

'You make it sound as if we're late.' Prudence pointedly did not look at the clock on the mantelpiece.

Lawrence made a play of digging beneath his jacket and removing his silver hunter from the small pocket in his waistcoat, flicking open the cover to study its face. He gave Prudence an approving smile that Patience knew would irritate her far more than a sarky reply would have, then flipped the watchcase shut and returned it to his pocket.

Lawrence performed the introductions, then Mr Wardle ushered them to his desk, where two chairs stood ready. Where was Lawrence going to sit? But he remained standing. Looking down on them.

'Thank you for attending, ladies,' Mr Wardle began. 'We are here to read the last will and testament of Mr Edwin Lawrence Hesketh, the father of Lawrence from his first marriage and Prudence and Patience from his second.'

'I have it here.' Prudence drew her handbag onto her lap and opened it.

'No,' Mr Wardle said in a measured voice. '*I* have it *here*.'

Prudence pulled out the envelope and removed Pa's will, thrusting it across the desk.

Mr Wardle examined it. 'This is indeed a will made by your late father, Miss Hesketh, but it isn't his *last* will. This, which I personally drew up,' and with a smooth wave of his hand, he indicated the document lying before him, 'is his last will. A new will, properly drawn up and witnessed, automatically takes the place of any and all former wills.'

'I'm aware of that,' said Prudence. 'Are you saying that my father—?'

'The old boy made a new will,' Lawrence cut in impatiently. 'Read it, Wardle.'

'But I had no idea...' began Prudence.

'He wasn't under any obligation to inform you,' said Lawrence, 'no matter how much you may think he was.'

'I never thought any such thing.'

'Just as well, since he obviously didn't want you to know.'

Mr Wardle cleared his throat. 'Perhaps we should proceed with the reading. It's very straightforward. To summarise, the house in Wilton Close is left to Lawrence Hesketh—'

'To *Lawrence?*' Prudence burst out.

'Lawrence?' Patience echoed. 'Oh, my goodness.' There was ringing in her ears. She couldn't breathe.

As if from a distance, she heard Prudence say, 'He can't do that.'

'On the contrary,' said Lawrence, 'he could and he did.'

How? As a loving father – how? Patience stared at her clasped hands. Her eyes filled; her lashes felt spiky and sticky.

'What I mean,' Prudence snapped, 'as you know perfectly well, Lawrence, is that the house belonged to our mother – *our* mother, not yours.' She started to point to the old will lying on Mr Wardle's desk, but dropped her hand almost at once. Was it shaking? 'Pa left the house to Patience and me. He couldn't leave it to you. It came from our mother's family.'

'It's true that the property once belonged to Mrs Florence Hesketh,' Mr Wardle said, 'but she left it to her husband, with no conditions attached. She might, for example, have bequeathed it to him on condition he left it to you and your sister, but she didn't.'

'Which means Pa was free to dispose of it as he saw fit,' Lawrence gloated. 'It's appropriate that he should leave his property – *his* property, note – to his son.'

'Mother would never have left the house to him had she thought for one moment—' Prudence began.

'Then it's fortunate for me that she didn't think.'

They were arguing again; they were always arguing. Childhood anxieties reared up in Patience's chest. 'Is there anything we can do?' She could barely get the words out; her mouth was dry.

'We'll contest the will,' Prudence declared.

'That's your prerogative, of course,' said Mr Wardle.

'Assuming you can afford it,' said Lawrence.

'But I must advise you that the will is watertight,' Mr Wardle finished. 'It won't do you any good.'

Patience's hand crept across, seeking her sister's. Prudence grasped it in a fierce, painful squeeze that seemed to run all the way up Patience's arm and into her chest, where it wrapped itself around her heart. How could Pa have done this to them? How *could* he?

'I'm sorry.' The others were talking. What had she missed? 'I didn't catch that.'

'Mr Wardle is about to explain how such a palpably unfair will can possibly be watertight,' said Prudence.

'Ah, but it isn't unfair, Miss Hesketh. The late Mr Hesketh knew that you and your sister are provided for. As well as owning the house in Wilton Close, your mother also had an annuity, which automatically passed to you and your sister upon her death. Because you were children at the time, arrangements were made for your father to have the use of the money to meet the expenses associated with your upbringing and care until you married or achieved the age of twenty-five, whichever came first.'

Whichever came first. Just think. There had been a time when she had expected marriage to come first. Oh, how young she used to be, how naive, how romantic... how foolish.

'We're aware of that, thank you,' Prudence said in the testy voice she reserved for tradesmen who thought a pair of middle-aged spinsters didn't know what was what. 'What you have neglected to explain is how our inheriting Mother's annuity somehow makes it appropriate that Lawrence should be given the house that belonged to her family.'

'I would remind you, Miss Hesketh, that the will in question is your father's, not your mother's, and your father had three children. The house in Wilton Close started out in the hands of your mother's family before becoming hers outright. She chose to leave it – quite properly, in my view – to her husband, and there her interest in it ceased. The house you insist upon referring to as your mother's has in fact been your father's since her early death. Naturally, your father wished to see all three of his children provided for. You and your sister have benefited from your mother's annuity for – ahem – a considerable number of years. What more could you expect? Your father was entitled to leave the house, his house, to his son. What right-minded man wouldn't?'

'But Lawrence already has a house,' cried Patience.

'Rented,' said Lawrence. 'Not the same thing at all.'

'And an income from his work,' Patience went on doggedly. 'If you take away our home, what will we be left with?'

'The annuity.'

'You say that as if it's riches, and it isn't. We...' Her voice faded away. How vulgar to talk about money. They might be what Grandma Hesketh would have called the genteel poor, but they had their pride.

'And Prudence's salary,' said Lawrence. 'Don't forget that. You'll have ample between you to rent a couple of rooms. What more do you need, a pair of spinsters like you? I have a wife and family and that house will suit us very well.'

'And then there's the other way of looking at it,' Mr Wardle said smoothly. 'Had you two ladies come into the house, your brother could well have had grounds to contest the will. For the two of you to have the annuity as well as the house – well, that's hardly fair, is it?'

'This is an outrage,' said Prudence.

'I'll take that as a professional compliment,' said Mr Wardle, 'though I believe you'll find it isn't an outrage. It is merely watertight.'

'I don't know how you talked Pa into this,' Prudence flung at Lawrence.

'Who says he needed persuading?'

'I advise you to be careful what you say next, Miss Hesketh,' Mr Wardle intervened. 'It would be highly unwise to suggest—'

'Let her suggest all she wants,' said Lawrence. 'There's nothing quite like committing slander in the presence of a solicitor.'

A charged silence rolled round the room before Prudence said stiffly, 'If that's everything, Mr Wardle, my sister and I will forego a formal reading of the will.' She stood up. 'Come along, Patience.'

'Yes, run along, Patience,' Lawrence said, 'but before you do, there's one more thing.'

'Well?' Prudence demanded.

Lawrence puffed out his chest. 'I intend to move my family into my new house and I'd be obliged if you would vacate it at your earliest convenience.'

Belinda pressed her lips together, then released them. She couldn't afford to look awkward or unsure, especially with her being older than the other candidates, not to mention lower class. Not that there was anyone to see her. After the two Miss Heskeths had been escorted upstairs, Mr Hathersage had invited her to come through. But before he could so much as wave her towards the chair, the young clerk with the boiled-ham cheeks had appeared at an inner doorway that led to a further room.

'Mr Hathersage, I apologise for the interruption, sir, but would you mind?'

'Excuse me, Miss Layton. I'll return directly.'

The door shut behind him. What should she do? He hadn't actually invited her to take a seat: should she remain standing? The door to the hall was still open: ought she to close it?

A few minutes passed. It felt ridiculous to remain standing so she sat and waited. And waited.

At last the inner door opened and the clerk stuck his head out. 'Fearfully sorry about this, miss. Mr Hathersage will be a while yet. Perhaps you could come back another time?'

'No, I'll wait.' She couldn't possibly have a second day off sick.

Hearing footsteps on the stairs, she glanced through the open door. The two Hesketh ladies were on their way down – and something was obviously wrong. Miss Sharp had a face like thunder while Miss Softer's eyes were fixed in a pained stare. She stumbled on the final step and grabbed the newel post to steady herself.

'Come along, Patience,' said Miss Sharp.

Miss Softer – Patience – looked like she could do with a breather. Belinda rose and went into the hall.

'Excuse me, but are you all right? Do you need to sit down? Not there,' she added hurriedly, as the two ladies glanced at the row of wooden seats. 'In here.' She indicated the office. 'I'm sure Mr Hathersage won't mind. And perhaps something to drink?' Mr Hathersage wouldn't begrudge his masters' clients a glass of water, surely.

'Little as I wish to remain on these premises,' said Miss Sharp, 'a cup of tea would be most welcome.'

Panic streaked through her. 'I'm – I'm sorry. I meant a glass of water.'

Miss Sharp gave her a look which combined outrage with disgust, at the very moment that the inner door opened and Mr Hathersage appeared.

'Ladies, may I be of assistance?'

'No, you may not,' replied Miss Sharp, 'unless you wish to train your staff to have better manners. A glass of water, indeed! Come, Patience.'

'Member of staff? This young person is not employed here, I assure you.'

But Miss Sharp wasn't interested. Taking her sister by the arm, she led her out. Mr Hathersage bustled after them, brushing past Belinda as if she was of no consequence whatsoever, and opened the front door for them, blustering apologies for whatever impertinence they had suffered at the hands of that young person.

The front door shut and he came back into the office. Belinda had heard of people looking down their nose at you, but she had always taken it to be no more than a form of words. Now, however, she knew it to be the literal truth. Mr Hathersage sneered at her down the length of his nose.

'How dare you thrust yourself forward in such an objectionable manner?'

'I only offered the lady a glass of water, sir. She looked upset.'

'That is none of your concern. No wonder you have been unable to secure an office junior position by your age, if that is how you behave. Kindly leave the premises.'

Belinda stared. All she had done was offer comfort to a lady in distress. Was that such a crime?

You could have been an office girl.

No, she couldn't. Not if it meant not caring about others.

Chapter Five

THE FRONT DOOR clicked shut as Prudence left the house.
Standing at the window, Patience watched her sister set off
for work. Prudence had made arrangements to go to the office
at half past ten, straight after the meeting at the solicitor's, but
instead she had felt obliged to bring Patience home, so now she
was late. Patience huffed a sigh, hating herself for getting into
a state. Yet who could blame her after the devastating news Mr
Wardle had delivered?

What were they going to do? They had lived in this house all
their lives. She felt cold right down to her bones. She went upstairs
to remove her funeral dress, stowing it away on its padded hanger
before donning her plain everyday dress. A plain dress for a plain
person. She looked at herself in the dressing-table mirror. Worse
than plain today. Haggard. Oh, Pa, how could you?

Being plain had never bothered Prudence, but it bothered
Patience, and if that made her shallow, then so be it. Prudence
was thin and upright, her facial features clearly defined – sharp,
some might say. Patience was thin too, but there was nothing
sharp about her. She was all soft edges. That summed up her
life: blurred round the edges. She hadn't had the life she had
longed for.

A thin, plain old maid, that was what she was. Soon to be a
thin, plain, homeless old maid.

Fear rolled through her. She went downstairs. Unhooking her apron from the back of the kitchen door, she put it over her head and tied it behind her back before seeing to the downstairs fires. Thursday was brass day. Was it still brass day even though they were about to lose their home? But what else was she to do, if not this?

She laid a sheet of newspaper on the kitchen table, along with the Brasso and a couple of cloths. Then she fetched the first batch of ornaments. The brass had been Mother's, and her mother's before that, so it ought to feel special, but it wasn't half so appealing as dainty porcelain would have been, preferably with roses or forget-me-nots painted on with a delicate brush.

She had barely started when the doorbell rang, followed, as she entered the hall, by a loud rat-tat on the knocker. Pulling her apron over her head, she opened the door.

Lawrence pushed his way in. 'You took your time answering.' He marched into the sitting room. 'Ah, there it is. Good, good.'

Hurrying behind, she found him stroking the lid of Pa's beloved old bureau as if it were a favoured dog. He pulled out the runners and lowered the lid to rest on them. Then he gave a humph of vexation.

'Look at all this!' His hand swept across Pa's papers, notebooks and goodness knows what else spilling out of the pigeon-holes. 'I thought you'd have cleared his things away by now.' He jerked open one of the drawers underneath. 'What have you been doing since he died? Nothing useful, by the looks of it.'

'Lawrence, what are you doing?'

'What does it look like?' He shoved the drawer shut. 'I'm taking what's mine. Don't stand there gawping. Empty all this rubbish from the bureau. The van will be here soon.'

'The van..?' Was she actually wringing her hands? She dropped them to her sides, then found them clutching at her side-seams.

'How else do you imagine we're going to transport everything? It's hardly going to fit in the motor. Is that bow-fronted chest of drawers still in Pa's room? I'll want that too.'

'Don't forget the pearl-handled fish-knives.'

Patience spun round to face Evelyn, beautifully turned out from her droopy-brimmed hat trimmed with a huge bow, and her cape-collared green wool coat handsomely adorned with embroidered braid to her slender leather shoes with their pointed toes. How she managed to cram her feet into them was anybody's guess.

'Good, you've got an apron,' said Evelyn. 'You'll be able to box things up for us. Didn't I tell you she'd be sensible about it, Lawrence? Shall we?'

The next thing Patience knew, the two of them were storming all over the house, throwing doors open and exclaiming in delight. All she could do was flutter after them, feeling hopeless and ineffectual in their superbly confident wake.

'The walnut bed and matching wardrobe and dressing table in your father's old room. Such a handsome set.'

'The painting of the seaside village. Our Lucy will love that...'

'This mirror – and that blanket chest...' crowed Evelyn.

'The clock on the window sill on the half-landing – and the monk's bench in the hall. We can always flog it if we don't want it.'

'The dining table and chairs,' cried Evelyn. 'I've always admired the carving.'

'The barometer...'

'The epergne...'

'The what?' Lawrence asked.

'This.'

Patience was just in time to see Evelyn making elegant waving motions with her pudgy hands, like a conjurer's assistant presenting an item to the audience.

'That old thing?' said Lawrence. 'It's hideous.'

'Only because your sisters fill it with bits of string and old tram tickets and pencil stubs. Properly polished up, with fruit in the dish and flowers in the little vases, it'll make a splendid centrepiece for our dining table.'

'Our new dining table.' Lawrence ran his hands over the back of a dining chair.

'And don't forget the dinner service,' Evelyn added, beaming. 'Where is it, Patience?'

'In the sideboard. Our everyday crockery is in the kitchen cupboard.'

'So you never use the good stuff?'

'We save it for best,' said Patience.

Evelyn looked at Lawrence. 'That means they never use it. You see, we're doing them a favour, really, taking it off their hands.'

'What's going on?' If it made her look stupid to ask so late in the proceedings, then she would just have to look stupid.

'What does it look like?' said Lawrence and muttered something under his breath, which brought a flush to Patience's cheeks even though she didn't hear it.

'Poor little Patience,' said Evelyn. 'You do understand that the house is ours now, don't you, dear? The contents are ours as well, so we're taking a few things away; you know, clearing the decks to make it easier for you and Prudence to pack up and move out. Do you still have the silver teapot and tea-caddy?'

'You… taking our things? You can't do that.' Or could they?

'We're taking *our* things, dear,' cooed Evelyn. 'Where's Prudence? At the office? There you are, then. That shows how sensible she is being about this. Now you must be sensible too.' Evelyn draped an arm around Patience's shoulders and squeezed. 'Do you think you can do that? There's a good girl.'

Evelyn released her and Patience stumbled on watery legs into the hall. Any moment now, the promised van would roll up and her home would be dismantled before her eyes. Why did this have to happen when Prudence wasn't here? Prudence wouldn't let Lawrence and Evelyn walk all over her. Even if she couldn't legally stop them taking items they now owned, she would at the very least have had a jolly good argument over it.

Patience shivered. A row was the last thing she wanted. She was the gentle one of the family, the peacemaker. The weak one.

Was that why Lawrence was here now, in Prudence's absence? Because he knew that soppy little Patience was no match for him? Well, she wasn't having that. She might be gentle, but she absolutely was not going to be walked over. It was up to her to do what needed doing.

Whatever that was.

Her thoughts seemed to be all squished together in her head and if there was a sensible idea in there, she couldn't find it. She might as well slump onto the monk's bench and drop her head into her hands. But she couldn't, she mustn't. There must be something she could do.

And there it was, crystal-clear in her mind, a possible answer to this vile situation. Would it work?

Lawrence and Evelyn were still in the dining room. Patience heaved herself to her feet and stood in the doorway. Evelyn was on her knees, rooting around in the sideboard cupboard.

'Lawrence,' said Patience, 'don't you think you should move your motor further along? You know, to make room for the van. You're parked right outside and your removal people might find it more convenient if they could park there.'

'Good point. Give yourself a pat on the back, Patience. It's good to see you taking this on the chin.'

He threw open the front door and disappeared. Goodness, he had fallen for it. Now for Evelyn.

'Did I hear you mention the fish-knives, Evelyn? Here they are.' Patience extracted the box from the sideboard drawer and thrust it into her sister-in-law's surprised hands. 'Don't you think it ought to be put in the motor rather than the van? So much safer.'

'Really, I—'

'Let's take it before Lawrence locks the motor again, and I'll bring the epergne.'

'Oh, very well.'

Patience grasped the epergne. It was heavy and awkwardly shaped; the cut-glass dishes and vases were going to come adrift if she wasn't careful. Lawrence had left the front door open. With a polite smile, Patience let Evelyn precede her. Evelyn stepped from the porch onto the path. Heart hammering, Patience stayed in the porch.

'Evelyn – take this, will you?'

She pushed the hideous object into Evelyn's arms. Evelyn did a little dance, trying to cope with the knife-box and the epergne, which made ominous tinkling sounds. Patience jumped back into the hall and slammed the door, then raced like a mad thing to make sure the back door was locked. The doorbell rang and didn't stop ringing. The knocker clattered.

She ventured through to the sitting room, nearly jumping out of her skin as Lawrence appeared at the window and banged his fist on the glass. She did the only thing she could think of: she drew the curtains. Then she sank into a chair, breathing rapidly.

The doorbell stopped ringing. There was no more knocking. She held her breath, not daring to let it go because that might make her relax and that wouldn't be a safe thing to do, not yet. If ever.

Then came the metallic whisper that usually heralded the arrival of the post.

'Patience!' Lawrence shouted through the letter-box. 'Don't be an idiot. Open the door this minute.'

She didn't move a muscle.

'Have it your own way. But you'll open up soon enough when I come back with the police.'

'Lawrence did *what?*' Prudence demanded. Freshly returned from work, she stood in the hall, still in her hat and coat, Patience having been unable to hold back even long enough for her to shed her outdoor things. 'How dare he force his way in and try to make off with our possessions?'

'He said – well, actually Evelyn said – it all belongs to them now.'

'But you outfoxed them, you clever old thing. I didn't know you had it in you.'

Patience felt a glow of satisfaction. Prudence didn't hand out compliments lightly. Life was a serious business for Prudence. Well, it was for Patience too, but whereas she might have enjoyed some fun, Prudence couldn't be bothered with flibberty-gibberty stuff like that. Was it a lifetime of office work that had endowed her with that air of authority? No. She had been born with it.

'Lawrence was fearfully angry,' said Patience. 'He threatened to send for the police.'

'He only said it to frighten you.'

'I wanted to sneak out and telephone you. I thought you'd be permitted a personal call under the circumstances; but I didn't dare leave the house.' It sounded stupid now. 'I thought Lawrence might be round the corner, waiting for me.'

'It's a pity you didn't telephone,' Prudence said grimly. 'I would have gone straight back to Rosemount Place and given Mr Wardle a piece of my mind. In fact, that's what we must do tomorrow.'

'We won't get an appointment.'

'We're not going to ask for one. I'll go into work and arrange to be absent for a while; then we'll simply turn up in Rosemount Place.'

Patience tried to ignore a faint tightening in her chest. 'Oh, Prudence, are you sure?'

Prudence had no interest in lily-livered dithering. 'Either Mr Wardle agrees to see us immediately or we insist upon seeing one of his colleagues. That will muddy the waters, mark my words. In fact, I've a better idea. Either Mr Wardle sees us or we make our way to the newspaper offices on Deansgate. Neither Mr Wardle nor Lawrence will want that. If he is ever to rise to the rank of alderman, Lawrence can't afford to have the slightest question mark over his character.'

'Oh dear.'

'Never mind "oh dear". This has to be done – unless you fancy repelling him and Evelyn again tomorrow. Now, let me get my coat off. What's for tea?'

Patience had meant to go to the fishmonger to purchase coley, but had ended up cowering inside the house, so there were no fishcakes this evening. Instead she had sacrificed the cooking apples that had been destined for tomorrow's apple pie and had made curried apple soup. As she heated it, worries fluttered round her. Pa, how could you?

The next morning, Prudence set off for the office as usual. Patience followed her later, meeting her near the corner of Rosemount Place at ten o'clock.

'You do realise today is Friday the thirteenth,' Patience said.

'It certainly is for Mr Wardle.'

'What if they don't let us see him?'

Patience almost had to break into an unseemly trot to keep up with her sister. Prudence marched round the corner – and there, heading for the black door to Grace, Wardle and Grace, was Mr Wardle himself. Prudence put on a spurt and overtook him, flinging herself up the front steps before he could mount them, with Patience pattering behind.

His mouth tightened, but he shifted his briefcase to his left hand and raised his bowler. 'Good morning, ladies. Might I trouble you to stand aside?'

'Not until I've said my piece,' replied Prudence.

'If your piece, Miss Hesketh, appertains to your father's will, you had ample opportunity to say it yesterday. May I remind you that you were the one who cut short our meeting? Now if you would kindly step aside...'

Prudence stayed put. 'Are you aware that my brother turned up at the house yesterday to remove the best furniture?'

'No, I was unaware of that, but had you stayed to hear the full contents of the will, you would know that your father's personal possessions now belong to him.' Mr Wardle took a step forward as if expecting Prudence to melt obediently aside.

Prudence did no such thing. 'The things Lawrence wanted belonged to my mother.'

'Wedding presents, no doubt, and therefore also the property of the late Mr Hesketh.' Mr Wardle took another step forward; Patience could have told him he was wasting his time.

'On the contrary, they're all items Mother inherited from her family. I believe you'll find she came into possession of most of them before she married my father.'

'Oh, well, that's different – assuming you are correct.'

'I make a habit of being correct, Mr Wardle. So in fact Lawrence was attempting to steal what is rightfully ours.'

'I'd be careful of making accusations if I were you, Miss Hesketh. How could your brother, who was a small child when his father remarried, be expected to know the provenance of every stick of furniture?'

'As his solicitor, I suppose you're obliged to spout claptrap in his defence.'

Mr Wardle's throat bobbed above his starched collar. 'Miss Hesketh, I do not conduct business in the street. If you hadn't flounced out of my office yesterday, not only would you have heard the full contents of the will, you'd also have been offered your own copy.'

'Then we'll come inside now and get one.'

'I'll arrange for one to be posted to you at the office's earliest convenience.'

'We wouldn't dream of putting you to such trouble, Mr Wardle, would we, Patience? We'll come in now and collect it.'

'It will have to be prepared.'

'No, it won't. You've just said you were going to give it to us yesterday.'

Prudence marched inside, Patience behind her. Patience looked round for the kind girl from yesterday: she would help them for certain but, no, there was sign no of her, just Mr Hathersage coming to his feet, a look of surprise on his face.

'We've come for a copy of our father's will, which was prepared for us to take yesterday,' said Prudence. 'Could you fetch it, please?'

'This is most irregular,' Mr Hathersage began.

'And here is Mr Wardle to vouch for us – isn't that so, Mr Wardle?'

Mr Wardle didn't actually growl, but looked as if he would like to.

Fifteen minutes later, having been obliged to sign receipts in triplicate, Prudence was in triumphant possession of Pa's will. Patience didn't feel triumphant. The whole business was shabby and upsetting.

'Do you think Lawrence really thought those things were his?' she asked as they walked away. They should be mourning Pa, not fighting one another.

'Of course not. He was trying to get his hands on the good stuff before we could pack it away, should we move out.'

Would it really come to that? Yet how could it not, with Lawrence so determined, and the law on his side?

The last thing Patience felt like was entertaining – well, you could hardly call it that when it was an hour with an old friend once a week for a chat and perhaps a couple of hands of whist. Miss Kirby always came to their house. Goodness knows, they weren't well off, but dear Miss Kirby barely had sixpence with which to scratch herself. She had been a schoolmistress, responsible for her invalid mother. When old Mrs Kirby passed away and there were no more doctors' bills to pay, just when things might have become easier for Miss Kirby and she could have spent a few final years at work building up a nest-egg, she was required, because of her age, to surrender her post to a returning soldier. Life could be hard for women. Miss Kirby would spend the rest of her life feeling the pinch.

Patience wished she could invite her to have her tea with them on Fridays, but Prudence had vetoed the idea.

'If we have her to tea, she'd feel obliged to invite us back and she can't afford it.'

'If we made it clear a return invitation wasn't necessary…'

'Then our invitation would be charity and you can't have charity between friends.'

So every Friday evening, Miss Kirby came to their house; and if Patience happened to have made some gingerbread or a cherry cake that afternoon, that wasn't charity, it was good manners and hospitality.

Anxiety twisted inside her. If Lawrence got his way and they had to leave this house, they would never be able to afford somewhere as comfortable – and it wasn't just physical comfort. There was social comfort too. This address gave them a certain standing.

When the doorbell rang, she hurried to admit their friend. Soon the three of them were settled around the fire.

'Thank you for attending the funeral,' said Prudence. 'We appreciated your support.'

She didn't thank Miss Kirby for her letter of condolence: that would be acknowledged by post. Oh, the rules they lived by! What Patience wanted was to envelope her old friend in a hug and thank her for the kind letter that had brought tears to her eyes.

'You'll miss him,' said Miss Kirby. 'I know how long it took me to get used to being without Mother.' She glanced at Pa's empty armchair. 'The house will feel strange for a long time.'

Would Prudence confide? They could trust Miss Kirby to keep their family troubles to herself.

'I regret to say that we might not be here to make that adjustment.' Prudence explained about Pa's will and Lawrence's determination to take possession of the house.

'Goodness me, what a shock,' said Miss Kirby. 'Your lovely home. Whatever shall you do?'

Prudence's jawline hardened, squeezing her narrow lips into a white gash. 'It hardly seems possible that Lawrence can require us to leave, but we have to face it.'

Patience slipped her hand into her pocket for her lace-edged hanky and sniffed delicately, though what she really wanted was a jolly good blow, but ladies didn't honk into their hankies.

'Well, I for one will miss coming here. Such a pleasant home; and… it sounds foolish, I know, but whenever I come here, I indulge in a little day-dream.' Miss Kirby's cheeks went pink. 'I spent my working life standing up in front of classes of sixty, remember; and I always thought, wouldn't it be wonderful, wouldn't it be a privilege, to teach a small class, just a few children, and really bring them on.'

'What has our house got to do with that?' asked Prudence.

'I can't help imagining your sitting and dining rooms as two little classrooms. There, I told you it was foolish.'

'They would be very little classrooms,' Prudence observed.

Patience jumped in. She often did when Prudence sounded dismissive. 'A harmless day-dream, not foolish at all. Naturally you see places through a teacher's eyes.'

'Wait a minute,' said Prudence. 'That's not a bad idea.'

'What?'

'Having a school here – not for children, but for adults; young women who want to work in offices. You sometimes see advertisements in the newspaper for a series of evening classes where you can learn to use a typewriter. Why not a series of classes to learn filing and letter-writing and... reading and writing invoices and delivery notes? I have years of experience.'

'What about Lawrence?'

'If we think this through carefully, he won't have a choice.'

Chapter Six

BELINDA TIPTOED AROUND the ridges of mud at their end of Grave Pit Lane, jumping with relief onto the cinder path and setting off with a cheerful swing in her step, her bag of library books bumping against her leg. It was another bitingly cold morning, but the January skies, overcast for so long, were a vivid blue and the sunlight had a dazzling edge. It was her first Saturday morning off after weeks of cleaning duty in the mill and it felt like a treat. Mind you, getting out of the cottage, with its air of I-told-you-so, would make anyone feel better.

After her disastrous interview, so disastrous that she hadn't even had an interview, Auntie Enid and Grandma Beattie had tried not to gloat, but Auntie Enid hadn't tried very hard, her crossed arms and tilted head, even the way she rocked on her heels, expressing in no uncertain terms her satisfaction that Belinda had come a cropper.

'I don't mean you no ill, lass, you know that,' she said after her smugness had a chance to subside, 'but this is where you belong, and I don't just mean here in End Cottage. You can't climb out of your life. Everyone has their rightful place.'

Was her rightful place to dress in black for the rest of her life, endlessly mourning with Auntie Enid and Grandma Beattie until they passed away and she was the only one left?

That was what they thought, just as they thought her rightful place was in the mill. In the mill, and in black.

Were they right? Was this the way her life would always be?

She dashed the thought aside. Nothing must be allowed to spoil this morning of fresh air and freedom, made all the more enjoyable because she was meeting Sarah. She emerged from Grave Pit Lane to see Sarah coming towards her, her green shawl wrapped warmly round her and her sandy hair, several shades lighter than Belinda's, swinging loose.

'We were meant to meet outside the library,' said Belinda, linking arms as they set off together.

Sarah rolled her eyes. 'I couldn't wait to get out of the house. Thad's being a right so-and-so and Jacob's just as bad. Mikey's been saving up his pocket money for summat-or-other, and it's gone missing, so he accused Thad, and... oh, you don't want to hear the rest. It's bad enough living there without talking about it as well.' Her pretty mouth formed a pout. 'You'd think being so close in age would make Thad and Mikey close, but they hate one another.'

'It's because of being in the same class,' said Belinda. 'You aren't old enough to remember, but when they were tiny boys they were fine together, but being born in the same school year meant they had to be in the same class and people thought they must be twins. Thad hated that. That's how the bad feeling started.'

'Let's not talk about them.' Sarah squeezed her arm. 'We haven't had a Saturday morning together for ages. I have to be at work by one, so let's make the most of it.'

They went to the library first. Sarah only ever borrowed one book at a time, which she kept inside her pillow-case, but she was happy to help Belinda choose.

'Let's go for tea and a bun,' said Belinda when they came out. 'My treat. I've still got some of what I earned last Saturday.'

'Mum didn't fleece you out of it, then? I know Dad tried to get his hands on it.'

'I did give her some, but only a shilling.'

'Only! And that's on top of what you give her anyroad out of your regular wages. I bet she tried to get more than a bob an' all.'

Belinda felt a stab of shame. Mum could be money-grabbing these days. 'I'd spent some of it already.'

'What on?' Sarah asked eagerly.

Talking about other people's purchases was often the closest they got to shopping; but it wouldn't be right to tell Sarah before she had told Auntie Enid and Grandma Beattie.

'Just some fabric from the market.'

Uncurling her arm from Sarah's, she pushed open the door to the tea-shop they frequented. It had seen better days, but then, had it been a top-notch establishment, they wouldn't have been able to afford it.

'A bun each today,' she whispered. 'A pot of tea for two, please,' she said as the perky young waitress appeared at their side, pencil poised over her notebook, 'and an Eccles cake and...'

'A lardy cake, please,' said Sarah, her lips twitching into a sunny smile. 'Thanks.'

Belinda returned the smile. 'If I can't treat my little sister.'

'Don't you get fed up of handing money over to Mum? You must have to tip up at End Cottage an' all. It isn't fair on you.'

She shrugged. 'I can't see my family going without, especially when I'm lucky enough to live at End Cottage. It used to be easier giving Mum money when the boys were smaller and...'

'...less objectionable,' Sarah finished. 'I'd be much better off if I was allowed to live in at the hotel. I'd have to pay bed and board and I'd still give Mum summat, obviously, but I wouldn't have to pay my fares every day. That's where all my money goes – all that I'm allowed to keep, that is.'

'Same here.'

If only Ben had come home and they had got wed, her financial situation would have sorted itself out naturally. She and Ben would have taken care of Auntie Enid and Grandma Beattie as and when they needed it, and she would have slipped Mum a bit now and then; but she and Ben would have had their own home and their own family, both of which she would have put first, and no one would have expected otherwise. As things were, she was caught in a financial trap and she would never have any money of her own.

What had Miss Kirby called girls like her? Surplus girls. No husbands and no training. Just a lifetime filled with responsibilities.

The waitress returned. She put down the teapot and milk jug. 'One lardy cake… and one squashed flies cake.' With a cheeky smile, she headed back to the counter.

Sarah bit into her lardy cake. 'Mm, this feels like a celebration.'

'It might have been, if this week had happened differently. Have you heard of surplus girls?'

'No. What are they?'

'Not "they", Sarah. We are surplus girls. The men we could have married died in the war.'

'Well, Ben, yes, but I didn't have a fellow. I wasn't old enough.'

'Think of all the men who died. Some of them were little more than boys. What if one of them was meant to be for you?'

Sarah's eyes widened. 'You make it sound like there are no men left.'

'There's not nearly as many as there should be.'

'I'm sure I'll meet someone.'

'I hope you do; but plenty won't. Without husbands to support us, we'll have to spend a whole lifetime at work, so…' She took a breath. 'I applied for a post in an office.'

'You want to leave the mill?'

'I want a better-paid, more interesting job that I'll be happy to do for the rest of my working life.'

'You're a two-loomer, aren't you? If you leave, one of the tenters will be made up and that'll make room for a new tenter. Mrs Sloan helped you get took on as a tenter. Do you think she'd do the same for me?'

This wasn't the way she had expected the conversation to go. 'You don't want to go there. It's hard work.'

'Well, you try cleaning for ten hours a day. That isn't exactly a picnic.'

'You go deaf and lots of weavers have bad teeth.'

'The hours are regular. No starting at five in the morning, no working till midnight. Do you know what it's like for me, getting to and from work at those hours? Do you know how often I have to walk because there's no buses or trams? Please say you'll help me get took on.'

'I didn't get the office job, so it's beside the point.'

Was she daft to feel disappointed? She had wanted to discuss the surplus girls. She had never given the future any thought, other than to boggle at the way all her hopes and plans had been wiped out the moment the telegram arrived. For the past four years, she had lived a day-by-day existence, dressed in black, being accorded the status of widow by Ben's mother and grandmother. For a long time, that had been sufficient; but recently her youthful spirit had reawakened... only to find herself facing life as a surplus girl. What had Miss Kirby said? Something about fending for themselves... *and what education, what training, do they have under their belts to equip them for that?*

A dart of fear passed through her.

'I don't blame you for wanting summat better, Sarah. It's what I want an' all.'

But if she couldn't get an office position, how would she make her way?

*

Patience did some light dusting, which was all the housework she ever did on a Saturday. Catching sight of Prudence walking through their garden gate, she returned the duster to the house-maid's box and opened the front door.

Prudence looked decidedly pleased. Healthy too, with an unaccustomed rosiness in her normally pale complexion. Colourless, they had been called all their lives. Washed-out. Other girls had been blessed with pretty curves, golden curls and properly blue eyes, but the stick-thin Hesketh sisters had straight hair of the palest fairness and their blue eyes were closer to grey. In middle-age, their fairness hadn't changed to silver but to faded pewter. Still, what did it matter? Two old spinsters: who cared?

Patience cared. She always had. Which just showed how silly and superficial she was.

Having shed her outdoor things, Prudence walked into the sitting room.

'It's our lucky day,' she announced. 'I found a typewriter in the second-hand shop on Beech Road. A bit battered, and the Z is wonky, but how often does one require a Z? They're delivering it later. And I asked at the post office about a post office box, but we have to go to the big post office on Wilbraham Road for that.'

'You've been busy and all I've been doing is dusting.'

'I called in at Brown's as well and bought a new typewriter ribbon and a dozen sheets of carbon paper. That'll get us started. And I asked about putting a postcard in their window, advertising our services.'

'They said yes?'

'Naturally. They don't care what the postcard says – well, as long as you aren't advertising anything indecent or illegal.'

Patience squeezed her fingers into fists. 'Is what we're doing quite legal?'

Prudence pulled down the corners of her mouth thought-fully. 'This house may not be ours legally, but it is ours morally and we're not going to stand by while Lawrence marches in and lays claim to it. I'll take postcards round all the newsagents when I sort out our post office box.'

A movement outside caught Patience's eye. 'It's Lawrence's motor.'

'Talk of the devil,' said Prudence. 'Is Evelyn with him?'

'Yes.'

'Here's what we do. Be polite, let their words wash over us, then wave them on their merry way.'

Unfastening her apron, Patience went to open the door. Evelyn, looking smart and expensive in a calf-length, rust-coloured coat with a whole family of foxes dangling from her shoulders, beamed at her from the path.

'You look like an old family retainer, opening the door as we arrive.'

'It's the least she can do after slamming the door in your face last time,' scowled Lawrence, waving Evelyn across the threshold ahead of him.

'I apologise for that, Evelyn.' Patience tried not to sound humble. 'It was a difficult situation.'

'It's all forgotten.'

Evelyn turned her back and started to shrug her coat off. It was tempting to let it fall to the carpet, but Patience caught it and hung it in the cloakroom, then moved swiftly away before Lawrence could require the same courtesy. There were limits to what this old retainer was prepared to do.

In the sitting room, Evelyn sat down, Lawrence remaining on his feet. Patience sat, but Lawrence stayed standing; so he hadn't been courteously waiting for her, he wanted to lord it over them. He planted himself with his back to the fireplace. He cut a fine figure in his dark blue suit and striped silk tie.

'I am most displeased—' he began.

'Patience has already apologised for slamming the door,' cut in Prudence.

'I'm referring to the manner in which you took it upon yourselves to upbraid Wardle in the street. Disgraceful! I know it was you, Prudence, rather than Patience. Carrying on like a common fishwife, and in public too.'

'Rosemount Place is hardly the most public place,' Prudence murmured.

'It's a place peopled by gentlemen of standing and means. What if your behaviour had been witnessed by somebody who knew you to be connected to me? I'm ashamed of you.'

Patience glanced at her sister, but Prudence's features had been wiped clean of all emotion.

'You might as well know,' Lawrence continued, throwing out his chest, 'that I asked Wardle to produce a written account of the rash and unladylike haranguing to which he was subjected, and you know what that means, don't you? It means I have an official record of what you did.'

He whipped out an envelope from his inside pocket and waved it under Prudence's nose. Patience held her breath, but Prudence remained impassive, though her pale eyes glittered.

A slash of colour appeared across Lawrence's high cheekbones. 'That'll teach you to make a spectacle of yourself,' he jeered.

'Have you quite finished?' Prudence asked, her voice tight.

'Almost. I've come to give you notice to quit the house.'

'Oh!' Patience couldn't help it. The cry slipped out.

'In spite of Prudence's tantrum in the street, I'm here to do the decent thing and give you until the end of the month.'

'The end of the month?' Patience's heart thudded. If their plan failed, then at the end of January...

'And this is the decent thing, is it?' said Prudence.

'It is indeed. You'll receive an official letter from Wardle early next week.'

'But out of the goodness of our hearts,' said Evelyn, 'we couldn't let that be the first you heard of it. We couldn't subject you to that shock.'

There was a burning sensation in Patience's eyes and she steepled her hands in front of her lips. How could Pa have done this to them? How could Lawrence?

'Don't imagine you can extend your occupancy beyond that. My coming here today to tell you in person goes in my favour. It demonstrates how tolerant I'm prepared to be even after you treated my good self and my lady wife, not to mention my solicitor, so shabbily.'

'Lawrence, please,' Evelyn murmured. 'I'm sure they understand what's expected of them.' Again, that beam. She smoothed the skirt of her crêpe-de-chine dress, spreading her fingers on her knees with a flash of precious stones. 'Obviously we'll leave you alone as much as we can to get your packing done, but you won't mind if we pop in to do some measuring, will you?'

'And to label the items that are to stay.' Lawrence rocked to and fro on his heels. 'We wouldn't want there to be any unfortunate misunderstandings.'

'Speaking of which,' said Prudence, 'I believe you walked off with our fish-knives the last time you were here. Could I trouble you to return them since they weren't Pa's personal property?'

'Well, really,' said Evelyn. 'Yes, of course.'

'But feel free to hang onto the epergne. Horrid old thing – I never did like it.'

'Finished gallivanting, have you?' Mum demanded the moment Belinda and Sarah walked through the door. 'Leaving me to work my fingers to the bone as usual, our Sarah. Well, I've left you a pile of darning, so you needn't kid yourself you've got off scot-free.'

'Mum, I won't be home before midnight...' Sarah began.

'I'll make a start on it,' said Belinda. She had intended to walk Sarah to the bus stop, but she would have to forego that.

Sarah had only a few minutes before she had to hurry on her way, flinging goodbyes over her shoulder. Belinda sifted through the darning. Boys' socks, mostly. Wouldn't life be simpler if boys were taught to sew? She rifled around in Mum's sewing-box and found the darning mushroom and some wool.

But instead of being pleased, Mum was nowty. 'I don't know why you have to help our Sarah when I'm here peeling carrots and chopping swede for a whole family.'

'If our Bel had been here to do the dinner, at least our Sarah would have set off for work with a hot meal in her belly,' growled Dad.

And that was all it took. Next moment, they were shouting at one another. Belinda felt her customary wretched hollowness. Fingers brushed her arm and, with a jerk of his chin, George signalled they should leave their parents to it. He handed her her shawl, took his coat from the back of the door and led her outside.

'Why have we come out here?' she asked. 'We could have sat in the bedroom.'

'No chance of being overheard out here.' He popped his tweed cap onto his head, his fingers brushing his moustache, which was still new enough that he couldn't leave it alone.

'Not much chance of it in the bedroom, the way they're yelling,' said Belinda. 'Anyroad, what have you got to say that's so private?'

His expression changed subtly. The muscles tightened around his jaw, hardening the youthful lines of his face. He wasn't a boy any more. He would be nineteen this summer. He had fought for his country.

His gaze locked on hers and she felt a tremor of apprehension. 'I've got a new job.'

Surprise made her laugh. 'Congratulations! Why so serious?'

'You think me getting a new job is a joke?'

'Of course not.' She felt slapped down. 'I didn't know you'd applied for something.'

He shrugged. 'No one does. Only you.'

She ought to feel honoured, but her skin prickled. 'What are you going to do?'

He drew himself up, his face lapsing into boyishness. 'I'm joining the post office. I'm going to be a postman. You know what that means? I'll be a civil servant.'

'Oh, George. That's summat to be proud of, that is.' She immediately pictured Ben as a postman, which was wrong and selfish when George was all puffed up with excitement, but she couldn't help it. She tried to make amends by making a fuss of him. 'You'll wear a uniform and have your own round. You'll be in charge of all those letters and postcards.'

'It's a responsible job. Folk rely on their postman.'

'It's more than a job, George. It's a proper, dignified occupation. Oh, let me give you a hug.' She threw her arms round him for a moment, then stepped away, feeling warm and relaxed, close to him in a way she hadn't been for a long time. 'My brother the postman. And I'm the first to know. I'm honoured.' She was too. How stupid to have felt wary.

Delving in his pockets, George produced a packet of Lagoons and drew out a half-smoked one, popping it between his lips as he fiddled with a box of Swan Vestas. The tip of the cigarette glowed as he inhaled. He threw back his head, exhaling a stream of smoke into the air.

'I'll be leaving home an' all.'

She frowned. For a moment, all she could think of was the attic dormitory in the Claremont Hotel. All the chambermaids and kitchen-girls slept there – all but Sarah.

'Do postmen have dormitories?' she asked.

'No, but you remember Harry Phelps? We were mates at school.'

'You were more than that. As I recall, you ran off together to join up.'

God, what a scare that had given everyone. Auntie Enid had received the telegram about Ben in the January and, a few weeks later, George and Harry had lied about their ages and joined the army. Hadn't Ben's death taught them anything? As for the authorities who turned a blind eye to lads telling blatant lies...

But George and Harry had both come home, that was the main thing.

'Harry's auntie is looking for a lodger to help make ends meet, so that's where I'll be living. It's all arranged.'

'And you've not told Mum and Dad?'

'I thought I'd tell you first so you can start packing to come home.'

'You what?'

'You heard. You was quick enough to bugger off when you got engaged, and you stayed buggered off after Ben copped it, but with me moving out, you'll have to come back. Mum will need your money.'

There was a heavy weight in her chest; she had to push her breath past it. 'I'm not coming back here.' She couldn't. Her skin crawled.

'I've done my fair share, Bel. Now it's your turn.'

'Belinda Layton! How could you?'

Grandma Beattie's voice, sharp and vexed but with an edge of hurt, suggested she wanted to come pounding down the stairs, but instead she had to creak her way slowly down, same as always. She reached the bottom and stood there, feet planted apart, eyes hard as flint, mouth bunched up. Belinda left off blackleading the range, getting up off her knees and scooping an errant lock of dark hair away from her face.

'What's wrong? Have I done summat?' Then she saw what Grandma Beattie had in her hand. Oh, heck. It was difficult not to slump with guilt; but she hadn't done owt wrong, she hadn't.

Would Auntie Enid and Grandma Beattie see it that way?

'What's the matter?' demanded Auntie Enid. She had just come in with their shopping and was putting their Sunday chops in the meat-safe.

'Eh, Mrs Sloan, you won't believe it,' said Grandma Beattie. She rounded on Belinda. 'I weren't checking up on you. I weren't nosing. I was just putting new lavender sachets in your hanging cupboard and one of 'em slipped through my fingers and when I picked it up...' She stopped, her breathing harsh. 'Oh, Mrs Sloan, you'll never guess what our girl's done behind us backs.'

Auntie Enid's gaze flashed from Grandma Beattie to Belinda and back again. 'What? Tell me.'

'The sachet fell behind summat at the bottom of the cupboard – a brown paper parcel. I never opened it on purpose, but when I fiddled around to get the sachet, the parcel fell on't floor and...'

Belinda's neck shrank into her shoulders.

Grandma Beattie brought out the piece of mauve material, waving it accusingly. 'You never said owt about wanting to break your black.'

Oh, why hadn't she been brave enough to tackle the conversation, preferably before she had bought the wretched stuff? 'I'm sorry if I've hurt you.'

Grandma Beattie might be riled up to boiling point, but Auntie Enid looked pale and perplexed, which was somehow worse.

'Oh, Belinda. Why, love?' Auntie Enid looked like she might collapse in tears. 'I thought... I mean, the three of us... Our Ben...'

'It's only a piece of mauve fabric,' Belinda said gently. 'I wanted to wear a bit of colour. It's been four years...'

Auntie Enid plonked down at the table, as if her legs had given way. 'I thought... Nay, I can't say it. Things will never be the same again if I say it.'

'Things 'ull already never be the same again,' snapped Grandma Beattie.

Anguish chilled Belinda's blood. 'If you mean that maybe I don't love Ben any more...' She clapped her hand to her mouth to stop a desperate keening pouring out.

'How can you want to leave him behind?' Auntie Enid whispered.

'I don't. I'm not. I only want to wear a little colour.'

Grandma Beattie flung the offending material on the table. 'I wish I'd never found it.'

They all stared at one another. Belinda was the first to look away. If they were this upset about the mauve, what would they be like when they saw the pink? Maybe they never would. Maybe she would never be brave enough to show them.

In the end, they all returned to what they had been doing before, because what else were they to do? It didn't matter how distraught you were five minutes ago. There were still lavender sachets to be popped in to drawers and cupboards; still turnips and potatoes to be tipped into the vegetable box; still a socking great range to be blackleaded.

Belinda rubbed vigorously at the smooth old surfaces. She was awash with grief and regret, but there was frustration and anger too. Wanting to add mauve to her black didn't mean she had forgotten Ben. Trying for an office job hadn't meant she was getting above herself. She felt hemmed in by other peoples' expectations. George said she had to move home – well, who was he to boss her about?

A knock at the door jolted the strained, busy silence. Belinda answered it. Miss Kirby stood outside, wrapped up in an overcoat, her hat pulled down over her ears against the cold.

'Miss Kirby! What brings you here?'

'I went to Cromwell Street and your mother gave me this address. I've something to tell you, following on from what we talked about last time.'

'You mean office work?' Oh, heck. Today of all days. She was tempted to grab her shawl and march Miss Kirby along the lane, but there had been enough secrets for one day.

'Who is it?' Auntie Enid came up behind her.

'This is my old teacher, Miss Kirby.'

'Where are your manners?' said Auntie Enid. 'Invite her in. How do, Miss Kirby. I'm Mrs Sloan, Belinda's honorary mother-in-law.'

'Please sit down, Miss Kirby,' said Belinda. 'May I take your coat?'

'No, thank you. I shan't stay long.'

'Who is it?' Grandma Beattie laboured down the stairs.

'It's Miss Kirby,' said Belinda. 'She's the teacher who—'

'Who wanted to send you to high school,' Grandma Beattie finished. From her tone, Miss Kirby might have wanted to send Belinda to the sewage works.

'What brings you here, Miss Kirby?' Auntie Enid asked. Was her voice a trifle more refined?

'I met Belinda recently and we talked about—'

'Office work,' said Grandma Beattie. 'Aye, we know. Filling her head with nonsense...'

Belinda flushed. 'I applied for a position, but I didn't get it.'

Miss Kirby brightened. 'So you're interested in bettering yourself? That's why I'm here.'

'Mrs Sloan,' Auntie Enid murmured, forestalling Grandma Beattie. 'Let's hear what Miss Kirby has to say.'

'Friends of mine, two very respectable maiden ladies, are about to set up a business school and I wondered if Belinda might be interested in taking lessons.'

'Yes,' said Belinda.

'And how do you propose to do that when you're out working all day?' asked Auntie Enid.

'It will be a night school,' said Miss Kirby, 'with classes in the evenings. One of the Miss Heskeths goes out to work herself, in one of the Corporation offices.' Her glance flicked round, landing on each of them. 'I've written down the address for you, if you wish to make enquiries. I'll leave you to discuss it as a family.'

'I'll see you out.' Belinda showed her to the door. 'Thank you for this.'

'You're welcome, dear. I hope...' Miss Kirby's gaze darted past her into the cottage. 'Never mind.'

Belinda shut the door and returned to the others.

'Well, I don't know,' grouched Grandma Beattie. 'First that material and now this. Look at her face, Mrs Sloan. She's already made up her mind, and never mind what we think. She leaving us behind.'

It was as if the breath had been snatched from her body. She threw herself on her knees at Grandma Beattie's feet, grasping the knobbly old knuckles and peering up into her face.

'I'd never ever do that. You're Ben's nan and that means you're my nan too.' Twisting, she reached a hand towards Auntie Enid. 'And you're my mother-in-law. I know how much you want things to stay the same – and I do an' all, here, in our home, in our little family. But I'm the youngest and one day I'll be on my own. I won't be able to keep End Cottage on my mill money. I'll have a better chance of supporting myself if I have an office job.'

Annoyance shot through her. She was tired of being the obedient daughter. Ben's death wasn't just the loss of the boy she loved. It had also robbed her of proper grown-up status. As a wife, no matter how young, she would have been accorded respect that was denied her as an unmarried girl. Was she destined to go through life not being taken seriously?

'Well, if you put it that way,' said Auntie Enid. 'But you're not going round there today. You must sleep on it. We all must.'

The thought of it hung in the air all afternoon and evening. At cocoa-time, when Grandma Beattie trotted out her determination not to go to bed on an argument, Belinda fiddled about inside her collar and drew out the dainty locket Ben had given her. It was warm from her skin.

'I remember our Ben giving it to you.' Auntie Enid smiled sadly. 'I remember him bringing it home when he bought it. "D'you think she'll like it, Ma?" Eh, what girl wouldn't?'

'He thought the world of you, our Ben did,' said Grandma Beattie. 'We think the world of you an' all.'

Her heart swelled and warmth filled her. 'I wear this locket every day, but you're the only ones that know. To me, it's a private thing between me and Ben. I wear it under my clothes, next to my heart. I don't parade round the streets with it on show; I don't invite people to say, "That's pretty. Where did you get it?" I know it's important to wear black and show respect, but I don't need to dress in black from head to toe to keep Ben's memory alive. I'm not asking to wear sunshine-yellow, just a touch of mauve. It's still respectful, but it's a bit of relief from all the black and it would make me feel better.' She gazed into their careworn faces, yearning for their approval. 'You want me to feel better – don't you?'

Chapter Seven

PATIENCE TOOK THEIR small joint of lamb out of the oven. It had reduced in the cooking. Would there be enough for rissoles tomorrow? It didn't matter if there wasn't quite enough: they would still have rissoles. It was important that the Sunday joint stretched to Monday. It was a question of standards.

She had set the table with the best china, the so-called good stuff that Evelyn had claimed, rightly, they never used. Well, why not use it? Why keep things for best if suitable occasions never arose? They didn't live a 'for best' kind of life. She had dug out the cut-glass tumblers and matching water jug as well, washing and polishing them before adding them to the table.

'Goodness, are we expecting visitors?' said Prudence, coming into the dining room.

'It's a waste, keeping the best things in the sideboard. A few days ago, I thought Lawrence and Evelyn were going to waltz off with them, so now I want to enjoy them.'

Afterwards, Prudence returned to the sitting room while Patience cleared away and washed up. She was responsible for all the housework, cooking and shopping, and always had been. Keeping house was what she had dreamed of as a child, though of course she had imagined keeping house for her husband and children.

She joined Prudence in the sitting room, where their small fire crackled away. Instead of reading, Prudence was jotting in one of Pa's notebooks.

'What are you doing?'

'Planning lessons.'

A frisson ran through Patience. Would Prudence's plan work? And if it did, what of their relationship with Lawrence and Evelyn?

Patience picked up her tapestried sewing-bag and withdrew her current piece; a tray-cloth she was working in crewel embroidery in a Jacobean design of curving stems and subtly shaded flowers and leaves. Sometimes it felt as though their house was covered from top to bottom in crewel-work.

The doorbell rang.

Prudence frowned. 'Who can that be? Sunday is meant to be a day of rest.'

'Says the person scribbling away at her lesson plans,' Patience said mildly.

Prudence made a *tsk* sound and carried on.

Loosely folding the tray-cloth, Patience left the room, the chill in the hall hitting her as she went to open the front door.

A girl stood outside. She seemed familiar – but where from? How could she possibly know a person of this sort? Her puzzled gaze took in the black shawl, the black collar and blouse-front underneath, the black skirt. Older shawl-women habitually dressed in black from head to foot, but not young ones like this. She must be in mourning. Poor thing.

The next instant, Patience placed her.

'It's you!'

'Miss Softer!'

'I beg your pardon? You've come to the wrong address, dear. Our name is Hesketh.' She glanced up and down the cul-de-sac, putting names to residences. 'I know no one of that name.'

She took a step backwards, ready to shut the door, but the girl spoke up.

'Please, miss. I'm sorry to get your name wrong. I'm here about the business school.'

'Who is it?' came Prudence's voice from behind and Patience stepped aside.

'This young lady has come to enquire about our business school.'

Prudence's raised eyebrow said *Young lady?*

'Our first enquiry.' Patience wasn't sure what to do with her voice. Sound pleased? To have a working-class shawl-girl on their doorstep? And yet – it was an enquiry. Already!

Prudence's features hardened. 'I know you. You're from Grace, Wardle and Grace. Have you been sent to spy on us? I'm not standing for this. Lawrence has gone too far.' But her annoyance melted into a pained stare. 'If he already knows about the business school, we haven't a hope.'

'To spy?' The girl sucked in a breath. 'Honestly, miss, I don't know what you're talking about. Anyroad, I don't work for them.'

'Don't tell lies,' snapped Prudence. 'We saw you in their office. We thought—'

Patience nudged her: no need to insult the girl with their assumption she was the cleaner. 'You offered us a drink. Only an employee would be permitted to do that.'

'I were there for an interview – for the position of office junior,' she added.

'Really?' Impossible not to sound surprised.

'Yes, miss, really.' She lifted her chin. 'Or do you think girls in shawls have no business wanting better jobs? I'm sorry to have wasted your time.'

She started to turn away. What was the right thing to do? Prudence made all the important decisions, but this one felt somehow too important to leave to her. Patience bit her lip.

The kindness this girl had shown when she was distressed deserved something in return, surely?

'Come in and we can talk about it.'

Prudence glared at her, but at least she had the common courtesy to turn her head away from the girl as she did it. Patience lifted her eyebrows in answer, feeling a flicker of uncertainty at what she had done. The girl looked clean, but you never could tell.

Prudence stalked to the sitting room. Patience stood aside, giving the girl an encouraging smile as she followed, bringing with her a swish of cold damp air. Entering the room behind her, Patience caught the girl's hesitation. Not a bold piece, then. How must their sitting room look to this girl? The crimson velvet curtains in the bay window may have hung there for donkey's years, but their fringing and lining testified to their quality. Did the armchairs in this girl's house have antimacassars and arm-caps, with a spare set in the sideboard? Her house wouldn't have a carpet, let alone one that covered most of the floor; and it probably had whitewash instead of wallpaper.

The girl's lips parted. 'You have electricity!' A rosy flush swept across her cheeks. 'I'm sorry. First the muddle over your name, and now your electric light switch.'

'First impressions are important,' said Prudence, 'and so far...'

'You're probably nervous, aren't you?' Patience gave Prudence a fleeting frown. 'Sit over here and we must perform introductions.'

'I'm Miss Hesketh,' said Prudence, 'and this is my sister, Miss Patience Hesketh.'

'I'm Belinda Layton.'

'How do you do, Miss Layton?'

'Very well, thank you.'

'That is the reply to "How are you?" The correct answer to "How do you do?" is "How do you do?"'

'Prudence!' Patience exclaimed.

'What?' Prudence gave her a look. 'If a girl doesn't have the social graces, she can't work in an office. It's my intention to give instruction in the skills necessary to office work, not to teach deportment and elocution.'

'If a girl is in need of a little polish, perhaps I could provide it.' The idea popped out of Patience's mouth. 'It makes sense when you think about it.' It would be good to contribute something. The teaching of business skills would be solely down to Prudence. Patience didn't have any skills to speak of, beyond the domestic. 'Then it will truly be *our* school and Lawrence will never be able to claim you pushed me into it.' She hadn't even known she was worried about that.

'Well, we'll see.' Prudence turned to their visitor. 'You aren't the sort of person we were expecting. It's all very well to present yourself on our doorstep claiming that girls in shawls deserve a chance, but so far I've seen no evidence of it.'

Miss Layton straightened her shoulders. 'My teacher wanted me to go to high school, but my dad wouldn't let me. She's the one who suggested I come here – Miss Kirby.'

'Miss Kirby?' Patience looked at Miss Layton, seeing intelligence in her expression and quiet resolution in her upright posture. She glanced at Prudence. Could she see it too?

'I was meant to get married,' Miss Layton continued, 'but my fiancé was killed in the war.'

'Oh, my dear,' Patience murmured.

'I've worked in a mill for a few years and I was expecting to stay there for ever, but Miss Kirby told me about surplus girls.'

'So sad,' said Patience. 'All those girls facing life alone. No husbands, no children.' She knew how that felt. The hopeless dreams; the love, unused and unwanted. The gnawing loneliness. The fear of an empty old age.

'Working in the mill is a good job,' said Miss Layton, 'but I don't want to stay there for the rest of my life, not if I'm capable of better. I'm a surplus girl and that means I need to think about my future and do the best I can for myself.'

Prudence leaned forward. Surely she wasn't going to tear the girl off a strip?

Prudence said, 'Thank you, Miss Layton. You've given me a jolly good idea.'

The rain slashed against the windows. Belinda had already placed pans around the cottage beneath the places where the drips came through, adding the smell of damp to the lingering aroma of lamb chops and mint sauce, mingled with the sharp-edged pungent smell of coal. For tea, they had feasted on oven-bottom muffins with grated Lancashire cheese – well, as grated as it could be when it was so crumbly – and apple-and-marrow chutney. It had been comforting to come home on a dark, rainy evening to something warm and tasty, even if Auntie Enid and Grandma Beattie weren't exactly jumping up and down with glee at her being offered a place at the business school.

'I have to go to Mum and Dad's,' she said. 'The Miss Heskeths want everything done properly; so, being as I don't get the key of the door until June, I need parental consent.'

'What's the hurry?' said Grandma Beattie.

'It's raining,' said Auntie Enid. 'You'll catch a chill.'

'If I wait for an evening in the week, there's no saying Dad will be there.' It was a polite way of saying he would be down the pub.

She pulled on thick woolly socks over her stockings and forced her toasty-warm feet into her ankle-boots before wrapping her shawl round herself.

'Here. Have mine as well.'

Auntie Enid put her shawl over Belinda's head and round her shoulders. Belinda examined her expression. Had she softened? No, she was just being a good mother. Guilt pierced her.

Auntie Enid and Grandma Beattie had been nothing but kind to her and they didn't deserve to be upset. Should she back down? What, and continue with their lives the way they were? No. It was hard fighting for something when no one was on your side, but she mustn't cave in.

As she opened the cottage door, cold wind rushed inside, leaving her no choice but to hurry out at once, the door resisting as she pulled it shut. Rain splattered her face as she peered into the deep darkness. There was no such thing as a lamppost in Grave Pit Lane. She couldn't stand here waiting for her eyes to adjust. Off she went – straight into the mud. She hurried to the cinder path, pulling Auntie Enid's shawl down further over her forehead, holding it bunched under her chin. Reaching the end of the lane, she ran through the wet streets.

In Cromwell Street, she thumped on the front door. It was unlocked during the day, but after dark someone turned the key. Belinda couldn't imagine anyone in her family bothering.

The door opened and there was Mrs Abbott from the first floor.

'Oh, it's you. Shut your noise.'

As she opened her family's door, Mrs Abbott shouted, 'Let your own visitors in,' and stomped upstairs before Mum or Dad could reply, though that didn't stop Thad yelling, 'Oy, you! Don't you tell us—' before George clipped him round the ear, prompting a different sort of 'Oy!'

'What brings you here?' asked Mum. 'Take off them shawls and sit by the fire.'

She wove her way across the crowded room. Thad was at the table with George; Mikey was hunkered down in a grimy corner by the range, so either there had already been a scrap or else Dad was taking preventive measures. Jacob sat cross-legged on the hearthrug.

'Budge up, Jacob,' she said.

'Jacob doesn't live here. I'm Jake.'

'You're a pain in the neck,' said George.

Oh, this was just what she needed, frayed tempers and a grouchy atmosphere.

'Is everything all right?' Mum asked.

'Actually, I've come to ask for Dad's permission.'

Dad sat up straighter. 'Oh aye?'

'I want to go to business school. There's one starting up in Chorlton.'

'You can't go back to school,' said George. 'What about your job?'

'It's night school.' She looked at Dad, willing him to like the idea, to ask questions, to want what was best for her. 'It's so I'll be able to get an office job.'

'Why do you need permission?' he asked. Then he scowled. 'I'm not paying any fees.'

'I'm not asking you to. I can pay for myself by working Saturday mornings. I have to get permission because I'm under twenty-one.'

'You'll earn more in an office job.'

'Probably not right away.'

He jerked his chin. 'You can forget that, then.'

'But, Denby,' said Mum, 'if she earns more in a year or two's time...'

'That's no good in the here and now. She can stop where she is.' He wasn't even looking at her. It was as if she wasn't in the room.

'But, Dad...'

His face swung round impatiently and he pinned her down with his gaze. 'Hand over more of your earnings and I might consider it.'

'No.'

His answer was a shrug as he turned away.

She left soon after. Why stay? Mum helped her on with her shawls. Her own was damp; Auntie Enid's was positively soggy.

'Sorry your dad said no, love, and I don't mean because of the money. It were rotten on you, losing your Ben. If anyone deserves a chance in life, you do.'

'Thanks, Mum.'

They smiled at one another. Mum's eyes were tired, but for once her mouth wasn't petulant. Belinda felt a rush of love, but George bustled over, stepping in front of Mum, more or less pushing Belinda out of the door.

'George,' she objected.

'I want a word.' He pulled the door to behind them. 'What's going on, our Bel? You can't pack in your job for summat lower paid.'

'It'll be better in the long run – or it would have been, if Dad had said yes.'

'Good job he didn't. Have you forgotten what I told you about moving back?'

'You can't tell me what to do.'

But he was already marching back into their room. Bracing herself, she set off through the rain, huddling inside her wet shawls, and without the promise of permission to keep her warm.

At End Cottage, Auntie Enid and Grandma Beattie drew her indoors, relieving her of the shawls and her boots, which Auntie Enid stuffed with screwed-up newspaper and put on one of the range's shelves to dry out. Then she was pressed into a chair and offered a hot drink, which her fingers were at first too chilled to hold.

'What did Mr Layton say?' asked Auntie Enid.

'No.'

She was aware of a look passing between them. They had got what they wanted.

But Auntie Enid said, 'Your father can't have it both ways. If he had wanted to hang onto his authority, he should have kept you at home instead of letting you move in with us. As your honorary mother-in-law, I'll write you a letter giving permission.'

'Oh, Auntie Enid.'

'Grandma Beattie and me have had a talk. Without Ben to take care of you, we can see that you have to be able to take care of yourself. You won't always have the two of us and we need to know you'll be all right.'

She filled with an inner glow. They were on her side after all. 'Thank you. This means everything to me. And I promise that going to night school won't change things here.'

Auntie Enid sniffed. 'It already has.'

Chapter Eight

I LIVE IN THE present, the here and now, right this moment. I used to have a past. Past, present and future – that's what you're supposed to have, isn't it? Your past life, childhood, parents, your family; going to school; getting your first job; everything that brought you to this moment, this now. And you have plans to take you towards your future. A better job? Marriage? Children? You're supposed to know what you want, what you're aiming for.

I don't know any of that. I have no past. Well, that's not strictly true. I'm building a past, little by little; starting with waking in a bedroom with a sloping ceiling. I remember the smells of lavender and iodine. Such familiar smells. In that moment, a hundred memories danced around me, so close I could almost touch them, but they were just – just – out of reach.

Lavender. A grandmother? A scented pillow? An English garden?

Iodine. Childhood scrapes? Grazed knees? A field hospital?

I know the kind of memories these smells might evoke. I just don't know my own memories.

And I have lived like that ever since.

The bedroom with the sloping ceiling is in a farmhouse in France. I don't know how I got there – or rather I do know, because I've been told. What I mean is, I don't know it of my own knowledge. Is that the correct expression? An expression that is widely used and generally understood? It could be a family saying, for all I know.

Anyhow, Monsieur Durand and his son Jean-Louis found me. I was conscious, apparently, though I don't remember. German soldiers had set a building on fire in the town; and there were men inside. No one could do anything to help, not in that situation. Monsieur Durand and Jean-Louis crept to the back of the building, standing on something to see over the wall. They arrived in time to hear a great shattering of glass. Thick black smoke poured through the opening; then – apparently – I clambered out of the window, dragging a comrade with me. I dumped him on the ground, coughing his guts up, and climbed back inside.

When Jean-Louis would have shinned over the wall, his father pulled him back. He had seen what his son had failed to notice: soldiers in a look-out position on the steps of the old stone cross that marked the centre of the market square. The soldiers couldn't see the back of the building, but they would have seen someone climbing over the wall. Discretion being the better part of valour – and that one has got to be a common saying; I refuse to believe my family coined it – the Durands, *père et fils*, jumped down and melted away.

They returned a few hours later. The Germans were gone and the building was a stinking, blackened shell. Round the back, they found me and a heap of others. A heap, yes. The others were dead, and I was as good as. We were dressed in the uniforms of the British Army, but beyond that there was nothing to identify any of us; no asbestos identity tags, no precious letter from home tucked inside a breast-pocket, not even a packet of cigarettes. Some had presumably died when the smoke invaded their lungs, others had been shot for good measure. I was the lone survivor and it didn't look like I was long for this world.

The Durands carried me back to their farmhouse, where, in due course, I awoke in the room with the sloping ceiling and the smell of lavender and iodine.

And that, in a way, was the beginning of my life.

I had no memory of what had gone before. I hadn't lost just the immediate past, those traumatic events that had brought me to this point. I had lost everything. My entire life, my name, everything. I tried not to worry at first. It would all come back before long. I just needed to recover.

Give it time, I told myself. It'll come back.

That was at the end of 1918. Peace broke out while I was convalescing. It's now the beginning of 1922 and my memory never has returned.

I still live at the farm, though I have not slept in the room with the sloping ceiling for a long time. These days I lay my head in the upstairs part of the barn, where an area was sectioned off for someone, a farmhand or a groom, who went off to war and didn't return. The idea was that I would stay as long as I needed, in other words until I regained my memory or until someone came for me, but neither of those things happened. The war ended and I... stayed.

I could have made my way back home to England – oh, I do know I'm English. If nothing else, so says Monsieur Durand, my excruciating French accent would have made that evident. The Durands call me Pierre. You have to have a name, don't you? It's odd, answering to a name I know is not mine.

I know plenty of other things about myself. I learned French at school – I know that. I don't take sugar. The first time I picked up a pencil, I knew without experimenting which hand to use. I knew I could get on a horse and ride it. I know how to ride a bicycle, how to tie a variety of knots, how to juggle (yes, really!), how to leap like a hurdler over a fence and how to make a paper dart. I know I love the scent of roses. That might sound ridiculous, because who doesn't? But I don't simply love it, I *love* it.

That piece of knowledge is deep down inside at the very core of my being, and at the same time, it is right up at the top, near the surface, immediate and necessary... and out of reach.

Did my family – does my family have roses in the garden? Was I a gardener before the war?

Whatever I was then, I'm a farmhand now. The Durands let me stay, thinking I would move on when the time came. I thought the same thing. But that time has never come. Am I a coward? Is that why I have stayed here this long? Would a braver man have thrown a sack of provisions over his shoulder and headed for his native country?

Was I a coward in wartime?

The locals are used to me. They think nothing of my presence now. I am... I am part of the furniture. Now there's an English expression, if ever there was one. I must tell the Durands. It will make them smile. No doubt there will be an equivalent French expression they will share.

We have managed pretty well, all told, as regards language. My schoolboy French and their limited English proved to be enough to get by on; and over time, my French has come on no end. I do a bit of English teaching in the village; and – very English – I play cricket with the children.

It is a new year. Am I going to stay here, to while away my life, making no attempt to seek out my identity? Was I a ditherer back in the days when I knew myself? Was I a weak fellow, incapable of making decisions?

Or was I capable and determined? Have I lost my character as well as my memory?

It is a cold day, but the skies are azure blue and the sun shines brilliantly. I pick up my pace as I walk into town. That blue sky, after a grey, wet winter, has infected me. I am as close to cheerful as I ever feel. I am heading for the *école* to do a spot of teaching. I have devised a counting game, a loud and boisterous game, I might add, and the children love it.

I have to pass the shell of the building where I was found, where my comrades perished. One day it will be pulled down and rebuilt but for now there are many other jobs that need doing all over the local area. Seeing the wreck of the building where I nearly lost my life does not distress me as such. It frustrates me; the not knowing frustrates me. I have no memory of the atrocity committed by the enemy soldiers. No hideous, nightmarish thoughts or impressions are awakened by my proximity to what remains of the building. I have been inside it, clambering my way through the internal ruins, trying to spark a memory, trying to force memories to the surface, but nothing ever happens.

Will my memory ever return to me? In the early days, I thought all I had to do was wait. Everyone thought so. But time passed and nothing changed. At this stage – what? Am I to accept that my mind will be for ever closed to me?

A man stands outside the building, looking at it. He is a stranger. His upright bearing speaks of the military, even though he is dressed in a suit with a double-breasted jacket. I change course so as not to disturb him, but he hears me and glances round.

'*Bonjour*,' I say.

He steps into my path. 'Excuse me.' He speaks to me in English. 'Isn't that an English accent?'

Something rushes through me. Fear? Elation? 'Yours is the first English voice I've heard in a long time.'

'You live here?'

'Since the war ended.'

'Can you tell me what happened here?' He looks at the building.

'Why do you want to know?'

'I may not be in uniform, but I'm an army man. There are a lot of unanswered questions about what happened here. I should like to find the answers.'

Am I standing on the brink?

'I was one of the soldiers trapped inside. I lost my memory because of it. I don't even know my own name.'

'Really?' He gazes at me. His eyes narrow, then widen again in acceptance. 'If that is the case, sir, then I'll be able to help you find out who you are.'

Chapter Nine

THE LIGHT DUSTING Patience normally did on a Saturday wouldn't be sufficient. Today was special. Today their plan was going to be officially announced.

'I don't know how you have the nerve,' she had told Prudence. It was a good thing she wasn't a nail-biter or she would have nothing left but stumps.

But Prudence exuded composure and resolution. 'We have to do it this way. Telling the press, making it public – how can Lawrence argue? He's going to be the hero of the hour.'

'He won't be fooled for one moment.'

'He doesn't have to be fooled,' Prudence said crisply. 'He merely has to want to be an alderman. His desire to be seen by the world as a jolly good egg will do the rest.'

The week had passed in a whirl. Instead of the packing that Lawrence and Evelyn were undoubtedly picturing, they had been busy preparing for their business school. Patience couldn't help feeling useless compared to Prudence, who had worked in an office for forty years.

Forty years! Where had the time gone? Prudence was going to be fifty-two this year. She hadn't seemed to mind about turning fifty, though Patience had minded quite awfully for her. She was dreading her own fiftieth birthday next year. At least Prudence could claim to have done something with her life. What did she, Patience, have to show for it? A life of domesticity wasn't all it was cracked up to be when it wasn't centred around a family of your own.

But this week had been different. Oh yes, there was nothing like the threat of losing your beloved home to ginger you up. But it wasn't all bad-different. Parts of this week had felt distinctly good-different. Like popping into the St Clement's sale of goods in aid of the local orphanage and finding, of all things, a telephone.

'It's only a replica,' said the anxious-looking woman behind the stall, as if customers routinely attended church sales looking for the real thing. 'Someone in the local amateur theatre company made it as a prop. Goodness knows who's going to buy it.'

Someone in the process of setting up a business school, that's who. Patience bore it home in triumph and Prudence was gratifyingly impressed.

'Now we can teach the correct use of the telephone; how to dial, how to hold it. The girls can have pretend business conversations. That'll be your responsibility. I'll give you guidance in what the conversations should be about. I'll be busy teaching typewriting, filing and so forth. We'll charge extra for book-keeping tuition.'

Patience opened her housemaid's box. They had had a maid once, but that was years ago. Pa had treated Mother's small annuity as if it had turned him into a gentleman of private means, and Prudence's wage stretched only so far. They still had a daily char, of course, to do the rough and keep their doorstep pristine. It was a question of standards.

Talking of standards, she wanted the sitting room gleaming this afternoon. From the housemaid's box, she took cloths and beeswax and polished all the wooden surfaces; well, not quite all, obviously, not the skirting-boards, as that was the char's job. Afterwards she ran the library-brush over the bookcase. As she put the box away, she was tempted to get out the carpet-broom, but that was the char's job – or was it, these days? You did see advertisements in which the lady of the house was using a vacuum cleaner. Mind you, if they had one of those, their faithful old carpet would probably disintegrate and get sucked up, never to be seen again.

She went into the dining room, where Prudence was writing busily.

'Putting the finishing touches to my lessons,' she said without looking up. 'We can't afford to be caught out when Lawrence challenges the validity of this venture.' She put down her pen. 'I've asked the girls to arrive for three o'clock. We've got four signed up so far.'

'It was a good idea of yours to put a postcard on the noticeboard at work. When the two Corporation girls apply for better jobs, that will spur others to join us.'

'In an ideal world, but I doubt the Corporation will be pleased to see its typing pool vanishing.'

'What time is the press coming?' Patience felt a thrill of delight. There was something rather racy in talking about the press.

'Three-thirty. I want the girls here in good time beforehand so I can talk to them about the tuition available to them.'

'And perhaps let them have a go on the typewriter and the telephone; you know, to break the ice.'

Prudence dealt her a withering look. 'This isn't meant to be a jolly jaunt.'

'Of course not, but I'm sure the gentlemen of the press are more likely to be interested if they find pretty girls with smiles on their faces.'

'The gentlemen of the press would do well not to be so susceptible.'

'I only meant that the girls will look eager and interested.'

'In any case, Miss Hunt and Miss Michaels are from the Corporation typing pool. They don't need to be introduced to the typewriter.'

'Then they can show it to Miss Shaw and Miss Layton. It would give Miss Layton a chance to be involved. We don't want her feeling overwhelmed because of her humble background.'

'I hope we haven't made a mistake by accepting a working-class girl. We don't want to give our other pupils the wrong impression.'

'Miss Layton may not be out of the top drawer,' said Patience, 'but she's a polite girl with a pleasant manner. Bright, too. I rather like her.'

'As long as you don't make a pet out of her.'

'She's the one who gave you the surplus girls idea. She deserves a chance.'

'Let's hope so.' Prudence clearly wasn't going to back down: she seldom did. 'As well as the *Manchester Evening News* and *Stockport Echo* reporters, there'll be a lady journalist from *Vera's Voice*.'

Patience leaned forward. 'Really?'

'She lives locally, apparently: Mary Brewer. She writes under the name of Fay Randall.'

'Fay Randall is coming to our house?'

'Mrs Brewer is coming to our house. Fay Randall doesn't exist. Please don't be an embarrassment.'

'I wouldn't dream of it.' It wouldn't be embarrassing if she happened to leave the latest copy of *Vera's Voice* lying around. It would be a compliment. And perhaps a little speech of appreciation would be in order. Nothing effusive, just a few words. 'Miss Randall—'

'Mrs Brewer.'

'Mrs Brewer, then. This is precisely the sort of article she writes: about women doing their best for themselves.'

'If you're considering leaving your most recent *Vera's Voice* in a strategic place, please don't.'

'As if I would.'

'And don't fuss over Mrs Brewer. That would be highly inappropriate.'

'Really, Prudence, I don't know where you get your ideas from.'

'That will be my brother now.' At the sound of the doorbell, Prudence rose to her feet, every inch the gracious hostess. If the occupants of the sitting room could have seen the real, brusque Miss Hesketh, they would have been startled, to say the least.

Patience glanced round. Lawrence had arrived at exactly the right moment. Much longer, and the press would have finished and left. The gentleman from the *Manchester Evening News* was making notes as Miss Hunt answered his questions, while Mrs Brewer was quietly drawing Miss Layton out of her shell. Little Miss Layton had arrived wearing a coat and hat, a tired-looking ensemble but an infinite improvement on last Sunday's shawl.

Prudence accompanied Patience to the front door. They shared a glance before Patience opened the door to reveal Lawrence, in his overcoat with the astrakhan collar, and Evelyn, resplendent in burgundy wool complete with those revolting foxes dangling down her front.

'Come in,' said Prudence. 'Thank you for coming, Lawrence; and you've brought Evelyn. How nice.'

'I hope you've seen sense at last,' said Lawrence.

'Patience will take your coats,' Prudence replied.

She threw Patience an apologetic glance, but it wasn't necessary. Patience was well aware that Prudence had to stage-manage every moment of this crucial meeting. As the others went to the sitting room, she dumped the coats on the monk's bench and hurried behind them.

Prudence entered first. 'Ladies and gentlemen, my brother has arrived: the man of the hour, Mr Lawrence Hesketh and his wife, Evelyn.'

'I didn't realise this was to be a social gathering.' Full marks to Lawrence for a swift recovery.

'This is no time for modesty, Lawrence. Evelyn, have a seat over here, dear. May I present Mrs Brewer, who writes for *Vera's Voice*, and these young ladies are the first pupils...' she drew a breath, '...for our business school.'

'Your... what?'

'Didn't I tell you he's modest?' Prudence steamrollered on, smiling ruthlessly. 'Lawrence, these gentlemen are Mr Cox and Mr Fielden from the newspapers. They and Mrs Brewer are anxious to write up the story of the generosity of Mr Lawrence Hesketh, that well-known businessman who is rising in the world and who has kindly offered to use one of his properties as a business school to assist those unfortunate girls who, because of the terrible loss of life in the war, have little hope of finding husbands and instead face a lifetime of fending for themselves.' She glanced at the journalists. 'Did you get all that?'

'Mr Hesketh, this is a magnanimous gesture,' said Mr Cox. 'Where did you get the idea?'

'You must allow my brother a few moments to recover,' Prudence said smoothly. 'He intended that the school should be set up without fuss. We're deeply proud of him – aren't we, Patience?'

'Indeed, yes.' And then, somehow or other, words spilled out of her in a torrent. 'Prudence and I, being spinster ladies ourselves, feel a particular concern for this young generation of surplus girls and we're gratified that our dear brother shares our anxiety.' Goodness, where did all that spring from? Might she read her words in a forthcoming issue of *Vera's Voice*?

'Mr Hesketh.' Mr Cox tried again. 'I've heard your name before, sir. There are those who suggest that one day you might be elevated to the position of alderman. Do you think this venture might assist in that?'

Patience poured a thousand blessings on Mr Cox's head. That word, *alderman*, was more powerful than *abracadabra*.

Lawrence lifted his chin and thrust back his shoulders. 'I'm glad to have the opportunity to answer that question, Mr – Cox, is it? – Mr Cox, because while there might be people who imagine that such honours can, as it were, be bought and paid for through good works, I take the view that one's good works have to emanate from one's own integrity and a deep-rooted desire to do one's best for one's fellow man, or in this case,' and he glanced round in an avuncular fashion at the girls, 'one's fellow woman; and in the truest spirit of philanthropy, I seek no advantage to myself from this, or indeed from any other venture with which I might have the good fortune to be associated, and I would never push myself forward into the public gaze, but prefer to take a private, modest satisfaction in whatever I do that might, in some small way, serve to benefit others, as indeed my sisters will testify, since this gathering here today was entirely at their instigation and my good lady wife and I had no notion of what we would be walking into when we arrived.'

Thank goodness: a full stop at last. Patience was almost breathless as Lawrence ceased pontificating for long enough to flash a dangerous smile at Prudence and herself. She felt a quiver in her stomach.

Had they done enough to secure their home?

Belinda almost skipped down Grave Pit Lane. She had been anxious about the afternoon and having to hold her own among her fellow pupils, whom she was meeting for the first time, and it had come as a massive relief to find there were only three others so far. After Mr and Mrs Hesketh had taken their gracious leave and the reporters had departed, Miss Patience – they had been instructed to call the ladies Miss Hesketh and Miss Patience – had invited the girls to have tea and cake with them, whereupon she had sprung to her feet, saying she was expected at home.

'I'll see you out, Miss Layton,' said Miss Patience.

She would much rather have seen herself out, but Miss Patience had helped her on with her coat – they had a little room just for coats: imagine that! – and nothing in her tone or manner had suggested that Belinda's, or rather Mrs Harrison's, old coat and hat were in any way inferior to the stylish coats belonging to the other girls.

She was dying to get home and describe to Auntie Enid and Grandma Beattie how the ladies had taken the girls into the dining room, with its polished table of dark wood and matching chairs, so they could try out the typewriter and pretend to have conversations using a toy telephone. Belinda had felt hopelessly self-conscious, but not for long. Encouraged by Miss Michaels, she had typed her name and address, using capitals and commas and everything, and Miss Michaels had applauded when she finished, though not in a snooty way, but rather as if she had managed something both clever and amusing.

Miss Patience had given her the piece of paper on which she had done her typing. 'To show them at home,' she said with a smile.

Warmth had radiated throughout Belinda's body. Might she fit in at the business school? Even though she was from a lower rank in life, did being surplus girls make them all equal? Might she really and truly earn the right to wear a hat and coat to work instead of a shawl?

Oh, Ben, you don't mind, do you?

Opening the door to End Cottage, she bounced in, wanting to regale Auntie Enid and Grandma Beattie with the wonderful details. They weren't as keen as she was, not by a long chalk, but surely they wouldn't be able to resist when she spilled out her description of this afternoon.

The grim faces they turned to her made her insides slump. Then she realised their sombre expressions weren't because of her.

Dad was here.

'Dad!'

He never came here. And Sarah was in the corner, her face rigid with misery. Belinda hung up her borrowed coat and hat. Would it look false to smile as she turned round? It would look strange if she didn't. You were supposed to be pleased to see your dad, weren't you? But she wasn't. She felt wary. Even if his unexpected visit, coupled with his uncertain temper and money-first attitude to life, weren't reason enough for wariness, Sarah's frozen posture and sidelong glances would have rung warning bells.

'Your father says he's come to take you home,' said Auntie Enid in a flat voice that held on tight to her thoughts.

'Aye, I have that.' Dad came to his feet. 'And not a moment too soon, if yon coat and hat are owt to go by. Frittering your money away on clothes, when you ought to be helping your family.'

'They're borrowed,' said Belinda.

'Where have you been that you needed to do yourself up like a dog's dinner?' His eyebrows drew together. 'You've not got yourself a new man, have you?'

Cries of denial met this, not just from her but from Auntie Enid and Grandma Beattie, their words clashing together, none of them distinct. Belinda didn't even know what her own words were. They just burst out of her; or maybe it had simply been a howl of protest.

'Get upstairs and get packed,' ordered Dad, 'since our Sarah weren't allowed to do it for you.' He glared at Auntie Enid.

'You can't come here, expecting to walk off with Belinda's things,' said Auntie Enid. 'As for her moving back in with you, it's the first we've heard about it.'

'So you keep saying, missus.' He jerked his chin at Belinda. 'Don't gawp at me like that, girl. George has left home, so you're to come back. He said he'd told you, so don't pretend not to know.'

'Sorry, Bel,' Sarah whispered. 'He made me come.'

Belinda stood up straight. 'I'm not coming, Dad. I told George I wouldn't.'

'There, then that's settled,' said Auntie Enid. 'This is Belinda's home. You agreed to let her come here and—'

'That were when she was going to marry your lad. Now she's just any old spinster and spinster daughters belong at home with their parents.'

'I stand in the place of a mother-in-law to her.' Spots of red appeared in Auntie Enid's cheekbones, sharpening her features.

'But you're not her ma-in-law, are you? That's the whole point. Unmarried daughters live with their parents.'

'And hand over their wages, I expect,' said Auntie Enid.

'What's wrong with that? Me and her mother fetched her up: now she pays us back.'

'She's not going with you. She wants to live here and her grandma and me want her to stay.'

Dad snorted. 'She's not Bel's grandma and you're not her mother-in-law. Our Bel's nowt to you, not since your Ben went. Ta for putting up with her this long, but she's coming home with me and she'll pay her way in my family, not yours. Sarah, Belinda, get up them stairs and pack Bel's stuff.'

Auntie Enid stood up. 'Belinda is stopping here.'

Dad swaggered across and thrust his face close to hers. Auntie Enid flinched but held her ground.

'I'm her father and I say what's what. That's the law, that is.'

With an ugly smirk on his face, he tapped the side of his nose, then pointed his finger at Auntie Enid. Belinda bunched her hands into fists as shame seared through her.

As he turned away, Auntie Enid breathed in, making her nostrils flare. 'It would be the law if you still had your parental rights, but you haven't got those any more.'

Dad swung round. 'What are you talking about?'

'When Belinda asked you for parental consent to her joining the business school, you refused.'

'As was my right, as her father.'

'All you wanted,' cut in Grandma Beattie, 'was for her to carry on earning at her present rate so you can squeeze a few bob out of her every week. The poor lass tips up here every Friday and then tries to help her family an' all. Me and Mrs Sloan know full well what goes on – and not because your Belinda has ever said a word against you, so don't be giving her any sideways looks.'

Dad wrenched his glare away from Belinda. 'Me and her mum are entitled to a share of her wages and if I don't want her to go to business school, she doesn't go.'

'But she does go,' said Auntie Enid. 'That's where she was this afternoon – because I gave my consent.'

'You did what, missus?'

'I'm the adult she lives with and that makes me her guardian. As such, I wrote a letter giving my parental consent. If you don't like that, Mr Layton, I suggest you pike off down Chorlton and take it up at the business school. They're proper ladies, they are, and they won't take kindly to you arriving on their doorstep, shouting the odds.'

Belinda saw her chance to jump in. 'Auntie Enid's right, Dad. The Miss Heskeths had the newspapers there this afternoon and their brother is a famous businessman. The school is all his idea. He won't let you spoil owt.'

Dad banged his fist on the table. 'She's still coming home with me.'

'No,' said Auntie Enid. 'This is her home and has been since she were a lass of fifteen. I have parental responsibility now and, if you don't believe me, we can take it up with them posh folk.'

'The Heskeths,' said Belinda.

'You keep out of this,' growled Dad.

'Aye, them Heskeths,' said Auntie Enid. 'And kindly don't thump your fist on my table.'

'Come on, Dad.' Sarah tugged his arm. 'Let's go home.'

He yanked his arm away, his elbow jerking up and outwards, making Sarah flinch away. Belinda took a protective step towards her. She hadn't seen him this riled up since she couldn't remember when. The blaming and bickering that would go on between Dad and Mum when he got home didn't bear thinking about.

'Aye, well, happen you can stay for now, our Bel,' said Dad, 'but you needn't think this is over.'

Snatching up his cap, he gained the door in a couple of strides and threw it open, letting the cold air pour in. 'Come on, Sarah. Let's go and tell your mum that our Bel has turned her back on her family.'

'If it helps,' Sarah whispered, 'he were just as angry with George.'

'Now!' shouted Dad and Sarah scuttled out. Dad followed, banging the door shut.

Belinda didn't know whether to crumple with relief or drop her chin to her chest in shame. How could Dad come here and make a show of her like that? There had never before been a word spoken against her family under this roof, but now the pretence had been dashed aside and she felt diminished.

'Now there's a lass who doesn't want to go home,' said Grandma Beattie.

'Thank you for standing up for me,' said Belinda.

'I didn't mean you,' said Grandma Beattie. 'I meant your Sarah.'

Chapter Ten

BELINDA WENT BACK to Saturday morning cleaning to pay her night school fees. She wished she could have used some of the money to smarten her appearance. It was surprising and rather shaming how quickly she had gone from feeling special in her borrowed coat and hat to feeling dowdy. The other girls wore such attractive clothes. Miss Hunt had a dark green cotton mackintosh that rippled around her when she walked down the Heskeths' path in that brisk way of hers; and Miss Shaw's wool-tweed, though by no means new, had been spruced up with braid around the collar and cuffs and along the tops of the patch pockets. And they wore *colours* too. Miss Shaw's tweed was a heathery shade and Miss Hunt's mackintosh was a mustard-yellow that Thad would take devilish pleasure in aiming mud-pies at, if Belinda had ever dared wear anything so bold.

Their dresses were lovely an' all. Miss Michaels had a linen dress in a fetching hyacinth blue that she wore with a navy cardigan; and Miss Shaw had a cream-and-cherry dress that would look a lot better if the waistline was in the proper place, but apparently your dress's waist being on your hips was the coming fashion.

All in black, Belinda felt a hundred years old. What must her fellow pupils must think of her? Not that she saw much of them, since lessons were conducted mostly on a one-to-one basis, with one girl at the dining table with Miss Hesketh and another in the sitting room with Miss Patience.

'We want to give our pupils our best attention,' Miss Patience told her.

When she reported this at home, Grandma Beattie said, 'You're getting your money's worth, then.'

Actually, Belinda wouldn't have minded group lessons in preference to working alone under Miss Hesketh's gimlet eye. At her first filing lessons, Miss Hesketh produced a stack of cards, rather like those in the catalogue drawers at the library.

'I've put a name on each one: surname, first name and middle initial. Your job it to put them into alphabetical order swiftly and accurately. If you have four beginning with B, what will you do? And if two people have the same surname?'

Each time she visited the house in Wilton Close, the pile of cards had grown and there were more duplicated surnames and several pairs of names whose only difference lay in their middle initials.

'You enjoy sorting the cards into order, don't you?' Miss Hesketh observed. 'Your interest does you credit.' But just as Belinda was feeling pleased with herself, Miss Hesketh remarked drily, 'I hope your interest doesn't wane when you've been filing for twenty years.'

'I hope you aren't putting Miss Layton off,' said Miss Patience from the door.

Miss Hesketh fetched a sigh. There was never anything sorrowful in her sighs. Her sighs were annoyed or scornful. She could even sigh in a contemptuous way, though, thank heaven, she had never directed one of those at Belinda.

'If you're ready for Miss Hunt, I'll send her through,' said Miss Patience.

'Certainly. If you'll tidy the table, please, Miss Layton.'

If Miss Hesketh's attitude was anything to go by, tidying up was an essential skill without which finding employment in an office was out of the question. Belinda tidied, then joined Miss Patience for her telephone lesson.

'Are you quite all right, Miss Layton? You appear a little distracted.'

'It was what Miss Hesketh said. Twenty years! I know the point of coming here is to set myself up for life. But – twenty years. I'll be forty, forty-one come the summer. Grandma Beattie will be long gone, and Auntie Enid will be in her sixties, hanging on at the mill for as long as she can.'

'It doesn't always do to look too far ahead. Of course, if you're anticipating happy things, it's different.'

Was there sadness in those pale blue eyes? A middle-aged spinster couldn't have much to look forward to. She couldn't have much to look back on either.

Oh, heck. That'll be me one day.

'If Ben – that's my fiancé's name – if he'd lived, then when I'm forty I could have had a daughter the age I am now.'

Was Miss Patience about to touch her hand comfortingly? Of course not. Ladies kept their hands to themselves.

'I'm sorry, Miss Patience. I didn't mean to speak out of turn.'

'No apology necessary; though you must get used to saying "I apologise" rather than "I'm sorry." I've also noticed that you have a tendency to swap "was" and "were" around. An employer will require you to use correct English at all times. My sister has prepared a telephone lesson about deliveries that have gone wrong, so here's an opportunity to practise your apologies.'

It never ceased to be a relief that the telephone lessons were done with Miss Patience, who was such a sympathetic lady.

With Miss Hesketh, Belinda learned about invoices and delivery notes, using real documents that would otherwise have been disposed of by the Corporation, where Miss Hesketh worked and probably terrified everyone under her. There were also money lessons. Belinda thought those pointless to start with, until she was presented with several pages of columns of money to check.

'See if you can find the errors,' said Miss Hesketh. 'If you show an aptitude for this kind of thing, you might be a suitable candidate for book-keeping. That's a responsible job, and is paid accordingly, even for a woman, though you wouldn't earn as much as a man, of course.'

'It's the same at the mill. The men are on a higher rate than the women. It's not fair.'

'It is, however, the way of the world,' said Miss Hesketh in a tone that closed the subject.

'Did I say the wrong thing?' Belinda whispered later to Miss Patience.

'My sister is in full agreement with you, never doubt that. Between you and me, she had to fight to keep her job after the war and was regarded by some as unpatriotic because she resisted handing her position to a returning soldier, even though the job had been hers all along and wasn't a temporary wartime placement. That was hard. Being thought of as unpatriotic was hard.'

Sometimes Belinda wondered about what the ladies' lives had been like, but when she raised the subject at home one evening, Auntie Enid snorted derisively.

'Their lives have been a damn sight easier than ours.'

And that was that.

'Go and fetch the hot-water bottles, there's a good girl,' said Grandma Beattie.

Belinda went upstairs. In her room, she put down the lamp she had brought to light her way and picked up her treasured photograph of Ben, gently fingering the paper poppy attached to the black crêpe sleeve. If only she could wear the poppy sewn onto her blouse, just for a dash of colour. Would she ever get to wear the pink patterned material?

'Ah, our darling boy.'

She jumped. 'Auntie Enid – I didn't know you were there.'

She put down the photograph. Auntie Enid picked it up.

'He'd be that sorry if he could see you now.'

'Sorry?' She went cold. Had Auntie Enid read her mind?

'Aye. Instead of living your life in his memory, here you are going to night school. He'd be sorry to have caused so much worry.'

'I think he'd be proud of me.'

'Nay, lass. You were the sun, moon and stars all rolled into one as far as our Ben were concerned, but no man could ever be proud of his girl getting herself all trained up for a lifetime of work. That's not what a decent fellow wants for his lass.'

Patience was in the sitting room, embroidering and feeling guilty. Prudence, after a day at work followed by an evening of teaching, was at the dining table, preparing more lessons. Patience bungled a French knot and had to undo it. If only she could be of more use to the school.

At last Prudence came into the room.

'Now we have lessons ready up to the end of next week.'

'Sit down and I'll make the Ovaltine.'

When she returned with the tray, they settled down for a chinwag.

'This is our third week of teaching,' said Prudence, taking a sip. 'I've been thinking. Now that we have a second type-writer, we can let the girls use it for practice outside their lesson-times. It's the only way they're going to pick up their speeds.'

'They wouldn't need to pay for that, would they? I can't imagine Miss Layton's pennies stretching that far.'

'If they don't pay, we can't call ourselves a business, although they could pay a lower rate. As for Miss Layton, I rather think the business school ought to recognise the need to support charity cases. That will make Lawrence look like even more of a philanthropist and will be of genuine benefit to Miss Layton.'

Patience's heart sank. 'We can't call her a charity case.'

'Can you think of a better name?'

'Not immediately, no.' But she would. She wasn't going to have Miss Layton known as a charity case. Even if she was one.

'And we should organise a few part-time hours for each girl, on Saturdays, so they can use their new skills in a real work environment. That means getting local businesses to take them on – at no cost, of course. The girls will be doing it to gain experience. It will look good on their letters when they apply for new positions. Plus, of course, it will make it harder for Lawrence to close down the school if we have local business-men on our side.'

It was a sobering thought. 'How sad to be doing everything with an eye to keeping Lawrence at bay. What would Pa have said?'

'It was Pa who put us in this situation,' Prudence said bluntly. 'We need to do something about Miss Layton's appearance.'

'What's wrong with it? She's a pretty girl, and clean. Her clothes aren't new, but they're always clean and pressed.'

Prudence gave a bark of laughter. 'Poor Miss Layton. Is that the best way you can describe her? A clean girl. I'm sure she'd be flattered.'

'Don't mock. It matters.'

'Of course it does. It's the first thing you look for in the lower classes: clean poor or dirt poor. I don't care for all that black, though. It's deeply unflattering and if her young man died in the war, then it's high time she came out of it. She can't go into perpetual black like Queen Victoria.'

'That's unkind.'

'It's practical. If she turns up looking like the Ghost of Christmas Yet To Come, it isn't going to endear her to a potential employer. I'll write to Mrs Sloan. I have the impression that our Miss Layton is kept on a tight rein, which is appropriate, of course, for a young, unmarried girl, but in this case, my guidance is required.'

'She's not as young as all that. She's twenty-one this summer. As I recall, you left home not long before you turned twenty-one.' Oh, what had made her say that? 'I didn't mean to speak out of turn.'

How crass. She had no business making remarks about Prudence's time away. Prudence never spoke of it. She had gone with such high hopes, declaring that since men weren't queuing at the front door, she was going to devote her life to her work and not only that, she was going to leave home. Her friend had married and moved to Scotland, where her husband's family had a smart hotel and the friend – Elsie? Elspeth? – had secured the post of receptionist for Prudence. The family owned a dozen hotels around England and Scotland and Prudence had ambitions to be the first lady-manager. If anybody could achieve that, she could.

Pa and Lawrence had done their utmost to prevent her leaving, but she was having none of it.

'Since you have both spent my whole life telling me I'm doomed to be an old maid, I've decided to be an old maid on the banks of Loch Lomond or in one of the other locations where the Waddens have their hotels.'

'Since one of their hotels is in Manchester, you may well end up back here,' said Lawrence. 'That would serve you right for leaving Pa in the lurch.'

To this, Prudence had given the most effective reply possible: she left home.

Eighteen months or so later, she returned, complete with a brittle temper that forbade questions. On the one occasion that Lawrence had goaded her for her spectacular lack of success in the hotel world, she had risen from the table, tipped a serving dish of boiled potatoes over his head and marched out of the room, with her back so straight she might have had the poker tucked down her blouse.

That poker had been there ever since.

'If you wish to apologise,' said Prudence, 'the best way to do so would be never to refer to the matter again. It was years ago. As I was saying before you interrupted with your ill-judged remark, I shall write to Mrs Sloan about Miss Layton's attire. You may spend the next few days enquiring in local businesses about the possibility of our placing our girls there for a few hours on Saturday afternoons to extend their experience.'

'I couldn't.' What? Approach strangers?

'You have to,' said Prudence drily. 'Do you want us to remain in our home or not?'

A run of dry days made Belinda's twice-weekly evening walks to Chorlton pleasanter, certainly a lot less muddy. Even though the air still had a sharp edge to it, there was a kinder note underneath, a hint of the coming springtime. In the next few weeks, the evenings would lengthen. Auntie Enid and Grandma Beattie didn't like her being out after dark.

'I have a letter for Mrs Sloan,' Miss Hesketh said at the end of her lesson, 'if you would be kind enough to deliver it.'

Belinda took the envelope. It felt thick; not stuffed-full thick, but luxuriously thick. Who would have thought there was such a thing as a middle-class envelope? *Mrs Sloan* and their address were written in neat, upright handwriting in black ink, with *By hand* in the top left-hand corner.

'I won't put it in my pocket. I'll carry it.'

If she had hoped Miss Hesketh might give her a clue as to its contents, she was disappointed. Miss Patience might have murmured, 'It's nothing to worry about,' but Miss Hesketh was made of sterner stuff.

She kept the letter in her hand all the way home. In End

Cottage, the golden lamplight wasn't nearly as bright at the electric light in the Heskeths' house. Not that she said anything. One thing she had quickly discovered was that, much as Auntie Enid and Grandma Beattie gobbled up details about the wonders of the Hesketh household, only one mention of each thing was permitted. To mention something twice – the electric lights, the cloakroom, the carpets not just on the floor but on the stairs – resulted in accusations of not being happy in her own home.

'Miss Hesketh sent you this.'

'What is it?' Grandma Beattie's knitting needles clicked away without her having to look at what she was doing. 'A school report?'

'I hope not. I'm not a child.' But she was under twenty-one, so maybe Auntie Enid was entitled to be informed of her progress.

They both looked at Auntie Enid while she read. When she finished, she looked at Belinda as if it was her fault.

'Did she tell you what this is?'

'No.'

'She's only gone and laid the law down about what you're to wear. Apparently, being all in black – except she calls it *unrelieved black* – isn't how you dress to work in an office. You're to have a white or cream blouse. Well, you can forget that.' Again, that look, as if it was Belinda's fault. 'And you can forget about yon business school if it means showing disrespect to our Ben.'

'Auntie Enid!'

'Now then,' said Grandma Beattie, 'this isn't our Belinda's doing and she'd never give up her mourning if it was left to her.'

Auntie Enid wiped a hand across her eyes and sighed. 'Sorry, chick. It's riled me, this posh lady telling us what to do. It's obvious she's never lost anyone she cared about.' A moment later, the look of blame was back. 'I suppose this means that mauve material you bought on the sly has got a use after all.'

Grandma Beattie laid her knitting in her lap. 'It says white.'

'I don't care.'

Belinda sat unmoving. Was this the end of her hopes?

'It sounds like a kind of uniform,' said Grandma Beattie.

'You what?' Auntie Enid radiated suspicion.

'If office girls are expected to dress a certain way, it's like a uniform and that's got nowt to do with who's lost someone and who hasn't. God knows, everyone's lost someone these days. I don't like it any better'n you do, but if it's just a uniform—'

'Well, she's not having a white blouse and that's flat.' Auntie Enid gave Belinda that look again. 'You can have a white collar and cuffs and that's as far as I'm prepared to go.' She made a choked sound and forced the letter back into the envelope.

Belinda felt jumbled up. Was she meant to be relieved? Grateful? Outraged, like Auntie Enid, at the idea of breaking into her mourning? All she wanted was to make a better future for herself by getting trained up for office work. Why did everything have to be such a fight?

Her next lesson was on Friday evening and Grandma Beattie saw to it that she had a white collar and cuffs attached to her black blouse. She should be glad to have shed some black at last, but she couldn't be, not when she saw that sorrow in Auntie Enid's and Grandma Beattie's eyes.

'There,' said Grandma Beattie. 'You look like a proper office girl now – doesn't she?'

'Aye,' said Auntie Enid with enough of an almost-sigh to make sure you knew she felt like sighing but bravely wasn't.

At the Miss Heskeths' house, she expected to be congratulated on her improved appearance, but neither lady commented. Part of her was pleased not to be fussed over, but another part was disappointed.

Would her family notice? Mum had been pleased for her when she started at the business school. Surely she would like to see her daughter looking like an office girl? And if Dad saw her in her office-white collar and cuffs, wouldn't he realise the importance of what she was aiming for? So the next day, after she got home from her Saturday cleaning, she changed into her black blouse with the office-white collar and cuffs.

'Where are you off to, wearing that?' asked Grandma Beattie at the dinner table.

'I'm going to show Mum and Dad. I'd like Mum to see me looking like an office girl.'

'Aye, well, just make sure you leave your purse at home,' advised Grandma Beattie.

Belinda flushed. Ever since Dad had come round here, wanting to drag her home, the unwritten rule that Auntie Enid and Grandma Beattie never uttered a word against him in front of Belinda had vanished like morning mist.

'And don't go making any fancy promises,' added Auntie Enid.

'What do you mean?'

'I mean don't go making fancy promises.'

After she had cleared away their dishes and washed up, she set off. It was a bitter afternoon, but at least it was dry.

Mum was on the front doorstep, sharpening a knife against the edge of the brickwork.

'Mum,' Belinda called, going through the permanently open gateway – and was then distracted because something wasn't quite right. The gate was missing. Not that it had been of any use, being rotten and hanging off its hinges, but even so. 'What happened to the gate?'

Mum jerked back her head with a throaty, exasperated sound. 'Our Thad, that's what. He only went and pinched it, him and Jacob. They chopped it up and sold it for firewood.'

'They're running wild.'

'Don't tell me. Tell your father. He's the one that should stop 'em.'

'Mum, look.' She let her shawl slip down her arms. She felt like twirling round, but didn't because she wanted to look like business-like. 'What do you think?'

Mum tilted her head on one side. 'What am I looking at?'

'*Mum.*'

'Oh aye.'

'What do you think?' She braced herself for the flow of compliments.

'About time too. I know how much you loved Ben, but he's been gone a long time. Is a white collar all you've run to? Honest, love, you should come out of your black now. It isn't healthy, the way them Sloans keep you in it.'

'It isn't to do with mourning, Mum. It's for the office; and it's white cuffs an' all... I mean, as well. This is how office girls dress.'

'Is it? Well, it's a shame they don't wear more white, that's all I can say. I'm sick of seeing you in black. Are you coming in?'

She ought to; but for once she wasn't going to do what was expected of her. She spent her whole life doing what other people expected.

'I just popped by to show you my office clothes. I'd best get back.'

'Probably just as well,' said Mum. 'Your dad were spitting feathers when he came home after yon Sloans wouldn't let you move back. It's hard, you know, with our George gone.'

'I know, but one day I'll have a better job and...'

Don't go making fancy promises. Was this what Auntie Enid had meant? But she would never be able to see her family go without, especially Mum and Sarah.

'...I'll be able to slip you a bit more.'

'Eh, you're a good lass. Come here.'

Mum drew her into a hug. Belinda let her body meld with her mother's. She smelled of soap and used frying pans. Belinda wanted to hug away all Mum's cares, her tiredness, her scratchy temper, the way Dad and the boys took her for granted.

'I'd do owt for you, Mum.'

'Except come home.'

Belinda drew back from the embrace, almost dizzy with shock and guilt.

'Nay, love, that were a joke.' Mum grasped her hands and held them so tightly it was like being caught in a pair of pincers. 'You mustn't come back here, whatever your dad says. This is your chance to make summat of yourself. You don't want to end up like me.'

'Oh, Mum.'

'It's true. Now, get away with you. I've got a rabbit to skin; and before you ask, it came from the butcher, not off the meadows.'

She had wanted to say 'I love you,' but couldn't now that Mum was going on about the rabbit. She started to leave.

'Hey, our Bel,' called Mum and she turned round. 'You look reet bonny.'

She laughed. 'I'm not meant to look bonny, Mum. I'm meant to look business-like.'

'Eh, my daughter, the office girl.' Her face changed. She walked after Belinda, eyes watchful. 'You haven't got any money, have you? I wouldn't ask, but you know how it is.'

Even before she walked inside, Belinda knew. She opened the door to End Cottage and she knew. It was like when she had walked in and found Dad, only that time she hadn't known until she set eyes on him. This time, opening the door was enough. The atmosphere was different. Heavy with politeness.

She stepped over the threshold, glancing across the room.

'Miss Hesketh!' Her hand flew to her chest. Miss Patience was here too. She looked round at the four women – no, not looked: gawped. 'Miss Hesketh – Miss Patience.'

'Good afternoon, Miss Layton,' said Miss Hesketh. 'I see you're wearing your white collar and cuffs.'

'I wanted to show my mum… my mother.'

'I hope she was pleased,' said Miss Patience.

'The Miss Heskeths have come to tell us they've made you into a charity case,' said Auntie Enid. She looked humble and furious at the same time.

'I've already explained, Mrs Sloan, that a charity case is the last thing Miss Layton is,' said Miss Hesketh.

'She is, in fact, our first scholarship candidate.' Miss Patience smiled at Belinda. 'You may not be aware, Mrs Sloan and Mrs Sloan, that our brother, Mr Lawrence Hesketh, is the brains behind our business school. He is concerned for the welfare of the surplus girls in society. Now he has had the idea of offering support to scholarship candidates.'

'Charity cases,' muttered Auntie Enid. 'It doesn't matter how you dress it up. It's charity.'

Miss Patience smiled bravely. 'Our brother wishes to assist girls who, at elementary school, never had the opportunity to sit the scholarship, though they would undoubtedly have passed the examination, had they done so. I believe I'm describing you, aren't I, Miss Layton? Didn't Miss Kirby say you'd have passed?'

'We'll ask her to write a letter to that effect,' said Miss Hesketh. 'Now that we teach on Fridays, she comes to our house on Saturday evenings, so we'll ask her today. Then you'll be our first scholarship candidate and your fees will be reduced accordingly – not out of charity, but because girls such as yourself are more likely to be in lower-paid employment when they come to us.'

Auntie Enid breathed out through her nose. She didn't utter the word 'Charity!', but it rattled round the room anyway.

Miss Patience addressed her. 'Mrs Sloan, we understand your reservations. That's why we've come in person to reassure you. We know you wouldn't dream of accepting charity, but Miss Layton shows promise and we're certain you must be as keen as we are that she has this opportunity to improve her prospects.'

'It'd be a feather in us caps if Belinda was the first scholarship whatsit,' said Grandma Beattie.

'She wouldn't have to pay so much in fees,' said Miss Hesketh, 'and consequently her wages would stretch further.'

If Auntie Enid sucked her cheeks in any further, her face would turn inside out. 'We can pay us way.'

'I'm sure you can,' said Miss Hesketh, 'but if Miss Layton receives this position as scholarship candidate, which is entirely dependent upon Miss Kirby's writing a letter in support, then any wages she saves as a result will be spoken for, to start with, at any rate.'

'How so?' asked Belinda.

'Your attire, my dear,' said Miss Patience.

'Her what?' said Grandma Beattie.

'Her office clothes,' said Miss Hesketh.

'We sorted them out,' said Auntie Enid. 'White collar and cuffs is as far as I'm prepared to go.'

'Unfortunately,' said Miss Hesketh, looking her in the eye, 'it isn't far enough. Black with white collar and cuffs is what shop girls wear in the better class of establishment. It is not what office girls wear. We require Miss Layton to wear a white or cream blouse. She's already at a disadvantage through coming from the working class – I mean no offence; I am merely stating a fact—'

'She must look the part,' cut in Miss Patience with her kindest smile. 'We realise, of course, that you suffered a terrible loss, all of you, and your bereavement continues to be as painful as ever, but the war has been over for four years and

– forgive me – but dressed as she is, Miss Layton would look rather an oddity in the office; and I can tell that you want her to have the best possible chance.'

'Aye,' said Grandma Beattie. 'We do.'

They all looked at Auntie Enid. She said nothing, but she almost nodded and relief swarmed through Belinda's veins.

'Thank you, Mrs Sloan,' breathed Miss Patience.

'Miss Layton's office apparel must be sorted out by this time next week,' said Miss Hesketh. 'We're in the process of finding office work in private businesses for our pupils to undertake on Saturdays; just three or four hours, so they can use their new skills in a working environment. This work will be unpaid, but it means the pupils will have experience to offer a prospective employer when the time comes.'

'Are you saying our Belinda will have to fettle on Saturday afternoons as well as all the rest of the week?' demanded Grandma Beattie.

Miss Patience spread her gloved hands helplessly. 'It will pay off in the end.'

'You hope,' said Auntie Enid. Belinda wanted to throttle her. Didn't she realise she was putting her in a bad light with her tutors?

But Miss Patience took no offence, or not outwardly, anyroad. 'We do hope,' she agreed in her soft voice.

'We've already found a placement for Miss Layton on Saturday afternoons,' said Miss Hesketh.

Office experience? She wasn't ready. Her heart beat faster. But it wasn't just alarm. There was also a touch of excitement.

'Where?' asked Auntie Enid.

'At the bookshop on Beech Road in Chorlton,' said Miss Hesketh.

'It's not far from Wilton Close, where my sister and I live,' said Miss Patience.

'You said office work,' said Auntie Enid.

'Mr Tyrell sells second-hand and antiquarian books,' said Miss Hesketh.

'Anti-what?' asked Grandma Beattie.

'Books that are old and special,' said Miss Patience. 'They have to be treated with respect and I believe Miss Layton would do that.'

'Well, she does love her library books,' agreed Grandma Beattie.

'Do you think a position in a bookshop would suit her?' asked Miss Patience as if Grandma Beattie had the casting vote.

'I don't see how it's meant to give her office experience,' Auntie Enid persisted.

Miss Patience smiled at her. 'It will provide Miss Layton with precisely the experience she requires. It's a quiet environment, which is perfect for her first foray into the world of office-related work. Mr Tyrell had a part-time assistant for a time last year, a gentlemanly man by the name of Weston. When he left, Mr Tyrell didn't replace him, which is one reason we thought he might appreciate another pair of hands. Miss Layton will not, I hasten to add, be required to work as an assistant in the shop. Mostly, Mr Tyrell will want her to type.'

'My typing isn't up to it,' Belinda exclaimed.

'That's the point.' Miss Hesketh sounded brisker than usual after her sister's conciliatory manner. 'Typing is precisely what you need.'

'Don't be afraid,' said Miss Patience. 'Mr Tyrell won't expect your fingers to fly, though I'm sure they will do after a few more hours of practice. Between ourselves, he'll be grateful not to have to do the typing himself.'

'You'll type lists of books and short catalogues,' said Miss Hesketh. 'Mr Tyrell sells some of his books by post and his customers need to know what he has in stock.'

'I'm not sure I like the sound of it,' said Auntie Enid. 'A young girl working for a man.'

'I hope you aren't suggesting we would condone an arrangement where a young lady might feel uncomfortable,' said Miss Hesketh.

'Mr Tyrell is as old as the hills,' trilled Miss Patience, obviously used to keeping the peace.

'We've arranged for Mr Tyrell to interview Miss Layton this afternoon,' said Miss Hesketh. 'Please be ready to go in ten minutes, Miss Layton.'

'I'll take her,' said Auntie Enid. 'If there's any interviewing to be done by a man, I'll take her.'

'That would not be appropriate, Mrs Sloan,' said Miss Hesketh. 'As her tutor, I will accompany her.'

Belinda had had her fill of being talked about as if she wasn't present.

'Thank you both for offering, but I'd prefer to go on my own.'

Chapter Eleven

I T IS FEBRUARY the fourteenth – Valentine's Day. See, I know that without being told. I know about cards and presents and red roses, but I don't know if I ever had a valentine of my own. In my past, was there a girl, a sweetheart? Did I give her roses on Valentine's Day? I don't even know if I'm the sort of chap who does such things. I'd like to think I am. Even if I never did it in the past (was I really so hard-hearted?), I know I will do it in the future… supposing the opportunity arises.

How can I contemplate getting to know someone else when I don't know myself?

My thoughts never stop. They chase themselves round and round, asking questions, wondering and speculating, finding something new to worry away at – and what's the point? Thoughts of a possible future relationship are worthless, but because it is Valentine's Day and I know its significance, I can't prevent the thoughts from appearing.

It is a crisp morning. Frost on the grass crunches underfoot as I take my morning tramp through the grounds. Snowdrops grow in clumps beneath the trees. This is a fine place. Parkland surrounds what used to be a manor-house, its windows criss-crossed with lead to form little diamonds, a handsome building, known to the locals, so I've been told, as Maniac Manor.

It is official. I am a maniac.

No, not really.

We're here – me and the other maniacs – because the doctors believe we can be treated. For those poor souls who can't be treated, there is an asylum a couple of miles away. The thought of it fills me with sadness for those poor beggars who have been put there. Maybe they'll stay there for ever.

Since I have no memory, my fellow patients delight in testing my Englishness by offering me Marmite, black pudding, trifle, Colman's Mustard, tripe. Do I enjoy them? For the record, yes, yes, yes, yes and I have no idea, as I can't imagine putting it in my mouth and swallowing.

I have more freedom than the others. For them, there is a strict daily regime. They are unlucky blighters who are still suffering from profound mental and emotional trauma caused by the war.

I say as much to Dr Jennings that afternoon. His office occupies a corner of the ground floor, and has windows looking in two directions. Perhaps it was a morning room before the war, or a sitting room.

Jennings looks at me. He is middle-aged, with a gaunt face and hooded eyes. 'Doesn't it occur to you that you too are suffering from the after-effects of trauma?'

'I don't think of myself like that, even though I know it to be the case. Is it possible to know it and ignore it at the same time?'

'You tell me. You say it's what you do. The brain is a complex creature.'

'Mine doesn't feel very complex. Mostly, it feels empty.' I say it in a jokey way.

'You've had a couple of days to settle in here. Has returning to England brought back anything?'

I shrug. 'Nothing.' My shoulders feel like caving in, but I don't let them. 'You know who I am.' I don't make it a question: they must know. 'Why haven't you told me?'

'I hoped you might remember for yourself. Leaving France,

coming here, was a big step. It might have started to open doors in your mind.'

'But it didn't.' I look at him expectantly.

A pipe-rack stands on his desk. He makes a move as if to choose a pipe, then withdraws his hand. A change of mind or a way of playing for time?

'It would be better if you remembered naturally. I could tell you a lot about yourself, but if I do, it is just a list of facts.'

'A list of facts sounds useful.'

'Yes, but only inside your head. What you need is to have those facts in your heart.'

I raise my eyebrows. 'You don't sound like an army doctor. Not that I have the slightest idea whether I've ever met one before.'

'Knowledge isn't just facts in your head. Knowledge is a feeling. We don't have a word for that feeling in the English language, but the absence of the feeling is—'

'Emptiness,' I say.

'...doubt.'

Doubt? Is that what I feel? When I chase my thoughts down long corridors of speculation, is it doubt that propels me?

'It isn't simply a matter of knowing in here.' Jennings taps his temple. 'That would give you some peace of mind, of course, but after you'd learned the facts about yourself, would you be truly satisfied? Wouldn't you move on from "I know nothing of myself" to "I know various things, but I remember none of them; I *feel* none of them."' He raps his knuckles against his chest. 'Knowledge is a feeling.'

'So your plan is not to tell me anything.' I imagine myself spending years here, not remembering.

He smiles. He has a sad smile, though maybe it is his professional expression. 'It would be better for you if we didn't have to, but clearly, if coming here hasn't jolted your memory, then we'll have to give you some information.'

'Is it possible my memory will never return?'

'It's unusual for amnesia to last this long.' It's the only answer he will give me.

So I'm in the same position I've been in since I woke up in the bedroom with the sloping ceiling. I thought that coming back to England would open the floodgates. It hasn't.

Either I will remember or I won't. And I have to face the possibility that I won't.

(I am tired of putting on a brave face.)

They give me a list of names. 'See if one jumps out at you,' Jennings says in a casual way, as if it is of no consequence. I scan the list, suddenly anxious, heart pumping. Is this the moment when—?

Apparently not. I go back to the top and read the names again, one by one. There's still a chance. If I concentrate, if I take my time, there's still a chance. Anticipation makes my palms break out in a sweat. I find myself considering the first names in preference to the surnames. There is a John, a Mark, a Henry. Good, solid names.

In the end, they tell me.

'Linkworth. You are Gabriel Linkworth.'

Not John, then, or Mark. Not a good, solid name. Gabriel: did I get ragged about it at school? I find the name on the list and stare at it, willing it to mean something. Do I feel like a Gabriel Linkworth? Do I look like a Gabriel Linkworth?

'It sounds like a poet,' I say and they laugh as if I've made a great joke. 'What do you know about me?' I ask.

'All in good time,' says Jennings.

Gabriel Linkworth.

I go outside and tramp across the lawns. The frost has vanished. The grass is wet. The clumps of snowdrops shine bravely as the day draws in.

Gabriel Linkworth.

Chapter Twelve

THE LITTLE BRASS bell overhead jingled as Belinda threw open the door and almost fell into the shop. What a start to her first afternoon working here. Mr Tyrell appeared, stepping out from between two sets of bookcases. His height had taken her by surprise when she came for her interview last week. Being told he was as old as the hills had made her picture a small, stooped gentleman, but he was a real lanky longlegs.

'I'm so sorry to be late, Mr Tyrell.'

It was a sparkling February day of clear skies and pockets of surprisingly warm sunshine, but the inside of the shop was gloomy in spite of the large window. Her boots clattered on the floorboards, the sound lifting into the sombre air before being absorbed into the bookcases that filled the space. The shop smelled of wood, studiousness and well-thumbed pages.

Mr Tyrell frowned at her, shaggy eyebrows creeping together. Had he forgotten? Having run all the way from Stretford, she was sweltering hot and longed to undo her coat buttons, but she didn't dare until she knew he was expecting her. Trying not to be obvious about it, she waggled her right arm, which was aching darkly after holding onto her hat all the way here.

'You assured me you could get here for two o'clock. I assume you have a good reason for your tardiness.'

Oh, she had that all right. Mr Butterfield, the so-and-so. He had been today's tattler and, wanting everything to run smoothly come Saturday, she had asked him earlier in the week if he would check her work first and pay her right away instead of her waiting with all the others.

'Hm, I don't know.' He had hesitated, as if considering. 'If I say yes to you, Miss Layton, what if the others come begging the same favour? I can't oblige everyone.'

'You aren't being asked to, Mr Butterfield. Just me.'

'You want me to oblige you?'

'Yes please, sir.'

How stupid could you get? This morning, as midday rolled into view and the cleaning was all but finished, he had come up behind her when she was bent over the bucket, cleaning her brush. Fortunately, she had glanced round and that had given her a split second to slip aside, but she was penned in a corner.

'You did say you wanted me to oblige you, Miss Layton.'

Dread consumed her. Had her luck run out? Then some of the others came to clean their brushes and Butterfingers melted away. Phew. But she hadn't a hope of receiving her wages at midday.

She hadn't bothered bringing her snap with her and the only money she had was her fare home, but Maggie, Annie and the rest had each given her a bite of their pies and pasties, though she had taken care to have only a nibble of each one. For the poorest women with the biggest families, this was likely their one and only hot meal of the week.

Having queued for her wages – and frankly, she was in such a state by then that Butterfingers could have picked up her hand and licked it and she wouldn't have cared – she had dashed for the tram, agonising over whether to go straight to Chorlton; but she had to go home and get changed into her new – well, new to her – cream blouse that Grandma Beattie had picked up off Urmston market in the week.

Arriving at End Cottage to cries of 'Where have you been?', she had flown upstairs to get changed, dimly aware of indignant comments following her about her lateness having ruined the dinner.

'You can't go without summat warm inside you,' said Auntie Enid, as she ran downstairs and headed straight for the coat-pegs.

'I've had some,' she called over her shoulder as she hurried out of the door and took off up Grave Pit Lane at a run.

Now, here she was, dishevelled, sweaty and late. Talk about first impressions.

'I'm sorry,' she said again. 'I was given to understand I could leave work at twelve, but I had to stay until one.'

He looked through his spectacles down his long, straight nose. The shaggy eyebrows disentangled themselves from one another and climbed up his forehead. Then he uttered a 'huh' sound and plunged back among the bookcases.

Creeping forward, not wanting her boots to clatter on the floorboards, she peered round the end of the bookcase. Mr Tyrell gazed at an upper shelf, which she couldn't have looked at without a box to stand on, but which was at eye-level to a beanpole like him. He had pushed his glasses into the top pocket of his jacket and his fingertips pattered along the spines of the books while he murmured under his breath. Then with another 'huh' – a pleased-sounding one this time – he pulled out a volume, tucked it under his tweed-clad arm and, using the edge of the shelf as a sliver of desk, made a note in pencil on a piece of paper. Then he turned round to examine the contents of a shelf behind him, this time having to bend down. His knees creaked.

What was she meant to do? Well, she had two choices. Interrupt him, probably earning another 'huh,' or, as Grandma Beattie would have said, 'Use some of what God gave you.'

At the back of the shop she found a windowless office. It was dusty and tired-looking and in urgent need of a thorough spring-clean, but at least it was tidy – and on the table stood the typewriter, a pile of books beside it.

She took off her coat. There were no pegs, so she folded it and placed it on top of a cupboard, with her gloves and Mrs Harrison's hat on top. She found paper in one drawer and carbon paper in another. The carbon paper looked like it had been used a hundred times. She settled down to work, winding two sheets, with carbon paper in between, around the drum. At the top she typed *Tyrell's Books, Beech Road, Chorlton-cum-Hardy*, then she put the books into alphabetical order by author and started to type, tapping hard on the keys to give the carbon paper as much help as she could.

A frisson of pleasure ran through her. Here she was, dressed in her smart office blouse, sitting up straight as Miss Hesketh had taught her, doing a proper job. Her pleasure didn't last long. The office was chilly and her blouse was no protection. Draping her coat about her shoulders, she carried on. Every time she paused to look at the next book, she flexed her fingers and rubbed her hands.

She was turning the knob on the side of the machine to bring the paper out when Mr Tyrell came into the office.

'I've listed these in alphabetical order,' she said. 'I've done two copies.'

Putting down half a dozen handsomely bound volumes, he held out a large hand. She removed the carbon paper and gave him her work.

'The bottom one is barely legible.'

'You need new carbon paper.'

'Huh.' From between a couple of the books he had put on the table, he produced a piece of paper. 'For a customer. Type an invoice and parcel up the books. Brown paper and string over there.' He started to turn away.

'Mr Tyrell, it's rather cold in here.'

'There's a gas-ring and a kettle upstairs.' A vague wave of his hand indicated a door.

Did he live over the shop? Through the door was a staircase, with a door at the top that didn't shut properly. Far from being a home, it was a storeroom for boxes and shelves of books. There wasn't even a chair to sit on. There was a ewer of water beside a battered old kettle. She wrinkled her nose. How fresh was the water likely to be? But all she wanted was a mug of boiling water to wrap her hands around. Next week she would wear two chemises and both her cardigans. Would Grandma Beattie have time to knit her a pair of fingerless gloves?

Carrying the hot mug downstairs, she put on her coat for good measure and set about her next task. The piece of paper Mr Tyrell had provided was a letter from a Mr Wilstone, containing an order for books. Beside each title, Mr Tyrell had pencilled the price. She typed the invoice and added up the prices three times to make sure she had got the correct total. Mr Tyrell hadn't said anything about an accompanying letter, but it seemed the polite thing to do.

Dear Mr Wilstone, and that meant it would be *Yours sincerely* at the end, because she had used his name. *Please find enclosed* (Miss Hesketh had taught her that) *the titles* – that sounded posher than books – *you recently ordered, which we have pleasure in supplying.* Businesses liked referring to themselves as *we*, according to Miss Hesketh. New line: *We look forward to being of service to you again.* Then, with a triumphant *Yours sincerely*, she took it to Mr Tyrell for his signature. Removing his pen from his distinctly inky-looking top pocket, he signed his name.

Belinda set about parcelling up the books. Mr Tyrell appeared with another couple of books and a customer's letter. She smiled to herself. She could come to like this.

The next hour passed with more customer orders. Once or twice she heard the bell jingle in the shop, though this didn't seem to be followed by anything much in the way of conversation. Were Mr Tyrell's customers as reserved as he was? She imagined them waggling their eyebrows at one another and grinned. Forget Mr Butterfield; forget being late. This had turned out to be a good day. Perhaps, when she had been here a while, it might be appropriate for her to sign the letters that went in the parcels. Imagine finishing a letter with *For and on behalf of Tyrell's Books*.

The mug had gone cold, so she nipped upstairs to boil more water. As she returned to the office, the shop bell pinged. A customer arriving or someone leaving? A voice – a woman.

'Are you Mr Tyrell, sir?'

Oh, heck. Auntie Enid.

'I'm Mrs Sloan and this is my mother-in-law, Mrs Sloan senior. You've got our Belinda working here – that's Miss Layton to you – and we've come to make sure everything is as it should be. You can't be too careful, not with her working for a man.'

Tuesday. *Vera's Voice* day. Would this be the day? Fay Randall – Mrs Brewer – had explained that, because the article that would include their business school was part of a series she was engaged in writing, it could be as much as a month before it was published, though that hadn't stopped Patience eagerly turning the pages every Tuesday since.

She adjusted her hat in the mirror before setting off for the newsagent's. The end of February was in sight now: this day week would be St David's Day. Snowdrops formed bright clumps in the flowerbed and it wouldn't be long before the daffodils bloomed. The hopeful scent of spring was discernible beneath the chill.

She had already been out once with her shopping basket, but she didn't like to put her *Vera's Voice* in with the Tuesday fish, so she always came home and put away the shopping, before undertaking a spot of housework to earn her trip to the newsagent's. She had her shopping basket with her. You sometimes saw a man striding along with a folded newspaper beneath his arm, but naturally a lady wouldn't do that. Her magazine would be conveyed home inside her basket. It was a question of standards.

She purchased her magazine and returned home as rapidly as befitted a lady. She removed her outdoor things and sat down with her magazine. Was today the day? She scanned the contents list and drew in a deep breath. There it was. *Something for the Surplus Girl. Consider a Business School, by Fay Randall.*

Flipping through the pages, she found the article, devouring it so swiftly it barely sank in. She read it again, with proper attention. It opened with general comments about the surplus girl's responsibility to make the best of herself and then, finally, came the details of *one such business school* and the benevolence of the Hesketh family – that was interesting. Lawrence wasn't singled out for praise: had Mrs Brewer seen beneath the surface of their charade?

That evening, Patience hummed as she prepared a cheese and bacon pasty, ready to pop in the oven when Prudence arrived home. She much preferred preparing tea for the pair of them to getting her own solitary dinner ready: it never seemed worth it just for herself. Prudence ate her dinner in the Corporation canteen, where they specialised in hearty main courses and what Patience thought of as school puddings – jam roly-poly, spotted dick, syrup pudding and the like.

Hearing the front door, she went to greet Prudence.

'Take your coat off and you can read the *Vera's Voice* article while I put tea on the table.'

'Is it a good article?'

'Oh yes, very good.'

'Then I'll save it until afterwards, like a glass of port.' Coming from Prudence, this was a joke.

After tea, Patience anticipated an agreeable half hour discussing Fay Randall's article and squeezing every ounce of gratification from it before this evening's pupils arrived, but her hopes were dashed when the doorbell sounded. Automatically she looked at the clock.

'Far too early for the girls,' she said, getting up.

It was Lawrence and Evelyn, done up to the nines in evening dress. Evelyn's satin-lined velvet cloak was fastened at the throat with a glittering brooch that matched her earrings and the combs in her professionally waved coiffure. Long white gloves encased her pudgy forearms.

'Good evening, Patience,' said Lawrence, ushering Evelyn inside. 'You have no objection to our coming into our own house, have you?'

Evelyn swished by, trailing heavy perfume. Lawrence was resplendent in a black wool evening coat with silk lapels, his black shoes buffed up to a high gleam. He removed his top hat and indicated to Patience to precede him. In the sitting room, Prudence's deadpan expression was a reminder to her not to wear her own surprise quite so blatantly on her sleeve.

'Do sit down,' she said. Or shouldn't she make the invitation, since it was their house?

Lawrence stayed on his feet. Evelyn lowered herself onto the sofa, wafting her hands sideways to spread out her cloak. Beneath it shimmered midnight blue, embroidered with crystal beads. Patience had always known that she hadn't been put on this earth to wear gorgeous gowns like this, but that didn't stop a wave of envy pulling at her stomach. She didn't sigh. There was no point. She was plain and that was all there was to it.

'You're looking very smart, the pair of you,' she said.

'You shouldn't have dressed for our benefit,' added Prudence.

'Evelyn, what a beautiful gown,' Patience said before Lawrence could rise to the bait.

'Thank you. It is rather glorious, isn't it? I had it made at Mademoiselle Antoinette's in St Ann's Square. That is simply *the* place to go. My friend Mrs Fairbrother goes there. Have you heard of the Fairbrothers? No, I suppose not. Mr Fairbrother is very high up in the legal profession.'

'He must be useful for you to know.' Prudence looked at Lawrence.

'It does no harm to cultivate the right people.' Lawrence was unabashed. 'We're on our way to dinner with our friends, the Palmerstons.'

'How nice,' Patience said quickly before Prudence could enquire whether the Asquiths and the Gladstones would also be present.

'But we've taken the trouble to stop off to see you – and we haven't done it so you can admire our evening dress.'

'Would you care for a sherry?' Prudence asked, breaking into Lawrence's flow.

'What we would care for,' said Lawrence, unfastening his evening coat to reveal a dazzling white waistcoat and black bow-tie beneath a tailcoat, 'is an assurance that you'll give up this ridiculous business school venture; but we realise that there isn't a hope in hallelujah of your seeing sense.'

'It makes perfect sense to me to keep our own home,' said Prudence.

'But it isn't yours, is it? It's mine. I know what this is.' He dived across the room and snatched up Patience's *Vera's Voice*. 'It's that rag that Lucy gets.'

'*Vera's Voice*,' said Evelyn in a patronising tone that suggested she would never stoop so low as to read it herself, though Patience knew for a fact that she did, because more than once she had offered Patience a housekeeping hint that had come straight from the *Household Hints for a Happier Home* page.

'A rag that today contains a most pleasing article about our business school,' said Prudence.

'I'm aware of that. Lucy showed me.'

'She actually wondered if she ought to come here for some training, the silly girl,' Evelyn said indulgently. 'It's out of the question, of course. She's bound to marry, a pretty girl like her, and with her father rising in the world.'

Patience felt a pang for her niece – for both her nieces. What guarantee did any girl have these days?

'You've put me in an intolerable position,' snapped Lawrence. 'Those pieces in the newspapers, and now this feature.'

'On the contrary, I think we've made you look like a splendid fellow,' said Prudence.

'I want this house. I want to be able to say I own the house I live in. Not many people can say that. It would make certain people look at me in a new way.'

'If certain people's good opinion relies on something so ridiculous,' retorted Prudence, 'they aren't worth cultivating.'

'We didn't come here to fight,' said Lawrence. 'We're here to make a generous offer.'

'Allow me, Lawrence,' said Evelyn. She smiled at Patience. 'You probably think we don't comprehend your situation, but we do. I admit that we didn't to start with; hence the unfortunate business of coming here the day the will was read. That upset you, Patience, and on reflection, I don't blame you.'

'You have a perfectly nice house,' said Patience.

'But a rented one.' Evelyn spoke in a jolly whisper, as if she was doing the voices in a bedtime story. 'Some of the people we mix with, some of the people we need to have on our side if Lawrence is to fulfil his dream of becoming an alderman, own their own properties and even those that don't, rent larger houses than ours. This is an attractive house in a good area. Residing here, in our very own property, would be just the ticket.'

'We realise you can't rent a home equivalent to this one,' said Lawrence, 'and so we've decided to make you a generous offer.' He smiled at them. 'Let's put all ill-feeling behind us. We've found a house in Seymour Grove – nearer to town, nearer to work, for you, Prudence – and we'll pay the rent for you.'

'You're offering us a house?' said Prudence.

Evelyn beamed encouragingly. 'Well, not the whole house, no. You'll be upstairs, so you won't have people walking about above you, and you'll have a bay window, Patience.'

Patience blinked. What had she ever said to make Evelyn imagine a bay window was essential?

'So you're offering us an upstairs flat...' said Prudence.

'A smart upstairs apartment with indoor plumbing.'

'And a bay window,' Patience murmured.

'And a bay window,' Evelyn cooed.

'...in return for an entire house that ought to be ours anyway.'

Silence blanketed the room.

'Now see here, Prudence—' Lawrence began.

'No, you see here, Lawrence. Pa had no business leaving the house to you. This was our mother's house and it should have come to us.'

'We've come here out of the goodness of our hearts—' Evelyn began.

'Save your breath, Evelyn,' said Lawrence. 'Prudence won't listen to reason. I feel sorry for you, Patience. You should stand on your own two feet for a change. Prudence can't continue with this business school nonsense if you withdraw your agreement.'

'The school is as much mine as it is Prudence's.' Patience sat up straighter.

'Perhaps you should go,' said Prudence. 'You mustn't keep your important friends waiting.'

Lawrence glared at her. 'You haven't heard the end of this. Come along, Evelyn.'

Evelyn rose in a swirl of velvet, satin and perfume. Patience saw them to the door – and not a moment too soon. Walking along the road was Miss Layton. Lawrence helped Evelyn into the motor. She fussed with her cloak, making sure it wouldn't get caught in the door. Lawrence closed the door and walked round to his side, then veered off and intercepted Miss Layton as she arrived at the gate. Anxiety stirred inside Patience, but it would be rude to stare, so she closed the door.

'Well!' Prudence exclaimed as Patience joined her in the sitting room.

'He's talking to Miss Layton.'

'What about?'

'I could hardly stand there with my ears flapping.'

'We'll ask her when she comes in.'

Patience frowned. Wouldn't that be intrusive? But she needn't have worried, because Miss Layton was only too happy to blurt it out without any prompting.

'I've just seen Mr Hesketh. He recognised me and came over to say good evening. Wasn't that kind? I thanked him for making me a scholarship candidate. I hope I didn't embarrass him: he did look a bit surprised. I told him it's made such a difference, me being a mill girl.'

'What else did you say?'

'He asked about the school and I told him what an inspiration Miss Hesketh is, her being a lady office-worker, and how we learn about filing and typing and invoices. Then the lady in the car opened the door and called to him.' She bit her lip. 'I hope I didn't gabble on too much.'

'I'm sure he found you charming,' said Patience. She looked round as the doorbell rang. 'That will be Miss Shaw. I'll send her to you in the dining room, shall I, Prudence?' That would give her the chance to share the *Vera's Voice* article with Miss Layton.

Might the article generate enquiries? The newspaper pieces had, and more girls had signed up. Patience clasped her hands to her chest. She was enjoying this far more than she had expected to – well, she hadn't expected to enjoy it at all. She must make a note of all her ideas for telephone lessons and list against them which girls had handled pretend enquiries about costs, invoices, discrepancies and dates. Really, life was far more interesting than it used to be.

Over the next couple of days, she jotted down ideas for various telephone conversations, including useful vocabulary for different situations. She wasn't having Lawrence claiming the business school was all down to Prudence. If he suggested it again, she would produce her paperwork. This evening, after tea, she would show Prudence what she had done.

Prudence arrived home from the office with a frown on her face. There was nothing unusual in that. Frowning was pretty well her normal expression.

When they settled down to eat their buttered leeks, Patience was all set to explain – and, yes, show off a little – about her lesson preparation when Prudence announced,

'The Corporation has received an anonymous complaint about missing documents.'

'Oh dear. Important documents?'

'The simple fact that they're missing makes them important. I don't know what they are. That hasn't been stated. The thing is…'

She shifted in her seat. Patience felt a frisson of fear. Prudence was never uncomfortable. Discomfort was for people who made mistakes. Discomfort was for people who did something wrong. Neither of those descriptions could ever be applied to Prudence Hesketh.

'…what if it's the old invoices and delivery notes I brought home?'

'It can't be. You said they were finished with.'

'And they were, or I wouldn't have dreamed of taking them. I think it best I own up tomorrow.'

'Own up? That makes it sound as if we've done something wrong.'

'Thank you for saying "we", but the fault, if any, is mine, however unintentional.'

Patience put down her knife and fork, then picked them up again. Prudence wouldn't thank her for getting in a state.

She saw Prudence off to work the next morning, wanting to wish her well but knowing Prudence wouldn't like any fuss.

'I hope things turn out satisfactorily.' It was the least fussy thing she could think of.

She kept herself occupied during the day, but her insides felt wobbly, as if she needed to tighten her corsets. If she felt like that, what must it be like for Prudence? She was such an upright person. Integrity was her middle name.

That evening, she was on watch in the bay window and rushed to open the door as Prudence came stalking along. Her face was grim, but that needn't mean anything. Prudence wasn't one for smiles.

Patience tried to assist her off with her mackintosh, but she shrugged free of the helping hands.

'Don't fuss. You know I can't bear a fuss.'

'What happened?'

'Sit down and I'll tell you.'

Patience felt a click of annoyance. Honestly, Prudence treated her like a child at times.

In the sitting room, they took their customary places.

Prudence looked her straight in the eye. That was Prudence all over: she never shirked anything.

'Yes, the missing documents were indeed the invoices and so forth I'd taken.'

'Oh, Prudence.'

'My explanation and apology were accepted by Mr Donnington, together with my assurance it won't happen again.'

'Oh, Prudence.'

'Kindly stop saying "Oh, Prudence". I had the foresight to think of what I would say to reprimand a junior colleague in the same position and made sure I said all those things before Mr Donnington could.'

Oh, Prudence. But she didn't say it aloud.

'I promised to destroy all the paperwork, so we'll have to devise our own in future, but that's easily done. It'll also give us the opportunity to incorporate errors for the girls to identify, so it'll work out rather well.' She sounded cheerful, but Patience wasn't fooled. This had hit her hard.

'Thank goodness you owned up before—'

'Quite so. Mr Donnington was sympathetic in view of my honesty and it isn't going to be put on my record.'

'That's excellent news. You always said he thinks highly of you.'

'This isn't thanks just to his good opinion. Apparently, the complaint was made, not to him, but to Mr Mansfield, who is his opposite number in a different department, and Mr Mansfield had taken pleasure in bringing the complaint to him. Fortunately for me, Mr Donnington was more annoyed with Mr Mansfield's crowing than he was with my conduct.'

'Who made the complaint?' Patience asked. 'And why make it to Mr Mansfield if it didn't involve his department?'

'It was made anonymously.'

'How cowardly. How hole-and-corner.'

'Possibly. Or… convenient.'

'What are you suggesting?'

'We know Miss Layton told Lawrence about her lessons, including the use of invoices,' said Prudence. 'What if she told him we use real invoices?'

'You mean, Lawrence..? He wouldn't…'

'Wouldn't he?'

Chapter Thirteen

'W HAT D'YOU MEAN, you're not being paid to work in that shop?'

Dad's voice rose and Belinda's heart quaked. She hated the perpetual squabbling and sniping in Cromwell Street. The only thing worse than being forced to be the audience was being on the receiving end. Why did she have to explain herself all the time? Why couldn't Dad take a friendly interest? A fatherly interest. Some hope. His only interest lay in what he could get out of her.

'Mr Tyrell is employing me so that I gain relevant experience.'

'Employing you?' Dad gave a bark of laughter. 'If he was employing you, you'd get paid.'

Oh yes, and he'd know all about that, wouldn't he? He had lost more jobs than he'd had hot dinners. But she had to keep the peace.

'Miss Hesketh says it's an investment in my future.'

'Oh, Miss Hesketh says, does she?' But a sullen tilt about Dad's mouth said he was backing down. He might resent the Miss Heskeths, but he was in awe of them too. They were quality.

'If you get another job and leave the mill,' Sarah piped up, 'you'll put in a word for me so I can be a tenter, won't you?'

She smothered a sigh. Even Sarah's principal interest in her ambition was centred on what she hoped to get out of it. Not that Belinda blamed her. Sarah worked God-awful hours at that hotel. But it would mean a lot if someone in her family would give her genuine encouragement. Or was she being soppy?

'If you leave the Claremont, you'll lose the extra coppers you get for working difficult hours,' Dad told Sarah.

'Exactly,' said Sarah. 'Coppers.'

'It all mounts up,' said Mum.

Sarah tossed her head. 'In the long run, I'd earn more at the mill.'

'You're too old to start at the bottom,' said Mum.

'If our Bel can be an office junior, I can be a tenter.'

'Don't answer back, young lady.'

And they were off. Belinda spoke loudly to make herself heard.

'Time for me to go. I've got an early start again tomorrow.'

'For all the good it does your family,' Dad muttered.

'You tell her, Dad.' Thad gave her an impudent grin.

'If you want more money coming in, Dad,' said Belinda, 'why don't you get the boys working half time? If Thad was out at work in the afternoons, it might buck his ideas up.'

'What's that supposed to mean?' Thad demanded.

'It means you need taking in hand. I remember how you knocked Miss Kirby down in the market – and I remember why you were running like mad an' all. And Mum told me how you chopped up the garden gate for firewood and sold it.'

'The garden gate!' Thad made a great show of laughing out loud. 'Hark at her. Garden gate, my eye. You've got to have a garden to have a garden gate.'

'It's a good job there isn't a garden,' she snapped, 'or you'd probably have stolen all the flowers as well.' She looked at Mikey. 'You should be working half time too. I surprised at you for not bothering.'

Mikey tossed his head. 'Who says I didn't bother? I tried getting a job as soon as I turned twelve, only no one will take me on, because I'm *his* brother.'

Thad smirked. 'You're too rotten useless, more like.'

'Is this true, Thad?' Belinda demanded. 'Is your reputation really that bad?'

Thad thrust out his chest. 'I don't know. Why not ask the nosy cow who wants to know what happened to the garden gate?'

'Don't call me names,' Belinda cried.

'Or what?' sneered Thad.

'I'll give you a clip round the ear. You see if I don't.'

'You lay one finger on me and I'll crack you so hard, you'll be flat on your back.'

'Dad, are you listening to this?' said Belinda.

'Aye, and I don't appreciate you coming round here, telling me how to run my family. If that's what they're teaching you in that fancy business school, I'll have you out of there before you can say knife, and don't kid yourself I won't.'

Belinda stared in disbelief.

'Didn't you say summat about being on your way?' asked Thad.

She pressed her lips together, breathing in sharply through her nose. She hated to let Thad get the better of her, but there was nothing to be gained by staying.

'Walk up the road with me, Sarah.'

She said stiff goodbyes and pulled on her shawl.

'You see what I have to put up with, living here,' Sarah said.

Belinda stopped on the step and turned to her. 'You never used to answer back. You mustn't become like them.'

'That's rich coming from you, after the fight you just got into.'

'I can't believe what Dad lets Thad get away with.'

'Oh aye,' came George's voice from the empty gateway. 'What's he been up to now?'

'He's given our Bel some almighty cheek, that's what.' Sarah's voice rose indignantly.

George chucked his spent cigarette on the path and ground it out beneath his shoe. 'It's better than thieving, I suppose.'

'How can you sound so casual about it?' Belinda demanded.

He shrugged. 'It's nowt to do with me any more, now I've moved out.'

'That's what you should do, Sarah,' said Belinda. 'Move into the hotel dormitory.'

'Dad won't let me.'

'Don't give her ideas,' said George. 'Things will be even harder for Mum if Sarah ups sticks... unless you were thinking of moving back in, our Bel? I meant what I said. It's your turn. Me and Sarah have put up with things getting worse, while you have it easy in Grave Pit Lane.'

'I wouldn't call losing my fiancé easy.'

'I never said it was, but he's been gone a long time. Ben's mum and his nan aren't your family. You've done your bit for them. You've stopped on with them and helped them through the worst of their grief. Don't you think it's time you came home and did your bit for your own folks now?'

'Oh, please, not another fight,' begged Sarah, catching hold of George's arm. 'I'm glad you've come... but only if you're going to be pleasant to everyone.'

A reluctant smile tugged at George's mouth. 'Even Thad? I don't think I can manage that, even for you.'

He dropped a kiss on Sarah's head and Belinda felt a pang of envy. He didn't do that to her. She was out of favour because of not coming home. Uncertainty shook her. What sort of person didn't want to be with their own family?

As she walked home, she felt ruffled and out of sorts, but she hoisted a smile into place as she opened the door.

'How's the family?' asked Auntie Enid, glancing up from knitting for the poor.

Belinda shot her a quick look, trying to read her mind. A simple polite enquiry, requiring nothing more than a 'Fine, thank you' in reply? Or – after Dad's refusal to give parental consent, followed by his coming here to lay the law down and take her home – an invitation to spill all the juicy details about the Laytons' sordid way of life?

'Fine, thank you.'

'How's Sarah?' asked Grandma Beattie. 'She doesn't have it easy, trailing to town and back at all hours.'

'She hopes I'll get her a mill job if I move on, but I don't want her working for Mr Butterfield.'

Auntie Enid laid her knitting in her lap. 'Do you think I want you working for him? It's the way of the world, love.'

'At least at the mill, it's only him,' added Grandma Beattie. 'There's a lot more scope for that kind of nonsense in a hotel.'

She had never thought of that. 'You mean, because there are more male employees?'

'And guests.'

'Sarah has never said anything of the kind.'

'Have you ever told her about Mr Butterfield?'

'Of course not.' It wasn't the kind of thing you talked about to your little sister. She wanted to protect Sarah from that kind of knowledge; but maybe Sarah didn't need telling because she had already found out the hard way.

The thought stayed with her at work, making her resent Mr Butterfield even more. When she did her Saturday cleaning, she stuck like glue to Annie as much as she could and held her breath while Butterfingers paid her. If she could hold her breath for that amount of time, if she didn't breathe the same air as he did, then having to submit to being touched by him wouldn't be so bad.

Yes, it would.

Horrible man.

She hurried home to change into her office clothes. It was a shame having to pile on the second chemise before she slipped on her cream blouse, and a further shame to smother it beneath a warm cardigan. She felt more like a polar explorer than the smart office girl she aspired to be. But it was nearly the end of February. Give it a few weeks and she could shed her additional garments.

When she entered the shop, Mr Tyrell was with a customer. She crept through to the office, removed Mrs Harrison's coat and hat and settled down to work. Mr Tyrell had left two piles of books for her to list; and a couple of times, he came in with a pile of books with a letter protruding from the top one. She made out the invoices and typed the accompanying letters. Before making up each parcel, she took the letter to Mr Tyrell for his signature.

'I'm sorry to interrupt you, Mr Tyrell, but would you mind..?'

'Huh.'

He plucked his pen from his inky top-pocket and, leaning the letter against a book, scrawled his signature across the bottom of the sheet. Would he ever instruct her to sign on his behalf? Should she suggest it?

'Mr Tyrell.' Would he complain to Miss Hesketh that she was getting above herself? 'The next time a letter needs signing—'

The door opened and the bell jingled. Mr Tyrell made a move as if to shield her from the newcomer's eyes, but not before she had glimpsed the most handsome man she had ever seen and her heart practically leaped out of her chest.

Patience fiddled around the back of her neck, fastening the clasp on her modest string of pearls, which she wore every Sunday. Leaning towards the dressing-table mirror, she ran her fingers down the line of her throat. Her neck wasn't as firm as it used to be. Oh, the small sorrows of growing older without the joys and compensations that went with a family of one's own. Goodness, what a ninny she was. She was not going to get upset by a saggy neck. She certainly wasn't going to sob her heart out like she had when her monthlies had dried up. She should have been glad to see the back of them but instead she had cried her heart out for the children she had never had. What a nincompoop.

Downstairs, Prudence was vigorously brushing her coat-sleeves and shoulders with the clothes brush. Soon they were ready to go. The mild morning brought a smile to Patience's face. Spring was her favourite time of year. The buds on the drumstick primulas were plump and ready to open. She felt a bit like that herself. Not plump, of course, she was as thin as a stick, but ready to open.

'After last week's service, Mrs Milton told me that her widowed sister might be interested in attending our school,' said Prudence. 'Maybe she'll have news for us today.'

But when they lingered outside St Clement's after morning service, the oddest thing happened. Mr and Mrs Holborne, with whom they normally passed the time of day, plunged deep into conversation with another couple; and Mrs and Miss Wentworth hurried out of the gate; while the Randalls, who lived in one of the big houses on Edge Lane, hurried straight past them.

Prudence turned her back on the remaining members of the congregation. 'We've been sent to Coventry,' she breathed.

'Let's go home,' Patience whispered.

They walked in silence. Patience could imagine Prudence's mind seething with thoughts; her own mind didn't seem able to pin down a single idea. Even her senses were stunned. The sweet-fragranced promise in the air that she had relished earlier had dissipated.

As they turned the corner into Wilton Close, Mr Morgan from across the road was on his way out. Instead of raising his hat to them as he went on his way, he headed straight for them. Patience felt pleased – but only for a second. There was a purposeful rigidity in his shoulders and a glassy expression in his eyes.

'Good morning, Mr Morgan,' said Prudence.

'Is it?' he demanded. 'I'll tell you what would make this a good morning, Miss Hesketh: your assurance that you aren't teaching lower-class types in that school of yours. It's all over Chorlton that you're training girls from the slums.'

All Belinda could think about was next Saturday. She could barely sleep for thinking about it... about him, about Richard. She had heard Mr Tyrell call him that, and she had heard Richard call him Uncle. Richard Tyrell. Well, he might not be a Tyrell; he might be the son of Mr Tyrell's sister. It didn't matter. Knowing he was Richard was enough.

Last Saturday afternoon her heart had filled with a golden, pulsating warmth that slowed her breathing and scattered her delighted senses. Richard had joined his uncle in one of the alcoves formed by bookcases, making it impossible for her to see him from the office where she had been obliged to retreat when he arrived, her mind clutching at the image of his figure; the dark hair that was revealed when he removed his trilby to shake hands; his dark eyes, oh, and that flash of smile. The thought of that smile had made her heart flip as if the smile had been for her.

She had sank down at the table that served as her desk, flexing her fingers as if about to start typing, but making no attempt to work. Instead she got up and moved the chair to the other side of the table, turning the typewriter and the pile of books to face the other way. Now she could see him when he emerged from the alcove. She strained her ears, but caught only the murmur of low voices. Mr Tyrell apparently had more than 'huh' to say to his nephew.

She had to type; she couldn't afford to sit there in silence. Besides, if she could finish the next invoice and letter, she could go to Mr Tyrell for his signature. Thank heavens she hadn't asked for permission to sign the letters herself. But this customer, curse him, had requested a whole stack of books and what if typing the invoice took longer than Richard's visit?

Her hand trembled as she turned the knob that rotated the drum and fed the finished letter out of the machine. Her heart took several beats in a rush, going so fast it stumbled over the next few. She breathed steadily, trying to calm herself.

She took the letter to the alcove, her heart hammering as she saw Richard, appreciating his dark brown eyes and straight nose. She cleared her throat, or tried to. She tried again.

'Excuse me, Mr Tyrell. Could you sign this, please?'

They looked at her. Richard smelled of tobacco and lemons – hair oil or cologne? Heat flushed through her. Please don't let her blush.

'Who's this?' he asked pleasantly.

'Saturday help,' said Mr Tyrell.

Belinda waited for him to add her name, but he didn't. With a wave of his hand, he signalled to his nephew to turn round so he could use his back as a writing surface. Richard gave Belinda an amused smile and she had to bite the insides of her cheeks to stop herself beaming back like an idiot. She couldn't be so forward as to introduce herself, but since his uncle clearly wasn't going to do the honours, maybe Richard—

The bell danced as the door opened and a well-dressed couple entered the shop. Mr Tyrell thrust the letter into Belinda's hands and she reluctantly withdrew into the office. Would Richard follow while his uncle was greeting the customers? She prepared a smile – friendly but not excessive. Then she fussed with the stack of waiting books before looking round, ready to... her smile wasn't needed. He hadn't followed.

The shop door opened again and in came a man, who held it open for two women who arrived behind him. Just when she needed the place to be empty, the shop was fuller than she had seen it before. She couldn't stand here gawping; she had to get on with her work. Each time she finished typing a book's details, she looked into the shop, hoping to see Richard. The bell jingled a couple of times; someone left, someone else came in. Finishing the list gave her an excuse to stand up and move around, gathering what she needed to make up the parcel, but she didn't glimpse Richard.

When at last all the customers had departed, she waited breathlessly for Mr Tyrell to resume his conversation with Richard, but he got on with his work in silence. Somehow Richard had left without her noticing. Disappointment dried her mouth.

But he would visit the shop again – wouldn't he?

It hadn't been until she was on her way home that she realised she could have approached him while Mr Tyrell was busy. 'Excuse me. Are you Mr Lomax? There's a book waiting for you in the office.' Simple as that.

Maybe next time.

There would be a next time, wouldn't there?

Thinking about it had kept her awake ever since. She ought to be bog-eyed and exhausted, but instead she felt alert like never before. Her senses sang as they embraced the world. The tiny flowers on the shepherd's purse that grew in Grave Pit Lane had never been whiter and the groundsel's flower-heads were fluffier than ever, like miniature shaving brushes. Everything was better.

'You're looking well, Belinda,' Auntie Enid commented. 'All this business work must suit you.'

'It does,' she whispered.

What would Auntie Enid and Grandma Beattie say? They would be devastated.

What would Ben say? She picked up his photograph with its poppy sewn into the black sleeve. Dear Ben. He had occupied her heart for so long. She had never thought to replace him. Goodness, that was why she was attending the business school: because she had expected to support herself for the rest of her life.

Had she replaced him? Did this wild awakening of emotion constitute replacing him? Or would it take an actual relationship to do that? She had never considered the possibility of another relationship. Was she considering one now, based on having seen Richard once? Surely not: she might never see him again. And yet…

What would Ben say? Would he mind? People always said of the departed: 'He would want you to be happy', but did they really mean that or was it merely a convenient way of justifying what you wanted to do? Auntie Enid hadn't said, 'Ben would be proud of you,' when she started to have ambitions about her work. Auntie Enid claimed Ben would be ashamed to think of his darling girl having to work for a living. By that token, would he prefer her to find another husband?

Another husband! Hark at her. She had seen Richard only once and they hadn't exchanged a word.

But they had exchanged a smile. Her heart pounded. Would he come back to the shop? Would she see him again?

Patience hadn't had a good night's sleep since Mr Morgan had attacked them on their way home from church. Poor Miss Layton: did everyone think her a slum girl? Their other pupils were obviously middle class, with their stylish clothes, while Miss Layton made the best of herself in an ancient coat and hat that presumably she shared with an older relative of a larger size. Neither did she have that confident spring in her step that the better-off sort of girl had.

And it wasn't just Mr Morgan. No one else had said anything, but Patience had been on the receiving end of some tight-lipped glances. Neither was it just the people in Wilton Close. She had caught whispers behind her back in the butcher's and the fishmonger's. Only this morning, a woman whom she knew by sight had stopped her on the library steps to demand, 'Is it true? I've heard about your school for husbandless girls. Is it true you're taking in drabs and draggletails from the slums? Send 'em back to the gutter, that's what I say.' And she had marched on her judgemental way, head held high, leaving Patience too upset to change her books.

'I'm tempted to knock on Mr Morgan's door and ask where he got his information,' Prudence said at the table.

Patience looked at her plate. She had come to the table with little appetite for the stuffed chicken thighs she had prepared, but even that appetite fled at the thought of Prudence striding into battle. 'Please don't. We don't want to cause trouble.'

'Don't worry. I've got more sense. We can't have people thinking we're ashamed or unsure of what we're doing. Besides, if, as I suspect, Mr Morgan's information came from our dear brother, I have no doubt Lawrence will have covered his tracks.'

'But after those pieces in the papers, and the article in *Vera's Voice*, he can't denigrate the school. I thought that was the whole point.'

'He can't denigrate it publicly, but who's to say what hole-and-corner nonsense he can get up to?'

After tea, Patience cleared away before joining Prudence in the sitting room.

'Did you find the letter? I see you did.'

Prudence had the bulky envelope in her hands. 'I thought I'd wait for you before I opened it. It's addressed to us both.' Inside the envelope was another envelope. 'It's addressed to *The Hesketh Business School, % Vera's Voice*. How interesting.'

Prudence opened the inner envelope and read its contents; then she looked up and smiled. It wasn't the wide smile you might get from someone else, but a relaxation of the lips and a brief softening about the eyes. That was as far as Prudence went.

'It's from two young women – I assume they're young – who saw the article about us in *Vera's Voice* and wish to sign up with us.'

'How splendid.'

'But they don't live in Manchester, so they want to know if we provide bed and board.'

'That's a shame.'

'Not a shame, Patience – an opportunity.'

Chapter Fourteen

SATURDAY. AT LONG last, Saturday. Belinda felt like singing as she hurried to the bookshop. Secretly, in the dead of night, she had dug out the rose-patterned material from the back of her cupboard and cut out and sewn two simple pieces, which she had smuggled out of End Cottage today, waiting until she had nearly reached her destination before slipping the band around the crown of Mrs Harrison's old hat and sliding the matching scarf underneath the back of the coat collar and tying it loosely in the region of her breastbone, a splash of colour on this early spring day. Just in case.

When she reached the shop, her foot was already on the step and her thumb was pressing down the brass lever to lift the latch as she saw the *Closed* notice. Closed? Mr Tyrell had said nothing last week. Even if he didn't require her, she should still let him know she had come, to show she was reliable. She knocked on the glass pane in the door, imagining his 'huh' when she disturbed him.

She caught a movement inside the shop and a figure came towards the door. Richard! Her breath hitched as he shot back the bolts and turned the key. She smiled up at him. The blank look he gave her might have crushed her, but then he nodded and all was right once more.

'Oh – the Saturday help. I forgot you were due.'

So he hadn't spent the week dreaming of seeing her again. He hadn't arranged to be here at exactly the right time. Had her smile slipped? She heaved it back into place. He would notice her today, with her pretty hat band and scarf, he was bound to.

And this was the perfect opportunity to introduce herself. 'The Saturday help – otherwise known as Belinda Layton.' Look: a nice smile and a sense of humour, not to mention a stylish dash of colour.

'You'd better come inside.'

He stepped back to let her in. Her skin quivered at his nearness. Behind her, he shut the door and locked it. She looked round for Mr Tyrell, but there was no sign.

'I'm Richard Carson, Mr Tyrell's—'

'Nephew. Yes, I know.' Did she sound too keen? Did he know his uncle hadn't told her who he was? Oh, heck.

'You'd better sit down. I've got something to tell you.'

Was Mr Tyrell ill? Poor fellow. She could offer to help Richard look after him. Her stomach fluttered in anticipation. She wanted to grasp Richard's lapels and demand, 'Tell me.'

With a courteous wave of his hand, he let her precede him into the office. Automatically she removed her coat and hat, then realised she was keeping him waiting and sat down, her coat folded across her lap.

'I'm sorry to be the bearer of bad news, Miss Layton, but my uncle – well, a couple of days ago he unexpectedly passed away.'

Patience stood beside Prudence, looking at Pa's old bedroom. He had occupied the largest room, as befitted the master of the house. The handsome suite of bed, wardrobe, chest of drawers and dressing table, all made from beautifully carved walnut, shone from regular polishing.

'If we put your bed and mine in here for the new pupils,' said Prudence, 'we'll be left with Pa's bed to share.'

'It would have to go in your room. It wouldn't fit in mine.'

'It's hardly convenient. It'd be a damnable squeeze in my room and there'd be a big empty space in yours.' She made a brisk making-up-her-mind movement. 'These two girls are obviously friends, so we'll leave the double bed where it is and they can share. I'll write to say we'll put them on our waiting list, but if they don't mind sharing, they can join us at once.'

'What if they say no?'

'Then we'll lose two potential pupils, but I think they'll jump at it. Either way, you and I will keep our own beds in our own rooms. If we're going to take in paying guests, that'll be important.'

As Prudence was writing the letter, the evening paper was pushed through the letter-box.

Patience fetched it from the hall floor. 'You read it and I'll take the letter to the pillar-box. It should catch the teatime collection.'

The days were noticeably drawing out. The spiky golden flowers of next door's forsythia arched over the garden wall and carpets of anemones were starting to unfurl their blooms in several of the gardens she passed.

Patience returned home, feeling pleasantly invigorated, to find Prudence sitting bolt upright with the newspaper standing to attention in her hands, as if it didn't dare relax and let its corners flop over.

Patience sank onto the settee. 'What is it?'

'An attack on me. According to what the writer is pleased to call "a source close to Miss Hesketh", my years of office experience apparently make me (quote) "an inspiration" to my pupils.'

'That's good, isn't it? Wait. Inspiration? Didn't Miss Layton—?'

'Tell us she had said that to Lawrence? Yes, indeed. There's more. It mentions how I declined to give up my post to a returning soldier—'

'But you didn't have to. It was your job all along and we needed the income.'

'There's no mention of that, though it does say I'm believed to be in favour of paying women the same rate men receive.'

'Ah.' Except for the fact that she had been taught to sit up straight, Patience would have sunk deep into the cushions. 'I'm afraid I may have said something of the kind to Miss Layton.'

Prudence gave the newspaper a sharp flick as if the pages needed straightening.

'I'm sorry, Prudence.'

Prudence blew out a derisory breath. 'You didn't write this article.'

'What else does it say?'

'It saves the best till last. If I am an inspiration, the parents of the girls who attend our school are entitled to know what kind of inspiration. Will their daughters go home believing they should be paid more? Should there, God forbid, be another war, will they hang onto their jobs regardless of the needs of returning heroes?'

'But the last time they wrote about us, it was flattering.'

Prudence pulled the paper onto her lap and looked at her. 'Lawrence is trying to squeeze us out of business. Well, let's turn the tables. As far as the world is concerned, he is the real force behind our endeavour and we're merely the obedient and grateful sisters putting his plans into effect. So.' She drew the word out thoughtfully. 'We'll write a letter, saying how distressed we are on behalf of our dear brother, whose good name may be tarnished as a result of this article. We'll say I've been in office work since I left school. Regarding the returning soldier, we'll say that even back then, our dear brother, with extraordinary foresight and social conscience, was already in the early stages of devising the idea of the business school, and therefore it was with his blessing that I continued working. He knew that my continued office experience would be essential to the success of his fledgling plan to help unfortunate surplus girls.'

'Goodness,' said Patience. 'After that, Lawrence will have to be publicly on our side about your keeping your job. What about the matter of women earning the same as men?'

'It's probably best not to mention it as such.'

Patience thought furiously. If she was going to put her name to this letter, she jolly well wanted to share its composition. 'We can say how concerned Lawrence is for these poor girls facing a lifetime as breadwinners. We'll call it a breadwinner's wage.'

'Bravo,' said Prudence. 'There's something else we should do, though you won't like it. I'm afraid we may have to throw Miss Layton to the wolves.'

'No!'

'Yes. She is the person who started this off by talking so freely to Lawrence and providing him with all this ammunition.'

'We don't know that for certain.'

'She said she told him about using paperwork and behold, an anonymous complaint is made about documents missing from work. Need I continue? That word "inspiration" was hers.'

'You've made your point. What do you mean about throwing her to the wolves?'

'It won't be as bad as it sounds, I promise. But there is one piece of damage done by Lawrence that we haven't addressed.'

'The missing paperwork, keeping your job... Oh.'

'Oh, indeed.'

'What are you going to do?' asked Patience.

'Ask what Miss Layton is going to do.' Prudence elongated her back and her neck so she could peer through the window without standing up. 'Talk of the devil.'

Patience came to her feet. Miss Layton was coming up the path. There was something different about her, though it took Patience a moment to put her finger on it. Yes – a dash of colour. About time, too.

She went to the front door, opening it before Miss Layton could ring the bell.

'Come in. We were just talking about you.'

'Really?' Miss Layton looked at her. 'You've heard, then?'

'Heard what?' Goodness, what now? 'Let me take your coat and we'll go into the sitting room. That's a pretty scarf.'

'Thank you.' But the compliment didn't seem to give her any pleasure.

'I'm glad to see you, Miss Layton,' said Prudence. 'Take a seat. We need to ask you something.'

'Prudence.' Patience injected a warning into her voice. 'I think Miss Layton has something on her mind. What is it, dear?'

Miss Layton looked from one of them to the other. 'I don't know if you already know.'

'Know what?' asked Prudence. 'Don't beat about the bush.'

'I went to the bookshop earlier on as usual and... Mr Tyrell has died. His nephew told me.'

'Gracious,' said Prudence. 'No, we hadn't heard.'

'Poor old gentleman,' breathed Patience. 'Though he wasn't as old as all that. Sixty-something, I suppose. And what a shock for you, my dear, turning up as normal and...' She wanted to enfold Miss Layton in a hug.

'You say there was a nephew there?' said Prudence.

'Yes. Richard Carson.'

'It is proper to say Mr Richard Carson.'

'Prudence!' This was hardly the moment to correct the poor girl.

Prudence raised her eyebrows at her before addressing Miss Layton once more. 'I wasn't aware of a nephew.'

'He says he's Mr Tyrell's heir.'

'Really?' Prudence's voice took on a sharp edge. 'Then he ought to have had the courtesy to let us know of his bereavement, so we could inform you that your services were no longer required.'

'In fairness,' Patience ventured, 'he possibly didn't know about Miss Layton.'

'I wrote a letter to Mr Tyrell, confirming the arrangements.'

'He can't have found that yet,' said Miss Layton. 'Otherwise I'm sure he'd have done the right thing. He told me there's a lot to be sorted out. Actually, he already knew I was the Saturday help, because he was at the shop last week.'

'All the more reason why he should have gone through his uncle's papers to find a way of getting in touch with you.'

'Prudence, please,' Patience murmured. 'Carson, did you say his name is? We shall, of course, send a letter of condolence.'

'He's inherited Mr Tyrell's cottage,' said Miss Layton.

'We don't have that address. The shop address will do.'

'He seems to have told you rather a lot of his business.' Prudence's voice was lofty with disapproval.

Miss Layton dropped her gaze and wound her fingers together. 'He... he offered me a job.'

'Does he intend to run the shop himself?' said Patience.

'I'm sure you'd make a capable assistant in a shop,' Prudence added, 'but that isn't what we're training you to be.'

'He doesn't want to keep the shop,' said Miss Layton. 'He wants to sell the stock.'

'That would take a long time,' said Prudence, 'and meanwhile the rent has to be paid on the premises.'

'I'm sure some of the stock will go to customers,' said Miss Layton, 'but Mr Carson mentioned selling it to other bookshops.'

'And what job has he offered you?' asked Patience.

'Typing letters and catalogues, generally helping with whatever needs doing...'

'And when the stock is sold?' asked Prudence.

'Well...'

'He has offered you a temporary post that may last no more than a few weeks.'

'But it's office work… useful experience… It could help me move onto something else.'

'Or you could find yourself unemployed.'

The girl looked crestfallen. Why did she want this post so much? 'You said you had a question for me.'

'Not a question so much as a request,' said Prudence. 'It's to do with your being our first scholarship candidate. I'm sorry to inform you there has been a misunderstanding.'

Miss Layton gasped. 'You mean, I can't be a scholarship candidate after all?'

'Your position is secure. We're happy to have you as a pupil. Our brother is happy too.'

Miss Layton brightened. 'You said the position was his idea.'

'The misunderstanding concerns people outside the business school, who – well, frankly there has been gossip about you. People think…' Prudence stopped.

'They think I'm getting above myself,' said Miss Layton. Her voice sounded flat, but not surprised.

'I'm sorry,' said Prudence and Patience poured a thousand blessings on her head for not mentioning slum girls. 'Miss Patience and I believe the best thing is for you to write a letter to the *Evening News*, explaining your humble but respectable origins and expressing your gratitude to our brother for his generosity in allowing a girl like you to have this opportunity alongside girls from better backgrounds. It wouldn't go amiss if you were to mention how your fiancé died for his country, leaving you to face a lifetime of fending for yourself and how much harder this would be but for Mr Hesketh's sense of social responsibility. Do you think you can do that?'

Miss Layton nodded. 'I'm sorry if I've brought the business school into disrepute.'

'Nonsense!' cried Patience. 'This is malicious gossip.'

'It has to be knocked on the head,' said Prudence. 'We could write the letter ourselves, but it would be more meaningful coming from you. I know that Mr Hesketh, when he reads your letter in the paper, will be certain to speak well of the scholarship candidate idea.'

'It's the least I can do in return for his kindness,' said Miss Layton.

Patience stirred uncomfortably. They were using the girl for their own ends. But Miss Layton stood to benefit as well, if the gossip stopped. She would keep telling herself that.

Chapter Fifteen

SHE HAD TO accept Richard's job: she had to. If she didn't, she would never see him again. So what if it was temporary? It was useful experience. All Belinda had done for Mr Tyrell was typing. Richard wanted more than that, although, to be honest, she would be hard pressed to say what.

'I apologise if this sounds vague,' he had said to her on Saturday, with a deprecating smile that made her heart turn over. 'The truth is, I don't know exactly what I'll need you to do. There'll be correspondence to deal with and parcels to send and I may need you to work in the shop. I've inherited my uncle's cottage and its contents, so I need to sort through his belongings. Things will have to be disposed of appropriately: could you organise that? Arrange for buyers to collect things, for example. In due course, I'll move into the cottage. I'm in lodgings at present.'

'The cottage will need a thorough clean.' She spoke eagerly and then blushed. 'I don't meant to suggest it's unkempt, but you should always spring-clean before you move in.'

He gave her an approving smile. 'I wouldn't have thought of that. You're in danger of making yourself indispensable, Miss Layton.'

How could she turn down the job after that? He saw her value. He needed her. And who could say where that might lead? Her heart raced. She had no business thinking like that. For all kinds of reasons, she had no business.

Auntie Enid and Grandma Beattie were impressed by the job offer.

'Eh, it shows what a capable lass you are.' Grandma Beattie made it sound as if she had never said a word against office work.

Their pride made it painful to breathe. They would be distraught if they knew that a man other than Ben occupied her thoughts. Neither did she mention that it was a temporary position. It made her feel a complete heel to withhold the truth, but she couldn't risk it. This was a good opportunity. She would work hard and build up experience; and if it also enabled her to spend a few weeks in the company of the handsome Richard Carson, where was the harm in that? She felt alive in a way she hadn't in years. In fact, she probably had never felt as alive as this. Meeting Ben and falling in love had been wonderful and exciting, but it had also felt natural; while this untamed feeling Richard had awoken was unexpected, unlooked for, startling.

On Sunday evening, she sat at the table, pen in hand, composing her resignation letter. There was a tight knot in her stomach. Was she making a mistake? Would she be doing this if she hadn't been bowled over by Richard? But she couldn't back out now. If she did, she would always wonder. Losing Ben had provided her with a lifetime of *if onlys*. She didn't want to store up more. She had to seize this chance.

At tea-break the next morning, she took her letter to the tattlers' room. The door opened and two of the tattlers came out. One of them leaned back into the room.

'Miss Layton's one of yours, isn't she, Butterfield?'

He left the door open as he and his companion walked away. Belinda hesitated. Mr Butterfield was alone in the room, seated behind one of the battered-looking old desks.

'Come to seek me out, have you?' he enquired. 'Close the door.'

That was the last thing she wanted to do, but she couldn't avoid doing so without being openly disobedient. She held out her letter, ready to snatch her hand away the instant he took it.

'What's this, then?'

'My notice, sir.'

'You're leaving?'

'Yes, sir. Giving you the letter before dinner today means I can finish on Friday.' She had double-checked with Maggie.

'We'll be sorry to lose a capable little worker like you. You could have had a good future here.'

'Will you write me a character reference, please?'

He nodded. 'I'll have it ready before you leave.'

He came round the desk. She edged backwards, trying to make it look natural and nothing to do with her speeding pulse.

'Don't look so alarmed,' he said gravely, as if he had never given her any cause to be wary. 'I only want to shake your hand to wish you well.'

She couldn't refuse, could she? Feeling trapped, she extended her hand. He took it, exerting a gentle pressure as he shook it and she just had time to be relieved that all he had wanted really was to shake hands, when his fingers tightened and he pulled her closer and kissed her mouth. His cold tongue brushed her lips. Ugh. Her body went rigid. Her senses screamed at her that he was about to make another lunge and a calm little voice in her head said that if she stayed put, she was asking for it. She stepped back just in time.

He smiled. Couldn't anything wipe the smirk off his face? 'You little tease. Never mind. There's always next time. Don't forget to collect your reference.'

Darting from the room, she headed for the canteen. Her mind buzzed with images. She pictured herself slapping him, no, clouting him good and hard. It was what he deserved. Why hadn't she done it? She despised herself for not retaliating.

'You all right, lass?' asked Maggie.

'It's not too late to change your mind, if you're having second thoughts,' said Auntie Enid.

Belinda smiled, but her skin was crawling. She didn't say a word about that kiss. There were some women who would say, 'Dirty bugger fondled my bum,' or 'Dirty sod grabbed my tits,' but they were the coarser sort. Decent girls didn't make a show of themselves. Decent girls kept quiet.

Decent girls felt dizzy with fear at the prospect of having to collect their reference.

As they walked home down Grave Pit Lane, Auntie Enid said, 'This time next week, you'll be coming home from work in Chorlton.' She sounded wistful.

Belinda linked arms with her. 'It's only the job that'll be different. Everything else will stay the same.' Liar! She couldn't wait for the heady experience of spending her days alongside Richard. 'I have to drop a note through the shop letter-box to say I'm starting next Monday.'

'Better sooner than later. You don't want him thinking you're not interested and offering the job elsewhere. You need to tell your folks too.'

Would her parents be proud? It was hard knowing that their first reaction would be to ask about the money.

As they walked into End Cottage, a fishy aroma greeted them. Grandma Beattie stood at the range, gently poaching a smoked haddock.

'Look who's here to see you, Belinda.'

Sarah flew across the room to hug her. 'Mrs Sloan says you've got a new job. Clever old you! So this is your last week at the mill. What will you be doing? I want to hear all about it. Mrs Sloan said the old bookseller died and his heir wants to sell up.'

So Belinda launched into an explanation of how she would answer enquiries, type an inventory, get things ready for sale and organise deliveries. Being vague with the Miss Heskeths had been a mistake, even though Richard had been vague with her. She had managed to make the details of the work sound more definite by the time she told Auntie Enid and Grandma Beattie, and today, after all the questions that had been fired at her in the canteen, she had discovered an unexpected talent for blathering on about nothing and making it sound like something.

'Are you going round to tell Mum and Dad?' Sarah asked.

'Not tonight,' said Belinda. 'I need to confirm to Mr Carson that I'm starting next week.'

'Can I tell them?'

'Feel free.' She was delighted that Sarah was so pleased for her.

'Good. And can I also tell them that you'll put my name forward to be the new tenter?'

There was an air of excitement in the canteen. Jessie had been told she was going to take Belinda's place as a two-loomer and, in turn, Hattie was being made up to a one-loomer.

'Steady on,' laughed Belinda. 'I haven't left yet.' Was it mean to feel the tiniest bit put out? A couple of days ago, she and her new job were all anyone could talk about. Now Jessie and Hattie were centre-stage.

'We'll get a new tenter an' all,' remarked Annie, knocking back the last drop of her tea. 'I heard that Minnie Ollerenshaw is hoping to get her lass took on.'

'Jenny Ollerenshaw-as-was is a bit old to be starting off as a tenter,' said Flo, 'but I suppose, as a widow with children, she's desperate.'

'I don't care who it is,' Maggie declared, 'as long as she isn't foisted onto me to train.'

Auntie Enid nudged Belinda. 'If you're going to put in a word for your Sarah, you'd best not hang about. I'd ask for you, but Sarah knows you're not keen. If you can't tell her, hand on heart, that you was the one who asked, she'll get in a snit with you.'

Auntie Enid was right. Little as Belinda wanted Sarah within a hundred miles of Mr Butterfield, if she didn't try to get her the job, Sarah would never forgive her.

'I'll ask Butterfingers as soon as the hooter goes for dinner.'

'Good girl.'

She expected to speak to Mr Butterfield in the weaving shed, but he crooked his forefinger and led her to the tatlers' room, where he held the door open. She scuttled inside, wanting to get safely past him. He shut the door behind them.

Facing him, she pressed her lips together. They felt cold where his slimy tongue had touched them last time.

'Come back for more, have you? Can't say I'm surprised. I always sensed you had a taste for it.'

She stood her ground. Don't show you're afraid.

'I'm here about the tenter position. My sister—'

'Pretty is she, like you?'

'She's a hard worker, sir.' She heard herself babbling about hotel work.

'Hm.' His eyes were thoughtful. It looked like he was considering it. 'She sounds promising.'

'She's keen, sir.'

'But how keen are you, that's the question.' He caught the side of his lower lip under his teeth, raising his eyebrows and tilting his head.

The suggestive expression almost made her choke. Jerking away, she collided with a chair. It went over backwards with a clatter. Her thoughts clattered too, instinct and fear and loathing all mashed up together.

Mr Butterfield reached out a hand as if to steady her, but if he really meant to do that, it would be a brief touch; but no, the touch tightened into a grasp.

'You could get your sister the job, right here, right now. You'd do that for your sister, wouldn't you?'

There was a knock and the door was thrown open – Auntie Enid.

'Excuse me, Mr Butterfield, have you seen— oh, here she is. Are you coming for dinner, love?' She eyed the tattler. 'If you've finished with her, sir?'

He was already on the other side of the room, as if nothing had happened.

'Yes, quite. Off you go, Miss Layton.'

'Have you got her reference ready, sir?' asked Auntie Enid.

'It isn't usual to hand it out before the last day.'

'Then I'll come with her to fetch it on Friday, me being her guardian an' all.'

Belinda felt like flinging her arms round Auntie Enid and kissing her.

'You all right, lass?' Auntie Enid asked as they walked away.

'Yes, thanks.'

She couldn't, just couldn't, say what had happened. Well, nothing had happened, not really, had it? Yes, it had. He might not have mauled her, but he had intended to and her stomach was still roiling. Did he truly imagine she would pay such a price to get Sarah taken on? What had she ever done to make him think her loose? Oh, she couldn't wait to leave this place!

She arrived home to find a postcard from Richard, asking her to report to the shop at nine the following Monday. She read it a dozen times, wishing he had said more, then she forced herself to set it aside for fear of looking too interested.

Just two days to go at the mill – and no cleaning on Saturday. No bookshop work either. When had she last had the whole weekend to herself? It was like looking forward to a holiday.

During her last two days at the mill, she felt Mr Butterfield's eyes on her, no matter where she was. Ought she to tell him she wasn't prepared to pay his price? Instinct told her to keep well out of his way but, on Friday, after the dinner hooter sounded and the women were heading for the canteen, Colleen caught her by the arm.

'Mr Butterfield says to go to the tattlers' room to fetch your reference.'

She looked round but Auntie Enid was nowhere to be seen. Her heart thumped. 'If you see my Auntie Enid, tell her where I am.'

She went to the tattlers' room. The door was open. Perhaps if she stood in the doorway, she needn't actually go in; but when she stopped, there was no one inside.

A hand landing on her waist from behind nearly made her jump out of her skin. She scuttled into the room to get away from the loathsome creep. He followed her in.

'Colleen said you've written my reference.'

'Isn't Mrs Sloan meant to collect it with you?' He made a show of peering into the passage. 'No guardian angel today? What a pity.'

He closed the door. Belinda glanced round, as if another exit might magically appear.

'Is it ready?'

'My, my, you're in a hurry. We have some unfinished business to attend to before that. What about your sister's position as tenter? All you have to do is earn it for her.'

His hand reached towards her, aiming for her cheek.

She ducked away. 'No.' No, you dirty old man. You're disgusting. You make my skin crawl. All the women here hate you. But all that came out of her mouth was, 'No.'

'No? Are you sure?' His hand stopped in mid-air. 'Such a little thing to do, and your sister's future is secure.'

'No.'

He stilled, then rested his hand on her shoulder and leaned in – to kiss her? No, to murmur in her ear.

'No matter. She can pay for the job herself when she starts.'

Belinda gasped.

'Tell her not to worry. I'll let her find her feet first.' He smiled. 'Unless, of course, you'd rather pay the debt up front, as it were—?'

The door opened and one of the other tattlers stopped in surprise at the sight of them. Belinda fled. No, no, no. Never. Sarah wasn't coming to work here. Even if Belinda had to tie her up and lock her in the cellar, she wasn't coming here. She hovered outside the canteen, getting her breathing under control before she went in.

'There you are. Where've you been?' Annie laughed. 'We thought you'd mistaken the dinner-hooter for the going-home hooter.'

'Have you heard the news?' asked Flo. 'Jenny Ollerenshaw-as-was is starting as the new tenter. That's good, isn't it?'

Belinda's mouth dropped open, then snapped shut. Mr Butterfield had tried to get her to give in by threatening Sarah when he had already promised the job to Jenny Forrester. The dirty old bugger.

Across the room, Minnie Ollerenshaw nibbled on a barm cake. What price had she paid to get her Jenny taken on?

Chapter Sixteen

MANIAC MANOR BOASTS an excellent library. I spend hours at a time in here, flicking through the books, trying to deduce information about myself based on what interests me. Time and again, I open an atlas of the British Isles. Where am I from? My vowels are northern. I sound educated. Was I a professional man before the war? Not knowing leaves me feeling flat.

Frustrated, too. Dr Jennings is no help. Seated behind his desk, he urges me to bide my time.

'I've bided enough time, thank you.'

'And why did you?' He steeples his fingers, watching me across the desk. 'You're an intelligent man, a highly capable man, yet you stayed on that farm in France for a little over three years. The fire took place shortly before the war ended. Even allowing time for your physical recovery, you remained for a significant time with the Durands. What made you do that?'

Waiting for my reply, he strikes a match and sucks on the stem of his pipe, gently encouraging the flame to catch the tobacco. The aroma rises from the bowl of the pipe, a pungent tang with an underlying sweetness. I inhale, enjoying it, recognising it – but then, who doesn't recognise the smell of pipe tobacco?

'At first I stayed because I was waiting for my memory to return. Then I stayed because it was a busy time, not just on the farm, but also in the town. There was work to be done and not many men left to do it. I owed it to the Durands to stay and help. And, finally, I stayed because what else was I to do? Had I returned to England, where would I have gone?'

He points the stem of his pipe at me. 'Where indeed?' It is a challenge, a quiet one, but a challenge nonetheless.

A police station. A hospital. A newspaper office. A solicitor.

'I suppose I stayed... because I stayed. The Durands and the other farmers and the townsfolk made it possible for me to stay and so I did.'

'Perhaps you stayed to recover from your wartime experiences. Many men would.'

I smile. Not a real, eye-crinkling smile, more a wry tug of the lips. 'Ah, but I don't recall my wartime experiences.'

'What is your greatest fear?'

I look away. What man wants to answer a question like that? Out loud, I mean. I know the answer, but I'm reluctant to give it voice. I don't want him to think ill of me. Even though he is a doctor and his function is to help, not to judge, I don't want him to think less of me.

When I look at him, I find his gaze on me. He appears thoughtful, interested. He looks as if he isn't going to be fobbed off.

'Is your greatest fear that your memory will never return?' Does he think my fear of this is so great that I cannot put it into words?

'No,' I answer. 'After all this time, I accept that it's unlikely to happen. My greatest fear...' And it is fear: the hairs on the back of my neck stand up one by one. '...is that I stayed put in France because I'm a coward.'

'There are many who will view your memory loss as a symptom of lack of moral fibre.' He uses the same tone that he might use to share the cricket scores. 'They, however, are fools. Your memory loss is the result of trauma and nothing to do with cowardice. Neither is cowardice a part of your general character, I can assure you of that. That fire, the men who perished: you were all part of a special unit of soldiers on a mission that went tragically wrong. You wouldn't have been selected to serve in that unit had there been any doubt as to your character. Does that reassure you?'

Does it? I consider. The mere fact that I have to consider gives me my answer.

'I'm glad to be told, obviously, but you were correct when you said that true knowledge is a feeling. You tell me I'm no coward and I trust you to speak the truth; but that in itself doesn't give me the knowledge inside here.' I rap my chest with my knuckles.

'Let's leave it there for today,' he says.

It is a fair old walk into Aylesbury. It is a market day: I can tell by the carriers' carts that overtake me, bringing people in from the villages. I walk past the shops on the High Street, past the statue of Disraeli outside the London Joint Stock Bank; past the statue, at the top of the market square, of John Hampden. He is pointing – I have been told he points the way to London. I pause beside the new war memorial to pay my respects. It is an elegant, dignified creation: a stone cross rising above a low curved wall with plaques of names. My heart reaches out to the local people whose menfolk are remembered here. Not knowing what I did in the war leaves me feeling shallow and inadequate. I turn away.

In the market square, stallholders cry their wares, gaunt bearded old men sort through ancient farming implements and mothers sift through piles of clothes. The flower-seller deftly makes posies and buttonholes and the toffee-man stretches his toffee. I'm not short of a bob or two. The army owed me money, apparently. I buy toffee and give it to some wistful-looking urchins, who should probably be at school.

I wander towards the canal and walk along the towpath. Coming across a bench, I sit down and stretch out my legs.

It is time for me to leave Maniac Manor. Not because Dr Jennings says so – he has said nothing of the kind – but because I say so. I know so. Staying won't make my memory come back. Maybe nothing will. That being the case, I need to get on with my life.

I will ask for information about myself and my old life and use it to help me decide what to do. If all else fails, I'll stick a pin in a map of the British Isles.

I slap my knees and come to my feet. I am... ready.

I return to Maniac Manor to find that Dr Jennings has been asking for me. That's unusual. It isn't my day to see him. But when I knock on his door, he rises from behind his desk and ushers me across the chessboard-tiled floor.

'Let's sit somewhere more comfortable,' he says. 'In here do you?'

He throws open the door to the common room. Other rooms have been plundered of sofas and armchairs and tables to make this a relaxed place. We inmates spend our evenings here. At this time of day, the room is empty, but there is a fire. Is there a fire all day every day, just in case someone needs it? Or was it laid for my benefit?

Jennings heads for the wing-back chairs to either side of the fireplace.

'I like sitting by the window,' I say. It is a small way of taking control.

He concedes the point and we sit down.

'Something's happened,' I say, not making a question of it.

'It has.' Out come the pipe and tobacco-pouch. 'I'm going to tell you something of yourself.'

'Does this mean you've officially given up on waiting for my memory to jump through hoops?'

'It means, Linkworth, that it's time to give you some information. You'll see why in a minute.'

Have they brought my family here? Is he about to rattle off a list of names and relationships, then the door will open and they will pour in?

'You were a schoolteacher before the war.'

A schoolteacher. Of all the professions I have toyed with in my mind, I've never considered that.

'It must have been quite a cushy life,' he observes. 'Small private school; boys up to the age of thirteen.'

I see myself in a black gown with a mortar board, standing beside the blackboard, chucking a piece of chalk across the classroom at Smithers Minor to wake him up.

'What subject?' I ask. From nowhere comes the thought: I was good at Latin at school. Latin and maths.

'You were the sports master.'

Sports, eh? Does that surprise me? I remember playing cricket with the local children in France.

'The school was in the Lake District,' says Jennings.

'Am I from there?'

'No, you're a Yorkshireman.'

Yorkshire. Walking boots and a rucksack. Sweeping landscape, endless skies. Memory or imagination?

'You had a brother.'

I note the *had*.

'He died at Passchendaele; and your parents have passed away as well, I'm sorry to say.'

If I hadn't remained in France, I could have come home and found them. Did the anguish of one fallen son and the other missing presumed dead help them on their way to the grave? A pang of sorrow and regret pierces my chest in the place where I imagine the knowledge-feeling would be.

'You should know that after your mother died of the influenza, your father made a will. In the belief that both his sons had fallen on the battlefield, he left everything to your Cousin Irene.'

'Irene?' I make a quick dash around the inside of my head, hoping Irene will pop out of a corner, but the name means nothing.

'Mrs Irene Rawlins, a war widow and the mother of five children.'

'Five? What ages?'

'The oldest was born in 1910.'

A quick calculation. 'So they're all still at school.' A widow with five dependent children. 'She has it hard. Did my father have much to leave?'

'Enough to keep the wolf from the door until the oldest starts earning.'

'Does Irene…?' Presumably I am entitled to use her first name since we're cousins. 'Does she know I'm back from the dead?'

'No. It's up to you to tell people. It isn't the army's job.'

'Well, she has nothing to fear from me. I shan't make any claim against her to retrieve my father's money. I'll write and tell her so, if you'll furnish me with her address. When she's had time to adjust to the idea of my being alive and well, I'd like to visit her.'

He puffs on his pipe before he answers. 'There's somewhere you need to go before that. Does the name Reginald Tyrell mean anything to you?'

Has there been a mistake? Am I not Gabriel Linkworth after all? I try Reginald Tyrell for size. 'It doesn't ring any bells.'

'Reginald Tyrell is – was – your uncle. He passed away recently. He made you his sole heir.'

Chapter Seventeen

'I APOLOGISE IF THIS makes things awkward for you,' said Miss Hunt, 'but you do see my point of view, don't you?' She sat on their sofa, looking poised in a cream blouse spotted with green, her feet tucked out of the way, trim ankles neatly crossed. She evidently expected agreement and apologies.

Patience's heart sank. Prudence would agree. She knew she would. Miss Hunt was upset because she shared Tuesday evenings with Miss Layton from the slums – only she hadn't called her Miss Layton, she had called her 'a certain person', and she hadn't let the word 'slums' sully her lips, referring rather distantly to 'a lower-class area'. Miss Hunt wanted to change her Tuesdays for another evening, though she probably expected them to change Miss Layton's arrangements.

And Prudence would. Patience knew it.

'Firstly,' said Prudence, 'you may not change your Tuesday evenings, Miss Hunt. That is your allocated slot and when you joined our school, you confirmed that it suited you. Secondly, I assume you've heard an unpleasant rumour. Let me tell you that Miss Layton is a respectable mill-girl. More to the point, she is a surplus girl, as are you. As such, it's appropriate for you to make the best of your personal situation, is it not? If it is, are you able to furnish me with one good reason why it is not appropriate for Miss Layton to do the same? We will not entertain snobbery in our school. All our girls are decent and capable and that is all you need to know about one another.'

Gratitude flooded Patience. She had been prepared for Prudence to do what most people would have done and let class make the decision. Poor Miss Hunt looked aghast. Patience felt sorry for her. How could she save the poor girl's dignity?

'It's most unfortunate that you heard this rumour,' she said. 'You aren't alone in having been taken in by it.'

Miss Hunt reddened. 'Obviously, I didn't realise—'

'I suggest you're more careful in future.' Prudence never knew when to let go.

'I'm sure she will be,' Patience murmured. 'We'll never refer to the matter again. The last thing we want is for you to feel uncomfortable here, Miss Hunt, dear.'

Later, she said to Prudence, 'I never thought I'd see you defend Miss Layton so energetically.'

'Miss Layton may be a lower-class girl, but she's *our* lower-class girl and I won't hear her spoken ill of.'

Patience was delighted, though she took care not to show it in case she was accused of crowing. Anyway, her delight was short-lived. Two girls who had been due to start with them next week were both withdrawn by their parents, who freely admitted to having second thoughts after seeing the piece in the paper.

'I'd almost forgotten that,' sighed Patience, 'what with Miss Hunt's fuss over the rumour.'

'Hasn't Miss Layton sent her letter?' said Prudence, vexed. 'She promised she'd write.'

'Maybe her letter wasn't considered of a suitable standard for publication. I should have insisted upon writing it myself.'

Patience was still receiving glances loaded with criticism when she went round the shops. She decided not to attend her monthly flower-arranging afternoon.

'You should have gone,' Prudence told her that evening. 'We have to hold up our heads.'

'I didn't mind missing it. All the other ladies talk about is their children and grandchildren.'

She cast a hopeful glance at Prudence, aching for some fellow-feeling, for understanding of how left out she felt when Mrs Keene went on about her Maud's two little boys or Mrs Trevor described the arrangements for Ellen's forthcoming wedding. It made her feel even more childless.

Prudence, however, didn't respond. Well, she had been silly to hope for it.

After tea, as Patience washed up, Prudence came in behind her. Patience looked over her shoulder. Prudence was holding the *Manchester Evening News*.

'Miss Layton's letter?' Patience asked, pleased.

'Better than that. They haven't published it, but they have followed it up.'

'Please don't say they descended on Miss Layton at home.'

'Better than that.' Prudence's face relaxed into her rare smile. 'They descended on Lawrence and showed him her letter, thus putting him in the position of having to babble on about the importance of this scholarship position and how Miss Layton is the perfect candidate, being clean and hard-working, with a good basic education, and her young man having given his life for his country.'

'Never!' Patience started to raise her hands in delight and dripped all over herself.

'Not only that, they also showed him our letter, so he's been forced to agree with everything we said.'

'Oh, that is good news.' But she felt a twist of unease. Lawrence wouldn't be pleased.

'He was even obliged to praise us. See here: *The business school was my idea, but I could never have put it into practice without the support of my sisters, who are working hard to ensure the success of the venture.* I rather think a small celebration might be in order. If you meet me off the tram tomorrow evening, we could go for a walk and perhaps a bite to eat. We have a little extra money now, thanks to our pupils.'

Patience spent all the next day looking forward to their excursion. Their outings consisted of walks at the weekend or listening to the band in the recreation ground on summer afternoons, but they never ate out, apart from a toasted tea-cake or a scone to celebrate a birthday. With Pa using Mother's small annuity to act the part of the gentleman of private means, leaving Prudence to provide the only salary, and a woman's salary at that, their household had long stood testament to the ability of the middle class to live on fresh air and an unswerving belief in appearances.

Patience met Prudence at the terminus and they strolled down Barlow Moor Road to Chorlton Park, which was open later now that the evenings were drawing out. Afterwards they crossed the road to a modest place to have their tea, where they enjoyed slices of pork pie with tangy chutney, followed by syrup sponge and custard.

'That was a splendid treat,' Patience said on their way home, but the biggest treat of all was that Prudence – reserved, keep-your-hands-to-yourself Prudence – linked arms with her as they walked.

Patience's happy mood lasted until they turned the corner into Wilton Close, when she saw Lawrence's motor parked outside their house. Before he could emerge, Mrs Morgan came hurrying out of her house, in an ankle-length blue satin evening dress. Patience had long since suspected that the Morgans were the sort who dressed for dinner. Keeping up with the residents of Wilton Close was rather a strain when you hadn't got sixpence to scratch yourself with.

'I'm sorry to bother you, but I have to apologise for my husband. I know he had words with you… on a certain matter.

The thing is, we saw yesterday's paper and I do apologise for what Raymond said to you. It came as such a relief when I saw the piece in the paper. I said to Raymond, "I *knew* the Miss Heskeths would never lend themselves to anything untoward." You won't hold it against us, will you? You're far too generous for that. Please come inside and have a sherry and you can tell me all about your business school.'

'Thank you,' said Prudence, 'but as you can see...' She indicated Lawrence, standing beside the motor.

'Of course. I mustn't keep you. You must come in for sherry after church on Sunday. I won't take no for an answer.'

She bustled back indoors and Lawrence marched across the road to confront them.

'Where have you been? You never go out.'

'Shall we go inside?' said Prudence.

'I ought to have my own key,' said Lawrence. 'Then I wouldn't have to wait in the motor.'

'Had you troubled to tell us you were coming,' Prudence answered, 'we could have put you off.'

She led the way indoors, where she and Lawrence heaped their coats and hats into Patience's arms before stalking into the sitting room to carry on arguing. Patience quickly hung everything up before following. Prudence was in her usual place, looking as if she had been there all evening, while Lawrence remained standing, waiting for Patience to take her seat before he too sat.

'What brings you here?' Patience asked in a pleasant voice, hoping to lighten the atmosphere.

'A reporter came to my house—'

'We know. We saw the result,' said Prudence. 'It's gratifying to know we're all so in tune as a family. Pa would be proud.'

Lawrence made a derisive noise. 'Very funny. What choice did I have? I hope you're pleased with yourselves.'

'Delighted,' Prudence murmured.

'We'll see how long that lasts,' said Lawrence. 'Since you had no compunction about putting me in that position, I've decided to return the favour. Evelyn and I will be hosting an evening for various acquaintances – businessmen, councillors, what have you – and their wives. You're both invited. You will attend and will sing my praises. There'll be three aldermen there, including Alderman Edwards, who is set to retire at the end of the year.'

'I see,' said Prudence. 'It's part of your grand scheme to rise in the world. And you trust us to say the right things?'

'If you don't, sister dear, you'll jeopardise my reputation and hence bring the future of your precious school into doubt; whereas if you say the right things, you'll make me look splendid and thereby oblige me to keep your school open.' He sat back. 'Your choice.'

Belinda couldn't remember when she had last been this happy. Maybe she never had. She didn't want to be disloyal to Ben, but loving him had been coloured by all sorts of considerations. The war had kept them apart most of the time, trapping her in the shadow of fear. This feeling she had for Richard was unfettered by any such darkness and she revelled in every tingle that shivered its way across her eager flesh. When he smiled at her or she caught his eye, her heart swelled and it was all she could do to keep her answering smile within acceptable proportions.

As for the work, she loved it. It wasn't as varied as she had hoped, but that was only for now. Her duties would be more interesting and responsible once Richard got things under way. At present, she was mostly typing and serving in the shop. Miss Hesketh would tear her off a strip if she knew.

It hadn't been easy telling her tutors she had accepted the post against their advice.

'I hope you haven't made a mistake,' Miss Hesketh said. 'I fail to see how Mr Carson can take charge of his uncle's property at this stage. The will has to go through probate.'

Belinda didn't know what that meant and didn't like to ask in case it made Richard look bad; but she mentioned it to him the following day.

'No need to worry about that,' he said breezily. 'I'm the sole surviving heir, so there's no harm done if I get the ball rolling.'

One of the wonderful things about her new life was the working hours. She started at nine instead of eight and Richard said there wasn't enough for her to do to remain beyond five.

'It's all right for some,' muttered Auntie Enid.

She did extra housework to make up for it, humming as she did so because she had so much energy now that she wasn't engaged in manual labour for forty-eight hours a week.

'I thought office work was meant to bring in more money,' grumbled Grandma Beattie.

'It will… in time,' said Belinda. 'This is my first position. I have to build up experience.'

She wasn't surprised when she had to make the same point to Dad, though at least Mum took an interest, asking her about her work while Dad grouched in the background about that ruddy business school being a waste of space.

'I'm glad for you, Bel,' said Mum. 'If it gives you a step up, it's worth it. Is our Sarah speaking to you again yet?'

There had been a rumpus when Sarah found out she wasn't going to be offered the position of tenter. She had accused Belinda of not bothering, while Dad had yelled the odds about disobedient children who didn't pay attention when they were told to stick at the jobs they had already got. Fortunately, Sarah saw sense after Auntie Enid assured her that Belinda had done her best.

'I'm sorry I'm not earning more, Mum,' said Belinda. 'You know I'd help out more if I could.'

'Course you would, love, and I don't mind.' But Mum's eyes said otherwise.

She cleared her throat in case the crack in her voice betrayed her guilt. The truth was that she had less money now. Richard had offered to match the mill's hourly rate, but she wasn't working as many hours. By the time she had given Grandma Beattie her housekeeping, and handed over the usual to Mum, she had hardly anything left.

But who cared? She had taken the first step along her new path – and she was with Richard. Richard! He was so handsome with his dark good looks and engaging smile. Oh, that smile. It came so easily to his face and melted her bones every time.

He wasn't at the shop all the time, which was disappointing, but at the same time it gave her the chance to prove herself. He still had to go to work, but he had arranged to have what he called leave of absence for five half-days each week to sort out his uncle's affairs.

'We need to make the shop more hospitable if you're to spend your days here,' he said. 'Judging by the lack of creature comforts upstairs, my uncle never took the weight off his feet. I'll bring a few things here from the cottage. I'll take you there tomorrow morning and we can look round. Mr Parker at the confectioner's tells me Jim the window cleaner will ferry large items on his cart, but we can carry a few small things ourselves.'

'We're going to Mr Tyrell's cottage?' She mustn't sound over-eager.

'To my cottage,' he corrected gently. Then he smiled. 'I don't mind telling you that it will make a big difference to me to have my own home.'

'I've never met anyone before who owns their own place – apart from Mr Tyrell, of course, but I didn't know he did.'

She turned back to the inventory of history books she was working on. She mustn't betray her excitement at the prospect of seeing Richard's new home.

'I'm not sure I like the sound of that,' Auntie Enid said that evening. 'A young single girl going to a man's house: it's not decent.'

'It's part of my job. Mr Carson expects it.'

'As long as work is all he expects.'

The next morning, she borrowed Grandma Beattie's wicker shopping basket. It was a mild day and she admired the daffodils' golden trumpets and the blue drifts of grape hyacinths in the gardens on Edge Lane as she passed. Arriving at the shop, she took out her key, but the door was already unlocked.

'Good. You're here,' said Richard. 'Leave your coat on.'

To her surprise, he started along the route she took to go home. When they passed St Clement's Church in its tree-shaded grounds, she couldn't keep quiet any longer.

'This is my way home.'

'Really?' But he didn't ask where her road was. Well, of course not. He must be thinking about his late uncle. Going to Mr Tyrell's cottage must make his uncle feel very close.

Along Edge Lane, on the other side of the road from Longford Park, he guided her round a corner.

'Limits Lane. So called because on one side, you're at the outer limits of Chorlton and on the other, you're at the outer limits of Stretford.'

Thatched cottages stood behind privet hedges along one side, each cottage standing alone in its small garden. Richard walked all the way to the end. Go any further and you would trot down the slope onto the meadows.

'Here we are,' he said.

Like the rest, Mr Tyrell's cottage was behind a privet hedge. Belinda couldn't see it until they went through the gate. Its thatch hung low and sections had had to be cut out to accommodate the upstairs windows. Downstairs, there was one window to the right of the front door and two to the left. Close by stood a shed – very close by. You'd expect a shed to be tucked away in the corner of the garden; not that this garden was of any size.

Richard caught her looking. 'There used to be a lean-to attached to the cottage. It was leaky and rotten, hence the new shed. I don't mind telling you, Miss Layton,' and Belinda drew in a happy breath that he was about to confide, 'my inheritance includes some money; not a huge sum but I rather think I'll purchase a motorcycle and it can be stored in the shed. What do you think of the cottage?'

'It's a funny mixture. It's an old cottage, and there's the thatch, but it has a fresh look about it.'

'I had it painted last year.'

'You?'

'I wanted to take care of my uncle. Besides, if you knew a property was going to be yours one day, wouldn't you be happy to contribute to its upkeep and improvement?'

'I suppose it's like being your own landlord.' She examined the cottage again. If she lived here, she would have window-boxes filled with brightly coloured flowers.

Richard unlocked the door. 'After you.'

Walking inside made her feel obscurely ashamed of End Cottage, which seemed poky and dark by comparison. In this cottage, the rooms, though low-ceilinged, were larger and the furniture was better. Not only that but downstairs there were two separate rooms, not like in End Cottage, where the whole of downstairs was crammed into one room.

There was space for a chintzy armchair and small matching sofa by the fireplace, above which was an imposing over-mantel arrangement of no fewer than three shelves, covered in a mish-mash of ornaments and books. A basketwork chair stood in one corner, a drop-leaf dining table under one of the windows. There was an abundance of fussy touches. Had Mr Tyrell been a collector of coloured glass and figurines? And there were enough lacy mats and antimacassars to open a market stall.

'My late aunt,' said Richard.

Embarrassed to have been caught gawping, she held the wicker basket in front of her. 'What are we taking?'

'What do we need to make life more bearable?'

'The tea-caddy, sugar bowl, a jug for milk. Cups and saucers. Plates, cutlery, if we're going to eat our snap there.' She would eat on the premises. Would he? Would they get to know one another during dinnertimes?

'Anything else?'

'What about a table? I don't mean the dining table, but perhaps that small one, and a couple of chairs.' Had she gone too far? 'You said you wanted to be comfortable.'

'We'll take the armchair and that one in the corner.' He nodded at the basketwork chair.

She had only meant the dining chairs. It seemed like taking advantage to waltz off with the good furniture, but if Richard wanted it, then why not? She pictured cosy chats as they sat together over a pot of tea. Grandma Beattie would probably let her take some home-made shortbread to work.

'May I look for a tablecloth?'

'Help yourself.'

All the tablecloths were decorated with embroidery. The late Mrs Tyrell must have had a lot of time on her hands. Belinda chose one, then took what she wanted from the pantry, adding a box of Carr's Assorted Creams, and packed her basket.

'What else?' asked Richard. 'We're going to be there for some weeks and you'll be there more than I will.'

'It would be nice to be able to hang up my coat.'

Richard homed in on the hat-stand and removed a jacket and an old mackintosh and drew an umbrella out of the space beneath. Belinda wanted to stop him. It didn't seem respectful to set aside Mr Tyrell's things. But they were Richard's things now.

'What do you think of my new home, Miss Layton?'

She wanted to enthuse but must be careful. 'If it was mine, I'd call it Huh Cottage, because that's what Mr Tyrell used to say – at least, he did to me.'

Richard smiled. 'He wasn't good at talking to the opposite sex.'

'*Huh* was all I could get out of him. It reminded me of our neighbour's cat. Mr Austen swears blind it has one meow for food and another for fuss and another for playing. If I'd worked for Mr Tyrell for longer, I might have worked out what each different *huh* meant.' She cringed inwardly. Stop babbling. She pounced on a figurine of a shepherdess. 'Was this your aunt's?'

'Aunt Victoria liked pretty things, as you can see.' He smiled and her heart twisted happily before springing back into position. 'My uncle liked fine things too, but they had to be practical, like this silver letter-opener.' He picked up it from the desk and handed it to her. It was a slender knife with a fancy, engraved blade. He looked through the desk's contents. 'Here's the companion piece.'

'Another letter-opener,' she said. Why have two?

'Look again.'

This item was heavier and the blade was sharper.

'It's a page-cutter,' said Richard.

'A what?'

'The sign of a smart new book is that its pages are fastened together. You use the page-cutter to slice them open.'

'Oh. I get all my books from the library.'

Picking up the letter-opener, Richard held out his hand for the page-cutter. 'They make a good-looking pair. I'll finish going through the desk, then we'll leave. Feel free to look at my aunt's ornaments.'

Fancy being paid to admire figurines and vases! Soon Richard was ready to go. Belinda found her basket weighty. Richard didn't offer to carry it and she didn't expect him to. Wicker baskets were for women.

The items from the cottage made the shop a more congenial place, especially when the window cleaner brought the pieces of furniture on his cart. The first time she hung up Mrs Harrison's coat on the hat-stand, Belinda felt brisk and professional. But meeting Miss Hunt in her daring mustard-yellow mackintosh at the Miss Heskeths' garden gate that evening reminded her how dowdy her borrowed togs were.

Was she shallow to set store by appearances? She still had her pretty hatband and scarf, though she felt shifty putting them on as she reached Chorlton in the mornings and taking them off again at the end of the day, but she couldn't bear to hurt Grandma Beattie and Auntie Enid.

She arrived one morning to find Jim the window cleaner outside with his cart piled with tea-chests. She wasn't expecting them but did her best not to appear fazed.

'I hope you didn't mind having them dumped on you,' Richard said when he breezed in later.

'Of course not.' Would he see that she could take the unexpected in her stride? But he was already delving inside one of them.

'Some items to sell.' It looked like a lot more than merely some. 'Here, unwrap these.'

Everything was wrapped in newspaper. She unwrapped a musical box, a pair of candlesticks and a figurine.

'To be sold in the shop?' She would love handling and selling these things.

'Some of the bigger pieces can be sold individually, but most of it isn't valuable. The smaller things can go into boxes of bric-a-brac and customers can buy a whole box. We'll have to advertise.'

'I can put postcards in shop windows.'

'I'll put an advertisement in the paper, but you can put up a few postcards as well, if you like.'

Richard produced a heap of cardboard boxes of various

sizes and she enjoyed compiling the collections to fill them. She was surprised to find not just Aunt Victoria's things, which she could understand Richard's not wanting to keep, but also some of his uncle's possessions, such as a slide rule and a telescope, as well as the matching letter-opener and page-cutter. Surely he didn't want to dispose of Mr Tyrell's personal items.

'Did these get into the tea-chests by mistake?' she asked, all set for him to pour out his relief that she had spotted the error, but he shook his head, hardly sparing them a glance.

She couldn't understand it. Her locket from Ben was her most precious possession, even though she had now met someone else. Should she put Mr Tyrell's things to one side, so she could produce them when Richard was sorry he had sold them? How grateful he would be.

But he came across them in the cupboard and took them out.

'Don't forget these.'

So she had no choice. She popped the slide-rule into one box, the telescope into another, then hesitated over the letter-opener and page-cutter. Together or separately? She kept them together.

Richard made it a rule that nothing was to be sold in his absence.

'It's because we're selling my uncle's things. As his heir, I ought to be present.'

'Perhaps we could let customers view the boxes when you aren't here,' she suggested. 'That would make the selling process much quicker and – well, less upsetting for you.'

He glanced at her. 'You have a kind heart, Miss Layton.'

A kind heart! He thought she had a kind heart. She almost took a step closer, but he returned to checking through Mr Tyrell's stock ledger. Still – he thought she had a kind heart.

The next morning was set aside for customers to examine the boxes. Several people popped in.

'It's an interesting idea,' said a motherly-looking woman. 'My niece is getting married and one of these boxes will make an unusual wedding present.'

'If you want to give her a bundle of tat,' a man muttered scornfully.

Belinda looked at him in surprise. He was well-dressed without being expensively smart and his eyebrows beneath the brim of his top hat – top hat! – were bushy and grey. Should she defend her wares or would it be considered impertinent?

'Nothing of any interest,' he declared and left the shop.

'Well!' the motherly woman said.

Tempting as it was to settle in for a good gossip, Belinda stuck to her professional standards. 'Is there a box you especially like? I could put it aside for you.'

'That would be kind.'

When she closed up, she tidied those boxes which hadn't been viewed so much as rifled through. The disagreeable man might not have liked what he found, but it hadn't stopped him having a good rummage. One of the boxes he had sifted through contained the letter-opener and page-cutter. Should they should stay together? Separated, they could make two boxes more appealing. After all, the idea was to make money, wasn't it? Tat, indeed!

When Richard arrived, he took a quick look through the boxes, setting a price for each. The bell jingled as the door opened. It was the man who had been dismissive. He went straight to the boxes.

Belinda whispered to Richard, 'He was rude about those earlier.'

'Shh,' he warned softly, but the glance he gave her wasn't annoyed.

The man indicated a box with a flick of his gloved hand. 'I'll take this, if you please.' With a glance at the label, he delved into an inner pocket, drawing out a leather wallet. He paid, watching closely as Richard counted out his change. 'Thank you. My man, Pike, will collect the box.'

He didn't look the sort to have a man. He looked smart but not *that* smart. He produced a card from his wallet, offering it to Belinda.

She looked at it. 'Mr Rathbone.'

'Indeed. And for your information, young woman, my previous rude comments, as you were pleased to call them, were a strategy. If you see something you want, you don't announce it to the world or the world might also wish to take a look.' He bowed his head to Richard. 'Good day, sir, and I suggest you train your staff to have better manners.'

The instant he left the premises, Belinda burst out, 'Richard, I'm so sorry.'

His eyebrows lifted. 'Richard?'

She caught her breath. 'A slip of the tongue. Mr Carson—'

The door opened again. She didn't know whether to be relieved or frustrated. Several customers came and went; then Richard vanished upstairs. She couldn't think straight for needing to get him on his own and apologise for her lapse, but she barely got a word out before he interrupted.

'Not another word, Miss Layton. It's forgotten.'

'Thank you, sir.'

'There's no need to call me sir. Mr Carson will do. Friendlier, wouldn't you say?'

He smiled and instead of turning her heart over, it filled her with gratitude, so much so that it was some time before she recovered sufficiently to dwell on his final remark. *Friendlier, wouldn't you say?* Dared she read something into it?

'Excuse me, miss.'

Her head jerked round: she hadn't heard the door. A small, thin man stood before her. Well, he wasn't really small, but he gave the impression of smallness. It was there in his scrawny body and stooped shoulders, his anxiously blinking eyes and twitchy half-smile, the nervy way he twisted his tatty old trilby in his hands.

'I'm sorry. I was miles away. May I help you?'

He shifted from foot to foot. 'I'm here for Mr Rathbone's box.'

So this was Mr Rathbone's man. Not very impressive. 'Mr Pike? I'll fetch it for you.'

She brought it from the office. There was a bit of awkward juggling as he took the box, then had to hand it back while he put his trilby on. She opened the door for him.

'Thank you, miss.'

Richard appeared. 'Was that fellow collecting Mr Rathbone's box? Good. I can't say I took to our Mr Rathbone.'

'Neither did I.' How wonderful to be in tune with one another, but before she could make the most of it, the shop door opened behind her and Richard's expression changed from affable to fixed.

'Bloody hell...' he breathed.

A chill seeped through her. She turned to see who had come in. Two men. One, a middle-aged gentleman – and gentleman was the right word, as his grey wool overcoat, black bowler hat, silk handkerchief protruding from his breast pocket, and serious demeanour all testified – the other, younger, not burly but strong-looking all the same, with hazel eyes above high cheekbones, and a narrow but firm jawline. His upright stature and clear gaze spoke of confidence, yet there was something vulnerable in the set of his mouth, as if he was unsure what expression to adopt.

The older gentleman stepped forward and Belinda slipped aside so as not to be in the middle. She ought to attend to her duties, but fascination held her captive.

'Allow me to introduce myself. I am Mr Turton of Winterton, Sowerby and Jenks. May I take it that you are Mr Richard Carson?'

Richard cleared his throat. 'I am.'

'Then may I ask why you are selling the possessions of the late Mr Reginald Tyrell?'

Richard stood up straight. 'What's it to do with you? You aren't my uncle's solicitor.'

'I'm not a solicitor at all. I am the senior clerk with Winterton, Sowerby and Jenks.'

'Not that it's any of your business,' said Richard, 'but I'm the executor of my uncle's will.'

'I agree that you would have been the executor, had you been the heir. As it is, Mr Gabriel Linkworth is both heir and executor; and so I ask you once again, sir, what you are doing, disposing of Mr Tyrell's estate?'

Colour blotched Richard's handsome face as he stared at the younger newcomer.

The stranger stepped forward. 'I don't know whether we've met. They tell me you're Reginald Tyrell's nephew and I am his late wife Victoria's nephew. Perhaps we met at her funeral...?' A slight movement of his shoulders, the faintest of shrugs. 'I apologise for sounding vague. I – I lost my memory towards the end of the war.'

His right hand moved. Preparing to shake hands?

Richard's jaw set. He addressed Mr Turton.

'I did indeed meet Gabriel Linkworth at my Aunt Victoria's funeral – but I've never seen this man before in my life.'

Chapter Eighteen

HELL'S TEETH! GABRIEL LINKWORTH, back from the dead. Gabriel flaming Linkworth. How many times had Richard prevailed upon Uncle Reg to change his will and get rid of all mention of his other nephew?

'No need,' Uncle Reg had maintained. 'If Gabriel predeceases me, which he evidently has, everything comes to you. Nothing simpler.'

'That's not strictly true.' Richard had sounded good-humoured, as if changing the will was for Uncle Reg's peace of mind. 'The most straightforward thing would be to remove his name.'

'What for? He's dead and gone, poor fellow.'

'Precisely – which is a great shame and all that. I know you thought highly of him. After all, you made him your principal heir.' Clever, that, recognising Linkworth's importance. 'But you say you want things to be simple.' He had adopted a thoughtful tone. 'When the moment comes, which I hope won't be for a long time yet, but when it does, there'll be the additional trouble of having Linkworth officially declared dead.'

'Huh.' Never a good sign, that. *Huh* was never a good sign. 'I've already asked my solicitor. When Gabriel has been missing for seven years, having him declared dead will be a formality; so, as long as I drag myself past 1925, you'll be all right.'

'I never meant—'

'I know, I know.' His voice was gruff. They were inches from another *huh*. 'You want simplicity. Here it is. Everything is left to Gabriel. If he predeceases me, everything comes to you. He has predeceased me. It's all yours. No need to change the will.'

And nothing short of dynamite was going to shift the old boy from that point of view. It hadn't been ideal, but at least it had seemed safe to leave things as they were. After all, Gabriel Linkworth was dead.

Except that he wasn't. He was standing here, in the shop, looking troubled. Older too, but then didn't they all look older, everyone who had been through the war, and not just because its length had piled a few birthdays on them. Linkworth looked subtly different – thinner in the face. Not that Richard really knew him. They had met just the once, at Aunt Victoria's funeral. All the Linkworths had attended: Mr and Mrs and the two grown-up sons. The other son had copped it in the war – really copped it. Not like his bloody brother, missing presumed dead all this time and turning up now, alive and well and ready to scoop up the inheritance.

Well, Richard wasn't having it. He wasn't ruddy having it. Claiming never to have seen Gabriel Linkworth before had been automatic, the instinctive response to keep his inheritance safe. Even if Linkworth hadn't lost his memory, he would still have said those words. Hell's teeth, Uncle Reg had believed him to be dead. Uncle Reg had been content for Richard to inherit. He had expected Richard to inherit.

Bloody Linkworth. Coming back, ruining everything.

Fury roared in Richard's ears. The cords tightened in his neck, but he mustn't show his anger.

I've never seen this man before in my life.

The words hung in the air.

Linkworth and Mr Turton looked at one another. Linkworth frowned, but Mr Turton's professional courtesy didn't slip.

'This is unfortunate, though it makes no difference in the long run. You will hear from the offices of Winterton, Sowerby and Jenks, Mr Carson. In the meantime, I must insist that you refrain from selling anything further. In fact, you should take steps to retrieve items you've already sold. Good day to you, sir, miss.'

He raised his bowler to Miss Layton and showed Linkworth out.

Richard couldn't move. A fierce coldness hit him right at his core. Bugger bugger bugger.

Gabriel Linkworth, back from the dead.

He had relied on inheriting. A healthy sum from flogging the book stock and whatever else he didn't want, plus ownership of the cottage, would have set him up in a tidy way.

'Mr Carson, that man – is he pretending to be the real heir?'

He looked at Miss Layton. Christ, he had even employed an assistant. What was he to do with her now? Sack her? No, let her do the donkey work of buying back the sold items, then stick Linkworth with the bill for her services.

'Mr Carson?' Miss Layton looked confused, as well she might.

It was tempting to tell her to get lost, but, much as he needed time to think and plan and curse, there was no sense in alienating her. She liked him and wanted to please him and there was no saying when that might prove useful.

'I've no notion who that fellow is; some trickster who knows my uncle had another heir.'

'So there is another heir?'

'Assuming he's alive, which seems highly unlikely, given how long he's been missing.' He didn't want to discuss it. 'Anyway, we'd best see what we can get back from the customers.'

Not that he intended to try very hard. Any money already in his pocket could jolly well stay there.

'I'll do my best,' promised Miss Layton. 'I've kept a record of everything that has been sold, including listing the contents of the boxes.'

'You have?'

'You told me to.'

Yes, of course. He had deemed it wise, because of being a bit previous over the probate.

'Though keeping a list of what was sold isn't the same as knowing who bought what and where they live.' Miss Layton was obviously determined to rectify the situation somehow. 'I can write to the people who bought books by post, but as for the customers who bought books or boxes in person, unless they pop in and we recognise them, those things are gone for good.'

'Oh well.' What else was he supposed to say?

'We've got Mr Rathbone's address,' she said as if expecting him to raise three cheers.

He rewarded her with a smile and her blue eyes softened adoringly. It was rather agreeable to have a pretty girl hanging on his every word, though he took care not to say or do anything that could be construed as encouragement.

'We'd better make a start. I'll compose a letter for you to send to the people who purchased books by post.'

That would keep her chained to the typewriter and out of his hair. He had to make a plan. Was there any point in devising a plan? Was there any plan on earth that could retrieve this damnable situation?

Gabriel Linkworth, back from the dead.

Hell's teeth.

The bell jingled frantically as the door was thrown open and almost slammed shut. Mr Rathbone marched in, his face dark with anger. This time yesterday, Richard would have felt concerned. This time yesterday, Gabriel Linkworth was still rotting in the ground somewhere in France. Today Richard didn't care one jot why Rathbone was upset. Whatever his beef, it was nothing compared to Richard's.

'I'm here to complain,' Rathbone began brusquely.

'Good morning,' Richard replied.

Rathbone blinked. 'Oh – good morning. That box I bought from you yesterday: something's missing.'

Richard felt like grabbing the fellow by the shoulders, spinning him round and propelling him through the door. All he said was, 'Let me find the list.' He couldn't be bothered with this. He stuck his head round the office door. 'Miss Layton, do you have the lists of what's in the boxes?'

Getting up from her typing, she handed him a file. 'The lists are in number order.'

He flipped through it as he wandered back into the shop. 'Do you know what number your box was?' he asked without looking up.

'Twenty-two.'

'Here we are. *Three Men in a Boat*, piano music, geometry set, blue bud-vase, pair of figurines: boy and girl water-carriers, silver letter-opener, glass trinket-dish and a volume of Thomas Hardy's poetry.' He looked up. 'Something was missing?'

'It certainly was: the page-cutter.'

'That's not on the list.'

'It was in the box when I examined it prior to purchase.'

Bloody typical: the one time the girl made a mistake and it had to be when his world was collapsing around him. She appeared by his side.

'Mr Rathbone is right. The page-cutter was in the box when he looked at it.'

'Ha!' Rathbone exclaimed, standing tall as if posing for a portrait. 'Now it's missing and my man swears he hasn't stolen it.'

Miss Layton gasped. 'He most certainly hasn't. It's in one of the other boxes. When you were so, um, dismissive, I thought you weren't interested in anything and I swapped some items round.'

'You did what?' snapped Rathbone.

'If you'd said you wanted a box—'

'Do you know which box it's in?' Rathbone glared at the boxes as if he might start ripping them open. 'Fetch it this minute.'

Anger raced through Richard and he stopped feeling distanced. He felt rejuvenated and more than ready for a fight. 'That's enough. I won't have you speaking to my staff in that hectoring manner. You're the one at fault here. You made a show of being scornful to put off other customers. You have only yourself to blame if your scheme worked too well.'

'How dare you?' Rathbone barked. 'I won't be spoken to in this manner.'

'Too late. It's already happened.' The air beside him quivered with Miss Layton's shock.

'The page-cutter,' snapped Rathbone. 'I thought my box contained both parts of the pair. I'm prepared to buy it as a separate item, if necessary.'

'Impossible. In fact, I have to ask you to return the items you've purchased. It's a legal matter.'

'That's preposterous. I refuse to return anything.'

'Either you return the items or I'll hand your card to Winterton, Sowerby and Jenks. They, I feel sure, will be only too delighted to pursue the matter.'

'This is outrageous. I bought that box in good faith.'

Mr Rathbone continued to splutter indignantly, but Richard barely heard. Either Rathbone returned the box or he didn't: Richard couldn't care less. All Rathbone stood to lose was the matching pair he coveted, while Richard was on the verge of losing the money and the home he had banked on for the past few years.

Bloody Linkworth, coming back from the dead.

*

212

When Richard returned to his lodgings in St Werburgh's Road that evening – the lodgings where he had jubilantly given notice to his landlady and had then had to claw it back – a letter awaited him. An official letter. He felt like chucking it into the fire. It was from Winterton, Sowerby and Jenks, informing him that there was no doubt that the gentleman whom he had met at Tyrell's Books was Gabriel James Linkworth, but that since he had apparently failed to recognise him and since he was himself an interested party, there would be a hearing in the magistrate's court to prove Mr Linkworth's identity.

Bugger bugger bugger.

He didn't want to go to the shop the next day. What was the point, when he was about to lose everything? He didn't feel like attending work either. He went to the cottage in Limits Lane, but that was unbelievably depressing, so he headed for the shop.

Miss Layton gave him a minute to take his coat off. 'Mr Rathbone sent his box back.'

'Good.'

She was still hovering. What now? 'He has kept the letter-opener.'

'So what? I've got far bigger problems than a measly letter-opener.'

She flinched.

Damn and blast. He caught hold of himself.

'I apologise. I shouldn't have spoken like that.'

'That's all right.' Instant forgiveness. 'This is a difficult situation for you.'

'That's putting it mildly – I'm sorry. That sounded snappish.' He threw up his hands. 'You're correct. It is difficult.'

'May I ask, will you get half – if this other man is who he is supposed to be, that is?'

He was startled to hear her doubting Linkworth's identity, but of course all she knew was that he had claimed never to have clapped eyes on Linkworth before. Being the trusting, adoring girl she was, she believed everything that came out of his mouth. He softened towards her. It was good to be admired. Hell, it might be all he had left.

'No, I won't – if this man is Gabriel Linkworth.' No harm in maintaining the deception. 'But we have to face the fact that coming here with a representative of a legal firm does suggest the fellow is who he is said to be.'

'And you're both Mr Tyrell's nephews, but you aren't cousins?'

'No. I'm my uncle's nephew, he's my aunt's nephew. What you have to understand is that he vanished late in 1918 and he's been gone ever since. My uncle had already made his will several years before that, leaving everything to Linkworth, with the condition that should Linkworth predecease him, everything would come to me. For the past few years, that's what everyone has expected. Linkworth was missing presumed dead and Uncle Reg was happy for me to inherit. He even gave me advice about having Linkworth officially declared dead. As far as he was concerned, Linkworth was dead and gone and he expected me to get everything.'

'I see.' She frowned, taking it in.

'And now this interloper has turned up and...' He shrugged, wanting to look as if he had taken it on the chin and didn't know the meaning of words like jealousy, fury or disappointment. 'What hurts is that Uncle Reg believed I was going to inherit and he was happy with that. Isn't that what a will is meant to be about? Making sure the dead person's wishes are respected?'

'And then there's the way you looked after the cottage.'

A dig at his grasping nature? No, a simple statement of fact. 'Uncle Reg was pleased for me to have a hand in its upkeep since it would one day be mine. I kept a friendly eye on him and he appreciated the company.'

'No wonder he wanted you to inherit.'

He forced a rueful smile. 'Except I haven't, have I?'

'This new person might turn out to be someone else entirely. After all, you met the real Mr Linkworth and you didn't recognise this man.'

He needed to pull back, though not too much, on his supposed rejection of the stranger. 'My aunt's funeral took place years ago, before the war, and frankly I was more concerned with supporting my uncle through the ordeal than I was with consorting with people I wasn't related to.'

'That must make it worse for you, knowing that Mr Linkworth isn't Mr Tyrell's blood relation.'

He put a thoughtful expression on his face. 'That's a good point, Miss Layton.'

His thoughts perked up, as if a crank was turning inside his head. Uncle Reg had believed Linkworth was dead and he had expected Richard to inherit – Richard, his blood nephew.

He wouldn't be able to prevent Gabriel Linkworth from inheriting; but, hell's teeth, surely he had sufficient grounds to make his own claim against the will?

Patience hummed to herself as she got out of bed and slipped into her dressing-gown. Last night's dress hung from the top of the wardrobe door, covering the inlaid mirror. The evening at Lawrence and Evelyn's had been something of a trial: all those important people, all those opportunities to praise Lawrence to the skies. Prudence had been rather a trial too, huffing and puffing under her breath whenever they had a moment together, looking so fierce that Patience had feared one of the guests would smell a rat.

Lifting down her dress, she turned the key to open the wardrobe. Her dressing-gown sleeve slid up her arm as she hung up her dress. Velvet brushed her flesh. The gown was pre-war, very dated, but it was the only one she possessed.

Spinsters didn't require evening gowns, especially spinsters with no money. Had it ever suited her? She must have thought so once. But now, the V-shaped neckline seemed designed to highlight the recently acquired suggestion of slackness about her throat, while the high-waisted cummerbund emphasised her want of anything resembling a curve. As for the scallop-edged sleeves that covered her upper arms, they had had her slathering cream on her elbows in an effort to blur the wrinkly bits.

She had felt dreary and old-fashioned last night in the company of Lawrence's grand associates and their beautifully dressed wives, with their ankle-length evening capes and almost tubular dresses. Ordinarily she might have cringed with mortification at the memory, but not now. They had pupil lodgers in the house now, two lively, agreeable girls in their twenties, and she was loving every minute.

Prudence had apologised to her for the extra work.

'I've been so preoccupied with getting the business school up and running, and finding ways to oblige Lawrence to lend support, that I didn't take into account the effect of paying guests on you.'

The effect? If only she knew! Prudence viewed it in terms of housework while Patience relished the sound of young voices about the house and quick footsteps on the stairs. It was like – not that she could ever say it out loud – it was like having daughters. Who cared about extra cooking and bed-making? If anything, they were a pleasure.

But Prudence cared, and not just on Patience's behalf.

'It's a question of standards. It's fine for you to do the cooking and dusting, but not the washing-up and bed-making.'

'I've always done the washing-up and bed-making.'

'It didn't signify when it was us and Pa, but it's infra dig in front of the paying guests. Perhaps Mrs Whitney would oblige if we offered her more hours.'

'Prudence, we can't have the char doing a maid's work.'

'Well, we can't afford a maid as well. Even if we could, they're scarcer than hen's teeth these days. Besides, it's only while we have the p.gs. No, it has to be Mrs Whitney. We'll provide a smart white apron for her to change into when she's finished doing the rough. Do you think she might be persuaded to wear a maid's cap?'

Patience almost laughed at the thought, but it wasn't funny really. You walked a fine line when you were hard up and had to pretend not to be. They hadn't bargained for agonising over appearances when they took in their pupil lodgers.

Starting tomorrow, Mrs Whitney, complete with starched new apron, was going to earn extra money while the girls were here. They had been friends 'for simply yonks' and were called Jill and Kate. At least, that was what they called one another and Patience would have loved to use their first names too, but it was out of the question. Standards. So she called them Miss Deane and Miss Russell, though she had started adding 'dear' to their names, wanting them to feel at home.

Prudence had put a great deal of thought into preparing for them. Miss Dean and Miss Russell attended the night school and during the day they had work to do that Prudence left for them, as well as lessons with Patience that Prudence had provided. Prudence had also prevailed upon the employers who were providing Miss Hunt, Miss Shaw and the others with unpaid experience, to permit the temporary pupils to visit their offices and warehouses to see their administrative systems.

'The girls are most impressed that you've made these arrangements for them,' said Patience. 'I heard Miss Dean say, "We're certainly getting our money's worth," and Miss Russell agreed.'

'That's good, but I think we've bitten off more than we can chew. These girls expected, quite rightly, to be taught during the day. We've cobbled together a fortnight's lessons and visits for them, but to cater for them properly, I'd need to be here during the day, and that's out of the question.'

'But I thought having pupil lodgers would increase our hold on the house.' And I want them here. They're young and cheerful and we have such cosy chats when we stop for afternoon tea. I'll shrink if they leave and aren't replaced.

'It was a good idea in principle, but in practice…' Prudence shook her head.

An ache formed deep in Patience's throat. No more girlish laughter, no more spritely footsteps running up and downstairs. No more lapping up their life stories.

No more… no more daughters.

Patience hovered near the bay window. The evenings were light now: it would be April next week. She had a clear view to the end of Wilton Close. Ah, here came Miss Layton, entering the close from the left. A moment later, Miss Hunt entered from the right, waiting as Miss Layton crossed the road and joined her. Good. Whatever Miss Hunt did or didn't think of Miss Layton's background, her manners were impeccable.

Before long, the pupil lodgers and Miss Hunt were ensconced with Prudence in the dining room, working on basic accounts, while Patience had Miss Layton to herself in the sitting room for a telephone lesson, although she first wanted to thank her for writing the letter to the paper. But, before she could say anything, Miss Layton leaned towards her, blue eyes wide.

'Miss Patience, have you heard what happened at the bookshop?'

'Not since Mr Tyrell passed away and his nephew took over.'

The girl sank back. 'I was hoping you'd heard. I don't want to gossip.'

'Of course not, but if it concerns your place of work, you must tell me. My sister and I will do whatever we can to assist you.'

'It is to do with the shop, although there's more to it than that. You see, Mr Carson might not be the heir after all. In Mr Tyrell's will, he left everything to another nephew called Gabriel Linkworth. This Gabriel Linkworth was meant to have been killed in the war, which meant that everything would go to Mr Carson instead, but now a man claiming to be Gabriel Linkworth has appeared and Mr Carson says he very likely is Mr Linkworth.'

'Goodness me.'

'Mr Carson has done the decent thing all this time, as a good nephew should, and now this Gabriel Linkworth is going to get everything. And he isn't even a blood relation. It isn't fair.'

She shouldn't say anything, of course. Prudence wouldn't. Prudence had a will of iron. But, oh, the temptation. Patience settled in for a good – she refused to call it gossip – a good chinwag.

'Wills sometimes aren't fair, I'm afraid. I completely understand the heartache that follows when someone who isn't a blood relation stands to inherit.'

'You do?'

'From my own experience. You are aware that this house is my brother's property.'

'Yes, and he wanted you and Miss Hesketh to turn it into a business school to help surplus girls.'

'Miss Layton, dear, I believe I may trust you to keep a confidence.'

The girl's eyes widened. 'Cross my heart.'

Out it poured. 'My father was married twice. Our brother, Mr Lawrence Hesketh, is really our half-brother, the son of Pa's first wife. She died and he married Mother and had my sister and me. This house belonged to our mother, who inherited it from her family. Mother died and left it to Pa and he should really have left it to my sister and me—'

'Because it was your mother's house.'

'Exactly, but he left it to Lawrence.'

'He never!'

'I fear so. Between ourselves, dear, that's why we had to set up the business school. We needed something that would oblige our brother to let us remain here.'

'So when you go on about his generosity...'

'It's all an act; as is his claim to have provided the school out of the goodness of his heart. And it's all because of the will.'

'I bet you used to wait hand and foot on your pa, didn't you?'

'As the daughter who stayed at home, it was my place to do so.'

'That's like Mr Carson. He didn't look after Mr Tyrell as such, but he was attentive and even paid for it when the cottage needed work doing.'

'Wills can cause such complications. What about your position, my dear?'

'It's secure for the time being. Mr Carson says that he's happy for me to stay; but if Mr Linkworth takes over, who knows?'

'How will it be decided about this Mr Linkworth?'

'It's to be put before the magistrate's court.' Miss Layton blushed. It made her look pretty. Prettier. 'Mr Carson said I was entitled to know.'

Patience felt a twinge of unease. She hated uncertainty. 'So we must await the outcome.'

'Mr Carson hasn't said in so many words that the outcome is definite, but Mr Linkworth arrived at the shop accompanied by someone from an important legal firm, so probably he is the real Gabriel Linkworth – though I hope he isn't, for Mr Carson's sake. He deserves to inherit, just like you and Miss Hesketh should have done.'

Something clicked into place. Miss Layton's support for Mr Carson went beyond that of a loyal employee. What had started as a legitimate enquiry into Miss Layton's work situation had bloomed into something altogether more personal. She would need to be careful how she reported the conversation to Prudence, who had a nose for the inappropriate.

'Perhaps we should start our lesson,' she suggested. 'I'm going to enquire about being a pupil here, but I warn you I'm going to pose some impertinent questions about the tutors.'

'Why don't you ask about being a pupil lodger?' Miss Layton said with a twinkle. 'Then you could be very impertinent – I'm sorry. Have I spoken out of turn?'

'Not at all. It's my fault for not hiding my feelings. It looks as if these two girls will be our only pupil lodgers.'

'I'm surprised. They can't stop praising you.'

'The trouble is they need to be kept occupied all day and of course my sister has to be at the office, so it isn't a feasible arrangement. Now, are you ready to answer the telephone?'

She glanced at her list of questions, but she didn't have the chance to ask more than a couple before Miss Layton dropped her hand, earpiece and all, into her lap. Her face was bright with pleasure.

'Miss Patience, I hope I'm not being forward, but if you want to carry on taking pupil lodgers, I have an idea.'

Chapter Nineteen

I T SHOULD HAVE been a pleasure, being able to see more of her family now she was working shorter hours. Had she belonged to a different family, maybe it would have been. Neither did seeing more of her seem to afford them much pleasure.

'What's the point of coming round more if you aren't going to help out more?' Dad demanded from the armchair. Annoyance lent a gaunt edge to his narrow face. Money, or the lack of it, was the one thing guaranteed to get his dander up.

'I've just helped Mum change the beds,' she pointed out, 'and I've swept the floors and put down fresh sawdust.'

He shook the newspaper. It rustled tetchily. 'That's not what I mean, as you well know.'

Thad sneered at her from where he was sitting at the table, reading *The Boys' Herald*. 'Aye, Dad means tipping up, like I do.' He spoke in a loud, showy-offy voice. 'I tipped up five whole bob last week, which is a darned sight more than you've ever given in one go, our Bel. Tight-fisted, that's what you are. Don't tell me it costs you much to bunk with them two old biddies. You know what your trouble is? You don't give a monkey's about your family, that's what. Not like me. I'm one of the men of the house and I tip up proper.' He waggled his shoulders importantly. Was it possible to swagger without walking?

Seated beside him, trying to look as though he was sharing the comic when really Thad was hogging it, Jacob threw in his twopenn'orth. 'He's a good bloke, is our Thad.'

'That's right, Jakey-boy.' Thad delivered a rough nudge that nearly shoved Jacob off his stool. Jacob righted himself and grinned, as if it was friendly joshing. Couldn't he see what a lout Thad was?

'Oh aye, and where did the money come from?' Mikey sat on the floor with his back to the peeling wall. His legs stuck out in front of him, one to the side of the coal bucket, the other underneath the linen-draped clothes horse. 'Anyroad, he never tipped up, not on purpose. Mum found the money under a loose floorboard under the bed when she emptied the chamber pot.'

Belinda's mouth dropped open. Had it come to this? Taking the house to pieces to hunt for hidden savings? Pink swept across Mum's face and she fiddled with her hair.

'Anyroad, I appreciate your help, love,' she said to Belinda. 'Lord knows, our Sarah is neither use nor ornament when she's home.'

Belinda was about to defend her sister, then changed her mind. Not in front of Dad, who quickly grew fed up of arguments that didn't issue from his own lips. Not in front of Thad either. He was too mouthy for his own good these days. Without George here to give him a clip round the ear, he seemed to fill more space. Was she going to be scared of him one day? The muscles tightened in her belly. What a thought to have about your little brother. She had changed his nappies and given him his bath when he was a baby.

She waited until she and Mum were in the bedroom, bundling up used sheets and pillow-cases.

'What have you got against our Sarah? She's a good girl.'

'She's a lazy devil. She doesn't pull her weight around the house.'

'Yes, she does.' How could she not? Mum was on Sarah's back the moment she walked through the door. 'She works hard at that hotel, don't forget, and she has all that travelling.'

'Oh aye, take her side, as always.'

'I'm not taking sides. I can see both points of view.'

'Well, when you're talking to her, I hope you stand up for me as energetically.'

Belinda smoothed the folds in the pillow-cases. 'Things would be better if you didn't get on at her so much.'

'You want me bowing and scraping to my own daughter, do you?'

'I'm trying to help.' She was also trying not to get het up. One day she would let rip and be rude and difficult in reply, and she dreaded that happening. It would mean she had joined her family in the trap of lower standards. 'If you're not careful, you'll turn her away and she'll leave home the minute she's twenty-one.'

'That's years off yet. You're not twenty-one till June. Eh, fancy that, my baby girl turning twenty-one.' Mum sounded nostalgic, but then the corners of her mouth turned downwards. 'You don't know what it's like for me.'

'Tell me.'

She sat on the bed, holding out her hand. It looked like Mum would ignore it, then she accepted it and sat beside her.

'We used to have a good life. Do you remember? Me and your dad and three kids in a house of us own. Denby was a warehouseman in them days. It was perfect. Food on the table, the rent book up to date, a little girl for me, a little lad for Denby, and another girl to make the family complete. We were so lucky – and I never took it for granted. I felt like I had to hold our life carefully so it didn't get broken. Only I can't have held it carefully enough.'

'More likely Dad broke it.'

Mum shrugged. Somehow the shrug lifted her hand out of Belinda's. 'Aye, he did, time and again. It's rough, Bel, being married to a man who lets you down. It were a good job, being a warehouseman, but he lost that; and then he was a drayman – or was he a cask-washer next? I forget. And then those other jobs, and now he's a street-sweeper, a rotten street-sweeper.'

'There's nothing wrong with that, Mum.' Or there wouldn't be if Dad had been proud to work for the Corporation and serve the public; if he had been the best street-sweeper a man could be... if he hadn't been a skiver. Layabout Layton was his nickname, according to Thad. Whether this was true, or something Thad had made up, Belinda couldn't say. She dreaded its being true; but she also dreaded Thad's being so openly insolent.

'All those jobs, all those nights down the pub. My life is nowt but being tired and ashamed and knowing I'm better than this but I'm the only one who remembers it.' She sighed. 'You aren't old enough to remember your grandparents, but they'd be ashamed – and I'm talking about your dad's parents, as well as mine.'

'Mum,' Belinda said gently, 'if you would just—'

'Just what? Pull myself together? That's a fine way to speak to your mother.'

'If you'd take pride—'

'In other words, pull myself together. Do you think I don't know that? I know if I took pride, if I could rise above the cheerlessness of it all, things would be better, and sometimes I make up my mind to do it – but what's the point? I'd still be here in this dump and I'd still be stuck with a no-good husband who's gone right down in the world and dragged me along with him.'

'Oh, Mum.'

'He's probably going to sink further before he's finished an' all.' Mum came to her feet. 'Let's get this bed done.'

There was clean bedding for Mum and Dad, but not for the boys or Sarah. When the double bed was made up, Mum tied the bundle of washing and thrust it into Belinda's arms.

'Put that by our Sarah's mattress. She can take it down the wash-house in the morning.'

Belinda felt like dumping it onto the floor. Would Mum never listen? But there was no chance to try again, because the door opened and George stuck his head in.

'Evening, Mum. Put the kettle on, will you? I'm gasping.'

'George! Oh, love, thank you for popping round.' Mum bustled out.

'What did your last servant die of?' Belinda asked.

'Hoity-toity. You do it if you don't want Mum to.'

She started to sigh, then changed it to a smile. She didn't want to be at loggerheads in front of the others, especially as everyone knew why there was friction between them. Dad would love to pounce on that, and how Thad would crow.

She needn't have fretted. The resident Laytons provided plenty of friction to keep themselves occupied, not least the beginnings of a punch-up between Thad and Mikey that saw George getting between them and shoving Thad into the hallway, slamming the door on him. The door shuddered as Thad banged his fists on it and, a moment later, the house shook as the front door crashed shut.

'Now see what you've done, George.' Mum wrung her hands. 'Lord knows what he'll get up to out there, and as for when he'll come home—'

'Good riddance,' snarled Dad.

When Belinda got up to leave, George said, 'I'll walk you home, Bel.'

An olive branch? Or an opportunity to have another go at her? The moment he shut the front door behind them, she spoke up.

'I know you want me to move back in, but can you really blame me for not wanting to?'

He stopped to light a cigarette, then set off. 'Yes, I can. It's your turn. But at the same time, no one in their right mind would choose to live there. I resented you before because you could come and go while I was saddled with it, but now that I've left, I understand even more why you stay where you are. Wild horses wouldn't drag me back.'

Gratitude expanded inside her. 'Does this mean we're friends again?'

He glanced sideways at her. 'I'm not sure about that.'

She punched his arm. 'You'd better make up your mind quick or I'll withdraw the offer.'

George grabbed her and swung her round and, just like that, they were back to normal. When she righted herself, she slipped her hand through his arm.

'I've got my eye on a girl, Bel.'

'You're walking out?'

'Only as friends. I want to get some money behind me to show I'm going to be a good provider.'

Her heart went out to him. 'Not like Dad, you mean.'

'It's my greatest fear, turning out like him. Don't say owt to anyone. I haven't told the family about her and I won't until it's official.'

'I won't. How are your new digs?'

'Comfortable. *Quiet*.'

'Is Harry's auntie a good cook?'

'The best, though I have to say she seasons everything with salt, pepper and fart-powder.'

'George!'

They laughed and kidded all the way to End Cottage. Belinda could have waltzed down Grave Pit Lane. It was such a relief to be back on friendly terms with her brother. They had grown apart when she left home at such a young age, but George had always been there in the background, her beloved childhood playmate all grown up; a steady, loved figure in the landscape of her life.

She was still feeling chirpy as she walked to the bookshop

the next morning, the birdsong and the scents of spring adding to her sense of well-being. Would Richard notice and ask why she was happy? After confiding in her about the will, why shouldn't he look for confidences in return? Might they be on the brink of drawing closer?

Richard, however, didn't arrive before mid-morning. She broke off from typing the endless inventory to turn towards the door, smiles at the ready, only for him to clump straight upstairs, looking distinctly peeved, but it was only to be expected when you considered what he had to come to terms with, poor fellow. It would be harder for him to get married if he didn't have the cottage.

Presently the door opened again. She was between two of the bookcases, a pile of volumes balanced against her hip, ready to take to the office. Richard had attached a notice to the shop door to say they were no longer open for business, but they still had to leave the door unlocked in case anyone returned something they had previously purchased. Sometimes customers came in without bothering to read the notice, expecting to browse.

She was well-versed in what to say to either type of visitor, but when she saw Gabriel Linkworth, she was lost for words.

He smiled. She stared back and his smile slipped.

'Good morning,' he said.

'What are you doing here?' She hadn't intended to be rude, but she wasn't sorry. This was the non-blood relation who had swanned in at the last moment to scoop up Richard's inheritance. Let him taste her disapproval.

'I was hoping to see Mr Carson. Is he here?'

'I'll see. He might be busy.'

'Thank you. May I lend a hand with those books? They look heavy.'

'I can manage, thank you.'

Resentment pricked her. She didn't want him to be polite.

He was the enemy. Setting down the books, she went upstairs, her footsteps tapping out the beat of her annoyance.

Richard stood at the window, looking out at Beech Road, a cigarette dangling between his fingers. It was a casual pose, but the set of his shoulders spoke of a crowded mind.

'Mr Linkworth is here,' she said. 'Well, the man who says he's Mr Linkworth.'

'I saw him crossing the road. Say I'm busy.'

She retraced her steps. Determination flared inside her. If Richard didn't feel up to facing Gabriel Linkworth, she would do it for him.

Mr Linkworth looked up expectantly. He was a good-looking chap, she'd give him that. His eyes were a soft hazel colour, serious and kind. His jacket hung well on him, suggesting well-used muscles in his slim frame.

'He doesn't want to see me, eh?'

She had wanted to be the one to say this. 'Mr Carson is occupied with checking the stock.'

'Maybe I'll come back another time. I'd hoped… Never mind.'

He opened the door. The bell jingled. She stared at his back, wishing him on his way. If her will-power had had anything to do with it, he would be halfway up Beech Road by now.

He turned back. 'If you've no objection, I'll stay.'

'Mr Carson is very busy.'

'I'd like to look round, if I may.'

No, you may not. She clamped her lips shut.

He came across the shop floor. He didn't smell of cologne, as Richard did. He smelled of soap and fresh air. He planted himself in the middle of the shop and turned slowly in a circle. Then he caught her gaze on him and gave her a rueful smile.

'I hoped something might jog my memory.'

'Maybe you never came here before.' *Maybe you're here only to inherit.*

He frowned. 'I must have done – surely. I knew Mr Tyrell well enough that he made me his principal heir.'

'If you are who you're supposed to be.' There: she had said it, but instead of making her feel courageous and vindicated, she felt mean.

He looked amused. Cheeky blighter. 'I think we can safely say I'm Gabriel Linkworth. Even if I don't remember, the army does.'

She was fascinated in spite of herself. 'Do you truly not remember anything?'

'Not a jot.'

'That must be hard.'

'I can't say it's something I've ever got used to, but I try to get on with things.'

Yes, like waltzing in at the crucial moment and bagging someone else's inheritance. She mustn't feel sympathetic about his memory loss. She gave him the polite farewell smile she saved for customers, but it didn't work.

'Don't let me take you away from your duties, Miss..?'

'Layton, Belinda Layton.'

'I assume you worked for Mr Tyrell.'

'In a manner of speaking.' That was an expression she had picked up from Miss Patience. So then she had to explain about the business school and the Saturday hours to gain experience.

'It sounds a jolly good idea. What sort of work did you do for Mr Tyrell?'

In the next few minutes, he asked her more questions than Richard ever had – no, she wouldn't think that way. Did Gabriel Linkworth imagine he could get round her? She pushed back her shoulders. But it had been pleasant to be paid attention to.

'Excuse me.' She injected a note of finality into her voice. 'I have to get on.'

'Of course.'

He smiled and it would have been churlish not to smile back, but instead of leaving, he took a step towards the bookshelves. She retreated to the office and resumed typing. Ought she to pop upstairs to tell Richard that he was still here? Or was that too flimsy an excuse? Besides, if Mr Linkworth twigged that she had disappeared upstairs, it might give the impression that Richard was hiding from him and she was reporting back.

'You're lucky to work here.' Mr Linkworth stood in the office doorway, a book open in his hands. 'Surrounded by books all day, all those stories, all that knowledge, and with the company of other book-lovers as they come into the shop.'

She couldn't help smiling: there was something almost boyish about his pleasure. 'Are you a book-lover?'

'I think I must be.' The grave hazel of his eyes seemed brighter.

'You'll have to join the library. That's where I get all my books.'

'What do you enjoy?'

'Stories. My favourite book is *Persuasion*.'

'Jane Austen.'

'You remember that, then.'

He nodded. 'Now I think of it, I know Jane Austen wrote *Persuasion*, Dickens wrote *The Pickwick Papers* and Alexandre Dumas wrote *The Count of Monte Cristo*.'

She was on her feet. When had she stood up? She placed her hand on the table to remind herself not to step closer to him. Closer? Don't be daft. Why would she do that?

'I'm sorry,' he said. 'I'm interrupting your work.'

He disappeared into the shop and she sank onto her chair. Good riddance.

If only Richard would chat to her like that. She sat up straight, as Miss Hesketh had taught her to, and positioned her fingers. Richard had so much on his mind.

But maybe Gabriel Linkworth wasn't so bad after all.

Maybe.

I could talk to her all day. When she forgets she doesn't like me, her face relaxes, her eyes grow warm and she is friendly and appealing. Interesting, too. She clearly loves going to the business school. Good for her. She has her future sorted out. I wish I could say the same. That sounds mawkish, doesn't it? It isn't meant to. I'm careful never to say such things out loud in case I sound self-pitying. It isn't self-pity: it's a statement of fact. I wish my future was clear to me.

Perhaps it is.

I can see myself as a bookseller. It delights me to be among these books. Did I visit Mr Tyrell here? Did I love the books back then? Is that why he made me his heir? Was it planned between us that I would one day give up teaching rugger and long jump to young lads, and become a bookseller?

The typewriter clicks away in the background as I move along the shelves. I remove my gloves so my fingers can wander along the spines of the books. I recognise authors, titles. *Three Men in a Boat* – I enjoyed that: I laughed out loud at the Hampton Court maze scene. I stand still. A piece of myself has returned.

The beginning of remembering? I must not allow myself to hope. (And yet – the beginning of remembering?)

I look round the shelves, all those spines facing me, tempting me. Might I take over the shop and succeed Mr Tyrell as the local bookseller? It would make a safe retreat for a man with no memory, but I do not want it for that reason. Want it? Have I gone so quickly from *Might I?* to *I want?* Yes, I have. This would suit me. It would be fulfilment of a kind.

Quiet certainty creeps into my heart. After more than three years of not knowing, of wondering about myself, of constantly asking questions for which there are no answers, finally I know something.

I'm going to be a bookseller.

I walk back to the office doorway. At least she hasn't shut the door on me. While she finishes the line she is typing, I look at the curve of her cheek, the way her eyes dart aside to check the words on the book cover without any need for her fingers to pause. Her hands are small; she is a small person, a breath above five foot. When I first saw her, I thought her hair was black, but now I think it's brown, but brown in the way mahogany is brown, so deep and dark that it's as good as black. Her eyes are the blue of forget-me-nots. How do I know the precise blue of forget-me-nots? For me, of all people, to know the colour of *forget*-me-nots!

She finishes her line and looks up. She doesn't want to be disturbed, I can tell. It is there in the quickness of her glance before her expression subsides to a polite near-blankness. Or maybe she does not want to be disturbed by me. She is loyal to Richard Carson. Lucky Carson!

'May I help you?' she offers.

'I wanted to say goodbye. But I have one final question, if you don't mind.'

Clasping her hands in her lap, she looks at me expectantly.

'You told me you came here to gain experience as a typist.'

'That's right.' A tiny smile tugs at the sides of her mouth: she is proud of her work.

'On Saturday afternoons. So what brings you here in the week?'

'I'm employed here now.'

'Mr Tyrell took you on?' It pleases me to think that my unknown uncle liked her and found her a good worker.

The tip of her tongue runs across her top lip. She has a sweet mouth, sweeter still when she smiles. I know she doesn't wish to smile at me, but she has smiled once or twice all the same. When she smiles, her cheeks plump up and her eyes show the true kindness that lies within.

'No,' she says. 'Mr Carson employed me,' and she lifts her chin, 'to assist him in winding up the estate.'

'I see.' But I'm not sure I do, not entirely. I say gently, 'You understand that I'm Mr Tyrell's heir?'

'I know it's going to court.'

'Perhaps you're not sure of the reason for that.'

'It's to ascertain your true identity.'

She doesn't understand. She thinks she does, but she doesn't. Has Carson not troubled himself to explain? Given that she works here, she is entitled to know.

'There is no doubt that I am Gabriel Linkworth.'

She cocks her head, not believing me. 'Then why is it going to court?'

'Because Mr Sowerby of Winterton, Sowerby and Jenks believes in dotting every I and crossing all the Ts. There is no doubt as to who I am, but because Mr Carson, who might be supposed to recognise me since presumably we met at our mutual aunt's funeral some years ago, did not recognise me, and because he is named in Mr Tyrell's will, it's in everyone's interests to have my identity proved in front of a magistrate. Mr Sowerby insists upon it.'

'Oh.' Her face pales. Her gaze drops to her hands. When she looks up again, her eyes are bigger. Shock and concern fill them. 'Someone should explain this to Mr Carson? He thinks... I mean, he hopes...'

I know that a letter was sent to him. I know it admitted no room for doubt as to who I am. It explained that going to court did not in any way whatsoever suggest that my identity was in question. It said the purpose of going to court was to ensure that no one would ever be able to question afterwards that Mr Tyrell's will had been properly executed.

In other words, it gave Mr Richard Carson a sharp slap in the face.

I understand why he expected to inherit. I sympathise with

his situation in a way I'm sure he does not sympathise with mine. As Mr Turton pointed out to me, even when Carson believed himself to be the heir, it shouldn't have been business as usual here at the bookshop yet. He got ahead of himself in that respect.

But it seems he has told his assistant none of this. No wonder she tries to be icy. Protectiveness flares in my chest. She deserves to know. Perhaps Carson hasn't deceived her on purpose; perhaps it never occurred to him to inform her that he isn't the heir. At any rate, she knows now.

Her eyelashes flutter. Panic, as she realises the precarious state of her position?

'Poor Mr Carson.'

Poor Mr Carson, my foot.

The door on the far side of the office opens and Carson walks into the office.

'Are you still here? I can't see you now.' As if he is a captain of commerce, with followers fawning at his feet, hoping for an audience.

I look at Miss Layton. Her gaze is fixed on him. In sympathy?

No. Her lips are slightly parted, her expression soft, and there is a faint flush in her cheeks.

She is dazzled.

The door shut and Belinda went into the shop to make sure Mr Linkworth had left. She stood at the window as he crossed the road and strode away. Her skin tingled as Richard appeared beside her. She had been about to go back to her typing but, with Richard so close, she stayed put, his familiar lemony smell teasing her nostrils.

She turned to him with a smile, wanting him to see her, really see her; wanting him to set aside his troubles and realise she could be more to him than his assistant. The sight of his stormy eyes and tight lips banished her smile.

'He could at least have waited until after the court case to eye up the stock.'

She was unwilling to speak out of turn, but Richard deserved to be told. 'He said he is definitely Gabriel Linkworth.'

'Naturally. It's in his interest to say so.'

She tried again. 'He says the matter is going to court because his solicitor is a belt-and-braces man, who doesn't leave anything to chance.'

'What else did he say? He was here a deuce of a long time.'

'He asked about my job and he stayed to look at the books.'

He jerked his cuffs down. 'He seems to have won you round.'

'I felt sorry for him, that's all, having no memory.'

Richard's mouth softened, though his eyes didn't. 'You're too kind-hearted, that's your trouble. I'll be out for the rest of the day, so you'll have to lock up. In fact, keep the door locked all the time. I'm not having the supposed Mr Linkworth wandering in and out as he pleases.'

'What if someone tries to bring back something they bought?'

'They can knock, can't they?'

'I'll keep my ears open.'

'I know I can rely on you.'

You can, oh you can. It was no use yearning for more. Richard left and she spent the rest of the day alone, working just as hard as if he was standing over her. He relied on her and she was proud to be worthy of his trust.

As she walked home beneath the young leaves and clusters of pink and white blooms of early blossom that adorned the trees overhanging the garden walls along Edge Lane, she couldn't stop thinking about Gabriel Linkworth and Richard. Dear Richard. What a blow. To spend so much time expecting the inheritance that Mr Tyrell was happy to be his, only to lose it. She knew what it was to have expectations that ended up being dashed in the cruellest possible way.

And poor Mr Linkworth with no memory. What must that be like? To have nothing of yourself left, to have to start again. She had had to pick herself up and start again after Ben died. It had been a long time before she could face it, but at last she was doing it. At least she still had her sense of self. Imagine not having that.

She discussed Mr Linkworth's memory loss with Auntie Enid and Grandma Beattie after she had helped wash up after their tripe and onions.

'I don't understand it,' said Auntie Enid. 'Having a bang on the head and seeing stars is one thing, but losing your memory for years on end—'

'If he has lost it,' Grandma Beattie said darkly. 'Men did all kinds to try to get out of fighting. *Some* men.'

Belinda didn't believe it of Gabriel Linkworth, though she couldn't have said why. 'If it was pretence, why keep it up all this time?' It was a poor defence and she felt obscurely ashamed.

'Maybe it is real,' retorted Grandma Beattie, 'but strong men don't suffer mental collapse like that. *Real* men. Men of honour and integrity.'

'Do you mean he lost his memory through..?' She couldn't believe what she was hearing.

'Cowardice.' Grandma Beattie stated it as if it was a fact. 'At least our Ben died doing what a brave man should.'

There was a silence; that moment of deep, warm quiet that always occurred at the first mention of Ben's name. The Ben-silence.

'All this talk of losing your memory.' Auntie Enid's shoulders shuddered. 'The worst part would be forgetting our Ben.'

'We'll never do that, Mrs Sloan,' said Grandma Beattie. 'No matter what.'

'Aye, of course not.' Auntie Enid's smile was watery. 'We'll have him with us always.'

Belinda averted her gaze as Richard's handsome face appeared in her mind. Yet it was true. She would never forget Ben, her darling first love, the man she would gladly have spent her life with. Her fingers moved to the neck of her blouse, where Ben's locket formed a small lump beneath the fabric. Dearest Ben. She would treasure his memory for ever.

Would she dare tell Auntie Enid and Grandma Beattie that her pulse now raced for another man? How could she, when their grief for Ben was as fresh as ever?

Chapter Twenty

A KNOT OF REGRET squeezed inside Belinda's chest as she arrived at Tyrell's Books. She enjoyed working here, and not just because of Richard. She had loved the quiet atmosphere and the way that customers came in, not because they needed to, like they did at the fishmonger's, but because they chose to, because their lives weren't complete without novels or they had a particular interest in the Battle of Waterloo or foreign countries or natural history. All that had stopped when Mr Turton had told Richard he mustn't continue selling, but she had loved it while it lasted.

It had disappointed her that Richard hadn't wanted to keep the bookshop. Would Mr Linkworth want it? He was a reader. But even if he did keep it, it was none of her business. She was Richard's assistant and if the court case next week wasn't to solve the riddle of Mr Linkworth's identity but simply to establish it in a formal way, then she would be out on her ear. She had been so busy hoping against hope that Richard would inherit after all, that she hadn't thought of the consequences to herself if Mr Linkworth inherited. And, without a doubt, Gabriel Linkworth was going to inherit.

With her pulse jumping at the base of her throat and a dozen questions for Richard crowding her mind, she let herself in. Three or four tea-chests stood in the most inconvenient place in the middle of the floor. Not that there was much floor to speak of, after the way Mr Tyrell had packed the space with bookcases.

Richard came out of the office. He had removed his jacket and she must have been worried silly about her job because the sight of him in his shirt-sleeves barely roused a ripple of response, even though he was very modern and daring and didn't wear a waistcoat.

She indicated the tea-chests. 'What's happening?'

'All the boxes of ornaments and whatnot have been returned, so everything must be sent back to the cottage.' He sounded brisk and not at all as though his dreams lay in ruins: admiration swelled inside her. 'If you pack the chests, the window cleaner chappy will collect them later.'

He disappeared into the office, returning with a stack of newspapers that he dropped on the floor. It landed with a loud slap.

'Packing paper. I'll be upstairs.'

'Did Mr Rathbone ever...' She was talking to thin air. '... return the letter-opener?' Oh well, she would come across it if he had.

She went into the office to remove Mrs Harrison's coat and hat and her rose-patterned scarf. What should she do when it grew too warm to wear a coat? Office girls didn't turn up to work in shawls. What she needed to look the part was a jacket, but even paying for the fabric was impossible at present, let alone finding a second-hand one at the market. And when she lost her position here – it didn't bear thinking about, except that she had to think about it.

Piled on the cupboards and tucked up against the walls were the cardboard boxes she had taken such pleasure in filling with treasures from the cottage. Some boxes had never been sold; others had been sold, chased and returned. She really needed to unpack them all to determine what was in each one, but there wasn't room for that. She carried a couple through to the shop and put them on the table where once they had been displayed.

The sight of the newspapers on the floor caused an unexpected stab of resentment. Did he have to dump them like that? What did he think she was? A servant? Yes, he was going through a difficult time, but that was no excuse.

The packing took well over an hour. When the end was in sight, Richard appeared.

'Nearly done? Thank you. After that, would you make a pot of tea?'

'While we have tea, may I ask you something?' She was scared of hearing his answer, but she had to know.

Her hands were grubby with newspaper print when she finished the packing. She washed them and set about making the tea upstairs, laying the embroidered tablecloth on the small table from the cottage. She had imagined herself and Richard sitting here together, but it had never happened. When the shop had been open, either she had been alone or else, at Richard's suggestion, they had taken their tea-breaks separately so one of them was always in the shop; and since the shop had closed, he seemed to want to spend his time undisturbed. Now they were to sit together at last, but instead of being a happy thing to do, the situation felt grim. Perhaps he would open his heart to her.

When he didn't appear, she ran downstairs, calling, 'Tea's ready.'

He looked round, obviously expecting to be presented with a cup.

'Upstairs,' she said.

'Bring it down. I have to be here when Jim arrives to collect the boxes.'

'Can't you leave the door unlocked?'

'I told you. I'm not having Linkworth dropping in as and when he feels like it.'

'Isn't that rather...'

'Rather what?' he asked stiffly.

Petty. Isn't that rather petty? Of course it wasn't. Richard was under great strain, his dreams in ruins. But she couldn't think of another word. Oh, heck.

'...inconvenient?'

'I don't see why. Fetch the tea, there's a good girl. I'm gasping.'

She brought the tray downstairs to the office. Richard hitched one hip onto the edge of a tea-chest, making himself comfortable in a casual way. He looked at her through the office doorway, so she took him his cup and saucer.

She waited for him to say, 'What did you want to ask?' but he said, 'I'll give you the key to the cottage and you can unlock it for Jim.'

'Oh – all right.'

'You don't mind?'

'Of course not.'

'You're a brick, Miss Layton.'

'I aim to give satisfaction.'

He drank his tea, one leg swinging. She could recall every word he had ever said to her, but he didn't remember what she had said not twenty minutes ago.

'May I ask you something?'

'Fire away.'

'I'd like to know what will happen to me if... if you don't inherit.' Her voice dropped. She felt oddly ashamed.

'If? Don't you mean when I don't inherit?' His leg stopped swinging. 'I apologise.' He slid to his feet. 'That was unnecessary. Here.' He thrust his cup and saucer into her hands and went past her towards the stairs.

She spun round, not ashamed any more but determined. She wasn't asking out of selfishness but from a serious need to know.

'Mr Carson! Wait – please. I need to know what to expect.'

She waited until he turned. His mouth was set in a line. It was a thoughtful expression but also made him look rather shifty. Shifty? Then he smiled; his expression changed to warm and rueful.

'It's a fair question. I employed you in good faith, but as to what happens next...' He shrugged.

'I see.' How calm she sounded, even though she was all fluttery inside. 'I'd better look round for something else.'

There was a knock on the window – Jim. Richard immediately turned business-like, and never mind that he had delivered her a dreadful blow, though when he handed her the key to the cottage, he had the grace to ask, 'Will you be all right?' And what could she say other than, 'Yes, thank you'? She had to be all right. She had to ignore the roaring in her ears and get on with her work. Her temporary post, which she had taken on so confidently, had turned out to be a lot more temporary than she had bargained for.

Fetching her coat and hat, she slipped her scarf beneath the collar to hang down the front. She set off, leaving Jim and Richard loading the cart.

The walk to Limits Lane had a curious dream-like quality, brought on by the shock and dread of imminent unemployment. How would she tell Auntie Enid and Grandma Beattie? They had been good about her earning less. Yes, there had been grumbles, but they had accepted it. How would they manage without her wages?

Turning into Limits Lane, she passed the row of privet hedges and came to Mr Tyrell's cottage at the end. The latch on the garden gate was stiff and called for a small effort to lift it. As she turned to close the gate, she sniffed. Tears? No, weeping wasn't allowed. Inhaling deeply to steady herself, she drew in the bright scent of the privet and the wholesome smell of the soil, containing all the hope and promise of spring, but they failed to lift her spirits.

'Good morning, Miss Layton.'

Startled, she looked round. Gabriel Linkworth stood on the lumpy patch of lawn. He was dressed in a blue cloth jacket and grey flannel trousers. He raised his homburg to her in formal greeting, then his face flickered and he took a step closer.

'You're distressed.'

She brushed a hand against her face. 'I'm fine, honestly.'

'Forgive me, but you're not. Would you prefer me to leave?'

What did he expect her to say? He reached out his hand towards the gate, then hesitated with it in mid-air, and looked at her again. What now?

'I've no wish to intrude, but I have some news that might make things look a little better.'

What could he possibly say that would help? His eyes were hazel, not gorgeous deep brown like Richard's, but there was warmth in them nevertheless.

'You told me Mr Carson employed you to assist in winding up Mr Tyrell's estate. Now that he turns out not to be the heir, that puts you in a precarious position. I've spoken with Mr Sowerby at Winterton, Sowerby and Jenks and asked if you can be kept on, just for a while, to allow you time to look round for something else.'

'Are you sure?' Her eyelashes were heavy with teardrops that lent a glaze of radiance to her vision.

'Positive. It's all settled.'

'Thank you. I can't tell you what a relief this is.'

'There's no reason why you should suffer because of this situation.' He smiled awkwardly. 'Well, I'd best leave you to it.'

As he started to go, she instinctively reached out to stop him. The moment she touched his arm, she dropped her hand. She should feel embarrassed at having behaved in such a familiar way, but she didn't. She smiled at him. His face was narrow and serious; his chin was sharp.

'You were right when you said I looked upset. That's what I was upset about. The worry…'

'No need to worry any more. I can promise you a few weeks' grace to find another position. You mustn't feel obliged to snatch the first thing that's offered. I expect the ladies who run your business school will be able to advise you.'

Goodness, he really had listened to her. 'What brings you here?'

'Curiosity. The vague hope that seeing Mr Tyrell's cottage might spark a memory.'

'Why do you keep calling him Mr Tyrell? He was your uncle.'

'It seems appropriate since I can't recall him; more respectful.'

She rather thought that Mr Tyrell would have approved of such reasoning, but it wasn't her place to say so.

'What about you?' he asked. 'What brings you here?'

'Work.' Warmth glowed in her chest: it was safe to feel happy about work again. 'Mr Carson removed things to sell and now he's returning them. They'll be here soon.'

'He really was keen to get the money, wasn't he? I shouldn't have said that. The last thing I want is to put you in an uncomfortable position.'

She ought to be hopping mad at hearing Richard criticised, but no resentment flared. Mr Linkworth wasn't being snippy and disagreeable the way Richard was when he mentioned Mr Linkworth. He was simply making an observation. Snippy and disagreeable? Richard?

She opened her handbag. 'I'd better unlock.' She darted a glance at him.

'Don't worry. I shan't ask you to let me inside.'

She nodded. Bizarre as it sounded, she immediately felt it would have been appropriate for him to come in. He was so transparently honest. Ben would have liked him. Ben had admired integrity.

A cheery whistling reached her ears, accompanied by the sound of wooden wheels crunching their way down the lane.

'I think the delivery is about to arrive,' said Mr Linkworth. 'I'll get out from under your feet.'

It was for the best: Richard wouldn't want him here.

He raised his hat to her. 'Goodbye.'

'Goodbye – and thank you from the bottom of my heart for making my position secure.'

'It's a pleasure.'

Jim looked over the gate. 'Ah, there you are.' He pushed the gate open. 'Are you on your way out, sir?'

'Yes. Wait. Are you supposed to manhandle those boxes into the cottage on your own? Let me give you a hand – I insist.'

Belinda scurried ahead with the key. Next news, the two men were carrying a tea-chest between them and she jumped aside to let them in. The unloading was soon done. It didn't feel right to leave Mr and Mrs Tyrell's belongings there like that, but Richard had given no instructions about unpacking and it wasn't as though she knew where anything went.

She couldn't help watching Mr Linkworth. Would he grab the opportunity to have a good old gawp? He concentrated on getting the chests inside without banging anything, then with no more than a swift glance round, he went out. He and Jim shook hands and Jim went off with his barrow.

It should have been Richard helping Jim.

'Are you walking back to the shop?' Mr Linkworth asked. 'Would you care for company part of the way?'

Richard wouldn't like it.

Did that matter?

'I'd like to hear about Mr Tyrell,' said Mr Linkworth.

'I'm not sure I can tell you much.'

His expression tightened. 'I see.'

'I don't mean that as a brush-off. I just didn't know him

well, but I'm happy to tell you what I can. I'll start by telling you why I think this should be called Huh Cottage.'

'Huh Cottage?' Opening the gate, he waved her through. 'That I have to hear.'

As they walked along Limits Lane, she marvelled that just minutes earlier she had walked in the other direction in such a state of shock and fear that she could have been anywhere. Now the birdsong was clearer, the tiny white flowers of the common chickweed growing in the verge were as bright as little stars, and the sunshine made her wish for a straw hat instead of her borrowed felt.

When they reached Edge Lane, Mr Linkworth walked on the outside, which Ben had said was the sign of a gentleman. They chatted more naturally and comfortably than she would have believed possible, given that this man was the evil inheritance-snatcher.

At the corner by St Clement's Church, they parted company. Belinda returned to Tyrell's Books, feeling light of heart. She still had a job!

'You look chirpy,' Richard said as she let herself into the shop.

Would it be tactless to tell him? But she wasn't going to lie.

'I bumped into Mr Linkworth.'

'Oh, you did, did you?'

She lifted her chin, refusing to be put down. 'He says I'll still have a job here after the court case, while I sort out another position.'

Would he congratulate her? Her breath sat poised in her throat, ready to pour out in a long sigh of pure relief when he was pleased for her.

'It didn't take you long to desert the sinking ship,' said Richard.

*

At five o'clock, Belinda locked up and left the shop. It was a pleasant afternoon to walk home and, thanks to Gabriel Linkworth, she had more such afternoons to look forward to. Richard had left after her dinner hour, saying he wouldn't be back today, and in his absence she had set the inventory aside, too excited and relieved about her new-found security to sit at the typewriter. Needing to be up and doing, she had removed books shelf by shelf, careful to keep them in order, then wet-dusted the shelves and, while they dried, dry-dusted the books.

Now, walking along Edge Lane, she was in better spirits than she had been since Gabriel the inheritance-thief had first pitched up. She had spent a lot of energy on being agitated on Richard's behalf. She still felt sympathy for him, of course, but…

He had told her not to expect him tomorrow. Yesterday that would have floored her with disappointment, but now it was a relief. She was cured of him. The man she had idolised didn't exist. The man she had idolised would have explained her job situation to her without having to be pinned down. The man she had idolised would have taken an interest in her night school training. He would have helped Jim deliver the tea-chests. And above all, no matter how deep his disappointment, he would have spoken of and to Gabriel Linkworth with restraint and civility.

At what point had Richard known that Mr Linkworth was the rightful heir? When he had talked about the court case as if the matter was in doubt, had he been stringing her along? Taking advantage of her loyalty to boost his position? The man she had idolised would never have done that.

Her infatuation was over. Infatuation: yes. Thank goodness she had never told anyone or she would look a complete clot now. The heady yearning had been both wonderful and excruciatingly painful while it lasted. How could she have been so vulnerable? Had her feelings for Richard been nothing more than a reaction to her long-overdue independence?

Well, she was cured now; and if Richard didn't appear tomorrow, she was free of him until Monday, which suited her just fine. Was it normal, after an infatuation, to go from longing to be with the person to not wanting to clap eyes on them? Talk about one extreme to the other.

A sudden need to see Mum came over her. Mum had described being repeatedly let down by Dad and now, in a small way, Belinda had been let down too. Much as she loved and valued Auntie Enid, she had never grown out of wanting to feel special to Mum. Might Richard's unworthiness somehow bring the two of them closer? It seemed unlikely, as she could never tell Mum about him, because Mum wouldn't keep it to herself and she cringed at the thought of Thad running amok with the news that their Bel had had a stupid pash for her boss.

Even so, she needed to be with her mum. Perhaps her experience would make her more understanding and Mum would feel closer to her without knowing why.

Grandma Beattie wouldn't worry about her being late, as long as tea wasn't held up. Now was a good time to go, because Dad wouldn't be home from work and Thad and Jacob would be off doing whatever questionable activities kept them busy between school and teatime. It would be just Mum and probably Mikey and, if she was lucky, Sarah.

When she walked in, the first thing she saw across the room was Dad sitting in the armchair, and the smile froze on her lips. Oh no, please no.

'What are you doing home at this time?' she asked.

Please let there be another reason.

'Dad's been sacked,' said Mikey.

'Don't say that,' cried Mum. 'You mustn't say that. He's had enough of street-sweeping and he's going to try his hand at summat else. That's what you say if anyone asks.'

'If anyone asks,' growled Dad, 'you tell 'em to mind their own sodding business.'

'Denby! Language.' But Mum's heart wasn't in it.

'What happened?' asked Belinda. Did she even want to know?

'It doesn't matter,' said Mum.

'He punched his boss,' said Mikey.

Belinda sucked in a huge breath. 'Dad! Why?' Stupid question. As if there could be an acceptable reason. There would just be the usual Denby Layton reason: the other bloke's fault.

'He asked for it,' said Dad. There. See. The other bloke's fault. Nothing was ever Denby Layton's fault. Belinda wanted to curl up and die of shame. Honestly, this family was going from bad to worse. Mr Linkworth wouldn't have been so quick to keep her on if he had known the kind of stock she came from.

She didn't stay long. She couldn't bear to. What would it take to make Dad face up to his responsibilities? He had a wife and family to provide for and all he did was cadge money off his eldest and set a bad example to his youngest.

And she had to go home and tell Auntie Enid and Grandma Beattie. Oh, the shame. Her chin trembled, but she tightened her lips. Best get it over with. She marched down Grave Pit Lane, the cinders crunching beneath her feet until she stepped onto the track. She didn't slow her pace, but years of experience made her take care as she trod the ridges, like a mountain range in miniature, that started out as humps and bulges and furrows created in the rain by footsteps and carts, and then solidified as they dried out, playing hell with your ankles if you didn't watch where you were going.

How was she going to tell Auntie Enid and Grandma Beattie? She struggled to find a way to word it. Pressing down the latch, she opened the door onto a fishy smell. Fish rissoles for tea; Grandma Beattie would have asked the fishmonger for a bag of tails. Auntie Enid was already home, setting the table. Good: that meant she need deliver the news just once.

They stared at her. Could they see the shock in her face?

'I never would have thought it,' said Grandma Beattie.

Had they heard already? How?

'You was seen earlier today by Mrs Harrison's Irma,' said Auntie Enid. 'She said you were walking along Edge Lane with a man.'

'Oh, that!' Relief poured through her. 'He's my new boss. It turns out Mr Carson—'

'It's not that,' said Auntie Enid. 'We knew there'd be an explanation for that.'

'What, then?'

'I didn't believe it when Irma said.' Grandma Beattie sucked in her cheeks.

'When Irma said what?'

'She admired it. A bit of colour, she said, and I said, no, never, not our Belinda. She wouldn't.' Grandma Beattie raised her hand and pointed. 'Look at you, stood there as bold as brass.'

Belinda hadn't the faintest idea what she meant. Then coldness rippled through her as she dropped her gaze and saw the rose-patterned scarf that still hung around her neck.

Chapter Twenty-One

PATIENCE ROSE EARLY that Saturday morning. Miss Deane and Miss Russell were going on a jaunt today and, although they had offered to see to their own breakfasts, she wouldn't hear of it. She wanted to get up and prepare it for them and wave them on their way to catch the tram that would take them to town, from where they would catch the Southport train from Victoria Station.

She crept downstairs, wanting to have their tea in the pot before they appeared. As always, she opened the cupboard under the stairs to place her bedside lamp on the shelf.

'Morning, Miss Patience,' said a cheery voice above her on the stairs.

'Why do you put the bedside lamps away every morning?' asked Miss Deane, as the girls arrived behind her, their own lamps at the ready. 'We can't make it out at all.'

'We've always done it,' said Patience. 'It was oil-lamps when we were children. They were brought down every morning and put on this shelf then, before we went to bed, they were got ready for us to take upstairs.'

'But you don't need to do that with electric lamps,' said Miss Russell.

'I've never given it any thought. We've just carried on in the same old way.' Two dried-up old spinsters, living their lives to the same old pattern. 'Maybe I'll have a word with my sister.

Would you like poached eggs for breakfast? That should set you up for the day.'

'You're an angel, Miss Patience.'

It afforded Patience a flutter of pleasure to stand on the doorstep, waving them off. They were such dear girls and she would miss them when they left. What would Prudence think of Miss Layton's idea about a different sort of pupil lodger? Patience hadn't mentioned it so far. She had tried to kid herself that she hadn't been able to, as Miss Deane and Miss Russell ate with them and had full access to the sitting room when it wasn't being used for teaching.

She would mention Miss Layton's idea this morning, but before she had a chance, Lawrence and Evelyn arrived. Patience followed them into the sitting room.

'Morning, Prudence,' said Lawrence.

'What brings you here?' Prudence asked.

'We've come to check on Pa's old room. That's where you've stowed your pupil lodgers, isn't it? I'm not sure I care for having strangers living in my house, so we've come to make sure they're treating the place – and Pa's furniture – with respect.'

'Of course they are,' Prudence spluttered.

'I'll be the judge of that.' Lawrence puffed out his chest. 'Are they in or out at present?'

'They're out for the day,' said Patience. Thank goodness for that.

'Then you can't have any objection,' said Lawrence.

Prudence looked ready to explode. Patience stepped in – literally. She headed off Lawrence as he made for the door.

'There's no need for both of you to invade our lodgers' privacy.'

'They aren't entitled—' Lawrence started to say.

'This is something that requires a woman's eye,' Patience said firmly. 'Evelyn, go and look, if you must.'

'Don't touch anything,' said Prudence. 'You have no business rifling through the lodgers' belongings.'

'As if I would,' sniffed Evelyn. 'That isn't why we're here.' Off she went.

'Make the most of it,' Prudence told Lawrence. 'There'll be no more pupil lodgers for you to check up on after this. It's too much work.'

'Aha!' crowed Lawrence. 'Do I detect a chink in your armour? The first sign of your inevitable failure?'

'Don't imagine you can capitalise on this.'

'Oh, but I do imagine. A carefully worded statement to the press about the business school's not being quite as successful as anticipated... the conclusion, sorrowfully reached, that no more pupil lodgers can be taken... the stress and strain on Miss Hesketh, working hard all day, then working all evening as well... my concern for my poor sister's health: have I asked too much of her? My own guilt and regret, et cetera, et cetera.' He looked round, as if ready to be clapped on the back. 'You'd be surprised how easy it can be to cast a cloud over something.'

Evelyn returned. 'The room is spick and span.'

'I hope you wouldn't expect anything less,' said Patience, nettled.

'Naturally not, dear. You're a good little housewife. You should have set up a housewifery school, not a business school.'

'Don't give them ideas,' said Lawrence. 'The business school has begun to totter. We don't want them starting up another hare-brained scheme.'

'The business school has most certainly not begun to totter,' said Prudence.

Lawrence snorted. 'You said yourself: no more pupil lodgers—'

'There is more to our school than that—'

'Tea,' said Patience and everyone stared at her. 'I think a cup of tea is in order. Prudence, will you lend a hand, please?'

In the kitchen, she shared Miss Layton's idea as she put the kettle on the gas.

'Why didn't you tell me this earlier?' Prudence demanded.

Patience fiddled with the tea-caddy and checked the level in the sugar bowl, hoping to hide her flush of embarrassment. She hadn't said anything because Miss Layton's idea had been all tied up with that confidential talk they had had about wills and non-blood relations. She had wanted to wait before telling Prudence so that there was no chance of her spilling out the whole truth of that conversation.

'The point is,' said Patience, 'we must stop Lawrence before he can speak out against us.'

'But why would pupils need to lodge with us if they're local? They can live at home.'

'That's what I said, but we mustn't make assumptions about their personal circumstances. People have all kinds of reasons for not living at home.'

The look on Prudence's face said she didn't want those dubious reasons under her roof.

Patience paused in the act of swishing the hot water around in the pot. 'It's either this or stand by while Lawrence runs rough-shod over us.'

'Well, I hope you have all the answers to his questions, because I won't.'

Patience hoped so too. She straightened her spine. It was up to her.

Prudence left her making tea. She counted the spoonfuls of tea: one per person and one for the pot. Standards again. But her spoonfuls weren't quite full. Economy. She assembled the tea-tray and took it to the sitting room.

It was rather bizarre, pouring tea and offering sugar in the middle of a suspended argument, but it wasn't long before Lawrence started up again.

'What desperate scheme did you dream up together in the kitchen?' He smirked at Evelyn and she made a little snickering sound as if she was too well-bred to laugh out loud.

Prudence could look pretty snooty herself when she wanted. 'We haven't dreamed up anything, but there is an idea we have been considering for the past few days. It isn't settled yet, which is why we were reluctant to discuss it, but since you're all set to do us down, we're obliged to confide in you.'

'Go on then,' said Lawrence. 'Let's hear this marvellous idea.'

'Our current system of having pupil lodgers—' Prudence began.

'Current system!' mocked Lawrence. 'That's rich. You make it sound like you've been having lodgers for months.'

'Our current system,' Prudence repeated, 'has its faults, therefore we are considering adapting it. Our next pupil lodgers will be local girls with jobs, who'll attend our night school just like any other pupils.'

'So they'll just be... lodgers,' said Evelyn.

'Pupil lodgers,' said Prudence. 'They'll live here with us for the duration of their learning.'

'But why would local girls require lodgings?' asked Evelyn.

'It doesn't do to make assumptions about people's personal circumstances,' said Patience. 'Take our Miss Layton, for instance. You might expect her to live with her parents, but in fact she lives with her late fiancé's family.'

'Take us, for example,' Prudence added. 'The outside world thinks we run this school at your behest.'

'And people probably imagine you're pretty well-heeled,' said Evelyn, 'though actually you're as poor as church mice.'

'Please don't let's be catty,' said Patience. It was hard work being the peacemaker. Unrewarding too.

'How respectable are these reasons for not living at home?' asked Evelyn.

'Naturally,' said Prudence, 'we'll enquire into each girl's circumstances.'

'It sounds dubious to me,' said Lawrence.

Prudence put down her cup and saucer. 'We're going to place an advertisement in the *Evening News* on Monday. I'll deliver it to their offices personally in my dinner hour.'

Patience felt a burst of happiness that almost made her laugh out loud. More pupil lodgers, and ones who might stay for some considerable time, depending upon how much they needed to learn. If Miss Deane and Miss Russell, staying for a fortnight, could be pretend-daughters, how much more daughterly might long-term lodgers become?

There was no Saturday morning trip to the library. Belinda went straight to Cromwell Street. The optimism that yesterday's promise of job security had brought might never have happened. She couldn't think where she least wanted to be, in End Cottage or at the family home. Dad didn't have a cat in hell's chance of finding another job now that he had punched his boss, so what was going to happen to the family? She and George were settled elsewhere and, if needs be, Sarah could move into the maids' dormitory at the Claremont, but that still left Mum and the boys. Poor Mum. She must be tearing her hair out.

She arrived at the house to find Dad in a sullen, so-what mood and Mum on the verge of collapse.

'I've sent Mikey to fetch George,' said Sarah. 'He's got this morning off, because of being on afternoon and evening deliveries.'

'I don't know what good you think he's going to do.' Dad scowled. 'I'm the man of the house, not him.'

Some man! Belinda concentrated on clearing away the mess of crumbs and dirty crockery and the smears of dripping that adorned the table: the boys had evidently been left to fend for themselves this morning. Annoyed as she was with them for leaving the table in a shambles, she was vexed to think that bread and dripping was all they had been offered to line their stomachs at the start of the day, though the tell-tale tang in the air said that Dad had had his usual Saturday kipper. Mum's face was grey, apart from a hectic pink in her cheeks. She was slumped at the table, her elbows dumped in the mess left by the boys. Dad hadn't even offered her the armchair.

'What will we do about the rent?' Mum asked. 'We're on a warning not to be late again or we'll be out on our ears.'

'We'll talk about it when George gets here,' said Belinda. 'Mind your arms, Mum. I need to clean underneath.'

The door was flung open and Mikey flew inside. 'George is on his way.'

'That's all we ruddy need,' grumbled Dad. 'George is coming. Hallelujah. Bring out the brass band.' He hauled himself up straighter in the armchair. 'If he imagines he can tell me what to do, I'll give him summat to think about.'

'What'll you do, Dad?' asked Thad in unconcealed delight. 'Deck him, like you decked Mr McCall? That'd be great, wouldn't it, Jakey-boy?'

'Why don't you two get lost?' said Belinda. 'You're normally running wild on Saturdays. Why should today be any different?'

'Because we want to see Dad land one on our George,' retorted Thad. 'Lay 'Em Out Layton – that's your new name, isn't it, Dad? Better than Layabout Layton any day.'

Mum clutched her hand against her mouth. Belinda felt close to despair herself. Dad wouldn't get another job: that was the long and the short of it. No one would be mad enough to employ him after this. Lay 'Em Out Layton: she closed her eyes in shame. Dad had degraded them all – except Thad, it seemed, and Jacob. Those two young louts in the making seemed more inclined to hero-worship him. No, not hero-worship. That wasn't what she had seen in Thad. He had sounded as if he admired Dad and was building him up, but there was derision in his manner.

George marched in, bringing a waft of tobacco with him.

'Go on, Dad,' crowed Thad. 'Tell George what you did.'

'I already know, thank you,' George said stiffly. 'Are you all right, Mum?'

She sat up, straight as a pencil, and nodded, her features a clump of hopelessness, then she crumpled again.

'The rent is the first problem,' said Belinda. 'Mum says it hasn't always been paid on time, so now the landlord says it has to be paid promptly every week.'

'The rent's been late?' snapped George. 'But I've been helping with money. So's Bel, as well as what you get off Sarah. There's always been rent money, Mum.'

Mum's eyes narrowed to slits. 'Tell your father that.'

George heaved a sigh that lifted his shoulders. He didn't look at Dad. 'How much do you need to make up the amount, Mum?'

'All of it,' Mum whispered.

All of it! Belinda's head snapped up.

'Dad were sent packing with no pay,' said Mikey.

A charged silence thundered round the room. Belinda and George looked at one another.

'Well then,' said George, 'me and the girls will stump up – just this once,' he added as Dad perked up.

'A whole week's rent?' squeaked Sarah.

'All twelve shillings.' The quiver in Mum's voice told of long-held shame. You had to be pretty badly off if twelve bob was all the rent you could afford. Poor Mum. What a dance Dad had led her, led them all, over the years.

George muttered under his breath. He glanced at the girls. 'We'll discuss it outside.'

A brisk March breeze caught at Belinda's hair as they walked through the gap where the front gate used to be. She expected them to stop there on the pavement, but George stalked up the road and round the corner, as if Dad, or possibly Thad, would catch every word if they held their council of war outside the house.

George's normally good-natured face was set in grim lines. 'This is the last thing we need, Dad losing yet another job and for flooring his boss, if you please. It reflects badly on all of us, especially on me as his oldest son.'

'We can't have Mum worrying about being evicted,' said Belinda.

'If we pay it this time, Dad will expect it every time,' said Sarah.

'This once and that's all,' said George in a voice that said he wouldn't look kindly on disagreement.

'I won't be able to contribute much,' said Belinda, 'but you can have everything I've got. How about you?' She looked at Sarah.

'I've got a tin of money in my locker at work. Don't look so surprised. It's not as though I can leave it safely at home.'

'Then you'll have to go into town and fetch some of it,' said George, more gently this time. 'If you girls can pay half between you, I'll stump up the rest.'

'I'm sorry, but you'll have to pay most of our half,' Belinda told Sarah.

'I thought your fancy new office work was meant to pay better.'

'Don't you start,' she said crisply. 'I've had enough of that from Mum and Dad as well as at End Cottage. I'm not having it from you an' all.'

'Well, I can't get my money today.' Sarah looked mutinous. 'I'm not back at work until tomorrow. I'll fetch it then.'

'You'll fetch it today,' said George, 'and we'll take it round to the rent man before I go to work this afternoon, all three of us, then we'll know it's been paid.'

Poor Mum. How demeaning, her children paying the rent behind her back instead of giving it to her to pay. But George was right. They couldn't risk handing over the money at home.

'George, this must be the end of your involvement,' said Belinda. 'You're a postman now, a public servant. It would look bad at work if anyone found out, so after today you're to keep well away. It'll be my job to sort it out.'

'Oh aye, and what do you think you can do?' Sarah challenged her. She was in a right nowty mood this morning.

'I'll think of something. I have to, because George has to be kept out of it, and you're too young.'

She wanted to travel into town with Sarah, but her contribution to the rent would be meagre enough, without frittering away a few more coppers. She went back with Sarah to fetch Sarah's handbag, then walked her to the tram stop, waving her on her way when she climbed aboard. Then she headed back to Mum's, squaring her shoulders before she went inside. She had promised George she would take on the responsibility for sorting things out, so she had better get started.

'Back again like a bad penny,' groused Dad.

'I want a word with the boys. They need to get themselves sorted out with jobs.'

'You what?' demanded Thad. 'Who the hell d'you think you're bossing about?'

'Thad! Language,' said Mum, but as tellings-off went, it was pretty feeble.

'It's not a question of bossing about.' Belinda looked Thad in the eye. When had he grown so tall? 'It makes sense. Dad hasn't got a job and the family needs money, so everyone has to do their share. You and Mikey should be working half time anyway, at your ages. It's only Jacob who isn't old enough.'

'I tried to get a job last July the day after I turned twelve,' said Mikey. 'I tried at the grocer's and the fishmonger's, but they wouldn't have me because of Thad's reputation and they said it wouldn't be worth trying any other shops. So then I went to the timber merchant, but they said a lad had acted as look-out when there was a theft and they couldn't prove anything, but they didn't want Thad Layton's brother working there.'

Her shoulders stiffened in shock. 'I didn't know any of this.'

'It's not the kind of thing you shout about, is it?' muttered Mum. Belinda stared at her. What had gone wrong with this family? How had Mum and Dad managed to raise three decent, hard-working children in herself, George and Sarah, and then gone so horribly wrong with Thad? Or would Thad have been trouble, no matter what?

'Well, you're going to have to try again,' she said. 'Who teaches your class?'

'Mr Harvey,' said Mikey.

She didn't know Mr Harvey. He had started after she left. 'Ask him to write you a character reference.'

'Oh aye.' Thad bullied his way in. 'Ask him to write a letter saying he's nowt like his good-for-nothing brother, you mean?'

'Yes, I do mean,' said Belinda. 'You let us all down, the way you carry on.'

'Pardon me for breathing,' he sneered. 'What a shame we can't all be jumped-up typists like you. You've forgot where you come from, our Bel. You think we're better than we are.'

'I'm a darned sight better than you, Thad Layton, and don't speak to me like that. Show some respect. I'm nearly twenty-one and you're still a kid at school.'

'Show some respect,' Thad mocked in a high-pitched voice.

'You tell her, Thad,' Jacob encouraged him.

'And you can mind your manners an' all.' She flung a look at her parents. They should be supporting her, pulling the boys into line, showing the right way to behave. But Mum looked exhausted and defeated and Dad – well, Dad just sat there in his flaming armchair and let them get on with it. He would only get involved if they bickered so much that he lost his rag and then his contribution to the discussion would be to shout the place down and chuck the boys outside.

'You can mind your manners,' parroted Jacob in a sing-song voice, trying to copy Thad.

Belinda wasn't having that. It was bad enough taking cheek from Thad, but she couldn't have young Jacob thinking he could get away with it. She clipped him smartly round the ear. He yelled, more for effect than from pain, and clutched the side of his head.

'Mum! Did you see what our Bel did to me? Mum!'

'Pipe down,' said Mum. 'My head's pounding.'

'Listen to me, you boys,' said Belinda. She tightened her fists, hiding them in the folds of her skirt. She had to look confident and in charge. She had to look as if she expected to be obeyed. What on earth had made her take on the responsibility for sorting out her dreadful family? 'This family needs money. Mikey, ask Mr Harvey for a reference. Jacob—'

'I can't work half time,' Jacob said at once. 'I'm not twelve till July.'

'No, but you can get a paper-round or run errands.'

'Where's the point in that?' jeered Thad. 'He'll earn next to nowt doing that.'

'But he'll earn something,' said Belinda. 'You've all got to earn something, even you, though it has to be honest work, Thad.'

Thad grinned. 'Nah. There's no money in that.'

What now? Her name was mud in End Cottage. How could she have been so stupid as to forget to remove her scarf and hatband? More to the point, how could she have been so deceitful? She had never intended to be deceitful; she had wanted to protect Auntie Enid and Grandma Beattie. The upset over the mauve fabric a few weeks ago was nothing compared to their devastation at the rose-printed cotton.

But it was better to have it out in the open – or it would be once the fuss died down. Her abrupt recovery from her infatuation, together with knowing her position at Tyrell's Books was secure for now, had given her a strong sense of a fresh start. Was it too much to hope that Auntie Enid and Grandma Beattie's knowing she had broken her mourning could be a part of her fresh start? It didn't feel possible at the moment. They had been distraught yesterday evening and she had lain awake in the dead of night, tortured by the sound of their muffled weeping, longing to go to them but knowing she was the last person able to offer them comfort.

Did she get it from Dad? He had let down his family repeatedly. Was she going to follow in his footsteps? Surely not. In fact, absolutely not. She might carry Denby Layton's name, but that was the only thing they had in common.

She marched home to End Cottage, almost running down the final stretch of Grave Pit Lane. She felt so energised and filled with resolution that when she opened the door, it was almost a shock to see everything the same as normal. Nothing ever changed in End Cottage. Not Grandma Beattie, in her black clothes and her black lace cap, standing at the range, stirring the stewed apple. Not Auntie Enid, fitting in a quick half hour of knitting for the poor after her Saturday morning housework. Not the long strip of black crêpe that hung from the front of the mantelshelf, just as it had done every day since the arrival of the telegram. Not the smell of beeswax that lingered regardless of what other aromas might be present. Not the black marble clock ticking away the sombre hours.

The place looked dark and grim and pathetic. Spotlessly clean. Tidy. You couldn't fault it on those counts. But dark and old, as if the world inside End Cottage had stopped.

Well, it had, hadn't it? Ben had died and the three of them had gone into mourning and Auntie Enid and Grandma Beattie had never come out of it.

But Belinda had.

'Oh, it's you.' Grandma Beattie looked up from her stirring.

'I'm going to return Mrs Harrison's coat and hat. I want to apologise to you again for the scarf and the hatband.'

'Apologies don't butter no parsnips,' muttered Grandma Beattie. 'That were downright deceit, that were.'

'Yes, it was,' she agreed. 'I want you to understand that I did it because I hated to hurt your feelings. I know what your mourning means to you.'

'We thought it meant the same to you an' all,' said Auntie Enid.

'It did – it does. But I'm young and I like pretty things. I just wanted to have a bit of colour. It doesn't mean I think any less of Ben. I cherish his memory every bit as much as you do and I'll regret his death until the day I die – but I don't want to dress in black from head to foot any more. You can understand that... can't you?'

Chapter Twenty-Two

MONDAY: A BRAND-NEW week, and she still had her job. Whatever upsets the weekend had doled out, it was time to concentrate on work. Belinda was preparing to resume work on the inventory when she heard footsteps coming down the stairs and Richard walked in, a cardboard box in his arms.

He stopped, then smiled. 'I thought I might get in and out before you arrived.'

'What are you doing?'

'I'm not the heir, so it's time to bow out gracefully. I've come to collect a few bits and pieces I left here.'

It would be a relief to see the back of him. 'What will you do?'

'Return to my work and my old life... minus expectations.'

Was he sorry for himself? Bitter? He sounded off-hand, though it was difficult to believe that was how he felt, but it really wasn't her business.

'Goodbye, Miss Layton.'

'Before you go: you owe me last week's wages.'

'So I do.' He eyed her speculatively. 'I employed you in anticipation of inheriting my uncle's estate. Now that I'm no longer his heir...'

Did he expect her to forego payment? 'I need the money.'

'Aside from not needing you, I can't afford you, Miss Layton. Perhaps Linkworth can give you an advance on your wages.'

The palms of her hands felt sore where her nails were digging in. The door opened and the bell jingled. Drat! Now she would lose her chance to get paid.

Gabriel Linkworth walked in, accompanied by Mr Turton.

'Good morning, Miss Layton, Mr Carson,' Mr Turton greeted them. 'I see you're removing your possessions, Mr Carson. Good, good.'

'What's the matter, Linkworth?' Richard asked. 'Didn't you dare come without reinforcements?'

Mr Turton said mildly, 'I insisted upon coming with Mr Linkworth this morning. I wished to make sure you had received the letter from Winterton, Sowerby and Jenks and that you had acted on it.' He nodded at Richard's box. 'It appears that you have.' He stood aside. 'We won't hold you up if you're ready to leave.'

'As you wish.'

'Excuse me.' Belinda stepped forward. 'We were discussing my wages for last week.'

'There's no call to make a song and dance out of it,' Richard hissed under his breath.

'I'll pay your wages,' said Mr Linkworth. To Mr Turton, he said, 'That's in order, isn't it? Good. Don't let us detain you, Carson.'

Richard thrust the box onto the table, took his gloves from his pockets and snapped them on, then snatched his trilby from the top of the cupboard and jammed it on his head. Grabbing his cardboard box, he started to leave.

'We'll see you in the magistrate's court on Friday, Mr Carson,' said Mr Turton. 'As the person who initiated this matter by casting doubt on Mr Linkworth's identity, your presence is essential.'

'Believe me,' said Richard, 'I have no intention of missing it.'

Gabriel Linkworth opened the door and Richard stalked out.

'Well,' said Mr Turton, 'that wasn't as unpleasant as it might have been.'

'How did you know he'd be leaving today?' Belinda asked.

'Winterton, Sowerby and Jenks wrote to him and suggested that, unless he seriously intends to dispute Mr Linkworth's identity, perhaps he should withdraw from the late Mr Tyrell's property.'

'I see.' Time to bow out gracefully, indeed!

Mr Turton turned to his companion. 'There's nothing else for me to do here, Linkworth, so I'll take my leave. Good day, Miss Layton. You'll shortly receive a letter from Winterton, Sowerby and Jenks, confirming your position here on a temporary basis.'

'Thank you, sir.'

She settled down to begin typing.

'What's that you're working on?' asked Mr Linkworth.

'The stock inventory Mr Carson asked for. I think it was something to do with selling all the books.'

'Well, I don't want to sell them. That is, I do, but not in the same way. I want to take over the shop and be a bookseller.' He smiled – a real smile that broke through his habitual gravity.

She smiled. She was glad for him. Glad for the shop, too.

'I'm pleased Tyrell's Books will continue. Or will it become Linkworth's Books?'

'Now there's a thought.' He laughed and the lines of his serious face relaxed. That cautious, guarded look vanished from his eyes.

On impulse, she said, 'You haven't seen upstairs yet, have you?'

He indicated for her to lead the way. Upstairs, she put her hand on the back of the chintz armchair.

'These chairs and the table are from Mr Tyrell's cottage,' she started to say, but he was already between the bookshelves, taking care where he put his feet.

'Are all these boxes full of books?'

He walked around the shelves for a minute or two, gazing at the titles.

'Forget the inventory, for now at least. We need to unpack some of these boxes and get as many books as we can onto the shelves, both downstairs and up here. Then the remaining boxes will need to have their contents listed.' He opened a couple of boxes, looking ready to get stuck in immediately.

She didn't want to sound work-shy, but she had to warn him. 'It's grubby work and neither of us is dressed for it. If you don't mind waiting, I can bring a pinny from home tomorrow, and I'll put my hair in a snood; or I could run home in my dinner hour and fetch them.'

'It can wait until tomorrow. Let's go to the cottage and unpack those tea-chests. It didn't seem right last week, leaving them dumped on the floor.'

'Before we go, do you mind if I pop down the road to Brown's for a new typewriter ribbon? I'll only be a minute.'

'Did Mr Tyrell have a petty-cash tin? I must top it up.'

She hurried along the road to the stationer's, where she found Mr Brown dealing with three customers at once and looking frazzled.

'Are you on your own this morning?' she asked when it was her turn.

'Our Jeanie is expecting a happy event, but she's having a bad time of it. The doctor has told her to rest with her feet up and no arguments, so Mrs Brown will be over there every day for the foreseeable future, doing the necessary and looking after the little 'uns for her.'

'I'm sorry to hear that.'

'Aye, well, you do what you have to, don't you, for your family.'

Yes, you did. Would the boys sort out jobs for themselves or would she have to do it for them? She made her purchase and returned to the bookshop.

As she and Mr Linkworth walked to Limits Lane, he said, 'May I ask a personal question? Please say if it's inappropriate. It's your black shawl: it's not very spring-like.'

'It's a mourning garment.'

'My condolences. I apologise for speaking out of turn.'

Condolences for the girl who longed for colour! She was accustomed to accepting sympathy and letting others assume she was deep in mourning, but it was time to be honest.

'My fiancé lost his life in the war.'

'And you still mourn him after all this time.'

'Yes, I do and in a way I always will, but...' How to express it? 'I live with his mother and grandmother. They are in deepest mourning to this day and...' Never mind all the ins and outs: get to the point. '...and it hurts them dreadfully that I feel ready to reduce mine.'

'You were wearing a pretty scarf last time I saw you.'

'That's what caused the dreadful hurt; well, and that I tried to keep it secret from them. I'm sorry. I didn't mean to foist my family troubles on you.'

'No one's life is straightforward.'

'True.'

But her spirits lifted at having shared her 'disloyalty' and not been slammed for it. Then she sighed silently as she thought of Dad, unemployed yet again and now unemployable. She could never share that with Mr Linkworth. And what did that say about her, that she picked and chose which shame to share? Then she realised. No longer being in mourning wasn't a matter of shame. It was the natural progression of a young, heartbroken girl as she gradually healed. She hadn't forgotten Ben, but she wanted to look to the future. She wanted to make a future – one that didn't involve dressing in crow-black from head to toe.

At Mr Tyrell's cottage, Mr Linkworth unlocked the door and stood back for her to enter.

'Let's have some fresh air in here.' He opened the windows, throwing up the sashes with no difficulty. 'I thought they'd be stiff, in an old place like this.'

'Homes need fresh air,' said Belinda. The cottage felt stale. It needed more than air. It needed someone to live here and love it. Would Mr Linkworth do that?

She started unpacking the tea-chests as Mr Linkworth looked round. He disappeared upstairs; she heard his footsteps overhead. When he came down, he went through the back door into the garden.

'The place is in good condition,' he remarked when he returned. 'Exceptionally so. The range in the kitchen is modern and there's a new water pump outside next to the old well.'

'Shall you move in?' Belinda asked, unwrapping a figurine.

'Yes.' He lifted a newspaper-wrapped object out of another tea-chest. 'I'm in digs at the moment. I'll run the shop and live here. You can't imagine how good it feels to have a purpose.'

'Do you have any family?'

'I have a cousin called Irene and she has children. When everything is settled, I intend to write to her and then visit.'

'Why wait?'

'At this point, she doesn't know I'm alive.'

She stopped in the middle of unwrapping a cut-glass vase. 'Then you must get in touch at once.'

'It's not that simple.' Mr Linkworth folded some newspaper and added it to the pile she had started. 'My father, believing me dead, left everything to Cousin Irene in his will. Her circumstances are such that she desperately needs the inheritance.'

'Oh. So she's got your inheritance and you've got Mr Carson's.'

'In a manner of speaking; the difference being that my father, thinking me gone for good, changed his will, whereas Mr Tyrell, thinking the same, didn't bother.' He unpacked some books and put them onto the bookcase. His back was to her – on purpose? – as he said, 'I know Mr Carson feels hard done by and I can't blame him. I sense you sympathise with him.' He turned to face her.

She leaned so far into the tea-chest, she almost fell in. 'Of course I sympathise. Who wouldn't? But I'm not on his side against you. I didn't altogether understand the situation to start with – not that it's any of my business.'

He stood with his hands on the edge of his tea-chest. 'I apologise if I've made you feel uncomfortable, but I don't wish there to be any misunderstanding between us.'

He smiled and it was impossible to feel awkward. She liked him – oh, not in *that* way. She just... liked him.

Tuesday: *Vera's Voice* day, and not only a fresh copy of the weekly periodical to enjoy, but also another thick envelope like that other one that had been sent to them from the magazine's offices. Another enquiry about pupil lodgers? Too late, of course, because they were now looking for local girls, but it was good to receive it even so – if that was what it was. Patience put it on the mantelpiece for Prudence to open that evening. Another letter came by the four o'clock delivery, in a neatly handwritten envelope of high quality. Was it too much to hope that they already had an application from a local girl?

She thrust the letters at Prudence almost the moment she walked in.

'You know we don't open the post until after tea,' said Prudence. 'But I think today should be an exception. Here: I'll have this one and you open that one.'

Patience waited while Prudence had first use of the letter-opener, then she slit open the envelope that had been entrusted to her. Hers was the local letter. Please let it be an application.

It was.

'It's from a Miss Wilhelmina Palmerston. Goodness, what a name. You'd have to be frightfully successful at whatever you did, with a name like that. She saw our advertisement and, oh,

Prudence, she wants to be a pupil lodger. Isn't that splendid? What about yours?'

'It was sent on by *Vera's Voice*, with a rather charming covering letter from the editor, a Mrs Newbold. Apparently, Mrs Brewer's series about surplus girls has generated a lot of interest and she has received a gratifying amount of correspondence.'

'Some of it has appeared on the letters page. And the letter she posted on to us?'

Prudence barely spared it a glance. 'From a Mrs Vivienne Atwood, a war widow living and working in London.' She dropped both letters on the table beside her armchair. 'What about Miss Palmerston? Does she look promising?' She took the letter and scanned it. 'Hm... address in Wilmslow: very nice... Clerical work in a voluntary capacity for a couple of charities... Wants to train properly and have a career.'

'She sounds ideal,' Patience ventured.

'But why lodge with us? Why not live at home?'

'It would be quite a trek for her to come just for night school.'

Prudence tilted her head from side to side in a sort of left-right nod. 'We'll ask her at her interview.'

'Good. I'll write to her after tea and pop out to the pillar-box before lessons. That will catch the ten o'clock collection and she'll receive it tomorrow. Should I invite her to come on Thursday?'

And then, after Miss Russell and Miss Dean went home this weekend, there would shortly be another girl to take their place. Perfect.

It was funny how you could change your mind about someone. Belinda liked Gabriel Linkworth. She liked the way he mucked in. Take yesterday. When she had arrived at the shop with her hair in a snood and a pinny in her bag, he had produced a warehouseman's coat and they had worked on the boxes all day. Not only that but they stopped for their tea-breaks together, sitting chatting in the chairs from the cottage.

And at dinner-time yesterday, when he had gone across the road to Richardson's to buy barm cakes, he had offered to get one for her as well, saying 'My treat' in such a casual way that there had been nothing inappropriate in it. It had almost been a shame to refuse, but Grandma Beattie had provided her with a slice of pork-and-apple pie.

Now, again, today, it was the same: another morning of working together, sorting through the boxes of books, shelving what there was room for and listing what had to be put back.

Mr Linkworth paused to glance through the window. 'Look at that sunshine. What do you say to a picnic in the rec?'

When he popped out to purchase his barm cakes, he bought a bottle of cordial as well.

'We need mugs,' he said, 'and don't forget the tablecloth. You can't have a picnic without a tablecloth. If the grass is damp, we'll spread it between us on a bench.'

The grass was dry. Mr Linkworth spread the cloth and they sat down. Belinda drew her shawl around her shoulders. The sun was bright but there was a snap in the air.

'Cold?' Mr Linkworth asked her. 'We can go back inside.'

She shook her head. There was a curious feeling of lightness inside her chest. It took her a moment to recognise it. This was fun. When was the last time she had had fun?

Afterwards they returned to the shop and were soon back at work.

'Latin grammar... Greek architecture...' Mr Linkworth lifted books from a box. 'Some rather handsome Anthony Trollopes... Oh, look, an illustrated guide to the flowers of the British Isles.' He flicked through the pages. 'These illustrations are beautiful. Do you have a favourite flower?'

'I always look forward to blossom in the springtime.'

'There's plenty of that around at the moment.'

'Do you have a favourite?' She didn't expect a yes. Women had favourite flowers, not men.

'Roses,' he said at once. 'I love roses. I adore their scent.' He closed the book. 'Perhaps my mother had roses in her garden.'

'Perhaps you were a gardener.'

'As a matter of fact,' he told her, 'I was a teacher. A games master, to be exact.'

He didn't look like a games master, but then what did games masters look like? And on second thoughts, maybe he did. The way he hefted those boxes around showed him to be strong and supple, and he had a way of running lightly up and down the stairs. Not like Richard, who had sat around much of the time, doing she knew not what.

'I used to work in a school,' she told him. 'I went half time when I was twelve, because we needed the money. Mum wanted to find me a job in a shop, but Dad came up with this school job. He knew someone who knew someone and that was how he heard of it.'

'What did you do?' Mr Linkworth had stopped to listen.

'Drudge. Did you have a drudge where you taught? It would have been all right in a nice school – topping up the inkwells, washing the slates on Fridays, mopping up after the little ones wet themselves – but I was in a rough place. The half-timers in the top class worked in the slaughterhouse in the afternoons: that's how rough it was. One of my duties was to stand outside each classroom in turn and if it sounded like the teacher was being murdered, I had to run for the headmaster. Once, he sent me for the police.'

'Sounds tough, especially on a young girl. After you left school, did you find a job elsewhere?'

She opened her mouth, then shut it. Had she really been about to say that, much as she had feared working at St Joseph's and been desperate for another job, Dad had made her stay; and she had been there until Auntie Enid had found her a place at the mill? As far as Dad was concerned, it wouldn't have bothered him if she had stayed at Holy Joe's to this day, as long as she handed over her wages.

The trouble with Gabriel Linkworth was he was too easy to talk to.

'I stayed for a while, then I went to work in the mill. You're lucky to have this.' She indicated the shop and its contents. 'Lots of people don't enjoy their jobs. They work because they have to. I'm lucky. I enjoyed the mill and I love it here.'

'I'm pleased to hear it, but you understand I can't make promises about the future. I don't know whether an assistant is needed or whether I'll be able to afford one.'

Afford one. Not *afford you*. Afford one. She bent her head over her work. It had been decent of him to keep her on at all. Was he warning her that, if he did require an assistant, the position wouldn't be hers?

Wilhelmina Palmerston was a stunner. Patience would have given half a dozen years of her life to have had looks like that when she was young. Miss Palmerston was tall and not thin, but willowy. Oh, to be willowy! Her hair was the colour of honey, her eyes almond-shaped, her complexion flawless. And her clothes! No wonder she was able to dabble in charity work, with a dress allowance like that. Her coat, currently hanging in their cloakroom, was a ruby-red wool of a softness that had made Patience want to snuggle it close to her face and there was a matching ruby-red flower attached to the side of her fashionable cloche hat. Her dress, with its stripes of soft brown and warm cream that melted into one another, had a large collar with fancy stitching; and her pointed-toed shoes were trimmed up the side with tiny buttons. She had arrived in a motor car that she had driven herself.

Patience showed her into the sitting room, where Prudence waited.

'I'm Prudence Hesketh, and this is my sister, Patience. How do you do? Thank you for coming at such short notice.'

'How do you do? I'm Wilhelmina Palmerston, but my friends call me Billie.'

'How nice for them. Do sit down, Miss Palmerston, and tell us about your voluntary work.'

Miss Palmerston folded her hands in her lap. Her upright figure was elegant, her carriage perfect. She talked confidently about writing thank-you letters for donations received. A lesser person might have said – Patience, in her position, might have said – 'That's the extent of my experience, I'm afraid. It probably doesn't seem much to you.'

'Do you write or typewrite these letters?' Prudence asked.

'A handwritten letter is so much more personal, don't you think?'

'While that is appropriate in the context of your charity work, it wouldn't be suitable in an office environment. Do you consider yourself to possess any office skills?'

'None at all, I'm afraid.' Miss Palmerston smiled disarmingly. 'That's why I wish to attend your business school. I – I find myself in a situation that requires me to earn a wage.'

Patience sat forward a little. Poor girl. She had clearly been brought up to better things.

'And why do you require lodgings?' Prudence asked bluntly. 'Why not simply attend our night school?'

'Well, the distance, you know. All the way here from Wilmslow and back again...'

They talked on for a while, Patience speaking in a soothing tone to show she was sympathetic to Miss Palmerston's plight, but when she expected Prudence to offer Miss Palmerston a place with them, Prudence merely thanked her for coming.

'We have some other young ladies to consider and we need to meet them before we make our decision. If we're unable to offer you a place as pupil lodger on this occasion, shall you wish to be added to our waiting list?'

Miss Palmerston blinked. 'I'm not sure. I rather thought... that is, I hoped...' The engaging smile reappeared, composure restored.

'Quite so,' said Prudence.

She rose. Patience and their visitor followed her lead. When Patience had seen Miss Palmerston out, she returned to the sitting room to find Prudence marching up and down, head bent in thought.

'Prudence, what's the matter?'

Prudence stopped. 'Our dear brother, that's what. We came this close,' she held a thumb and forefinger a breath apart, 'to having a spy in our midst.'

'Miss Palmerston?'

'Yes. Palmerston: don't you remember? That evening when Lawrence and Evelyn descended on us with that generous offer of a flat in Seymour Grove, they were en route to have dinner with their friends, the Palmerstons.'

Patience frowned. It rang a bell.

'It came back to me while we were talking. I knew there was something iffy about her, I *knew* it. That drivel about hand-written letters: a real applicant would have said something about wanting to learn to use a typewriter.'

'Now you mention it, she was vague about wanting to come here.' That hadn't happened before. All their girls, quietly, sometimes with a trembling lip, but always with dignity, had spoken of a dead fiancé, of being the breadwinner for a widowed mother, of pulling her weight in her brother's household now that their parents had passed away and she had had to move in with him and his family.

'She didn't know what to say about being added to our waiting list,' Prudence added. 'No one had coached her in that one, had they?'

'Do you really think that Lawrence...?'

'A spy in the camp, that's what he wanted.'

'We must write to Miss Palmerston and put her off.'

'Not immediately, though,' said Prudence. 'Give it a day or two. Let Lawrence stew.'

'That reminds me. I must write to Mrs Atwood.'

'Who?' said Prudence. 'Oh, the *Vera's Voice* enquiry. I put her letter behind the clock.'

Patience retrieved it. She cast her eye over it, then read it again. 'Prudence, did you read Mrs Atwood's letter?'

'She lives in London.'

'Didn't you read the rest of it?' Her pulse quickened with the first stirring of excitement. 'She's coming to live up here. She has a job with the new Board of Health – I haven't heard of that.'

'There are moves afoot to do away with the workhouses,' said Prudence. 'The new Boards of Health will gradually take on the responsibilities of the Boards of Guardians... assuming the Boards of Guardians can be prevailed upon to let go of the old ways.'

'Mrs Atwood is to take up her position towards the end of April.' She let out a huge breath. 'You realise what that means? She'll be out at work all day and come to night school.'

'Let me see.' Prudence read the letter. 'This is precisely what we were hoping for: a girl working locally, with a genuine reason for requiring lodgings. Mrs Atwood may have solved our problem.'

'You're going to court? Ruddy heck, our Bel! What have you been up to?' There was no censure in Thad's voice, just surprise and a healthy dose of admiration.

Belinda swung round, glaring at him across the bedroom, where she and Mum were squeezing a stack of ironed clothes into the chest of drawers.

'You shouldn't be listening,' she said.

'Come off it, Bel. Tell us what you've done. I never thought you had it in you.' Thad yelled over his shoulder, as if Jacob was up the other end of the road instead of sitting at the table, 'Hey, Jakey-boy, come and hear this. Our Bel's only got herself nicked by the police and she's up before the beak tomorrow.'

There was a scrambling sound, then Jacob bobbed up beside Thad, followed by Mikey. For once, Thad managed to be in close proximity with Mikey without attempting to throttle him.

'What have you done, Bel?' Jacob demanded. 'When I think of the times you've had a go at me and Thad—'

'I haven't done anything. I might be required as a witness, that's all.'

'A witness?'

'Witness to what?'

'A bank robbery?'

'A murder?'

'Was there loads of blood?'

'Just wait till I tell the lads at school.'

'There was no robbery and no murder and not so much as a speck of blood.' She had to raise her voice to make herself heard.

'Aye, and she hasn't done owt wrong neither,' said Mum, 'so don't you go telling everyone she has. Bel, these boys will have us the talk of the wash-house, just you wait.'

'No, they won't, because if they say anything, they'll end up looking like idiots.' Hands on hips, Belinda stared at Thad. 'You wouldn't want that, would you? If I'm called as a witness – and it's only an if – it'll be to describe how a man came into the bookshop and another man didn't recognise him, and that's all.'

'You what?' said Thad. 'That's stupid, that is.'

'Not as stupid as you'll look if you try to make something of it – but if you want to run round telling all and sundry, be my guest.'

Muttering, the boys melted away. Belinda shut the door on them.

'So go on,' said Mum. 'Why are you really going to court?'

'It's like I told the boys.'

'No, I don't mean what you said to them. I mean the real reason.'

'That is the real reason.'

'I thought you said it just to fob them off.'

'No, it's true. When Richard first saw Mr Linkworth, he didn't recognise him.'

'Richard? Is there summat you're not telling me, young lady?'

'Slip of the tongue.' She shoved the drawer closed. Was she blushing? 'I meant Mr Carson.'

'I should hope so.' Mum's voice was sharp. 'I wouldn't want to think there was anything untoward going on.'

'Keep your voice down.' She couldn't have the boys hearing that. Forget the blood and murder they had hoped for. They could do a lot more damage if they spread it round that their Bel was cosying up to her old boss.

'So you're to go to court in case you're needed to say that your old boss didn't recognise your new boss?'

'I don't suppose I'll be needed,' said Belinda. 'There's no doubt as to who Mr Linkworth is.'

'Then why does it need to go to court at all?'

'Because of the will. If Mr Carson wasn't named in the will, it might not matter, but because he started off thinking he was the heir, Mr Linkworth's solicitor wants to prove Mr Linkworth's identity beyond doubt and he wants Mr Carson there when he does it.'

'So he can't cause trouble in the future.'

'Something like that.' How could she ever have fancied herself in love with him? 'Have the boys found jobs yet?' Or was it too much to hope for? Mikey would have found a job if he could, if being Thad's brother didn't hold him back, but as for the other two...

'I don't know. I've got too much else to worry about.'

'If they brought some money in, that would ease the worry.'

'Don't go on at me, Bel. You don't know what it's like.'

'I've got this court matter tomorrow—'

'Ooh, hark at you. Very grand!'

'All I meant is that I'll be back on Saturday to see what the boys have done.' And clearly there would be no support from Mum on the subject. Oh well. 'I'll give you a hand to get started on the tea before I go. Where's Dad?' He couldn't be down the pub. It wasn't opening time.

'He's got a job.'

A job? Lay 'Em Out Layton had a job? It couldn't be one that required a character reference. Should she be pleased or worried?

'Where?' she asked. The mere fact that Mum had left it till now to mention it didn't bode well.

It came out on a whisper. 'At the Bucket of Blood.'

'The Bucket of Blood? Oh, Mum!'

Despair gushed through her, drying her mouth. The Bucket of Blood wasn't the pub's real name, but it was what everyone called it. It was a rough place with a violent reputation and only the most hardened characters drank there. Belinda had thought that clobbering his boss had been the lowest point of her father's increasingly dismal working life but, no, if he had been taken on at the Bucket of Blood, he had sunk yet further.

'I want you to fetch his wages,' said Mum. 'I made him promise to get Mr Reece to hand over half the money to me.'

'You want me to go to the Bucket of Blood?'

'It's the only way them wages will make their way home. Your dad 'ull drink 'em otherwise or else gamble 'em away.'

Belinda had heard the rumours. Hadn't everyone? Mr Reece used to be a prize-fighter and it was said he now organised bare-knuckle fights in the pub yard in the dead of night. The word was that the police stayed well away.

'Mum, I can't. It's a rotten area. If I'm seen there, a girl on her own, people will think... y'know.'

'Take our Thad with you,' Mum urged.

'Thad? Don't be daft. I know he's a thug, but he's only a kid when all's said and done.'

'I have to have that money, Bel, and who else is there to fetch it?'

Belinda felt a sour ache in the back of her throat. She was the one who had told George to stay away. She was the one who had declared she would sort things out.

'We'll go together,' she said.

Mum's face blanched. 'I can't go there.'

She clenched her hands as annoyance flared. 'What, you can't, but I can? I'm not going alone.'

She bundled Mum into her hat and coat and hustled her out of the house, linking arms with her and hurrying through the streets. Did they look guilty? Ashamed? Did they look like they were headed for the dark, rank, disease-ridden streets where only the desperate and most hardened lived? Beneath the sheen of wariness, a mixture of anger and humiliation bubbled in her stomach. What sort of husband and father was Dad to reduce them to this?

'You're late home, love. Everything all right?' Grandma Beattie asked as Belinda unlatched the door and walked in.

'I'm sorry. I had to go somewhere with Mum.'

'Well, if you had to be late, you chose the best day,' said Grandma Beattie. 'It's poached eggs, so I weren't going to start them until you got home, anyroad.'

'How are things at your mum's?' asked Auntie Enid.

She turned away to hang up her shawl. She had practised a pleasant, non-committal expression as she walked up the lane. She turned to face them.

'Oh, you know. Mum's in a fret about money but Dad's picked up a few hours' work. Thad and Mikey managed to stand beside one another without war breaking out. Wonders will never cease.'

'Were your Sarah there?' asked Auntie Enid.

'No, she's working till eleven.'

'We wanted to have a word about Sarah,' said Grandma Beattie. 'We've had an idea, haven't we, Mrs Sloan?'

'Aye. We don't want to speak out of turn about your family, but things are hard for your mum, with your dad out of work. Even if he's found a few hours, that's just casual, not like having a proper job.'

'And with all of them crushed into two rooms an' all,' Grandma Beattie added.

'And you said there's no room for your Sarah in the bedroom, which can't be easy on a lass.'

Belinda swallowed a cold lump of humiliation. Yes, her family's circumstances weren't anything to be proud of, but did they have to spell it out?

'So we'd like to offer your Sarah a home here with us,' said Auntie Enid. 'It'd be a squeeze, especially for you, sharing that single bed, but she does work them odd hours, so you'd both get the bed to yourselves sometimes.'

'It'd be easier on your mum,' said Grandma Beattie, 'one less mouth to feed.'

'And Sarah would have a bit of privacy away from those lads.' Auntie Enid's mouth set in a thin line. 'Her having to dress and undress in the kitchen-sitting room: it's not nice.'

'So we're offering to have her here.' Grandma Beattie made it sound like they were offering Belinda the greatest gift of all. 'What do you think? We won't do it if you don't want it.'

What did she think? She stared at their expectant expressions. It was a generous and considerate offer and Sarah would leap at it. She wanted to hug them and laugh and cry and thank them from the bottom of her heart for their kindness in offering her sister a stable and appropriate home.

But…

But if she said yes, wouldn't it make her more beholden to them just when she was trying to establish a measure of independence from their life of mourning?

Chapter Twenty-Three

FRIDAY IS THE last day of March. Tomorrow, April Fool's Day, might be a more appropriate day for my court hearing. I'm going to have a job not to look foolish, I'm sure. Mr Sowerby has told me that witnesses have been lined up to prove who I am. By the close of proceedings, I'll be the only person who won't know for certain. My head knows I am Gabriel Linkworth. By the end of this court case, presumably my head will know it even more so, after the witnesses have done their bit.

But will my heart know?

Will listening to the witnesses saying whatever they say make me know who I am?

I enter the offices of Winterton, Sowerby and Jenks in Rosemount Place. Mr Turton greets me with a handshake. He has a cool, no-nonsense manner that he adopts when dealing with the likes of Richard Carson, but when it is just him and me, his natural friendliness shines through. He once mentioned his family in passing and I sense he is a devoted family man.

Mr Sowerby is on his way downstairs, looking magnificent in a black wool overcoat with a carnation in his buttonhole, and a silk top hat. He is not a young man. He must have been wearing a topper all his professional life. I imagine younger colleagues consider themselves appropriately dressed in a bowler.

We walk to the magistrates' courts. The foyer is lofty, the expanse of floor tiled; there is a wide staircase with shallow treads. We head upstairs and walk along a couple of corridors.

A clerk greets us and shows us into – a room.

'Oh,' I say. 'I was expecting a courtroom.'

'There's no need for one,' Mr Sowerby says. 'The matter in question isn't in question at all. Your identity is a certain thing. We merely need to prove it with bells on, so that Mr Richard Carson will understand that he has no means of challenging the will.'

'Has he attempted to challenge it?'

'No, but when he met you, he claimed not to recognise you, which might or might not have been the truth. Either way, as the usurped heir, as it were, he needs to have your identity made crystal-clear to him, to the world in general, and, most importantly, to the court.'

In other words, he needs to have his nose rubbed in it.

'He believed himself to be the heir for some considerable time, and Mr Tyrell must have believed it too,' I observe. 'I wonder if I should offer him a share.'

Mr Sowerby looks straight into my face. 'Mr Linkworth, please do not say or do anything that gives Mr Carson the smallest hold on the late Mr Tyrell's estate. It is my professional opinion that Carson is a slippery customer. This is the man who commenced the sale of his uncle's goods without waiting for probate. I strongly suggest you make no concessions.'

Well, that's put me in my place.

There is a large desk in front of a wall lined with shelves of leather-bound books. Behind the desk is a handsome shield-backed chair. Beside the desk, presumably where the witnesses will sit, is a plain wooden chair that wouldn't be out of place in any decent kitchen.

Mr Turton stands at a table on the other side of the room. He places his briefcase on it and starts removing papers. There are three chairs. He glances up and signals to me: this is where he, Mr Sowerby and I are to sit.

Other chairs have been set out, but no other table. Of course not: my identity is not in question. Carson does not merit a table of his own.

The clerk walks in and gives Mr Sowerby a sheet of paper. Sowerby glances at it.

'All the witnesses have arrived,' he says. 'I've decided not to call Miss Layton, but the magistrate may wish to ask her a question or two.'

'Does she have to wait outside with the other witnesses?' I ask.

'No. It is the people who are here to contribute to the issue of your identification who have to remain outside until they're called.'

'Then let's ask her to come in. As first Mr Carson's employee, and now mine, she has a vested interest in this matter.'

Miss Layton is shown into the room by the clerk. Yesterday I gave her the money for her bus fare. Expenses, I called it, wishing I could have given her the money for a taxi; wishing I could have collected her from home and escorted her.

I don't know what she makes of being asked to attend. Her manner towards me has softened, I know that; and I know she now understands that I have not stolen Carson's inheritance. But I cannot forget the radiance in her expression when she looked at him. If she is called upon to describe our first meeting, will she feel she's being made to speak against him?

Talk of the devil. In he walks. Pausing to glance about, he looks confident, untroubled. He hangs his trilby on the hatstand and takes a seat, peeling off his gloves. He looks well turned out and (dammit) handsome.

Dr Jennings enters the room. I rise to shake hands before introducing him to Messrs Sowerby and Turton. Handshakes all round.

'Are you a witness?' I ask.

'Not necessarily,' he tells me. 'Only if the magistrate wishes to ask questions about your loss of memory.'

'Dr Jennings and I have been in correspondence,' says Mr Sowerby. 'He has advised me not to divulge to you the identities of the witnesses. He hopes—'

'I know what he hopes,' I say.

Jennings smiles wryly. 'You never know.'

There it is: that spark of hope. I crush it. It can lead only to disappointment.

'But you're permitted to know who the first witness is,' says Mr Sowerby, 'since he is unknown to you. Chap named Hardy, a handwriting expert.'

There is no time for more. The magistrate walks in and takes his place. I had expected iron-grey hair and whiskers, an old fuddy-duddy. This fellow won't see fifty for a few years yet and his bright eyes and ruddy cheeks give the impression he has marched five miles in the spring sunshine to get here.

'Good morning.' He addresses the room. 'My name is Sturgeon and I'll be hearing this matter. We're here to establish formally the identity of Gabriel James Linkworth. Mr Sowerby, have you any opening remarks?'

'No, sir. I'm happy for the first witness to be invited.'

Mr Eric Hardy is announced. This is the handwriting wallah. Mr Sturgeon asks him questions. They talk about upward strokes and downward strokes, closed and open loops, casual and formal capitals. Mr Sturgeon might look as if he is going to sprint out of here at the close of proceedings and swim twenty lengths before lunch, but he has clearly prepared for today.

At a nod from Sturgeon, Mr Sowerby comes to his feet.

'Mr Hardy, you were provided with two letters and asked to perform a comparison. Please can you inform us of your findings.'

'What letters?' I whisper to Mr Turton, my eyes on Mr Hardy.

'One that you wrote to Mr Sowerby; and one you wrote some years ago, before the war.'

My head snaps round. Turton keeps his gaze fixed on Mr Hardy.

'What letter?'

And how the hell did they get their hands on it? My gaze meets Carson's. For one moment we look at one another, then his glance flicks aside, back to Mr Hardy, who is busy answering questions I haven't listened to. I feel at a disadvantage. The feeling builds up, a robust mixture of impotence and anger and – yes, fear. It is not an unknown feeling – ask anyone who has complete memory loss – but I have never experienced it so strongly before. All these bloody people who know about me; and I don't know a single damn thing.

What letter?

Mr Hardy stands up. Mr Sturgeon thanks him. I have missed everything he said. He quits the room, the clerk holding the door open for him.

Mr Sturgeon looks at me. 'I've been requested not to call for the remaining witnesses by name. Is this acceptable to you, Mr Linkworth?'

Is it? I don't know. The room contains only Messrs Sturgeon, Sowerby, Turton, Carson and myself, plus Miss Layton and a couple of clerks, but I feel as if a thousand eyes are on me; and they will remain fixed on me when the door opens for the next witness to be admitted.

Impotence, anger and fear.

'Fine by me,' I say.

Mr Sturgeon signals to the clerk. He opens the door and nods to someone outside. A woman appears in the doorway. Tallish, with a thin face. She looks at me and gasps audibly. Her eyes fill with tears. The clerk indicates the wooden chair and she sits down, her gaze swinging straight back to me. She presses her lips together as she delves in her handbag and produces a hanky. She sniffs discreetly into it and clears her throat.

Mr Sturgeon looks at me. Everyone looks at me: I can feel it.

Sturgeon turns to the woman. 'You are Mrs Irene Rawlins?'

'Yes, sir.' It is barely above a whisper.

'A little louder, if you please, madam. It is important everyone can hear you clearly.'

'Yes, sir.' Louder this time.

'Can you please tell me how you are related to Mr Gabriel Linkworth?'

'We're first cousins, sir. His father and my mother were brother and sister. I've known Gabe all my life.'

Gabe?

'I believe I already know the answer to this from seeing your reaction, but I must ask you nevertheless. Do you recognise the gentleman seated in the middle there?'

A whoosh of breath escapes her. Her face lights up. 'Oh yes, sir. That's him, that's my cousin Gabriel Linkworth. I thought you were dead,' she says to me. 'We all thought you were dead.'

Mr Sturgeon clears his throat, drawing eyes to him. 'Thank you, Mrs Rawlins. I realise this has been an emotional experience for you. The clerk will show you out.'

She rises to her feet, throwing me a tremulous smile before she leaves. I swivel in my seat to face Mr Sowerby.

'I want to know who the other witnesses are and I want to meet them before they walk in here.'

Sowerby doesn't look at me. He comes to his feet and addresses Mr Sturgeon.

'Might I have a word with Mr Linkworth in private?'

'I'll allow you five minutes.' Mr Sturgeon leaves the room.

I follow Sowerby out. Turton and Jennings come too.

'This plan for me to be jolted into recognising people has gone far enough. I want to meet the other witnesses. There's no reason why we should be kept apart in advance, is there?'

'Only for the purpose of awakening your memory,' says Jennings.

'If my memory is going to wake up, it can do it in a private room.' I'm sick of being at a disadvantage. I live my whole life at a disadvantage.

'The next witness is your old CO.' Sowerby is brisk. 'Do you wish to meet him?'

'No, I was thinking more of... what you might call personal witnesses.' I see the looks that pass between the three of them. 'You saw how hard that was for my cousin.'

'Very well.' It is Jennings who steps in. 'But there isn't time now. We'll ensure you meet the final witness in advance, you have my word, but please don't ask who it is at this stage. Please let the meeting involve no prior knowledge on your part.'

'You never give up, do you?' I turn to Mr Turton. 'Please find my cousin and take her somewhere quiet.'

'Of course,' he says. 'I'll make sure she has a cup of tea and I'll remain with her while she composes herself.'

'Thank you. Don't let her leave. Tell her I want to see her when this is over.'

He nods. I know Cousin Irene will be in good hands.

Jennings, Sowerby and I return to the magistrate's room. Mr Sturgeon comes in and takes his seat. Dumping his elbows on the desk, he clasps his hands and looks expectantly at Sowerby.

'Are you ready to proceed?'

'By all means, sir. The next witness is Mr Linkworth's former commanding officer...'

My heart is still jumping from the business with Cousin Irene. I must ensure she goes home knowing that her inheritance from my father is safe and I shan't chase her for it. Most of all, I live again the moment when she smiled at me; that breathless dazzle of amazement and joy in her face. She didn't just recognise me – she was thrilled to see me. I feel as if I have run a victory lap in front of cheering crowds.

When he rises to leave, I realise I have barely attended to the evidence of my former CO. Who is the other personal witness I am to meet?

Mr Sturgeon waits for the door to close. 'We'll stop for now and resume after lunch.' He says it as if it is a suggestion he hopes everyone will find convenient. A quick nod to the room and he departs.

I catch Miss Layton's eye before I speak to Mr Sowerby. 'I'll find somewhere to take Miss Layton for lunch. I don't want to leave her high and dry. I also need to see my cousin—'

'First of all, there is someone you should meet.'

I sense a new alertness in Dr Jennings. My senses spring to attention. I signal to Miss Layton to accompany us and we leave the room. We stand in the anteroom; Mr Sowerby waits until Carson has walked past us and left. He glances at Miss Layton, then sends a look of enquiry my way.

'Miss Layton may stay,' I tell him.

'If you will kindly wait here, Mr Linkworth,' says Sowerby.

He leaves the room. The air is heavy with anticipation.

The door opens and Mr Sowerby ushers a lady inside. Yes, a lady. Roughly my own age, she is beautifully dressed in a blue costume with a dashing indigo feather in her hat. She walks towards me. How beautiful she is, how graceful. Yet when she comes closer, I can see the marks of strain about her lovely face; tiny lines etched at the corners of her mouth; and crow's feet: not laughter-lines, but lines of sadness. Her eyes are brown, warm but wary; they seem to gaze deep inside me. I am supposed to know her. It hurts her that I do not. She knows me. That is evident. I stretch into myself, into my mind, trying to find the memory of her, the knowledge she wants me to have – but it isn't there.

And then she comes closer still and – there it is! That scent. Sweet but sophisticated. A light fragrance with heady depths.

I smile at her. I can't help it. I smile so little in this new life. I have so few reasons to smile, other than out of politeness.

'Do you know me?' Her voice trembles. 'Do you remember me, Gabriel?'

In the troubled warmth of her brown eyes, I see how much it matters.

My smile widens. My face seems to crack open. There is lightness inside my chest. I know that later I will be consumed by frustration at my lack of memory, but here, now, right this moment, with this beautiful creature standing in front of me, willing me to know her, and with her fragrance teasing me and enfolding me, I am... happy. Yes, happy.

My senses are consumed by her perfume. Certainty radiates through my entire body.

'I know you,' I tell her. 'You are the scent of roses.'

Richard strode away from the magistrates' courts in search of a meal. Why couldn't the whole bally matter have been dealt with before lunch? Yes, all right, so Linkworth really was who he said he was – or rather, who everybody else said he was. He wasn't capable of saying whether he was Gabriel Linkworth, the court jester or the governor of the Bank of England. Richard wasn't trying to claim he wasn't Linkworth. Yes, he had 'failed' to recognise him that first time, but what of it? Any fellow would have done the same. Christ, what idiot would leap forward to shake the hand of the man whose return from the grave would overturn all his own long-held hopes and expectations?

But old Sowerby had insisted on dragging Richard here to listen politely while a hundred and one witnesses trailed in to establish Linkworth's identity. And there were yet more witnesses to come this afternoon. All Richard wanted was to state his own case.

God, what a mess. He still hadn't told his colleagues in the office that his good fortune had crumbled to dust, though he would have to soon. Why climb down before you were forced to? Bloody hell. All his hopes and expectations.

But he still had his own case to make. He had clawed back all the boxes of Aunt Victoria's treasures and as many of the sold books as he could – or Miss Layton had. Her efforts should make him look good. Cooperative. Disposed to do the decent thing. Sturgeon should look on him with an accommodating eye. After all, he wasn't about to ask for anything unreasonable.

He ate some chops and mashed potato at a dark corner table, then went for a brisk walk. At last it was time to resume his seat in the magistrate's room. The others were already there.

Mr Sturgeon came in and took his place. 'I believe we have one more witness.'

Mr Sowerby rose. 'That's correct, sir. I should like to ask Mrs Naomi Reed to join us.'

Old family retainer? The shopkeeper who sold him gobstoppers when he was a nipper with scabby knees? Please not another dewy-eyed cousin with trembling lips and a wobble in her voice.

The clerk opened the door and Richard sat up straighter as a beautiful creature dressed in blue entered the room. Crikey! What a peach! The clerk, who had merely waved the previous witnesses in the direction of the chair, escorted Mrs Naomi Reed to it.

Mrs Reed lifted her head and the feather in her hat shimmered.

'My name is Sturgeon,' said the magistrate. 'I'm in charge of these proceedings. Could you please confirm your name and address.'

'Certainly.' She gave her name and an address in the Lake District.

'Is the gentleman over there known to you, Mrs Reed?'

'Yes, sir. He is Gabriel Linkworth.'

'And in what capacity do you know Mr Linkworth?'

She looked directly at Linkworth, almost as if expecting him to answer on her behalf. Then she turned her face towards Sturgeon.

'Mr Linkworth... Gabriel and I... were once engaged to be married.'

Richard sat up straighter, aware of Miss Layton doing the same close by.

'This was some years ago, before the war.' Mrs Reed spoke softly. 'Shortly before the war ended, he was posted missing presumed dead.'

And she had married another man. Richard could almost believe her situation was worse than his own – almost. But just look at that rig-out and those amethysts: Mrs Reed had undoubtedly done well for herself out of her disappointment.

'Thank you, Mrs Reed,' said Sturgeon. 'And thank you for coming all this way.'

She looked at Linkworth. 'Of course I came.'

Ooh, interesting. Did she still carry a torch? And Linkworth, poor sap, presumably couldn't remember her. What a waste. And where was Mr Reed? Lurking outside, ready to spirit his lovely wife back to the Lakes, both of them gallantly pretending she wasn't heartbroken all over again?

Mrs Reed was shown out and Mr Sturgeon addressed Linkworth's solicitor.

'I believe Mrs Reed was your final witness. In that case, I will confer with the clerk of the court and then I will state my findings.'

He and the clerk conversed in low voices. It didn't take long.

'It is my belief,' Sturgeon announced, 'that it has been shown beyond all doubt that this gentleman is Gabriel Linkworth. I should like to place on record my thanks to the witnesses and I declare this matter closed.'

This was his moment. Richard came to his feet.

'Pardon me, sir. May I speak?'

'You surely don't intend to dispute Mr Linkworth's identity?' Mr Sowerby exclaimed.

It gave him a certain satisfaction to say, 'No, sir, I do not,' and see the flicker of uncertainty that crossed the other men's faces. 'I should like to lodge a claim, not on my uncle's estate, but against Mr Linkworth personally. As my uncle's sole heir, he stands to gain substantially from my own investment in my uncle's property. I believe that money should be reimbursed to me.'

Sensation, as they used to say in Victorian novels of a certain kind. There was a sharp intake of breath around the room.

'Preposterous!' exclaimed Sowerby. 'Mr Sturgeon, this fellow,' and coming from an old boy of such dignity, *fellow* was an insult, 'has already attempted to muddy the waters by claiming not to recognise Mr Linkworth at their first meeting.'

'I didn't recognise him.' Richard spoke calmly. 'Why should I? The one and only occasion we came across one another prior to that was at our aunt's funeral.'

'Mr Carson,' said Mr Sturgeon, 'if you wish to make a claim on your uncle's will, this is not the forum in which to do so.'

'I have already stated that I don't wish to do that. The will leaves everything to Linkworth. I freely admit I never expected him to turn up and claim the inheritance – and for that matter, neither did my late uncle – but here he is and my uncle's goods and chattels now belong to him. My claim is against Mr Linkworth personally.'

Sowerby inflated like a bullfrog. 'I suggest, Mr Carson, that you instruct your solicitor and I will await his letter.'

'I'd prefer to raise the matter now, if Mr Sturgeon has no objection. After all, I've just sat through all of your evidence – evidence which was unnecessary in my view, given that I have never attempted to contest the will on the grounds of mistaken identity. I've done you the courtesy of paying attention: now I ask the same of you. May I have my turn, Mr Sturgeon?'

He felt relaxed and sure of himself, the more so when he observed the discomfort in the faces of Sowerby et al. Would

Sturgeon permit him to speak? It would give his case greater impact.

The clerk was at Sturgeon's side. A quiet conversation ensued. Sturgeon nodded and the clerk stepped away.

'Mr Carson, you understand I have no authority in this matter, but I believe it's in Mr Linkworth's interests as well as your own to have this matter out in the open so it can be dealt with as soon as possible. Do you object, Mr Sowerby?'

What could the old codger say after that except, 'No'? The look on his face suggested a severe bout of indigestion.

'Very well,' said Sturgeon. 'Say your piece, Mr Carson.'

Richard surveyed the faces that were turned his way. He didn't care if he appeared smug. He ruddy well deserved to be smug.

'I make no claim on the books in the shop or on the furniture and what-have-you in the cottage; but I have a serious claim on the cottage itself. In recent years, I've had work done on it, partly to do my best for my late uncle and partly – I admit it freely to save Mr Sowerby the bother of admitting it on my behalf – partly because I saw it as an investment. I believed Gabriel Linkworth to be dead; as did my uncle. I believed the cottage would one day be mine; as did my uncle. In this belief and expectation, I organised repairs and improvements to the property. I now respectfully request that Mr Linkworth reimburses me for my lost investment.'

'Do you have paperwork, invoices and such, to support your claim?' Sowerby demanded.

'Indeed I do.' So you can take that snooty look off your face, old man. 'In fact, I can do better than that. I've written to the various tradesmen who did the work, asking them to confirm that I'm the person they dealt with. I have their replies here.'

'If I might—' Sowerby began.

'I'm happy to show these letters to Mr Sturgeon and to this gentleman,' he indicated the clerk, 'but I'd prefer not to hand them over to Mr Linkworth's solicitor at this stage. Mr Sowerby himself advised me to instruct my own man. Until I have done so, it would be inadvisable for me to make the documentation available to Mr Linkworth's solicitor. Isn't that so, Mr Sowerby?'

The clerk came to him for the pieces of paper.

'Before you see them, Mr Sturgeon, I should explain that I wrote to each tradesman asking him to confirm that I was the one who made all the arrangements for each piece of work to be done. In my letters, I said there was no need to write back at length, but that a brief confirmation, signed and dated, on my own letter would be sufficient. I hoped that by making it straightforward to reply, I would be rewarded by swift responses.'

Magistrate and clerk looked over the papers, then Sturgeon addressed Linkworth and his legal lackeys.

'It is as Mr Carson says. Each letter is addressed to a tradesman with a request to confirm that certain specified work at Mr Tyrell's cottage in Limits Lane was organised by Mr Richard Carson; together with dates and costs incurred; and each tradesman has written *That is so* or *Agreed* against the details and signed and dated it.'

'If I might have the letters back, please.' Before anyone looked at them too closely. 'Thank you.'

'Do I take it,' asked Linkworth, 'that you were responsible for the new water pump that replaced the old well?'

'Indeed. Also the new cords in the sash windows; and the new compact kitchen range that replaced the old Victorian monstrosity. I also had the outside of the building repointed and painted and I had boards laid in the attic, which not only make it possible to store things up there but also keeps the cottage warmer in winter.'

He savoured the moment. He had outwitted Mr Sowerby; but he didn't waste his time looking at the solicitor. He fixed his gaze on Gabriel sodding Linkworth. Now you see how it feels to lose something, matey. He didn't gloat – well, he did, but only on the inside. Outwardly he was civil and pleasant.

'I've totted up the account of expenditure for you, Linkworth, though I don't have it with me. Would you like me to post it to you or should I send it to your solicitor?'

What was the right thing to do? It didn't feel polite to get up and walk out. Belinda opened her handbag and pretended to search through it. Not that anyone was watching her. Mr Sturgeon and the clerks had gone and Richard also had departed, leaving Mr Linkworth and the two legal gentlemen huddled together. The other gentleman, the doctor from down south, had excused himself and left.

Being here today hadn't been a comfortable experience. No one had looked down on her or anything like that – no one had really noticed her at all – but there was nothing quite like being in a smart, official room with well-dressed, well-spoken gentlemen to make you tingle with awareness of your simple shawl and your working-class origins.

Well, there was nothing to be gained by sitting here like a lemon. Rising, she drew her shawl around her shoulders. Part of her hoped to be noticed so she could say a polite goodbye; another part wanted to slip out unseen. The three men were deep in conversation. She made for the door.

'Miss Layton, are you leaving?'

Drat. Now she looked rude for not saying goodbye. She turned, faking a smile. 'I'm not needed here, am I, Mr Linkworth?'

He crossed the room to join her. His smile was kindly but his eyes were grave. 'I hope you haven't been bored.'

'Not in the slightest. It's been very interesting.' Especially the bit with the ex-fiancée.

'If you don't mind waiting while I finish with Mr Sowerby, I'll walk you to your bus stop. I won't be coming back to the shop. I want to spend the rest of the day getting to know my cousin.' His smile softened his hazel eyes into a colour approaching caramel.

She warmed to him. 'I'll wait out there for you.'

He opened the door for her. As she walked into the ante-room, a figure rose from a chair on the opposite side – Mrs Reed. She stood motionless, looking straight past Belinda. Behind her, in the doorway, Belinda sensed complete stillness. Ought she to duck out of the way? But her presence was imma-terial: she might feel like piggy-in-the-middle, but to these two people, she was invisible.

Mrs Reed came forward. There was a table in the centre of the room. It looked as if she might walk into it, or possibly through it, like a ghost, but, without a glance, she skirted round it, her gaze on Mr Linkworth. She halted. Her face was pale, but there was a hectic slash of colour across her cheekbones.

'I wanted to see you before I leave,' she said.

Belinda silently stepped aside. Mrs Reed wore a pretty perfume, light with an underlying warmth, floral – roses.

'Thank you for coming,' said Mr Linkworth and Belinda felt like slapping him. Thank you for coming? He had been engaged to this woman, for pity's sake. She deserved more than that; and yet, if he honestly didn't remember her, what more was there for him to say? Especially as she was now the wife of another man.

'Of course I came.' It was what she had said in the magis-trate's room. Did she still love him? 'The letter – the old letter from before the war, that was used as evidence...'

Realisation flickered in his face. 'One I wrote to you.'

'Yes.' The word was so soft, it was almost a sigh.

A love letter? Did her husband know she had kept Gabriel Linkworth's love letters?

Mr Linkworth shook his head. 'I feel I ought to apologise for not remembering.'

'It's hardly your fault you lost your memory.' She sounded sensible, but there was pain in her eyes.

Across the room, the door opened. 'I believe you'll find her in here, sir,' said a clerk as a gentleman entered. He was smartly dressed and had that confident air the well-to-do were born with.

'Naomi, there you are. They tell me the matter is finished. Are you ready to go?'

Belinda's lips parted on a minuscule intake of breath. The man she married when the fiancé she loved didn't come home. Did she now love her husband?

Mrs Reed turned to him. 'Mason – yes, I'm ready. Let me introduce you to Gabriel Linkworth, the... the man I came here to identify. Mr Linkworth' – and she blushed: was it difficult not to use his first name? – 'this is my husband, Mason Reed.'

Mr Reed strode across as if the room belonged to him, and shook hands. 'How do you do? I was sorry to hear of the trouble you're having with your memory. I hope today's case will help you get on with your life. Now, if you'll excuse us, we have a train to catch.'

To Mrs Reed, Mr Linkworth said, 'Thank you – again.' He bowed his head to her, making no attempt to shake hands, but she offered hers and he took it. Then he raised it to his lips and dropped a kiss on her fingers.

Belinda's heart swelled with indignation. The inside of her chest burned.

She did like Gabriel Linkworth in *that* way after all.

Chapter Twenty-Four

BELINDA DIDN'T SLEEP. Hell's bells, how had this happened? It was barely five minutes since she had been in thrall to Richard Carson and now her heart was beating faster at the thought of Gabriel Linkworth. But it was different this time. She hadn't really loved Richard. Perhaps she had been in love with the idea of being in love. The recent changes in her life together with her first taste of independence had left her susceptible to his good looks and easy smile. Thank goodness she had kept her pash a secret.

It wasn't like that with Gabriel. Far from being dazzled at first sight, she had gradually learned to like and respect him. After being deliberately put off him by Richard, she had found out for herself that he was a decent man, who treated others with honesty and consideration. There was, whatever Richard had tried to make her believe, nothing underhand in the way he had come into his inheritance. And then there was the way he had given up his claim to his father's money, so as to leave it with Mrs Rawlins, who needed it. Would Richard have done that in his position? Not likely. Richard had been so keen to get his hands on his inheritance that he had ignored the proper procedure and hadn't waited for probate.

But Gabriel was kind, hard-working and searingly honest about the difficulty of living without his memory.

Was she falling in love with him?

Oh, this was ridiculous. She twitched over onto her other side. If she could get comfortable, she might fall asleep. Some hope. Her mind was wide awake, as were her senses. Naomi Reed's perfume was lodged in her nostrils. Could Gabriel smell it as well? Was he lying awake at this moment, tortured by thoughts of the woman who ought to have been Naomi Linkworth?

She swung out of bed and planted her feet on the floor. Might as well get up and make a start downstairs. She poured water from her jug into the china bowl. Would Sarah soon be sharing this room with her? She wanted the best for Sarah, she truly did. She loved her sister and enjoyed her company, regarding her as a friend. But having her here in End Cottage, while it might be best for Sarah, didn't feel like the best thing for herself. What might it do to her chances of having some independence? She already owed Auntie Enid and Grandma Beattie so much on her own account. She didn't want to owe them on Sarah's account as well. Was that ungrateful of her? Selfish?

She raked out the ashes, scooping them into the dustpan before hurrying outside to pour them into the box of earth and ashes they used to keep down the smell in the earth-closet. It was a fine morning, bright and cool. She wouldn't see Gabriel again until Monday. All these weeks she had rejoiced in not working on Saturdays, and now she would gladly go to the shop today. Not that she would be able to, even if that option was open to her. She must get the boys sorted out.

Would they have found work for themselves? Mikey would have, assuming anyone would take Thad Layton's brother. Would Thad have made an effort? She doubted it. Let alone he had a dodgy reputation, she could imagine him digging his heels in simply because it was her doing the asking. As for Jacob, he would copy Thad, more's the pity. He would do better to follow in Mikey's footsteps.

Grandma Beattie came downstairs, delighted to find the early morning jobs – raking out and making up the range, polishing the boots and cleaning the step – had already been attended to. Auntie Enid followed a minute later.

'Sit down,' said Belinda. 'I've made eggy bread.'

'That'll stick to us ribs,' said Grandma Beattie approvingly.

'Are you going to the library this morning?' asked Auntie Enid.

'Yes, then I'm going round to Mum's. I told the boys they have to get jobs.'

'Aye, it's hard when the breadwinner is out of work.'

'Maybe the place that gave your dad a few hours will tek him on properly,' said Grandma Beattie.

Full time at the Bucket of Blood? Mum would die of shame and Belinda wouldn't be far behind.

'Will you be seeing your Sarah this morning?' asked Auntie Enid.

'I don't know. She might be at work.' At least she hoped so. Anything to postpone having to make the offer of a new home. She was a rotten sister as well as a rotten daughter- and granddaughter-in-law.

After breakfast she washed up, then set off to change her library books before going to Cromwell Street to tackle the boys. As she stepped through the empty gateway, a movement at the window drew her eye; and just before she reached the front door, it was thrown open and Thad practically knocked her off her feet as he barged past, followed by a whooping Jacob. Belinda staggered but snatched hold of Jacob's collar, jerking him to a halt. He wriggled but she held on with both hands.

'Thad!' he yelled.

Thad was halfway up the road. He stopped and turned, roaring with laughter at the sight, then he was on his way again.

'He's not going to rescue you.' Belinda gave Jacob a shake. 'That shows what he thinks of you.'

She pushed him inside. Muttering rude comments, Jacob slouched into their kitchen-sitting room; Belinda stayed right behind him in case he intended to make a dash for freedom. Dad was in the armchair as usual; Mum was drooping over the range.

'Mr Harvey gave me a reference,' said Mikey, 'but it hasn't made any odds. I've been after a couple of half-time jobs, but they were given to boys whose brothers haven't gone to the bad.'

'Don't talk about our Thad like that,' said Jacob.

'Shut it, pipsqueak,' Mikey retorted. 'Thad isn't here to protect you now.'

'No fighting: I haven't got time,' said Belinda. 'I said if you didn't get jobs, I'd do it for you.'

'Not for me, you won't,' said Jacob.

She swung round to confront him. 'Grow up, Jacob. This family is in trouble. Dad hasn't got regular work any more. There's what he can bring in, plus what Sarah, George and I cough up. Give me one good reason why I should help support a snotty little brat like you.'

'Because it's your duty, miss, that's why,' said Dad. 'I let you move out and live with them Sloan women, but that doesn't mean you aren't obligated to your family no more.'

'See,' Jacob sneered in exactly the way Thad would have done.

Thanks for the support, Dad. 'Jacob, listen. There's less money coming in. The rent has to be paid without delay, so that means other things have to be cut back. Do you fancy having less to eat because there's not enough money?'

'I'm not having less on my plate, I can tell you that for nothing,' Dad blustered. 'I'm the breadwinner and I'm entitled.'

Belinda raised her eyebrows at Jacob. 'There are kids in your class who sit at the table and watch their dad eating the one proper meal there is. Do you want to be one of them? If not, you need to help out.'

Mum looked round. 'What a thing to say, our Bel. We're not like that. We may have come down in the world compared to where we once were, but we're nowhere near that low. How dare you?'

Belinda closed her eyes. How was she supposed to make Jacob fall into line if their parents undermined everything she said? She opened her eyes. Jacob was about to speak, but she beat him to it.

'If Thad's name crosses your lips, so help me, I'll clock you one. You're a sheep, Jacob Layton, and you've made a poor choice of who to follow. Now put your cap on and come with me. You too, Mikey, and bring your letter from Mr Harvey.'

Ten minutes later, they were outside the newsagent's on the corner near the library. Belinda indicated a notice in the window.

'They want paper-boys. You can do that, Jacob, and if there are extra errands that need running, you can do that an' all.'

Jacob assumed a bored expression, looking away with a loud sigh. 'You can't make me.'

'Oh, but I can.' Instinct urged her to stand up straight, the picture of authority, but Jacob was accustomed to taking orders from Thad, with his cocky slouch and taunting sneer, so she shifted her weight onto one hip, dropped her shoulders into a don't-care attitude and plastered a look of amusement on her face. 'Either you take this job and do it properly or else I'll take you to live at End Cottage. Dad won't care and I'll tell Mum she'll have one less mouth to feed.'

'Thad won't let you.'

'Don't kid yourself. He'll be too busy relishing having one less pair of arms and legs crammed into the bed.' Catching the flicker of uncertainty in his eyes, she pushed her advantage. 'At End Cottage, you can sleep on the floor beside the range and you'll have jobs to do before and after school. Auntie Enid and Grandma Beattie won't put up with any nonsense. They'll see it as their Christian duty to turn you into an upright citizen.'

Jacob's expression changed from bored to sulky. Grabbing his arm, she propelled him into the shop, putting on her best smile for the tired-looking man behind the counter as she explained why they had come.

'...and before you ask, yes, he is Thad Layton's brother, but we have an understanding, me and Jacob, and he's willing to work hard – aren't you?' She dealt him a sharp dig with her elbow.

'Ow. Aye, I mean yes.'

'You say "Yes, sir," when you're talking to your employer,' said Belinda.

'Yes, sir,' Jacob muttered.

'I'll pop in every few days to make sure you have no complaints, Mr Eccles,' said Belinda, 'but I'm sure there won't be any. Jacob is turning over a new leaf.' She felt a bright warmth inside: success! 'Right, I'll leave you to hear about your duties, Jacob.'

'That was impressive,' said Mikey as they left the shop.

'Not really. He's just a silly boy. Now, if I could strong-arm Thad into toeing the line, that would be impressive.'

Mikey laughed. 'Where are we going? Have you found me summat?'

'I hope so. It's in Chorlton.'

'Chorlton! I'd never get there in time.'

'You'll have to. The half-timers have their dinner dead on midday. Then you'll have to run.'

'But—'

'It's one thing to get Jacob taken on as a local paper-boy, but half-time posts are more important. You aren't going to get one near home. You know that.'

Mikey nodded. 'I'll do whatever I have to.'

When they reached Chorlton, Belinda took him along Beech Road, past Tyrell's Books and along to the stationer's.

'This is where I hope to place you.' She grabbed Mikey's arm as he tried to go in. 'We have to go somewhere else first.'

She took him to Wilton Close and knocked on the Miss Heskeths' door. Please let them be in.

The door was opened by Miss Patience. 'Well, this is a nice surprise,' she said and Belinda's heart filled with gratitude. She had done the right thing in coming here.

'I've come to ask for help – yours and Miss Hesketh's.'

'Of course, dear. Come in. And who is this?'

Soon she and Mikey were sitting shoulder to shoulder on the settee in the sitting room, Mikey's eyes practically out on stalks at being in such a smart room.

'Mrs Brown at the stationer's is going to be busy for some weeks looking after her daughter. I'm sure Mr Brown could do with another pair of hands and our Michael needs a half-time job.'

'Don't you live in Stretford?' asked Miss Hesketh.

Belinda's heartbeat quickened. 'Yes, but Michael can't get a job there because of my other brother, Thad. He's a ruffian.'

'And what about you, young man?' Miss Hesketh looked penetratingly at Mikey.

'I'll work hard, miss, I promise. I'm nowt like our Thad.'

'Michael has a reference from his teacher.'

Belinda nudged Mikey to make him hand it over. She held her breath while Miss Hesketh read it. Then Miss Hesketh gave it to Miss Patience to read.

'You said you'd come for our help,' Miss Patience prompted.

'If you come with us to Brown's, it would go in Michael's favour.'

'We've never met Michael before,' said Miss Hesketh. 'I shan't pretend to be in a position to recommend him.'

'No,' agreed Miss Patience, 'but we can thoroughly recommend you, Miss Layton – isn't that so, Prudence? It must count for something that Michael has a hard-working, respectful and pleasant sister.'

'I won't let our Bel down,' said Mikey.

'And if you do, she'll be just along the road in the bookshop for Mr Brown to complain to,' said Miss Hesketh. 'And, believe me, if I'm to play even the remotest part in assisting you to get this job, I'll be deeply displeased if there are any complaints. Do I make myself clear?'

There was an audible gulp from Mikey.

'Very well,' said Miss Hesketh. 'We'll accompany you when you make your application, Michael.'

'Mr Brown hasn't actually advertised a job,' Belinda said. 'I hope that, with Mrs Brown being busy for some time to come, maybe he could be persuaded...'

'I see,' said Miss Hesketh. 'You want us to support a boy we've never met before in getting a job that doesn't exist.' Silence rattled round the room as the others gazed at her. She rose to her feet. 'Let's go and explain to Mr Brown that he's in need of a willing and capable lad, shall we?'

Belinda arrived early at the shop on Monday but, even so, Gabriel was there ahead of her.

'You're bright and early.' He smiled.

Her heart melted. 'It's a beautiful day,' she replied as if this was reason enough. 'Have you moved into the cottage?'

'Unfortunately not. I'm still in lodgings. I've been advised not to move in until after this business with Carson is sorted out.'

'Him having paid for all the improvements?'

'Exactly.'

Chilly fingers pattered down her spine. 'But it's all right to be here in the shop?'

'Don't worry. Your position here is safe.'

Her cheeks felt warm. 'I didn't mean that. Well, I did, but I'm concerned for you too.'

'Thank you. No, it's only the cottage that's out of bounds. The shop is mine, all mine.'

She felt a glow of pleasure on his behalf. 'I'd best get on with some work, then.'

'Do you mind tackling the boxes upstairs on your own? I want to open the shop for business, so I need to be down here. Give me a shout if anything needs to be carried downstairs.'

Disappointment screwed up inside her as she went upstairs. She had been counting on their working closely together. But maybe it was no bad thing that they were on different floors. Much less distracting!

Having the shop open meant having different tea-breaks, but at least they had the same dinner hour when the shop closed.

'Shall we make the most of the fine weather and take a picnic to the rec?' Gabriel offered.

He must feel they got along well, to suggest it. That was something – an important something. She might not be beautiful and elegant like Naomi Reed, but there was something special about being friends as well as sweethearts. She knew that from being with Ben. They would have been best mates as well as man and wife.

Was she making a twit of herself by feeling all fluttery and self-conscious in Gabriel's presence? Would the man who had once been engaged to a lovely and well-spoken lady like Naomi Reed look twice at an ordinary girl like Belinda Layton?

They went to the rec for their picnic but, far from revelling in her scintillating conversation, Gabriel seemed thoughtful. Preoccupied, even.

With thoughts of Naomi?

'Penny for them,' said Gabriel.

'What?'

'You haven't said much the past few minutes, but all kinds of thoughts have been flitting across your face.'

'You can talk. You've been pretty quiet yourself.' Had that sounded churlish? She gave a belated smile to show she was joking.

'Things on my mind, I'm afraid,' he said. 'I apologise if I haven't been good company.'

'I didn't mean—'

'It's ten to. We'd better head back.'

Gathering their things, they walked to the gate. Gabriel made small talk, presumably to make up for his earlier quietness, and she responded in kind, but she felt let down. This wasn't the easy camaraderie they were capable of. Had her new-found feelings for him spoiled their friendship?

They passed through the gate in time to see, further along, where the shops were, a young lad flying down the pavement at top speed. Mikey! Belinda dodged back inside the rec.

Gabriel turned in surprise. 'Are you all right?'

'Yes, thank you. That boy: where is he now?'

'He's knocking at Brown's and... he's been let in.' Gabriel frowned at her. 'What of it?'

'That's my brother. It's his first day as a half-timer for Mr Brown.'

'Why hide from him?'

He wasn't going to let this go, was he? 'I didn't want him seeing us together.'

'Why not? We aren't doing anything improper.'

'I know, but if he went home and told the family...' Oh, heck. 'What I mean is, of course we've done nothing wrong; but I – I mentioned Mr Carson to my mother, only I called him Richard by mistake and...' Oh cripes, she was making this worse by the moment. 'I can't have questions being asked about you and me. Not that there is a you and me.' Her insides squeezed in a painful cringe.

'I see.' Gabriel looked along the road; she couldn't see his face. 'He's disappeared inside, so shall we return to the shop? Or would you prefer to walk on your own?'

'Of course not.' He really had taken it the wrong way, hadn't he? But was there a right way to tell someone you mustn't be seen with them? And now she thought about it, had she over-reacted to the sight of her brother? She might not want to face any family gossip or teasing, but she was proud to be in Gabriel's company.

He unlocked the shop door. Once inside, she turned to him.

'Please let me apologise...' she began.

'There's no need. Perhaps we'd better call a halt to the picnics.'

'Oh, but—'

'The last thing I want is to put you in an awkward position.'

'You haven't – ever.'

'If your brother takes any tittle-tattle home, please explain to your parents that, because of my memory loss, I couldn't possibly have any involvement with a girl. It wouldn't be appropriate.'

What made me say that? I don't want to put her off. I know she has eyes only for Richard Carson but even so, I don't want to put her off. And yet wasn't I right to say what I did? How can I possibly seek a relationship with a girl when I am handicapped by my lack of memory?

But with the right girl, would it be such a handicap? Wouldn't the right girl accept me as I am, empty brain and all, and take my hand as we make our way into the future together? Wouldn't the right girl concentrate on making memories with me, so that in the end the lack of my younger years would seem more bearable?

Belinda Layton would do that. She is kind and compassionate; gentle and strong at the same time. But she doesn't want me. She wants Richard Carson. All I am to her is the kindly heir who took pity on her and gave her job security for a spell. I would like to be so much more than that, but I know I never will.

It's a relief to leave her in the shop while I go to town for a meeting with Mr Sowerby. What news will he have for me?

Mr Turton greets me almost as an old friend and escorts me upstairs.

'Good afternoon, Mr Linkworth.' Mr Sowerby walks round his desk to greet me with a handshake. 'You don't mind if Turton remains in the room? He is fully au fait with the matter, as you know.'

'By all means.' I smile my assent at Turton.

'Have a seat,' Sowerby offers.

There are two armchairs beside the fireplace. Being invited to sit here rather than opposite Sowerby at the desk feels like a sign of approval. The chair is splendidly comfortable. Turton stands to the side of Sowerby's chair.

'Have you any news for me?' I ask, though the question is redundant. His expression is grim and I know that what follows won't be good.

'We've contacted the tradesmen on the list Carson sent, along with his statement of expenditure, and they have confirmed that they did indeed do the work in question, as authorised by Mr Carson.'

It surprises me what a blow this is. After all, why would Carson lie about such a thing? Yet I had obviously hoped, without realising I was hoping, that his claim would be disproved.

'Tell me the worst.'

'Do you have much in the way of savings, Mr Linkworth?'

'I haven't got much behind me. When I came back to England, Dr Jennings arranged for me to receive some back-pay from the army, but what savings I had from before the war were handed over, rightly or wrongly, to my parents by my bank manager when I was presumed dead.'

Naomi flits into my mind. Not just her beauty, her poise, her haunting fragrance, but her appearance. That hat alone with its dashing indigo feather cost a pretty penny and her elegant blue costume wasn't run up by the local dressmaker. She doesn't look like the wife of a schoolmaster.

'I assume you're asking because I owe a considerable sum to Richard Carson.'

'I fear so. Do you have the account, Turton?' Mr Sowerby takes the sheet of paper Turton offers, but instead of handing it to me, he leans forward, his eyes sharp and serious. 'He has a strong case for reimbursement. We could challenge him in court on the grounds that anybody who puts money into a property that doesn't belong to him is taking a significant risk – and certainly Mr Carson's risk has failed to bear fruit. On these grounds, we could argue that you shouldn't have to repay the full amount of his speculation. On his side, the argument would be that he had good reason to believe he was investing in his inheritance and is entitled to full recompense for his disappointment.'

'What do you think the outcome would be?'

'Even if the judge tells Carson he is an idiot for having spent so much on a cottage that didn't belong to him, the chances of your being let off the financial hook are remote, I fear. At the very least, you would be ordered to repay a proportion of Carson's money, and possibly all of it. There would also be the question of legal expenses. If the judge ruled that you owed Carson the full amount, he might also rule that you should pay Carson's legal costs.'

I give a low whistle. 'Sounds expensive.'

'It would be.'

He hands me the piece of paper. The hairs on the back of my neck are already standing on end before I look at it. 'I haven't a hope of repaying this. I suppose I'll have to let Carson buy the cottage – at a reduced cost.' Will my landlord agree to my turning the rooms over the shop into living accommodation?

'You could indeed offer to sell Carson the cottage, with these costs deducted from the price, but I doubt he could afford it. I'm surprised he was able to pay for these improvements. He is only a clerk, you know.'

I feel a stab of sympathy for Richard Carson. He must have saved hard and then sunk the lot into the cottage he expected to be his one day. All the same, I don't care for the idea of letting him have the cottage. I may be sympathetic, but I'm not *that* sympathetic. I don't like the fellow.

'So he can't buy me out and I can't reimburse him. That leaves selling the cottage and splitting the proceeds.'

'That avenue isn't open to you,' says Mr Sowerby. He glances at Turton.

'I looked into that possibility this morning,' says Turton. 'It's difficult to see who would purchase it. In spite of the improvements, it's still a humble dwelling in a lane of run-down cottages, and people in that walk of life don't buy their own homes. I took the liberty of speaking to the landlord who owns the rest of the properties in Limits Lane and he has no interest in buying the Tyrell place. The improvements would make it more costly to purchase and the likely tenants couldn't afford the higher rent.'

'So I can't sell it?' Am I stupid to be pleased? Whatever happens, I'll keep the cottage. My cottage. My future home. 'That still leaves the problem of reimbursing Mr Carson.'

'The cottage isn't your only asset,' Sowerby reminds me.

'If you're referring to the bookshop, the premises don't belong to me.'

'But the stock does. I understand Carson had some buyers lined up, who were interested in purchasing the books to boost their own bookshops. If you were to sell the books, you might settle your debt.'

Sell off the stock? But I want to run the shop. This is my dream, my new ambition, a source of comfort and excitement. Last week, I looked forward to today, believing it marked my new beginning. With Richard Carson's nonsense behind me,

I thought today, the start of the new week, would be the start of my new life.

Instead, it is the end. I have lost Miss Layton. Not that she was mine in the first place, but I have lost her all the same. And now I have lost the bookshop and, with it, my future.

It was five o'clock, Belinda's finishing time, but Gabriel hadn't yet returned and the shop was meant to stay open until six. It wouldn't look good if it shut early on its first proper day under its new owner. That settled it. She would stay till six, if necessary.

Presently, the door opened and Mikey walked in. 'Do you want to walk home together, Bel? I thought you finished at five.'

'I do, normally.'

The door opened again and Mikey scooted out of the way. Gabriel entered. The set of his face was grave. Hadn't things gone well at his solicitor's?

Gabriel looked from her to Mikey. 'You're Miss Layton's brother, aren't you?'

'Yes, mister. I'm Mikey. I thought Bel finished at five. I wasn't trying to get her to bunk off early, honest.'

'She does indeed finish at five.' Gabriel turned to her. 'I'm sorry I couldn't get back sooner. You'd better go.'

When she came back from fetching her shawl and handbag, Mikey was chattering easily to Gabriel about his first afternoon at Brown's.

'I'm going to work hard for him,' said Mikey, 'and that will help me get a job when I leave school next year.'

'I can see you're a hard worker like your sister.'

Pleased as she was to see Mikey holding a sensible and polite conversation with an adult, Belinda cringed at the memory of how she had made a fuss over not being seen with Gabriel earlier. Was he remembering, too?

'Goodbye, Mr Linkworth.' She ushered Mikey towards the door.

'Thank you for staying,' said Gabriel. 'I appreciate it.'

She felt like saying, 'Of course I stayed,' the same way that Naomi Reed had said, 'Of course I came,' in that quiet, steady voice; but all she did was smile as she left.

'That was your boss?' asked Mikey. 'I like him.'

'He's a nice chap,' she said casually, hugging to herself the knowledge of just how nice, before diverting Mikey's attention by getting him to tell her about working at Brown's. She liked the thought of their walking home together in future.

Mikey accompanied her to the end of Grave Pit Lane, then plunged across the road and went on his way. Belinda walked up the lane, appreciating its firmness underfoot thanks to the dry weather and enjoying the speedwell's wonderful blue. In amongst the stinging nettles were the purply-pink flowers of the red deadnettle, which Grandma Beattie swore by as a remedy for diarrhoea.

Inside End Cottage, Grandma Beattie for once in her life was sitting with her feet up, a pile of sweet-smelling, freshly ironed linen beside her on the table. Belinda felt a pang of guilt. Her work at the bookshop was a doddle compared to the physical effort Auntie Enid put in at the mill; and Grandma Beattie, when she wasn't on the go in her part-time job at the shop, was on the go at home. This being Monday, she would have spent all morning at the wash-house, possing, scrubbing, wringing and doing battle with the heavy handle on the mangle.

She started to get up, but Belinda pressed her down again.

'Rest a while. It isn't right that a lady your age should have to work so hard.'

Grandma Beattie snorted. 'Hard work is what it's all about, my lass. That's why I'm glad you've bettered yourself by training for office work.'

'Really?' Auntie Enid and Grandma Beattie had blown hot and cold so many times over her ambition that she never knew what to think.

'Aye. Women in our class fettle all us lives one way and another. I like to think of you having an easier time of it than some. You'll appreciate it when you get to my age.'

'I appreciate it already. Stop where you are and I'll prepare the tea. What are we having?'

'The butcher let me have some bits and pieces of lamb's liver, so I thought I'd do liver and onion.'

Belinda fried the onions, but even before she could add the seasoning, Grandma Beattie was up and fettling. In her world, only drunks and slatterns put their feet up before the evening meal.

A loud knocking on the door made Belinda jump and almost spill the dry mustard powder. The door opened and Mikey almost fell into the cottage. He righted himself, face flushed, chest heaving. He turned huge, frightened eyes on her.

'You've got to come, our Bel. Dad's gone. He's left us.'

Chapter Twenty-Five

SIX O'CLOCK HAS come and gone. I'm still here in the book-shop. My bookshop – but I can't afford to think of it as mine. I'll have to sell off the stock to settle the debt on the cottage. It's my only means of paying Richard Carson. My mouth dries; I rub the back of my neck. How much this shop and the prospect of a future as a bookseller has come to mean to me in such a short time.

A knock at the door makes me look round. Although I have turned the key and shot the bolts, I haven't yet pulled down the blind. A gentleman stands on the step, hands cupped around his eyes as he peers inside. He steps backwards as I approach and unlock.

'Good evening.' He raises his hat. 'My name is Miles. I work for Mr Dawson, your landlord.' His voice sounds as if his throat is filled with barbed wire.

I shake hands. 'Gabriel Linkworth. Please come in.'

'Excuse my voice. I'm coming down with a bad cold.'

'It sounds it.'

'I was on my way home when I glimpsed movement through the window. You have taken over the shop from Mr Tyrell?'

'He was my uncle.'

'My condolences, sir. You will find Mr Dawson an excellent landlord. He believes in taking care of his properties. Are there any matters you wish to report?'

It hardly seems worth it, since I am unlikely to be here for long, but the work will need doing whether I'm here or not. 'The door at the top of the stairs doesn't shut properly.'

He goes upstairs and returns, making a note in a small book. 'I'll get Perkins and Watson round. They do most of our jobs for us. They have someone in their office until seven, so I'll go now.'

'There's no need—'

He smiles wryly. 'It's now or not until after I surface after a day or two in bed, getting over this wretched cold.'

'Where are they?'

'Not far. Near the station.'

'Then allow me to call there and make arrangements. Give me the page from your notebook and scribble a line of authorisation.'

I see Mr Miles on his way and walk briskly to the station. It is a pleasant evening. If I didn't have the loss of the bookshop hanging over me, I would enjoy the walk.

I find Perkins and Watson easily enough. There is a yard with pallets of bricks in the corner, lengths of timber leaning against the wall, and a small building. I knock and open the door. A man sits behind a desk, head bent over some papers. His hair is silver. He looks up as I enter; his face is considerably younger than his hair colour suggests. Younger than I am; maybe not even thirty yet. Did his hair lose its darkness in the war?

'Good evening,' I say. 'I've come to arrange for a small job to be done locally.'

He rises for long enough to wave me into the seat opposite him. I hand him the sheet from the notebook.

'Ah yes, Tyrell's Books. I was sorry to hear he had passed on. So was my father – they were at school together.' He raises himself slightly from his chair, extending a hand. 'Tom Watson, son of Thomas Watson.'

I raise myself likewise and we shake hands across the desk.

'Gabriel Linkworth. I've inherited the bookshop. You can do this job?'

'I'll send someone round on...' He consults a diary. 'Thursday suit you?'

'Perfectly.'

'Decent old cove, Mr Tyrell. We've worked on his cottage as well. He always paid on the nail. Not like some.'

'You mean Mr Carson paid on the nail.'

'No – Mr Tyrell. He paid for everything.'

'I think you're mistaken. It was his nephew, Richard Carson, you dealt with.'

'Carson: yes, I remember him; full of ideas for bringing the cottage up to snuff.'

I lean closer. 'Do you mean Carson made the arrangements but Mr Tyrell footed the bill?'

'Steady on. I'm not suggesting anything improper. Mr Tyrell was in possession of his faculties and was happy for the work to go ahead.'

'And he paid for it?'

'Yes. Look, what's this about? This is a reputable firm. Everything we do is above board.'

'I don't doubt it.' My heart beats faster. Could it be...? 'Carson wrote to you recently, didn't he, asking you to confirm that he arranged for the work to be done at Mr Tyrell's cottage in Limits Lane?'

'Aye.' His voice is cautious. He wonders what I'm driving at.

'But he didn't ask you to state that he paid for the work?'

'Of course not. He didn't pay and we'd never have said he did.'

What a rat. What a devious, manipulative rat. My muscles tense, but the anger comes and goes in a moment, swept aside by elation and relief. I will keep the cottage after all and that means I will keep the shop and be a bookseller. A dream come true. A recent dream, but a deeply rooted one.

Any sympathy I might have entertained for Richard Carson's disappointment fades like morning mist as his deception sinks in.

What a rat.

Followed by Mikey, Belinda rushed into the kitchen-sitting room, stopping dead with a suddenness that took away what little breath she had left. It was no good being quick in this crowded space. You had to move carefully or everything went flying.

Mum sat at the table. She was shaking but not with sobs: she was just shaking. Jacob hovered anxiously, the cockiness he copied from Thad quite gone. He looked like the kid he was. And Thad – well, wouldn't you know it, Thaddeus Edward Layton was sitting, no, lounging in Dad's armchair, a smug expression plastered across his face.

Belinda pulled a chair close to Mum's, its legs scraping the floor. Sitting, she put her arms round Mum, wanting to scoop her into a safe, warm cuddle, but maybe she should have stayed on her feet to do that, given that her five foot two was a good three inches less than Mum's height.

'Mum, what happened?'

'Didn't Mikey tell you? He were s'posed to tell you.'

'I want to hear it from you. All Mikey knows is that he came home to hear an almighty row going on, so he scarpered for a while and when he came home, Dad was gone.'

Mum dissolved into tears. 'He's not coming back. He said – he said… He's took the money an' all. He said he were sick to death of having all of us hanging on his coat-tails and we can fettle for ourselves in future.'

A knot tightened in Belinda's tummy. 'Are you certain he's not coming back?'

'Positive. He wrapped all his stuff in a sheet. He said he'd a friend who'll let him bunk down for a night or two and then he'd just... go.' Mum lifted dazed eyes. 'Oh, Bel, what are we to do?'

Think, think. 'Well, the rent is paid up till Saturday, so we've got a few days. What?'

Mum froze, then wriggled free, turning her shoulder on Belinda so as not to meet her gaze. Mikey and Jacob had gone dead still as well.

Chill trickled through Belinda's veins. 'Mum, you and I went to the Bucket of Blood last Thursday especially to get half Dad's money. I told you the rent had to be paid.'

'Aye, but your dad took the money out of the jar on Friday and he were out God knows where all day Saturday. When the rent man came on Saturday afternoon, the boys were out; Mikey were in Chorlton with you; and me and Sarah had to climb out of the bedroom window to get away.'

'You had to escape from the rent man?' Shame tingled under her skin.

'He's got keys to all the rooms, so we had to climb out the back.' Mum's voice faded to a whisper. 'I spent most of today trailing round the shops so as not to be here.'

'You must be worn out.'

'Aye, and not just because I'm tired.' Mum perked up, eyeing Belinda sharply. 'Can you, George and our Sarah help out again?'

'No, I'm sorry, we can't. I've got next to no money and George and Sarah – well, their money is their business. Even if we did pay this week's rent, there'd still be another week due on Saturday.'

'Mikey and Jacob will have their wages by then.' Mum gave her a pained stare.

'That's nowhere near enough.'

'Then George will have to come home.'

'He can't support a whole family.' Not without making himself poor for years to come, and it would put paid to his hopes regarding his young lady. 'Come and sit in the armchair, Mum. Thad, shift yourself.'

'Not likely,' Thad crowed. 'The man of the house has the best chair and the best of everything, and that's me now Dad's gone.'

'You?' Belinda stood up. 'You're the one member of this family that doesn't bring in any money. You know what that makes you? A scrounger.'

Thad came to his feet so quickly that the armchair shunted backwards and hit the cupboard behind it. He glowered at Belinda. She steeled herself. She couldn't have him throwing his weight around.

Before she could say anything, George walked in.

'George!' Mum cried, as if her saviour had arrived.

'My landlady said our Jacob had been round. Is something wrong?'

Belinda watched incredulity take possession of her brother's face as the situation was explained to him.

'So you've got to come home and take care of us, George,' said Mum. 'We need you.'

'No.' Determination made Belinda speak loudly. 'I told you before, George. I'll sort this out.'

'You?' Thad curled his lip.

'I've got an idea. It'll tide us over for a few days while I find something better. I can't say more than that in front of you, George, because it's best if you don't know, you being a public servant in a responsible job.'

For all her fine words, she quivered inside. It was a daring plan. Would it work?

A note from Gabriel awaited her when Belinda let herself into Tyrell's Books. He would be out all morning and possibly all day: good. Much as she longed to be close to him, she had far too much on her mind at present. If he were here to witness her worry and distraction, he might decide she wasn't worth her salary.

That was yet another worry, on top of all the rest. It would slice her heart in half to give up working for Gabriel, but she urgently needed a better-paid job. Would the Miss Heskeths consider her sufficiently well trained to recommend her? And would her salary contribute a large enough amount to the rent on somewhere suitable for her family? She had to continue paying for her bed and board at End Cottage as well – or would she not be able to afford both? Might she have to leave End Cottage in order to do the right thing by her family?

Panic swelled inside her at the enormity of the responsibility she had taken on. She had to find a new home for her family that was affordable on what she and Sarah earned, plus what Mikey and Jacob could contribute. What were the chances of Thad being shamed into helping out? But before any of that, she had to get the family out of that fleapit in Cromwell Street.

The morning passed in a blur. She made some silly mistakes in her typing and had to force herself to concentrate. She closed the shop for dinner and went upstairs to eat the egg barm cake Grandma Beattie had provided, then, unable to settle, she paced the floor – well, in so far as you could pace a floor that was cluttered with bookcases and boxes.

There was a loud knocking at the shop door. She went downstairs and looked across the shop.

'Mikey!'

She hurried to unlock the door and pull him inside. Nothing else could have gone wrong, surely. But Mikey's wide eyes and heaving chest said otherwise.

'I skipped school dinners and went home. Mum's in a right state.'

'The rent man never caught her, did he?'

'No, but the truancy officer did.'

'Oh no, not Thad again.'

'Aye, but, worse than that, someone from the means test came round.'

Horror poured through her. Only the most wretched got swooped on by the means test. It was among the most shaming things that could happen. The proud poor were forced to sell their few precious mementoes to qualify for assistance and disabled soldiers were labelled work-shy. And now, her own family...

'Who brought them in?'

'Dunno. Mum reckons it were one of the neighbours. None of 'em wants to live under the same roof as Thad; and with Dad gone, it's a chance to get rid of us. But that's not the worst. The rent man came—'

'You said Mum avoided him.'

'She did, but he let himself in and left a note to say the bailiffs are coming tomorrow.'

'The bailiffs!' That was even worse than the means test.

'He wants this week's rent in full, plus next week's up front, or the bailiffs will take all our stuff.'

'They can only take goods to the value owed.'

Mikey dealt her a pitying look, as if she was too simple to understand the ways of the world. 'They don't care about that. What are we going to do?'

Fear threatened to overwhelm her. She pushed her shoulders back.

'We'll have to put our plan into action tonight instead of tomorrow.'

Sowerby can't apologise enough. Hands clasped behind his back, he marches up and down on the red-and-blue patterned carpet in his office, huffing and puffing. 'Carson has made fools of us all. Well, not you, Linkworth, but you're the only one.'

'I found out purely by chance.' A shiver feathers its way from my core through all the layers of my skin, leaving a scattering of goose pimples across my flesh. If Miles hadn't been going down with something... if the door hadn't needed fixing... if I hadn't spoken to Tom Watson...

Turton and I have spent the morning visiting the other tradesmen who worked on Mr Tyrell's cottage. They all said the same as Tom Watson: Carson arranged for the work to be done and Mr Tyrell paid the bills. No doubt about it. Every time.

'So cunning,' fumes Sowerby, 'to get the tradesmen to scrawl a line on his own letters to them. All they were in fact agreeing to was that he instigated the work, whereas if they had written letters of their own, they would have expanded on the details and said who paid. As it was, we made the natural assumption. A devilish cunning fellow.'

He has chuntered on in this vein for some time. I cut in.

'What happens next?'

He pauses mid-stride, as if I have posed a conundrum.

'We have to collect written statements from all the builders. What a schemer that young man is – and when I say "schemer", I mean, of course, out-and-out liar. First, he pretends not to know you – and at this stage, I am positive it was sheer pretence – thus obliging us to prove your identity; and now we have to prove that Mr Tyrell paid these bills. We shall expedite matters to ensure you come into your inheritance as soon as possible.'

'Thank you. Do you know where Carson works?'

After all the trouble he has put me to, I have a fancy to be the one to tell him his scheme has failed. Revenge? Why not? I have earned it.

Armed with the address of Carson's employer, off I go. He works in one of the vast warehouses on the Manchester Ship Canal; great, grim buildings, with banks of small, dark windows. As I approach, I bump into a young lad, an apprentice, probably, and ask for Carson. I don't give my name and the boy is too inexperienced, or possibly too shy, to ask for it. He runs inside and, as I wait, I feel my shoulders relax for the first time since this mess began. A smile tugs at the side of my mouth, but I pull my lips into a straight line. I mustn't be grinning like an idiot when Carson sees me.

The door opens and he steps outside. I see the exact moment when his expression changes from dark-eyed curiosity to annoyance and distrust. He isn't quite such a handsome blade any more.

I'm going to enjoy this.

Bloody hell. Bloody bloody hell. He had lost it all. From the moment Uncle Reg told him in a letter to the trenches that Gabriel Linkworth had been posted missing in action, Richard had hoped; and when, in the subsequent letter, *missing* had been bumped up to *missing, presumed dead*, his hopes had been bumped up into solid expectation. That was the moment when he knew, he *knew*, he was going to survive this blasted war. How could he not, when he had so much to look forward to? Not riches, no, but a cottage, a small pot of money and the contents of a bookshop, which he would soon convert into more money. Independent means: the holy grail to a shipping clerk such as himself, with years of toil ahead and no useful family connections to give him a leg-up.

Once he returned from the war, he had done his level best to persuade Uncle Reg to change his will and eliminate Gabriel Linkworth, but to no avail; though Uncle Reg had been most amenable to the idea of having the cottage improved.

'I'm my own landlord,' he said with a chuckle as he signed a cheque for a magnificent sum after the new water pump had been installed, 'and a jolly good landlord too.'

Richard had watched with well-concealed proprietorial satisfaction as his future cottage was updated and brought into the twentieth century.

When Uncle Reg died, he had felt a pang of sorrow, but it was soon lost in the swell of complacency at coming into his inheritance at a considerably earlier date than he had dared contemplate.

He had known exactly what to do: quit his lodgings and move into the cottage, sell the books and build up a nest-egg; and that would be him set up for a comfortable future. Lord above, he had even taken on an employee to help him get rid of the books and Aunt Victoria's knick-knacks. How confident he had been.

And then Gabriel sodding Linkworth had come back from the dead. He had made a last-ditch attempt to grab some money by pretending to have paid for the improvements on the cottage out of his own pocket, but now his ruse had been found out and he was left with nothing. Zero. Not a jot.

Bloody hell. Bloody bloody hell.

And maybe it wouldn't end here. Maybe he would be reported to the police for attempting to gain money by fraudulent means. Linkworth hadn't mentioned informing the authorities, but what were the odds against that old fogey law-man doing so?

Oh, this was impossible. He couldn't return to his ledgers and continue working as if nothing had happened. He needed to get out of this damn warehouse and consider his position. Feigning toothache, he made his excuses and departed. When had his life taken such a wrong turn? No point in dwelling on it. It had happened. Look to the future. But he couldn't let it go. When had his life gone so drastically wrong?

When Gabriel Linkworth came back from the dead, that's when.

Well, he would give Linkworth something to remember him by.

Richard headed for Limits Lane, instinct taking him by a roundabout route. He alighted from the bus at Chorlton Green, walked past the disused churchyard and rounded the corner into Hawthorn Road, its long lines of red-brick terraced houses and corner shops stretching away before him. Down at the end, he could get onto the meadows and walk across to the slope that led up to the bottom of Limits Lane. Quite what he would do when he reached the cottage, he didn't know. Frankly, he felt like blowing it to smithereens. After all the effort he had put into it, after all the hope he had invested in it, it stuck in his craw to think of Gabriel Linkworth living in it, benefiting from his efforts and hopes.

He strode down the street, glancing at the corner shops: a tobacconist, a newsagent, one of those shops that sold everything from Shredded Wheat and Crawford's Currant Puffs, to Vim and metal polish, to paraffin and night-lights. The name over the door said Trimble's: it ought to be a confectioner's, with a name like that. As he passed by on the other side of the road, the door opened and a fellow emerged, thin and wiry, not badly dressed but untidy.

At the far end of the road, Richard stopped. The meadows lay before him, the air bright with the tang of grass and sunshine. Delving in his pocket for his packet of Grand Parade, he bent his head to light a cigarette, inhaling deeply and blowing out a stream of smoke.

'Excuse me, sir. Have you got a light?'

It was the fellow from outside the shop. Close up, his wiry build had nothing puny about it and his clothes were decent enough, though they were on the way to being threadbare. There was something rumpled about him, as if he had slept badly and got dressed in the dark. If this had been first thing in the morning, Richard might have thought him hungover.

He struck a match and the man leaned towards the flame, shutting his eyes as he drew on his cigarette.

'You look like you needed that,' Richard remarked.

'Aye.' The fellow blew out his smoke even more fiercely than Richard had. 'Family troubles, work troubles, money troubles, you name it.'

'Down on your luck?' He knew how that felt.

'Not through any fault of my own. A damn officious boss, who had it in for me. A miserable nag of a wife, older kids who won't pull their weight, younger ones running wild. Well, I'm done with the lot of them. I'm making my own way from now on.'

'I don't blame you.'

The fellow eyed him; a sharp, sideways glance. 'Troubles of your own?'

'You might say that.' Richard chucked away his cigarette, grinding it beneath his heel. 'I must get on. Good luck to you.' He turned away, but the man continued talking and he turned back, not troubling to hide his impatience.

''Tisn't luck I need. It's a few bob in my pocket so I can move away and start again. I've got half what I need from doing a job for... well, least said soonest mended.' He tapped the side of his nose.

Richard felt a twist of dislike, but the feeling untwisted and turned out to be... anticipation. Could he make use of this fellow, who sounded to be already on the wrong side of the law?

He proceeded carefully. 'Sounds as if a fresh start is what you need.'

'Chance 'ud be a fine thing.'

'If you've already got half the funds...'

'Aye, but there's no more where that came from. T'other fella got nabbed, didn't he?' He coughed, a forced sound, as if he thought he could hide his wrong-doing behind it. 'You didn't hear me say that.'

'I'm in a bit of a hole, myself, as it happens, so I'm in no position to judge.'

Another of those sideways glances. 'It happens to the best of us.'

'Indeed it does.' Should he, shouldn't he? Go on. Take the chance. 'If your friend hadn't got himself nabbed, what were you going to do?'

'I don't know as I should say.'

Richard shrugged. 'Two strangers passing the time of day. We'll never cross paths again.'

A long pause. A blackbird sang in a nearby bush. Was the fellow cursing himself for getting embroiled in this conversation?

'We'd have done another job or two and I'd have got enough money together.'

'Enough to...' He was about to say *disappear*. '...start again elsewhere.'

For answer, the fellow dragged deeply on his cigarette, his gaze roaming over the meadows, as if he and Richard were nothing to do with one another... which, of course, they weren't. That was the beauty of it.

'What if I give you the chance to earn what you need?'

No reply beyond a quick glance.

'Correct me if I'm wrong,' said Richard, 'but it sounds as if the job you and your unfortunate colleague undertook wasn't legal.' He waited. 'As I said, correct me if I'm wrong.' He wouldn't utter another word until this man had admitted it.

'You're not wrong.' The fellow sounded sullen.

'Good. Then we understand each other. I'm prepared to pay you the sum you require if you'll undertake a small commission on my behalf.'

'You what?'

'I'll pay you to do a job. I want you to burn down a cottage.'

The man bridled. 'Never!'

'It's empty, I swear, and it stands on its own, so there's no danger of the fire spreading. I want it done tonight.'

Now the fellow looked at him, eyes narrowed, interest piqued. 'Where is it?'

'Not far from here. Do you know Limits Lane?'

'I know the name, though this isn't my usual stamping ground.' He frowned. 'Limits Lane: someone mentioned it at home recently.' His mouth tugged this way and that. 'I dunno. Boys fighting, women gassing: who listens? Not me.'

'The cottage is the last one in the lane, just before it slopes down onto the meadows. I want you to provide sufficient paraffin, rags and matches to get the job done. You can purchase what you need at that shop you went into a while back: Trimble's. The cottage is thatched. If you can get the thatch ablaze, that'll do the trick. There's a wooden shed right next to it; that'll go up like a firework.'

The fellow gazed at his feet. Richard let him mull it over.

'Tonight?'

'It has to be tonight,' he said, 'and tomorrow you can be on your way to start your new life. Do we have an agreement?'

Chapter Twenty-Six

L OCKING THE SHOP on the dot of five, Belinda waited for
Mikey to emerge from Brown's and they hurried on their
way, separating when they reached Stretford.

'Go straight home and tell Mum to start packing,' she said.
'You all have to help, including Thad. I'm going to see Mr
Harrison in his yard.'

Would Mr Harrison be able to help at such short notice?
Her original idea had been to ask him today if he could do it
tomorrow, but now that the bailiffs were coming tomorrow,
their moonlight flit had had to be brought forward to tonight.

Their moonlight flit: her chest tightened. They had done
a moonlight flit once before, years ago, so long ago that she
could almost pretend it had never happened. Now once again
the Layton family would disappear into the darkness, leaving
their rent unpaid. And it was her idea. Not her fault, though.
The fault lay squarely with Dad, wherever he was.

A tall wooden fence surrounded the rag-and-bone yard.
There were two big gates for the horse and cart, but these
were securely fastened. Close by, a door was set into the
fence. She had to pick her feet up as she stepped through,
because there was a plank of wood across the bottom. The
yard was piled high with items of all kinds – sticks of furniture, cracked basins, wheels, the empty case of a grandmother

clock. Under shelter, boxes were stacked, containing goodness knows what.

Mr Harrison appeared from behind an old washing copper.

'If you want another lend of the hat and coat, you'll have to talk to the missus.'

'It's not that. I've come for your help.' Shame clogged her throat and she had to force herself to continue. 'It's my family – not the Mrs Sloans. My mum and my brothers and sister have to move house urgently and we need a cart for the furniture.'

'A moonlight flit? Nay, don't go all hot and bothered. You aren't the first and you won't be the last.' Mr Harrison frowned. 'You didn't mention your dad.'

'He's gone. Left us.'

'Nay, he never has. That's a bad business. When is it to be, this moonlight flit? Soon, I expect.'

'Tonight. I'm sorry for the short notice.'

'Moonlight flits are like that. Don't fret, lass. You tell me when and where and I'll be there.'

She scrabbled inside her handbag. 'I haven't got much, but I'll pay what I can.'

'Keep your money, lass. I'll help thee without that. If your dad's cleared off, your family needs all its coppers.'

Oh, the relief that something was going right at last. She went home, stopping to smooth her features before entering End Cottage.

Presently, the three of them were tucking into rollmop herrings. Well, Auntie Enid and Grandma Beattie tucked in while she tried to look equally keen. As they ate, she explained – lied – about the move.

'Now that Dad's gone, Mum and the kids have to move, so I'll go round there after tea to help pack. I'll stay overnight.'

'Eh, your poor mam,' said Grandma Beattie. 'If you fetch back a couple of her dishes, I'll do her vegetable stew and an apple pie.'

'Where are they moving to?' asked Auntie Enid.

'I don't know the details. It's all happened so quickly, with Dad doing his disappearing act.'

She pretended not to see the look that passed between Grandma Beattie and Auntie Enid; a look that suggested they had already had plenty to say about Denby Layton and that after she had gone, they would say it all over again.

When she started washing up, Grandma Beattie gently pushed her aside.

'Off you go, love. Your mam needs you.'

Gathering her night things, she kissed them goodbye and rushed along Grave Pit Lane, her heartbeat detonating inside her ears. Entering the house in Cromwell Street, she found their two rooms in a state of quiet chaos and her heart cracked open with anguish at how Mum must be suffering. Her early married years, before Dad's working life started going down the drain, must seem like heaven on earth compared to this.

'Mikey!' she exclaimed at the sight of fresh purple bruising around his eye-socket. 'What happened?'

'It's Thad's idea of being the man of the house,' said Mikey. 'But I never hit him back. I know how important it is for us to get packed.'

Aye, and wasn't it a pity they couldn't leave Thad behind? That boy was nowt but trouble. The thought of taking him into their temporary home made Belinda's blood run cold, but what choice did she have?

She and Sarah stripped the beds. Mum emptied out the chest of drawers and the hanging cupboard, then the clothes and linen were bundled inside a sheet. Cutlery went inside one pillow-case, the clock and ornaments from the mantelpiece in another, packets of Oxo and Cooperative Tea and tubs of Bisto and cocoa in a third. Mikey stacked the saucepans and crockery on the table and Jacob wrapped the plates in newspaper.

Thad took down the curtains, complete with brass rings.

337

'Those curtain-rings aren't ours,' said Mum.

'They are now. Give me a minute and I'll have them curtain-poles off the wall too.'

'Thad,' Belinda objected, 'we aren't thieves.'

He gave her an insolent look. 'I could take the doors off the hinges in two ticks.'

'Mr Harrison is a law-abiding citizen. If he thinks anything is stolen, he won't help us.' Would that be sufficient to keep Thad in order? 'Jacob, put the brushes and the fire-irons in the pail. Mum, is the fender ours?'

Darkness fell and Mum lit one of the gas-lamps. It came to life with a soft *pop*.

At last, they heard the steady clop-clop of hooves coming down the street and stopping outside their house. Belinda went to let Mr Harrison in. He looked round at their piled-up possessions.

'We need this door and the front door propped open, prefer-ably with summat that won't go clang boom crash if someone knocks it. We'll get the furniture loaded first, then the small stuff. I've brought a couple of tea-chests. If the girls get them filled, me and the lads can do the furniture.'

For once, Belinda was grateful that Thad was a big brute in the making. He and Mr Harrison moved the bulky pieces and Mikey and Jacob helped get them into position on the cart. Then it was time to take the smaller pieces and the family ferried everything outside while Mr Harrison loaded up. Out and in, out and in they crept, like a line of ants.

When they finished, Belinda put the keys on the mantelpiece and shut the door behind her.

Thad was sculling eagerly around the front of the cart.

'Nay, lad.' Mr Harrison spoke softly but with authority. 'Yon hoss has enough to pull without lugging a squad of healthy boys an' all. The missus can sit up here with me and you young 'uns can walk behind.'

'Where are we going?' Mum asked.

'Yeah, our Bel, where are we off to?' Thad demanded and was met by a chorus of shushes from all sides. 'You've got no business not telling us.'

'If no one knew, no one could let it slip out.' She felt a thrill of fear. What she was about to do was inappropriate, to say the least. She desperately hoped her family wouldn't let her down. 'We're going to my boss's cottage in Limits Lane – just for a day or two while I sort out something else.'

'Really? That's generous of him,' said Sarah.

Belinda turned to Mr Harrison. 'We'd best get moving.'

'Here, missus, let me give you a hand up.'

Mr Harrison helped Mum onto the seat and they set off. The boys tried to ask Belinda about the cottage, but she dodged their questions by reminding them to keep quiet. By the time they reached Limits Lane, they were all flagging. Mr Harrison drew in the horse while he set a flame to a couple of lanterns to make up for the lack of street-lamps.

The cart halted by the garden gate and Mr Harrison helped Mum down.

'It's good of Mr Linkworth to give permission for us to stay here,' she said.

It was time to own up. 'He hasn't. Not exactly.'

'Not exactly?' said Mum. 'What's that supposed to mean?'

'It means not at all,' Thad crowed. 'It means our Bel is the biggest liar and cheat of us all.'

'I am not,' she hissed.

'Oh no?' Thad retorted. 'That's what you'd have called me if this had been my idea.'

'It's only for a few days while I find something permanent. Now listen. If anything gets broken in the cottage or goes missing,' she stared at Thad, his face devilish in the mixture of lamplight and shadow, 'I'll end up losing my job and then we'll be in an even worse position than we are already; so you must all treat the cottage and everything in it with respect.' She rolled her shoulders, trying to shake off her tiredness. 'There's a shed our furniture can squeeze into. I suggest we take only our bundles of clothes and food indoors. Mum, you put the food away while Sarah and I make up the beds. Boys, help Mr Harrison stow the furniture. And after that, you must all go to bed.'

'You an' all,' said Mum.

She nodded, but she didn't mean it. She was far too edgy to sleep, so when they had said goodbye to Mr Harrison and the boys disappeared into one bedroom, under pain of death if they dared to fight, and Mum and Sarah went to bed in the other, she crept downstairs under the pretence of locking the door.

She ought to feel triumphant for having rescued Mum and the children from the bailiffs, but bringing them here to Gabriel's cottage weighed heavily on her. It was wrong, whichever way you looked at it. Should she have sought his permission? But that would have involved telling the truth about Dad and the rent and the means test and the bailiffs, and she could never do that. She had only told Auntie Enid and Grandma Beattie because it would have been impossible not to. Besides, what if Gabriel had refused? Then she would not only have shamed herself in front of him, but she would still have needed to find somewhere for her family. No, doing it on the sly was the only way.

A lump filled her throat. On the sly was the only way: what did that say about her? She wasn't a bad person, she really wasn't. She was just trying to do her best for her family. Anyroad, what was done was done. She needed to concentrate on what was coming next. She must look in the *Evening News* for a job with a better salary; and somehow she must find a new home for her family. It wouldn't be easy without a man's wage coming in, but there must be so many widows these days in need of homes. Surely landlords were used to totting up a family's combined wages and seeing what they came to.

A wave of tiredness engulfed her. Sitting at the table, she laid her head on her arms. She would rest her eyes for five minutes. Just for five minutes.

I am wide awake, flat on my back in bed, hands linked behind my head. It is the middle of the night, but I am as wide awake as if this were a glorious morning of golden sunshine. Is it foolish to say I feel sunshiny? Maybe, but that doesn't prevent its being true. True: wonderful word; as in, dreams coming true. That is certainly the case for me. The cottage is mine to keep, which means the bookshop is as well. My future has been saved.

I roll out of bed and stand up. I'll walk to Limits Lane, to my cottage, my new home. Maybe I will sleep when I get there, maybe I won't. Either way, when the sun comes up, that's where I'll be.

I was advised to keep my distance while the Richard Carson affair was in full swing, but that is now resolved – practically, anyway. The various tradesmen will be asked to make formal statements. Very likely Mr Sowerby would advise me against taking possession of the cottage until every detail has been double-checked, signed, counter-signed and sealed with a loving kiss, but I don't intend to wait for all that. I have waited long enough. I can live without my memory because I have a future to embrace. A cottage to live in, a bookshop to run, new memories to build. What more could a fellow wish for?

I know the answer to that.

I scribble a note for my landlady, then creep down the stairs as stealthily as any burglar. I unbolt the door and escape into the cool darkness of a spring night. There is a sharp edge to the coolness: it is only the first week of April. I have excitement and purpose to keep me warm.

I have a mad fancy for walking to Limits Lane across the meadows, my strides brushing up the night-time scents of grass and leaves and cowslips, but I don't have my torch with me and could well end up blundering my way as far as the Bridgewater Canal, not to mention the possibility of breaking my ankle down a rabbit-hole. So I go via the roads, running the flat of my hand along privet hedges and savouring the crisp, wholesome aroma.

The street-lamps inform me when I arrive at Limits Lane. I turn the corner and, as I do so, I see the glow of sunrise. My heart leaps – and then crashes. Not sunrise, you fool, not at this hour. Fire! I take to my heels, pelting along the lane. It's my cottage – my cottage. I veer off towards another of the dwellings, barging through the gate, hammering on the door until it is opened.

'Fire! My cottage is on fire – the end one, Mr Tyrell's old place. Rouse everyone in the lane. Bring buckets. I have a water pump in the back garden. I saw a bobby near St Clement's Church. Send someone to catch up with him. We need the fire brigade. Do it, man!'

I throw myself through his garden gate and race the final yards. Oh, my cottage. The thatch is ablaze in several places; the sound of crackling flares through the night, the acrid smell invading my nostrils. *God almighty, Jerry has set the place on fire.* I fumble for my key. There is a bucket in the kitchen. I hold my breath and shove the door open. A cry in the darkness. I stop mid-stride.

'Who's there?'

'Mr Linkworth!'

'Miss Layton? What the... Come on!'

I grab her arm, yank her to her feet. She stumbles. *I grab Roy Coster by the arm. He stumbles. I pull him up. Eyes stinging, throat raw, head spinning.* I haul her from the building. We burst into the garden.

342

She gasps, a huge inward breath of shock. 'Fire! I was fast asleep. I woke with a jump when you came in. My mum – the boys – they're upstairs.'

She darts for the door, but once more I grasp her arm. She spins round.

'Let me go!' she cries.

'Let me go!' I yell.

'You can't go back in there – you mustn't!' Coster shouts – or tries to. His voice is hoarse and heaving, as if he is about to throw up. He makes a grab for me.

'Let me go!' I have to fetch the others. I can't leave them in there to choke and burn.

If the Layton family is upstairs—

'Look!' I point to the thatch, ablaze in several places. Smoke streams upwards from the flames.

'I have to,' she insists.

I have to. I can't leave them to die like that.

I know what to do, but my head is teeming with images and words, another fire, another place, another heart pounding in panic – no, not another heart, my heart; my heart pumping fit to explode in two times, two places, both in the same moment. Two fires, two emergencies. *I have to do it. I have to save them.* I have to do it. I have to save them.

'Come with me.'

Seizing her hand, I drag her round to the back garden. Pulling off my jacket, I thrust it at her.

'Hold it under the water.'

I take the pump handle and thrust it down hard. Water spurts out. She holds the jacket inside the cold flow. Letting go of the handle, I throw the sopping garment over her head and round her shoulders. As we race to the front door, others appear in the garden, brandishing buckets, empty coal scuttles, a chamber pot.

'The pump is round the back,' I yell.

At the door, Miss Layton is about to shoot inside ahead of me. I hold her back.

'Stay behind me.'

Here, downstairs, I can smell smoke, a sharp, filthy smell. At the foot of the narrow staircase, it intensifies. It will be bad upstairs. I turn and place my hands on her shoulders. In her face, in her eyes, I see how she hates me for preventing her.

'Listen. There's no noise up there. With luck, they're asleep, but they may be unconscious. How many are there?'

'Mum and Sarah in one room, three boys in the other.'

We hurry upstairs. The staircase is barely two feet across and the top is clogged with smoke. It is madness to come up here. The landing is small, just a square. I am holding my breath, but my throat burns. *Burning throat, bursting lungs, foul smoke. Desperation, determination, desperation, determination.*

I throw open a door and the two of us almost fall into the room. It isn't too bad in here. Ribbons of smoke curl through the air. Miss Layton propels herself at the bed, shaking its occupants.

'Mum – Mum! Sarah!'

They stir, exclaim, sit up – realise.

'The boys!' cries the mother.

She and the girl scramble from the bed, getting tangled in their haste. Miss Layton throws the wet jacket over her mother's head and shoulders.

'Get them downstairs,' I order.

'My brothers—'

'I'll fetch them.'

I have to rescue them, my men, my comrades, my friends, my brothers, fastened inside to die. I bundle the Layton women out of the room. Their exclamations of shock and distress as they meet the murky smoke on the landing are cut off as their breathing catches. Coughing, gasping, they head downstairs.

I push open the other door and plunge in. The room nestles beneath the thatch, its window inside a cutaway section. Outside, around the window, the thatch is ablaze. Inside, the room is filled with the deadly stench.

Two boys lie in the bed – wasn't it meant to be three? I shake them but they don't stir. My foot catches on a lad asleep on the floor. He groans, rolls over, wakes.

I bend down to him. 'The cottage is on fire. Get downstairs and outside. Now!'

He scrabbles away. I heave a boy from the bed and pull him over my shoulder. Dizziness swoops through me. I sway but force myself to stay in control. I find the stairs and carry him down. *Endless stairs, my back straining. When I get him out, I'll have to go back in again. Just one more time, just one more time.*

I dump the boy on the lawn. There is a scuffle as someone tries to hold back his mother. She breaks free and hurls herself at her child.

Back I go. *One more time. You can do it, you can do it.* Across the room, up the stairs, into the bedroom, eyes streaming, *skin prickling*, throat raw, *lungs ready to explode*. My men need me; this boy needs me. Come on, soldier-boy, help yourself, can't you? I can't do this without a bit of cooperation. But he is unconscious. I have to do this. Lift him, lift him, drag him up and over my shoulder. I stagger. My knee gives way, an old injury – rugby. 'You wait,' says my father. 'That injury will catch up with you one of these days.'

Down the stairs, down, down, away from the worst of the smoke. *Private Stoneley is the last. Family man, three nippers: I have seen the photograph. I'm sure I've got them all out. My head is swimming, confused, panicked, but in my heart I'm certain I've got them all. As for our mission, our reason for being here – mission not accomplished. Sorry, sir.*

Out of the cottage. People, people. A human chain, wielding buckets. Some brave mad idiot is up a ladder, chucking water on the thatch, trying to save my cottage. Hands take the child from me. My head is swimming, confused, panicked, but in my heart I'm certain all the family is out of the cottage. Mission accomplished.

A thousand images inside my head, an explosion of colour and sound and laughter and memory and confusion.

A hand on my arm. I look down. A pretty face in the fire-light. A scared, anxious face – but a pretty one.

'Come this way,' says Miss Layton. Belinda. Pretty Belinda. I try to walk, but—

Chapter Twenty-Seven

I T WAS MOST unlike Miss Layton not to turn up for her lesson yesterday evening, so Patience walked to the bookshop to see if something was wrong. And here was another mystery: the shop was shut.

'It won't be open today,' said a woman coming out of the grocer's next door but one. 'Haven't you heard?'

Patience went cold all over. 'Heard what?'

'Mr Tyrell's cottage caught fire last night and the young chap who took over the bookshop and his family were all burnt to a crisp.' The woman shivered elaborately. 'Doesn't bear thinking about, does it?'

Patience caught her breath. Poor Mr Linkworth. Wait a minute. He didn't have any family, surely, or if he did, he didn't remember them, so what was this woman talking about? Seeing the eager horror in the woman's face, Patience recoiled from discussing the matter. She set off for Mr Linkworth's cottage. Perhaps Miss Layton was there, helping to clear up. She knew where the cottage was because Miss Layton had described going there with Mr Carson, undoubtedly having no idea how her eyes shone when she mentioned his name.

When she reached Limits Lane, her heart turned over at the sight of the dirty cloud that hung in the air at the other end.

Her stomach turned over too. Even from this distance, the stink touched her nostrils.

'Come to gawp, have 'ee?' demanded a wrinkle-faced old man, leaning over the garden gate at the top of the row.

'Not at all. I'm looking for someone who I thought might be clearing up after the fire.'

'Not much clearing up to do. Once the fire got hold of the thatch, that were it for the cottage.'

'Oh, I'm sorry.'

'The folk got out safe, that's the main thing.'

'Someone told me it was the new owner's family.'

'Don't know who they were, missus. All I know is that young Mr Tyrell were taken off to hospital on account of the smoke he breathed, saving their lives, and the family went piking off to Grave Pit Lane.'

Grave Pit Lane! Then the stricken family must be Miss Layton's – but what could they have been doing in Mr Linkworth's cottage?

'Thank you,' said Patience. 'You've been a great help.'

She hurried to End Cottage. When she knocked, the older Mrs Sloan opened the door.

'You're one o' them Miss Hesketh ladies. What brings you here?'

'I'm looking for Miss Layton.'

'She'll be back soon. Come in and wait.'

'If it's no trouble.'

'We've had half Manchester through this door in the past few hours. One more won't make any odds.'

Patience stepped inside. The already cramped quarters seemed full to bursting with people. Faces turned towards her – a dozen at least, or so it felt. Then she looked properly and realised there was a woman; a pretty, sandy-haired girl of sixteen or seventeen; and three boys, one of whom was a strapping creature with a surly mouth.

'This is our Belinda's family,' said Mrs Sloan. 'That's her mother, Mrs Layton.'

Mrs Layton was a wretched-looking individual with worried eyes. The whole family was dressed in nightclothes: Patience didn't know where to look. The room smelled smoky, and not because of a mishap on the range.

'This lady is one of Belinda's teachers,' Mrs Sloan introduced her.

'Pleased to meet you, miss,' said Mrs Layton. 'You've done a lot for our Bel and I'm grateful.'

Patience rose to the occasion. 'It's been a pleasure. She's a diligent pupil.'

'Please have a seat,' said Mrs Sloan. 'You, boy, Thad, give the lady your seat.'

Patience sat down. Thad gave her a sulky look, which she chose to ignore. 'Might I ask? I've come from Limits Lane.'

'Our Bel's gone to buy us new clothes,' said Mrs Layton. 'The Mrs Sloans put up a bit of money for it.'

'Just doing our Christian duty,' said Mrs Sloan.

Mrs Layton's chin wobbled. 'We lost all ours in the fire.'

'We're not having new clothes,' the smallest boy piped up. 'Just new-to-us.'

That was as far as he got before his sister gave him a swipe, her pretty face marred by embarrassment and annoyance.

Patience was dying to ask why they had been in the cottage. The door opened and Miss Layton came in, arms full of a vast bundle.

'Oh – Miss Patience.'

'You didn't attend your lesson yesterday and I was concerned.'

The girl's mouth opened in an O. 'I clean forgot. My – my family needed me.'

'We did a moonlight flit,' announced the youngest.

'Jacob!' His mother buried her face in her hands.

Miss Layton's face flushed, but she held her head up. 'We had no choice. Dad's left us.'

'My dear girl.'

One heard of such things, but she had never met it head-on before. She wished she hadn't come. No, she didn't. Her duty as an educated, middle-class lady and a churchgoer was to do her best to assist this family. Besides, she was fond of Miss Layton.

'Will you permit me to help you, Mrs Layton? You must be exhausted. Firstly, everyone needs to get dressed. Is there somewhere?'

'You can take turns to use my room,' said Miss Layton. 'Then the boys must go to school. That means you an' all, Thad.'

Three voices groaned in protest.

'We'll get the cane for being late.'

'Not if your mother writes you a note,' said Patience. Would there be a pen and paper in this humble dwelling?

'Mikey and Jacob, go and get dressed,' said Miss Layton, 'while Mum writes you a letter to take.'

'I don't know what to say...' Mrs Layton began.

Miss Layton produced a pen. 'Here you go, Mum. "Please excuse the boys being late, but we were in a fire last night." No one can doubt it. They're going to whiff of smoke until they have a bath.'

Soon the boys were dressed and gone and the cottage felt big enough to contain those left behind. Mrs Layton and her younger daughter went upstairs one at a time and came down, looking self-conscious, dressed in their new clothes.

'Where are we going to sleep tonight?' asked Mrs Layton.

'I'll think of something, Mum,' said Miss Layton. 'Right now, I ought to go to the bookshop. I'm meant to be at work.'

'I wonder if Mr Linkworth has been let out of hospital,' said her sister.

'If he has, that's where he'll be,' said Miss Layton, 'and I owe him an explanation.' She glanced at Patience. 'I... borrowed his cottage for my family.'

'And it burnt down?' said Patience.

Miss Layton made a helpless movement with her hands. 'The boys swear it wasn't them, but...' Poor girl. She had taken a chance, taken a liberty, and now she was paying a frightful price.

The door burst open and, with an almighty clatter, the three boys fell into the cottage. The room seemed to flinch.

'Bel! Mum! Mr Carpenter says if we've got nowhere to live, he's going to send for the Board of Guardians.'

Belinda went cold, but there was no time to be distressed or ashamed, because Mum let out a wail and dissolved into exhausted whimpering. Miss Patience rose to her feet, looking crisp and tailored in their lowly home. She was about to make a run for it and Belinda couldn't blame her.

'I'm sorry you had to see us like this, Miss Patience.'

Miss Patience gave her a look of such warmth that she had to stiffen all her muscles so as not to crumple.

'My dear, this is a difficult situation, but I hope that between us, we can sort it out.'

Belinda had thought it would be up to her alone to cope and her mouth dropped open in surprise, whereupon uncertainty flickered across Miss Patience's gentle face.

'I know I'm not a managing sort like my sister, but I'll provide whatever assistance I can – if that is acceptable to you, Mrs Layton?'

Mum gulped and nodded. She wouldn't care who sorted it out as long as it was somebody else – Belinda caught her breath. What a horrid, disloyal thought. But years of managing in ever-worsening circumstances had ground Mum down. She would pick up again once things got better. Wouldn't she?

And how on earth was Belinda supposed to make them better?

'The boys must return to school,' declared Miss Patience. 'If they don't, the truancy officer will be involved.'

'And that will be another reason for the Board of Guardians to get involved,' Belinda realised.

'If the Guardians are involved,' said Grandma Beattie, 'you could all end up in't workhouse.'

Jacob stood huddled close to Mum, for once not standing cockily side-by-side with Thad. Thad looked sullen, but there was a gleam of wariness in his eyes.

'Have you any money?' asked Miss Patience.

'Hardly any,' said Belinda, 'and no possessions.'

'Then…' Miss Patience lapsed into silence. Was that the sum total of her usefulness?

'Young Sarah can stop here,' said Grandma Beattie. 'Our Belinda told you that me and Mrs Sloan have offered to have your Sarah, didn't she, Mrs Layton?'

Oh, heck.

Mum looked bemused. 'Did you, Bel? No, I'd have remembered.'

'I never got round to it.' Belinda ignored a sharp look from Sarah.

'Is there room for us?' Jacob asked hopefully.

'Nay, lad,' said Grandma Beattie, 'not even if you could sleep standing up. You can see how we're fixed.'

'We'll go up before the Panel,' said Mikey, 'and they'll send us to the workhouse.'

'Then we have to provide a reasonable alternative, so they leave you alone.' Miss Patience came to life. 'There's an orphanage on the corner of Church Road and High Lane in Chorlton. Do you know it? St Anthony's. I suggest taking the boys there.'

'St Anthony's?' cried Mum.

'It's better than being up before the Panel,' Belinda pointed out.

'But we're not orphans,' said Mikey.

'Not all children in orphanages are orphans,' said Miss Patience. She looked at the boys. 'I wonder: smelling of smoke to show the urgency of the situation or having had a good wash to show what a clean family you are. Mrs Sloan, may we trouble you for some hot water?'

Belinda couldn't help smiling as cleanliness won out over drama. 'I'll fetch a towel. Give yourselves a good rinse down, boys,' she added before Miss Patience could ask for soap. The Sloan household had soap, of course, but not in such quantities that it could be squandered on boys who would be grubby again in five minutes.

The boys squeezed into the cold scullery to sort themselves out.

Belinda spoke quietly to Miss Patience. 'I can't tell you how much this means.'

'It helps to share difficult decisions. I should know. I've always been able to rely on my sister.'

'When were you going to tell me I could move in here?' Sarah demanded.

A yell and a crash from the other side of the scullery door had Belinda leaping across the room to yank the door open, exposing Thad and Mikey, half-dressed and locked in a wrestling hold. Stuffed into a corner, a naked Jacob gave a howl and grabbed the towel.

'I can't trust you to behave, so this door stays open,' Belinda flared. 'Act your age – or do you want to be taken away by the Welfare?'

Fuming, she turned away from them, astonished to find that in a strange way she was relieved Thad and Mikey had got into a scuffle. After the horror of last night, it was their normal behaviour. Did other families have nice-normal?

Disagreeable-normal seemed to be the way for the Layton family and had been for a long time.

'I'll accompany Mrs Layton to the orphanage with the boys,' said Miss Patience, 'and I suggest you go to the bookshop. If it's still closed, perhaps you can find out which hospital Mr Linkworth was taken to last night. Is there something useful Sarah can do?'

'Go to the sorting office and wait for George to come in off his round,' said Belinda. 'He needs to know what happened.'

Mum perked up at the mention of George's name. No matter how much Belinda did to support her, it was always George she wanted.

'With you girls living here, and the boys going to the orphanage, I can go and live with George in his lodgings and that will be all of us settled.'

Gabriel sat in Mr Sowerby's office.

'Are you certain you're well enough to be here?' that gentleman enquired.

'Quite sure, thank you. Taking me to hospital was merely a precaution.'

'And your memory is returning, you say? Extraordinary.'

'I lost my memory after pulling my men one by one from a burning building, and the fire last night...'

'Extraordinary,' Sowerby repeated. 'You may wish to know that Mr Richard Carson has an alibi for the time of the fire.'

Gabriel weighed that in his mind. It didn't automatically mean Carson wasn't responsible. Had he organised the fire that destroyed the cottage? It was such an extreme thing to do. Gabriel didn't know him well enough to guess what he might be capable of.

'Then there's the question of his fraudulent attempt to acquire funds from you to repay his so-called expenditure on the cottage.' Sowerby steepled his fingers. 'Given that he didn't succeed, and there is no reason to suppose he has made a career of committing fraud, the police won't be interested. If you wish to pursue the matter—'

'I couldn't afford to – and I want to move on from it, anyway.'

His mind was teeming with information, memories, images; yet it was like examining it all through a window. He felt separated from it. Dr Jennings would probably say it was his mind's way of breaking him in gently.

'Frankly,' he said, 'I have enough problems without taking my chances on a legal tussle with Richard Carson. I'll be happy to forget him.'

Interesting turn of phrase. Inaccurate too, now that his memory had returned in full force.

'There's no doubt, however,' Sowerby added, 'that the fire was arson, not accidental. It was started outside the cottage, not inside. Turton has been in touch with the police and they are certain.'

'So no one from Miss Layton's family...'

'Precisely.'

'Good. I'll ensure she knows.'

'What was her family doing there anyway?'

'I've no idea. I was never more astonished in my life than when I went into the cottage and she sprang up out of nowhere.'

How long had the Laytons occupied his cottage? Not long, obviously, as there hadn't been the opportunity, but why were they there? Before this, he would have sworn he could trust Miss Layton with his life – and now it turned out she had moved her family into his property behind his back. He didn't want to discuss it with Sowerby. He didn't want to hear all the laws Belinda Layton had broken. He couldn't rid himself of his belief in her honesty. Were his feelings for her clouding his judgement? No, Belinda Layton was a good person.

'Actually,' said Sowerby, 'it would be better for you if one of them had set the place on fire by mistake. Your uncle insured the cottage against accidental fire, but not against arson, so you'll receive no recompense.'

He absorbed this. 'That's a blow, I admit, but not such a great one as it would have been if my memory hadn't returned. Other matters don't seem as important as they would under normal circumstances. Something I'm determined to do is clear the land. I haven't seen what remains of the cottage, but I assume there's rubble and ruin left. I want it cleared.'

'The cottage occupies the final spot in a run-down lane. The remains of a ruined building will be of no inconvenience to anybody.'

He sat up straighter. Wasn't Sowerby listening? 'I wish to pay for the land to be cleared.'

He had to do it, had to. In France, time and again he walked past that burnt-out ruin where he had come close to losing his life, where he had saved his men only for them to be executed by enemy soldiers. That ruined building had represented the great empty hole where his sense of self was supposed to be. He could never walk past it without wishing it could be flattened.

Now, he was going to make good the plot of land at the end of Limits Lane. He couldn't live with himself if he didn't. Now that he remembered the death and destruction he had witnessed in the war, he couldn't be responsible for letting a ruined eyesore remain.

'It would be a costly business,' Sowerby cautioned him.

'There is some money in the inheritance. I'll put it towards that purpose.'

'And what of the bookshop? I fail to see how you could afford the rent if you use all you have clearing the land.'

Gabriel waited, giving himself time to change his mind, but he remained resolute. That piece of land had to be cleared. He imagined the cleared land reverting to grass and wildflowers. That was how he wanted – needed – it to be.

'The land will be cleared,' he stated quietly.

'For what it's worth, Linkworth, you won't receive a bill from Winterton, Sowerby and Jenks. After the oversight on our part that, had you not uncovered the truth about Carson's skulduggery, would have led to you struggling to pay him off, there's no question of our submitting a bill to you.'

'Thank you.' Gabriel came to his feet. 'Now, if you'll excuse me, I must return to the bookshop. I hope to find Miss Layton there.'

'Ah yes, the mystery of the secret visitors.'

He felt a twist of annoyance. He owed Sowerby a great deal, but that didn't give the old fellow the right to make sarky remarks about the girl he loved. Yes, loved. He loved Belinda Layton, but she was in thrall to that snake, Carson.

He left the building, popping into William Turton's office for a few words of thanks and farewell, and headed for Chorlton, his heart taking him to the bookshop. Would she be there?

He opened the door. There was a flurry of movement as she rushed towards him. Delight coursed through him, but he had the presence of mind to step aside. She was only acting out of relief at seeing him on his feet. She stopped awkwardly, her face flushed. His arms ached with emptiness.

'You're all right,' she exclaimed.

'As you see.'

'I need to apologise for putting my family in your cottage.' Her fingers twisted together. 'My father walked out on them and they had to do a moonlight flit before the bailiffs came. I didn't know what else to do – but it was only going to be for a day or so, I promise.'

Bailiffs? A moonlight flit? She must have been beside herself. 'You could have sought my help.' But she couldn't, could she? The girl who was in love with Richard Carson wasn't going to turn to Gabriel Linkworth when she was in a tight spot.

Colour crept across her cheeks. 'I'm so sorry. It was nasty to go behind your back like that, but I was at my wits' end.'

'You took a liberty, but you were desperate. I understand that. I'm not going to hold it against you.'

She caught her breath. 'Oh, thank you. I've been so...' She tried to mask a tiny sniff as she collected herself. 'I swear I don't know how the fire started. My brothers—'

'It was arson. Someone set fire to the cottage from the outside.'

She paled. 'If you hadn't come along, we'd have – we were all so tired—'

'You're safe, that's what matters.'

'Thanks to you.'

The look she gave him melted his heart. Her eyes sparkled with tears. He wanted to wipe them away and hold her. Clearing his throat, he made a show of looking round the shop, all business-like.

'I shan't keep this place.'

'I thought you wanted to be a bookseller.'

'I do, but at present I can't afford the rent. What funds I have will be used to clear the remains of the cottage. I don't want that land defaced by a ruin.'

'And what about you?'

Oh, what a girl. Anyone else would worry about themselves, but her first thought was for him.

'If you're feeling sorry for me for losing the shop, don't. My memory started coming back last night. One thing I now know about myself is I'm not the sort who wants everything to be handed to him on a plate. I've been given so much because of my lost memory: a home and a job in France by the family who took me in; then I was taken on by the army and seen by a specialist doctor; then I inherited this shop and the cottage. But now I've got my life back and I don't need to settle for what I'm given. I want to go out and earn it for myself.'

She stood straighter, looking him in the eye. Was she proud of him?

'All these books are still mine. And there will be another bookshop one day, I promise you.'

One day. Yes. He was sure of it.

Shortly before five o'clock, George entered the shop. In his collar-attached shirt and well-worn jacket, he wasn't as well dressed as Gabriel, but he was smart and handsome in his sister's eyes. He went straight to Gabriel, hand outstretched.

'Mr Linkworth? George Layton. You saved my family's lives last night and I'm grateful.'

Gabriel accepted the warm pumping of his hand and asked, 'Have you come to escort Miss Layton home?' He glanced at her. 'I don't mind if you leave early.'

Did he want to get rid of her? She couldn't blame him. After that first conversation, he hadn't referred to the liberty she had taken, but she had looked for hidden criticism in everything he said.

'If you don't mind,' George told Gabriel, 'it would help if Bel could come now. Our mother has an appointment with Mrs Rostron at the orphanage. She wants me to go with her and I think Bel should come too.'

She fetched her things. Mum was waiting outside, wearing the linen dress, lightweight coat and felt hat that Belinda had found at the second-hand stall that morning. Her skin was colourless, her eyes bruised with tiredness and shock. Belinda squeezed her arm, but it was George Mum attached herself to. They walked to the corner and turned into Church Road, passing the long line of low brick walls and tall terraced houses with netted windows. At the far end, behind walls smothered in thick ivy, was St Anthony's, a sprawling building that looked more like a school than a home. Parts of it had those horribly high-up windows that classrooms had, which you'd have to be a giant to see out of.

'This way,' said Mum.

They went through the gates, across the playground and up some stone steps to haul on an old-fashioned bell-pull. A maid in a dark blue dress beneath a long white apron let them in, not into a pleasant hallway, but onto a short corridor. She led them round a corner and up a flight of stairs. Everything smelled of wood and disinfectant. The babble of voices suggested the children were cooped up together close by. Teatime, presumably.

The maid knocked at a door and stood aside for them to crowd into an office. A woman sat behind a desk. She looked up as they came in, but didn't rise to greet them. She didn't smile either. She was middle-aged with a serious face and keen eyes. Her dark hair was long and worn in a loose bun that looked like it might shake free at any moment, though Belinda rather thought it wouldn't dare.

'Good afternoon, Mrs Layton. Thank you for coming back.' Mrs Rostron's gaze flicked from George to Belinda. 'And you are?'

'George and Belinda Layton,' said George, removing his cap. 'Mrs Layton's eldest.'

'I see. I have two chairs for visitors. You don't mind standing, Mr Layton?' Mrs Rostron's tone suggested it wouldn't matter if he did mind. 'I have this afternoon received the school reports and references for your boys, Mrs Layton. I see that Michael and Thaddeus are due for another year at school after this year, and Jacob another two years. Let's start with Michael. Very good reports: I'm happy to accept him. I see he has a half-time job on Beech Road and I've been made aware as to why he had to travel so far afield to get it.' Her gaze ran over the three of them, cool and assessing. Blaming them for Thad's behaviour? 'Now then: Jacob. A silly boy, easily led and, in the process, I understand, of being led severely astray. I'll accept him too, but I'll have words with him – and I suggest you do the same – to the effect that he must make a choice. Either he pulls his socks up or he goes to the bad: his choice, and whether he remains here will depend upon what he elects to do.'

Mum stirred, but didn't get a chance to speak.

'Which brings me to Thaddeus. A trouble-maker, according to this.' Mrs Rostron indicated the papers in front of her. 'And a trouble-maker according to my staff, I might add. He has already provoked a fight as well as taking more than his fair share of the midday meal. I'm not prepared to accept him. I'll make arrangements for him to be sent to the reformatory, where they'll keep him until he's fourteen, at which time, if he has reformed, he'll be found an apprenticeship. Otherwise, he'll be put in the army. Don't look so shocked. It could be the making of him.'

'A reformatory?' breathed George.

Mrs Rostron glanced at her papers. 'Fighting, bullying, lying, insolence, cheating, theft... Need I continue? I cannot have behaviour like that in my establishment. Do you accept my recommendations for your boys, Mrs Layton?'

'Well, for Jacob and Mikey, yes, but—'

'You may not pick and choose. If you don't send Jacob and Michael here, my assessment of their needs will be put before the Panel; and the Panel will look at the entire family, not just them.'

'But – a reformatory...'

Mrs Rostron sighed. 'Your slack parenting enabled Thaddeus to run wild and now you must bear the consequences. Michael, on the other hand, is a credit to you. I suggest you take what comfort you can from that.'

Belinda felt winded as she, George and Mum stumbled off the premises. She wanted to dislike Mrs Rostron, but her assessment of the three boys had been spot on; and maybe the reformatory would turn Thad round. They would have to cling to that hope.

'I must call on the Miss Heskeths,' Mum said wearily. 'The one who came this morning said they would try to help me.'

'I'll take you there,' said Belinda.

'Will you come an' all, George?' Mum asked.

'No. My landlady will have my tea on the table shortly.'

'Does she have an empty room?' Mum asked.

'Let's see what the Miss Heskeths say first,' said Belinda. 'You cut along, George.'

'I were only asking.' Mum sounded plaintive.

Belinda hurried her to Wilton Close and Miss Patience let them in.

'My sister is home from the office and I've explained the situation to her.'

Mum was all eyes as they entered the sitting room. Invited to sit down, she smoothed the skirt of her dress and straightened her shoulders. She looked like she was in her element.

'A bad business,' said Miss Hesketh. 'I'm glad you're all safe and well. We must be grateful that Mr Linkworth appeared when he did.'

'Yes, miss,' Mum agreed.

'As I understand it, the rest of the family is taken care of, so there's just you to be placed, Mrs Layton.'

'I keep saying: I can live with our George. He's my eldest. He's a postman.'

Belinda swallowed her frustration. 'No, Mum.' She hated to wash the family's dirty linen in public, but it had to be done. 'George has his eye on a girl and he needs to save up to get married. If he was already married, with a house, maybe there'd be room for you; but he can't support you at this stage, or he'll never get wed. Maybe one day, when I've got a better job and can afford a room, you can live with me, but that's some way off, and you'd still have to go out to work.'

'Mothers aren't meant to go out to work. A mother's work is in the home.'

'It's not as though there are any children at home now,' Belinda said gently. 'There's nothing wrong with going out to work. Look at Auntie Enid and Grandma Beattie; they've worked all their lives. Miss Hesketh goes to the office every day and she and Miss Patience teach in the evenings.'

'I can't cope with all this,' Mum whispered.

'You used to cope,' said Belinda. 'I remember us having a nice little house and you keeping it spick and span.'

'I were younger then.'

'You cared how you looked and you cared how we looked and how we behaved.'

Mum glared from beneath lowered lids. 'Not in front of the ladies, Bel.'

She reached for Mum's hand. 'You've been so unhappy and ground down for such a long time that you've forgotten what you used to be like, but I remember.'

'I may have the answer,' said Miss Hesketh. 'You require an income and a roof over your head, Mrs Layton. You have years of experience of looking after a home. I wonder if Mrs Morgan would be interested.'

'Oh, *yes*.' Miss Patience was all smiles. 'She's our neighbour across the road. She used to have a live-in maid before the war. Their house is much grander than ours; the same size, of course, but a great deal smarter, and,' she added impressively, 'they have a vacuum cleaner.'

'Imagine looking after a posh house, Mum,' said Belinda. 'Imagine all the nice things Mrs Morgan must have.'

'You want me to clean for her?' said Mum.

'It would be housework, not charring,' Miss Hesketh said, 'and if you show yourself willing, there might be the chance of cooking too.'

Miss Patience sat forwards. 'If it helps you decide, our daily once told me that when you have regular work cleaning a house, you come to feel in a way as if the house is yours.'

'Would you like me to put a word in for you?' Miss Hesketh asked.

To Belinda's dismay, tears welled up in Mum's eyes. 'All I ever wanted were a family and a home to take care of, and when I got it, Denby went and ruined everything.'

'He's gone now,' said Belinda. 'You deserve a fresh start, but turning up on George's doorstep isn't the way. You've spent years complaining about Dad. Now you have to set the family a good example. Show us what you're made of. What do you say?'

Chapter Twenty-Eight

GABRIEL VOWED TO concentrate on packing up the books. It would distract him from thinking about Miss Layton – Belinda. Some hope. She was in his thoughts the whole time. He was torn in two. He had to leave the shop, but when he did, he would never see her again. She didn't want him, so he would be better off not seeing her. So he told himself.

Maybe she wouldn't require a new job. Was this the moment when Richard Carson scooped her up and put a ring on her finger? Did she still feel the same about Carson after his financial skulduggery? Surely not. And yet... that starry-eyed look she had bestowed on him...

Gabriel kept a discreet eye on her over the next day or two. She looked pale and tired. He knew she was running around like a mad thing after work, walking Mikey from Brown's to the orphanage at five o'clock, then scooting round to Wilton Close to knock on the back door of the house where her mother had been taken on, to have a few minutes with Mrs Layton before going home; and then this evening, Friday, she would walk back to Chorlton for her lesson at the business school.

And if he happened to be strolling along Edge Lane this evening on his way to Limits Lane, and if it happened to be around the time when Belinda might be coming to Chorlton, who was to know what a prize ass he was, other than himself?

He walked briskly to start with, eager to see her, then slowed for fear of reaching Limits Lane too soon. Even so, he arrived at the corner without seeing her. As he hovered at the top of the lane, a woman emerged from the first cottage. Judging by her worn, lined face, she could have been anywhere from forty to seventy.

'You're young Mr Tyrell, aren't you?'

'My name is Linkworth, but, yes, I'm Mr Tyrell's nephew.'

'We've got some of your things in our place. After you collapsed, us neighbours saw there were nowt to be done for the cottage, so we rescued what we could from downstairs.'

'I had no idea or I'd have come sooner.'

'We've all got stuff, all us cottagers. Crockery, ornaments, pictures. She loved her figurines, did Mrs Tyrell. And some bits and pieces of furniture an' all, though the upholstery stinks summat dreadful from the smoke. We've had to keep it outside. It's a mercy it hasn't rained.'

'That's very good of you all. I'll arrange for everything to be collected.' Was Belinda on her way? He wanted to look over his shoulder, but couldn't be so rude.

'Come and see what we've got.'

Nothing would satisfy her but that he should knock at every door to thank each family personally. Being familiar with the standard of comfort his uncle had enjoyed, it was sobering to see how humble the other cottages were, not even boasting proper floors downstairs, just compacted dirt. Aunt Victoria's beloved figurines looked like priceless ornaments in such settings.

He would hang onto a couple of ornaments as keepsakes, but he didn't want to cram his lodgings, or his house when he eventually got one, full of them. Carson had intended to sell them, hadn't he? Perhaps that wasn't a bad idea. Properly boxed, they could be stored alongside the book stock... when he had somewhere suitable to keep them.

'If the furniture is of use to you, please keep it or pass it on to someone in need,' he told the cottagers. The kitchen table, the armchairs, the sideboard, the cupboard with glass doors, would make a difference to these folk.

With good wishes ringing in his ears, he took his leave, cheered by the cottagers' decency and kindness. Their humble dwellings had brought home to him just how much he had, in spite of what he had lost. He still possessed the wherewithal to stock a bookshop, and once he had found work and got some savings behind him, he would be able to look for a shop to rent.

The cottagers had done him another favour too. They had prevented him from making a jackass of himself over Belinda Layton.

Patience made their nightly Ovaltine and carried the tray to the sitting room. They mulled things over while sipping their bedtime drinks.

'I hope we'll be able to help Miss Layton,' said Patience. Their working-class pupil had become the most dear of her pretend-daughters.

'She was foolish to take on a temporary post in the first place.'

'I do think you were a little harsh with her this evening. She only asked for a character reference and a testimonial as to her office skills. There was no need to say we couldn't magic up a job for her like we did for her mother.'

Prudence shrugged. 'It's preferable for people to know where they stand.'

With a quiet sigh, Patience let it go. Nothing was going to soften Prudence's judgemental nature this late in life.

'Might there be vacancies in the Corporation typing pool?' she ventured.

'It doesn't matter if there are. I can't put Miss Layton forward. Imagine what poisonous remarks Lawrence would drop in the ears of anyone who would listen. *Business School Pupils Given Corporation Posts by Tutor* – that's what the papers would say. Meanwhile Lawrence would be giving interviews left, right and centre, apologising for his foolish sister who has brought his business school into disrepute and the only honourable course of action is to close it down.'

Patience shivered. Minuscule ripples passed across the surface of her drink. 'It's beastly having to think of Lawrence's likely response every time we want to do something.'

'We're managing pretty well. The school seems safe enough for the time being.'

'And we've got Mrs Atwood coming soon.'

Another pretend-daughter, and one who would be living with them for some time to come while she attended the school on a once- or twice-weekly basis. A vase of fresh flowers on the chest of drawers would be a welcoming gesture.

And if things went well with their new lodger... why, only this morning she had stood in the box-room doorway, considering the possibilities. A single bed with a rug beside it; pretty curtains... well, why not?

'I saw Mrs Morgan this morning,' she told Prudence. 'She's delighted to have live-in staff again.'

Prudence snorted. 'Live-in staff! She's lives in Wilton Close, not Tatton Hall.'

'We must send a couple of lines to Mr Linkworth to say how sorry we are about his cottage.'

'One feels one ought to offer assistance, but what could we possibly do?'

'He went straight back to work, you know. Miss Layton told me. She said he has eyes for nothing but the books.'

'Like Mr Tyrell before him,' said Prudence.

'Miss Layton seemed dismayed by his dedication to his work.'

'Nonsense. It's an admirable trait.'

'I suppose,' said Patience, 'she's worried about her own position. The harder he works on packing up the shop, the sooner
it will close. He wants to put the books in storage, apparently,
and start up again when he has earned some money.'

'Where will he store everything?' Prudence sat up straighter.
'Maybe we can assist him after all. Our cellar is spacious, dry,
ventilated – and empty. He can use it, for a peppercorn rent.'

'What if Lawrence finds out?' asked Patience.

'You saw the piece in the *Evening News*. Mr Linkworth
carried one boy downstairs through thick smoke, then went
back for the other. Just you wait. Lawrence will tell his cronies
how he has used his premises to assist a local hero. We'll call
at Tyrell's Books tomorrow and make the offer.'

By half-seven in the morning, Gabriel was at Perkins and
Watson's yard, where two or three fellows were getting ready
for work, including, he was pleased to see, Tom Watson, who
greeted him with a cheery wave and walked across to him.

'Would you take a look at the cottage,' he said, 'and let me
know the cost of clearing the land?'

'Is it covered by insurance?'

''Fraid not.'

'Tell you what. Tell the folk in Limits Lane it's all up for
grabs.'

'They've already saved the small possessions and the
furniture.'

'I don't mean that. I mean bricks, doors, window-panes, the
kitchen range, the slop-stone. You'd be surprised what people
can make use of; and what they can't use, they can sell. It's
Easter next weekend. Tell them they've got until close of play
on Bank Holiday Monday. After that I'll give you a price to
clear what's left.'

Gabriel cut along to the shop and got to work boxing up
books. At nine, he lifted the blind on the door and turned the

sign to Open. He had barely returned to his packing when the bell jingled, summoning him to greet his customers, a pair of faded-looking ladies, who looked the same... only not quite the same. One was taller, all angles, straight and sharp; the other had a gentler face.

'Good morning, ladies. May I help you?'

'Mr Linkworth?' enquired the sharp-looking one. 'As a matter of fact, we may be able to help you.'

By the time they left, his head was whirling. How good people were. The Limits Lane folk had rescued his belongings; Tom Watson had come up with a way to cut the cost of clearing the land; and now the Miss Heskeths had offered to store his books.

The bell rang again and William Turton walked in, genial and smiling.

They exchanged greetings, then Turton said, 'I've brought a proposition for you to consider.'

'Come and sit in the office.'

Turton removed his bowler, unfastened his double-breasted overcoat and sat in the chair Belinda used when she typed. Gabriel leaned against the wall.

'Mr Sowerby informed me of your plan to clear the land in Limits Lane. A worthy endeavour, if I may say so.'

Gabriel inclined his head. Turton was building up to something.

'And you won't be able to keep the shop on. A shame.' It was said in a matter-of-fact way, proffering neither censure nor pity: Gabriel liked him for it. 'Would I be correct in supposing you find yourself in need of a job?'

Surprise made him laugh. 'Yes.'

'I may have found one for you. Clerking work with one of the principal landlords in town. They've been clients of ours for years and will accept you on our recommendation.'

'That's jolly decent of you.'

'Think nothing of it. When are you due to quit the shop?'

'Mr Dawson called personally yesterday. Out of respect for my late uncle, he'll let me out on a week's notice.'

'Has Miss Layton had any luck finding employment elsewhere?'

'Unfortunately not. I told her, of course, as soon as I knew I wouldn't be keeping the shop, so she is aware her days here are numbered.'

'As indeed they were all along,' Turton reminded him.

Gabriel's pulse slowed. It really was going to happen. The shop would shut and she would disappear from his life.

Turton came to his feet. 'Will you accept a word of advice from a fellow who has been happily married for over twenty years? Tell her how you feel.'

'I – what?' He stood up straight.

'Your face fell a mile at the thought of her leaving here. Talk to her.'

'She likes someone else.'

'And has that someone else put a ring on her finger? Then what are you waiting for?' Turton fastened the buttons on his overcoat. 'I loved another girl once, not Mrs Turton, I mean. My feelings for her were real enough, but then I realised what had been in front of me all along.' He put on his bowler. 'My point is, Linkworth, that you may not be Miss Layton's first love, but what of it, so long as you are her lasting love?'

It wasn't until a customer alerted him to the time that Gabriel realised he had stayed open beyond midday. He rang up the gentleman's purchases and closed the door behind him. His eyes felt gritty. He hadn't slept well recently, his brain too busy turning over a lifetime of memories. Awarding himself an extra-long dinner hour, he wrote *Back at 2 o'clock* on a piece of card and propped it in the window beside the door.

He chose a couple of barm cakes in Richardson's and went to the rec. Sitting on a bench to eat, he wrote a letter in his head to Cousin Irene. They had spent a couple of hours together at the end of his day in court. She had wanted to tell him about his family, but hearing about his parents and his brother had been profoundly unsettling and he had encouraged her instead to speak of her children and her late husband. Now, though, he was eager to see her again and have a proper chinwag about old times; about attending the village school and flicking ink pellets at one another behind the teacher's back; about her wedding and Auntie Mabel, who had got drunk and danced on the table; and about Great-Granny Linkworth, who had gleefully celebrated her hundredth birthday with all her descendants around her, only for her to pass away the following year, leaving behind family papers that showed she had in fact been a stripling of ninety-two.

Should he tell Irene about the fire and the destruction of his hopes? No, not the destruction; far too dramatic. Postponement: that was better. He wanted to be open with her, but what if, hearing of the fire, she offered up her inheritance from his father? He couldn't have her falling on her sword. Neither did he want to reassure her – again – that he wasn't after his father's money. To do so might give the impression he wanted her to be grateful – again. He didn't want her feeling beholden.

He glanced round the rec. A group of children ran about, playing tag with much squealing; older boys were playing cricket. A woman trotted along the path with her shopping basket, probably hurrying home to get the dinner on the table; and over by the rose-beds that flanked the bowling green on three sides were... Belinda and her family.

He sat up. 'Tell her how you feel,' said William Turton's voice in his head. He got up, stuffing the paper bag that had held his lunch into his pocket, and headed in their direction.

'Good afternoon.' He raised his homburg to Belinda and her mother. 'I haven't seen you since the night of the fire, Mrs Layton. I hope you're recovered.'

'Yes, thank you; and thank you for what you did that night. You saved all our lives.'

'I gather you've made arrangements for your children and yourself.' He knew from what Belinda had said and, more to the point, what she hadn't said, that Mrs Layton leaned heavily on others. If Belinda walked out with him, giving her mother a helping hand would become part of his life.

'But we've all been separated,' said Mrs Layton.

'Only for now,' said Belinda.

'Have you settled in at the orphanage?' he asked Mikey.

'It's takes a bit of getting used to, mister, but we're all right, aren't we, Jacob?'

'I miss Thad,' said the younger boy.

'Aye, like a hole in the head,' said Mikey.

Gabriel didn't know all the ins and outs, but he remembered Belinda referring to Thad as a ruffian. 'Do yourself a favour, son,' he advised Jacob, 'stick with Mikey. He's a good lad.'

Mikey stood taller at the praise. 'Have you got the time, mister? Dinner is at one o'clock on Saturdays and Sundays and we have to be back in time to wash our hands and line up.'

'You'd better scoot, then,' said Gabriel.

Mrs Layton's face crumpled, then she put on a smile. 'I'll walk down the road with you.'

After a flurry of goodbyes, the others hurried away, leaving Belinda looking forlorn. Gabriel's heart reached out to her, but he felt a surge of joy too – and nerves. This was his moment.

'I have to get home,' she said.

'May I accompany you as far as Limits Lane?' He immediately struck up a conversation so as not to give her an opportunity to refuse. 'Where is your sister living?'

She fell in step. 'At End Cottage. She's sharing my room. It's a terrible squeeze, but it'll bring us closer... in more ways than one.' She laughed. 'Sarah wants to go to the business school. We hope she can be the next scholarship pupil. She's a chambermaid in a hotel, but she's decided she wants to work in the office and perhaps be a receptionist one day.'

'Good for her.' What was he doing, talking about the younger sister? He wanted to talk about Belinda, about his feelings, but nerves got the better of him and all he asked was, 'Have you seen any positions to apply for?'

'I'm going to write some applications this afternoon. Miss Hesketh has kindly agreed to recommend me and you have too, of course.' She glanced shyly at him.

'It's the least I can do – and only what you deserve.' He couldn't have her thinking he was providing the reference out of guilt. 'I may not have known you long, but I can vouch for how efficient and reliable you are, not to mention being punctual and hard-working.' Shut up, shut up. That isn't what you say to the girl you want to marry.

They continued on their way, his praise having killed the conversation stone dead. He cast about for something else to say.

'Have you seen my uncle's cottage since the fire?'

'No. I can't help noticing you call him "my uncle" now. You used to refer to him as Mr Tyrell.'

'It seemed only polite, since I couldn't remember him. To call him Uncle Reg would have felt presumptuous.'

'Uncle Reg?' She smiled.

'He was a bit grumpy, but good at heart. He and Aunt Victoria had no family of their own, so they always took an interest in my brother and me.'

'He must have thought well of you to make you his heir.'

'Yes,' he agreed simply. He knew now why Uncle Reg hadn't removed his name from the will.

'It's a good job I've got Victoria's nephews,' he had said once. 'I'm not keen on my own. Out for what he can get, is Richard. I'm leaving all my worldly goods to you and Frank. Only if you both predecease me will anything go to Richard.'

Later, after Frank was killed, Uncle Reg had told Gabriel on his next leave, 'I've changed my will and left the lot to you. I'm not changing it again, my boy, so you'd better make sure you stay alive. I've kept Richard in, because he's the sort to contest the will if he's left out, but by keeping him as first reserve, as it were, he can't claim he was overlooked.'

All that, however, was a private matter, to be shared with no one. It gave Gabriel a warm feeling to know he had been valued by Uncle Reg. Mr Sowerby had once been sharp with him for suggesting sharing the inheritance with Carson. Now he knew Uncle Reg would also have had a few pertinent words to say on the subject.

What was he doing, thinking of Richard Carson? The man was like a burr, clinging to his brain. Here he was, with the girl of his dreams, and he had talked about her job prospects, her sister and Uncle Reg. 'Tell her how you feel,' William Turton had advised. But suppose he did and it was the end of everything.

At the corner of Limits Lane, she stopped. They had come all this way and he hadn't said his piece.

'Come and see the cottage.'

'I don't think I want to. I've had dreams about it.'

'I'm not surprised after what you and your family went through. The mind is a funny thing. Mine shut down my memory after the fire in France and then it allowed my memory to wake up again after this fire. If you're having bad dreams, seeing the cottage as it is now might help your mind to accept that what happened is over and done with.'

They walked down the lane. Beside him, she slowed. He opened the gate and waited for her. She stood a short distance away, peering through. Her colour had fled.

'If you hadn't arrived when you did…'

'But I did, so you and I together got your family to safety. Try not to think of the alternative.'

'When you said you were going to clear the land, I thought you must be mad. I thought you might as well chuck your money down the drain. But now, seeing this... You're right. I want what's left of the cottage, and all those memories, swept away for ever.' She lifted her chin. 'If my family had died, it would have been my fault for bringing them here.'

'No. The fire was the fault of the person who committed arson.'

'If I could get my hands on them...'

'I'm sorry. I didn't bring you here to upset you. I brought you to... to...'

'Yes?'

Leaving the gate to swing shut, he went to her, walking round her so that, in turning to face him, she had her back to the cottage.

'I didn't want you to come here at all. It merely provided me with an excuse to walk with you. Miss Layton – Belinda...' It had been so easy when he did this with Naomi. There had been no doubt on either side. 'Ever since I met you, I haven't been able to stop thinking about you. I know I don't stand a chance.' Don't say that, you fool. What if she agrees? 'I know there's someone else you're interested in.'

Her lips parted. He had to say something quickly before she could cut him off. *My point is, Linkworth, that you may not be her first love, but what of it, so long as you are her lasting love?* And all at once, the panic subsided and he knew what to say.

He caught her hands in his, fingertips holding fingertips.

'Belinda Layton, I love you. I tried not to, because I saw your interest in Carson, but I couldn't help it. You're clever and kind and you think of everybody else before yourself. I saw Mr Turton today and he said something about first love and lasting love. I've been so preoccupied by your possible feelings for Carson that it made me forget he isn't your first love. Your first love was your fiancé, that brave chap who gave his life for his country. You aren't a helpless girl to be scrapped over. You're an independent young woman, with a sense of responsibility, and you've shown your mettle at every turn. I can imagine no greater honour than to be your lasting love; and so, even though I honestly can't tell what you think of me, even though I know that Richard Carson dazzles you, I'm going to say: forget him and marry me. I will cherish you and do my best for your family. I'll work hard and one day we'll run a bookshop together. It'll take time, because I haven't any money. All I have is the books to stock a shop I can't afford to run. But that's just for now. Mr Turton has found me a decent job and I'll work hard and save up. Running a bookshop is my dream – one of my dreams. My other dream is running that bookshop with you.' He dropped to one knee. 'Will you marry me, Belinda? Or at least give a chance. Say you'll think about it.'

Her eyes were starry. Well, that would be the surprise, of course. Or possibly confusion. Her lips parted. That wasn't a good sign. An immediate response wasn't a good sign.

'I don't need to think about it.'

Of course not. An instant no.

'Yes,' she breathed.

Elation almost drained his body of power, but he lurched to his feet. 'Yes, you'll think about it?' He wanted to dance her up the lane and back again. She was going to consider him, give him a chance to prove himself.

'Yes, I'll marry you.'

'Say it again. Say it a thousand times.'

But she didn't get the chance. He leaned down – she was tiny, only a whisper above five foot – and took her face gently in his hands before he kissed her.

Chapter Twenty-Nine

BELINDA PICKED UP Ben's photograph, her fingers trailing over the black crêpe and the red poppy. Darling Ben. Her first love. Not so long ago, she had expected to love him for ever, and in a way, she would. But her life had moved on and now a new man occupied her heart. Not Richard Carson. He had never set foot in her heart. He had been a mad fling, her emotions having bats in the belfry. She shook her head, casting him aside for ever.

It was Gabriel who mattered now. Her love for him was real and lasting. She had to tell Auntie Enid and Grandma Beattie, but first she had to tell Ben. How handsome he was, with his dark hair and dark eyes, looking serious in his photograph. And yet he hadn't been a serious person. He had been lively and full of fun. And a hugger. When he had hugged Grandma Beattie and Auntie Enid, they had pretended to bat him away, but really they had loved it. She had loved it too. Her own family wasn't affectionate and she had tingled all over every time Ben had held her hand or given her a cuddle; not just because she was attracted to him, but because she adored the closeness, the warmth of two people showing they cared. After he went away and never returned, the hugging had stopped. Was Gabriel a hugger? It didn't matter if he wasn't, because she intended to be and he would learn.

Pressing her finger to her lips, she kissed it, then pressed the kiss onto Ben's photograph. She felt no sense of conflict. She could carry him in her heart at the same time as loving Gabriel.

It was time to go down and tell Ben's mother and grandmother.

She descended the dark staircase. Grandma Beattie was beside the range, patting herby dumplings into shape on the bread board while Auntie Enid applied lavender polish and elbow grease to their old dresser.

She ignored the nerves in her tummy. 'Come and sit down. I've got something to tell you.'

They joined her at the table.

Here goes. 'It's... it's Ben.'

A ripple passed through the other two, a quiet resettling of shoulders, thoughts, feelings.

'You know how much I loved him and that I've mourned him as deeply as you have.'

'Aye, love, we know,' said Auntie Enid. 'It's such a comfort to us.'

Maybe she shouldn't have started with Ben, but how else was she to do justice to this situation? She had to tell them straight out. She mustn't appear ashamed.

'Mr Linkworth and me... we want to walk out together.'

Their mouths fell open. Grandma Beattie's double chin wobbled as she gulped. Auntie Enid's face paled and then flushed. Then, against Belinda's every expectation, she laughed.

'Don't be silly. He saved your family from that fire, which was very brave, and you're grateful and you admire him, but that's all it is. It's not real feelings.'

'It isn't gratitude.'

'Yes, it is. It's not real, not compared to your feelings for Ben.' She gazed at Belinda with a pained stare.

'It started before the fire,' said Belinda.

'Behind us backs?' Grandma Beattie exclaimed.

'No.' She tried to sound firm, but her heart was pounding. 'We had feelings for each other, but neither of us said a word until today.' Today. See, you are being informed immediately. 'We – we love one another.'

'I knew it,' said Grandma Beattie. 'I knew nowt good would come of you leaving the mill and going to that business school.'

'You told me you were glad I'd have a better future.'

'Aye – in an office. Not putting yourself about, looking for a man.'

'I haven't put myself about—'

'Fancy leaving our Ben high and dry.'

'Ben will always be dear to me, but I've...' It was a moment before the words would come. 'I've moved on. It's the same as wanting to wear some colour.'

'It most certainly isn't!' Auntie Enid leaned forward, eyes glinting. 'Comparing a coloured scarf to walking out with a new fellow – how dare you?'

'So that's it, then,' said Grandma Beattie. 'We lost our Ben when he didn't come home from the war and now we've lost him all over again, because his fiancée has "moved on". There's nowt more to be said, really, is there?'

Belinda didn't go to church with Auntie Enid and Grandma Beattie. She had arranged with Mum to attend St Clement's in Chorlton, because that was where the orphanage children went. She felt torn. She ought to be with Auntie Enid and Grandma Beattie to show she was still part of their little family, but she also needed to be with her other family, to create a feeling of togetherness; herself, Mum and the two boys, coming from different addresses, but going to the same church service. Two boys, not three. She wanted to feel a sense of good riddance at Thad's removal, but she was too shocked that such drastic action had been taken.

She stood outside the church, wishing for Sarah's presence, but Sarah had taken on extra shifts to earn more money.

As she waited, she saw Miss Hesketh and Miss Patience coming along the road. She smiled politely at them, but didn't want to presume. Then Mum arrived. She wanted to tell Mum her news about Gabriel, but Mum kept looking over her shoulder, so she kept it to herself for now and joined Mum in gazing down the road for the orphans. A crocodile appeared, headed by an adult, with another at the far end. Beside her, Mum stirred and brightened. Mikey and Jacob smiled and nodded as they went past, but there was no time for more. No time for mothers and sisters of non-orphans to have a hug and a few words, no time for a mother to produce a hanky with an order to spit, before scrubbing away at a grubby face. Not that Mikey and Jacob or any of the children looked grubby or crumpled. Dressed in their sober uniforms, they looked neat and clean and all the same, the boys in grey shirts, shorts and jackets, the girls' grey capes shifting as they walked to reveal glimpses of white pinafores over grey dresses.

It was no different when they left at the end of the service. Belinda and Mum had sat near the back of the church for a quick getaway in the hope of a minute with the boys when they came out, but the orphans walked out in twos and didn't stop until they reached the kerb. A young woman led them across the road and a man brought up the rear.

'It's the way things are going to be,' said Mum. 'I'll have to get used to it.' She sounded in control, almost flippant, but her mouth twisted. Was she cursing Dad?

She had to hurry off to do the vegetables and serve the Morgans' dinner. Belinda hadn't expected that.

'But I've got something to tell you,' she tried to say.

'It'll have to wait. Tell me next time.'

And she hurried off. Not even a goodbye kiss. Belinda stared after her.

'You look taken aback, if I may say so,' said a gentle voice.

'Oh – Miss Patience. I was hoping for a word with Mum, but she had to get back. I've got something important to tell her.'

'A new job?'

'No.' She held her breath for a moment. 'I'm engaged. To Gabriel – Mr Linkworth.'

'I thought you liked Mr Carson.' Miss Patience's eyes widened. 'I do apologise.'

'And you call me tactless,' remarked Miss Hesketh.

'Many congratulations, my dear,' said Miss Patience. 'This is unexpected, but very happy news nonetheless.'

But Miss Hesketh was all reserve. 'I wish you well, obviously, but it'll be a shame to see your new skills going to waste.'

'They won't! We can't get married for some time. Gabriel needs to save up – we both do – and eventually we'll rent another shop to sell the books.'

'In that case,' said Miss Hesketh, 'there's a job going at the funeral parlour. The paperwork has to be accurate, as you can appreciate, and you have a quiet, respectful manner that – what's the matter?'

'I've just told you I'm engaged and your response is to tell me about a job.'

'Well, you still need one.'

'She wants us to be happy about her engagement,' said Miss Patience, 'don't you, dear? And we are, even if my sister has an unconventional way of showing it. Who else have you told?'

'Auntie Enid and Grandma Beattie – and they were desperately hurt.'

'Ah,' breathed Miss Patience.

All the disappointment she had kept bottled up since yesterday afternoon came pouring out. 'They want me to carry on living a life of mourning with them. They think I'm betraying Ben.'

'I'm sorry to hear that,' said Miss Patience.

'It's difficult for you,' said Miss Hesketh. 'And now you must excuse us. Patience, we should be getting home.'

Belinda stepped aside. 'Of course. Thank you for telling me about the position at the funeral parlour. I'll certainly apply for it. And thank you for your good wishes.' They had given her their good wishes, hadn't they?

She trailed home. She was going to see Gabriel this afternoon, but instead of being able to tell him jubilantly of Mum's joy, there would be no enthusiasm to offset the grim reaction in End Cottage. Auntie Enid and Grandma Beattie would spend the afternoon feeling betrayed and abandoned.

But she wasn't going to let it stop her.

'It's rather seedy, isn't it?' said Prudence as they walked the length of Grave Pit Lane. 'Miss Layton has done well for herself.'

'I hope you aren't suggesting that's why she has attached herself to Mr Linkworth,' said Patience, shocked.

'Actually, I was referring to her commitment to better herself through professional training.'

'Do you think we're doing the right thing?' The closer they drew to End Cottage, the more nervous Patience felt.

Prudence dealt her a sideways glance. 'It was your idea.'

'I know, but one doesn't like to interfere. Is it interfering to the help the course of true love?'

'If you're going to talk twaddle, I'll turn round and go home.'

At End Cottage, the younger Mrs Sloan let them in. There was no sign of Miss Layton, which was probably for the best. The older Mrs Sloan heaved herself off the battered old sofa.

'Please sit here, ladies,' she offered.

'Don't let us disturb you,' said Patience. 'I'm sure the two of you were comfortably settled for the afternoon. My sister and I are quite happy to sit at the table.'

They all sat, the Mrs Sloans looking self-conscious in the best seats. Oh dear. Should she have let them give up their places? Too late now.

'Pardon us for interrupting your Sunday afternoon,' said Prudence, 'but we're here about Miss Layton and Mr Linkworth.' Trust her to get right to the point.

'Oh aye?' said Mrs Sloan the elder, deference dissolving. 'She's wasted no time spreading the word, then.'

'And why should she?' Prudence replied at once. 'It isn't every day a girl gets engaged.'

'Engaged!' cried the younger Mrs Sloan.

'She never told us that,' said the elder.

'Oh my goodness.' Patience's heart thumped. What a blunder.

But Prudence appeared unruffled. 'I'm not surprised she didn't tell you. It sounds as if you were hard enough on her simply for looking at another man.'

'Prudence!' Patience exclaimed.

'You're the one who wanted to help the course of true love. How did you propose to do it without a bit of plain speaking? Mrs Sloan and Mrs Sloan, please consider this. You've already lost your son and grandson. Do you intend to lose your honorary daughter- and granddaughter-in-law as well? She has mourned her lost love for several years, but now she has met someone else. You can accept it or fall out over it. Which is it to be?'

'You can't come here telling us what to do,' blurted the elder Mrs Sloan.

'Please don't take offence,' said Patience.

'Easy for you to say,' came the swift retort, 'a pair of old maids like you.'

Dots of anguish flashed before Patience's eyes. 'Have you any idea what a cruel thing that is to say? Some women are destined to go through life alone. Is that really what you want for Miss

Layton? Ladies, please, I know how much you care about her. The fact that she lives with you testifies to it. You're frightened, aren't you, of losing her? And not just because of the precious link to Ben. You love her in her own right. I know how affectionately she speaks of you and I'm sure the feeling is mutual.'

The two women glanced at one another.

'Well, of course we care about her,' said Mrs Sloan the younger, 'but there's nowt to be frightened of. I don't know what you're talking about.'

'You've lost so much already,' said Patience. 'Please don't lose Miss Layton as well. Surely you know her well enough to know she wants to share her happiness with you and keep you as her dear mother-in-law and grandmother-in-law.'

'Steady on,' murmured Prudence. 'You're not in a position to make declarations on Miss Layton's behalf.'

'Aren't I? I think I know her well enough to rely on her generous nature.'

'I think we know her better'n you do, miss,' said Mrs Sloan the elder.

'I'm sure you do,' Patience agreed, 'so I appeal to you. Is she the sort to turn her back on you because she has got engaged to Mr Linkworth? Or will she be true to her long-standing relationship with you?'

As Belinda entered the shop first thing Monday morning, Gabriel came out of the office and they walked into one another's arms. This was where she wanted to be, now and always.

'I haven't stopped thinking about you,' said Gabriel. 'Did the Mrs Sloans make things difficult for you again after you got home yesterday afternoon?'

Putting her hands on his chest, she pushed herself a little away, but not so far that he had to let go. 'Not at all.' She could still hardly believe it. 'Their attitude has changed completely. They've accepted our relationship.'

'What a turnaround. What prompted that?'

'They said they'd had time to think and they don't want to lose me. And listen: they want to be mother- and grandmother-in-law to you once we're married.'

Gabriel laughed. 'I'm marrying into a bigger family than I thought.'

'You don't mind?'

'Why would I? I promised you yesterday that I'll do my best for your family, and that includes the Mrs Sloans.' He stepped away from her with obvious reluctance. 'We must get to work.'

He disappeared upstairs to finish packing the books stored there while Belinda settled at the typewriter to continue the inventory. The bell jingled and the postman came in. He handed her a letter and a packet.

She called up the stairs, 'Post's come. Do you want to open it or should I?'

'You do it. I'll put the kettle on.'

She opened the letter first, an enquiry about a history book. She found the book on the shelf and set it aside, then turned to the packet. It proved tricky to open, then suddenly it slit straight across and the contents spilled out over the table. It was a collection of envelopes – no, opened letters. Her heart forgot to beat. The letters were addressed to Miss Naomi Colby.

Naomi.

With them was a letter; high-quality paper, folded in half. She picked it up, holding it still folded. Was it her imagination or was there the faintest scent of roses? She shouldn't read it. It was for Gabriel's eyes.

She read it. Of course.

Mrs Naomi Reed, Naomi Colby-as-was, Naomi Linkworth as she had expected to be, had returned Gabriel's letters. Letters: that was what she called them. Love letters was what she meant.

Had she chosen to return them? Had her husband stood over her as she penned the letter and made up the packet?

Gabriel's love letters to the woman he would have married after the war, if he hadn't lost his memory. Oh, heck.

His memory had come back now, which must include his memories of Naomi, beautiful, elegant and poised, with her well-bred loveliness and cultured voice and her subtle, enticing floral perfume – roses.

I love roses. I adore their scent.

'The tea's brewing. What have you got there?'

She pushed the envelopes to the edge of the table. It took him a moment to realise.

'Oh,' he said.

He picked up Naomi's letter, releasing the tiniest waft of sweet fragrance. Either he read it more than once or he was giving himself time to think. Or maybe he was overwhelmed by memories of that happy, hopeful time in his life. Perhaps he was drowning in the scent of roses.

Belinda sat frozen in misery. She wanted him to say something, though she didn't know what. She wanted Naomi not to matter – but what would it say about Gabriel if he could discount his old love so easily? Hadn't she promised to carry Ben in a special place in her heart? She expected Gabriel to understand and respect that. Would he now require the same understanding and respect on her part?

But this was different. No, it wasn't. Yes, it was. Naomi was still alive. What had it cost her to appear in the magistrate's room to speak on Gabriel's behalf? She had conducted herself with such gravity and poise. The perfect lady.

Aye, a lady; not a working-class lass, trying to better herself.

Gabriel hadn't been able to remember her that day, but he could remember her now. *I love roses. I adore their scent.* And the fact that Naomi Reed was married and unattainable needn't make any difference to that.

'These are old letters I sent to Naomi – Mrs Reed. You know she and I were once engaged.'

Tears burned the backs of her eyes. She had herself once been engaged. She had no business being thrown into turmoil by Gabriel's former engagement.

'She's kept them all this time,' he said.

After he was supposedly dead – well, that was fair enough. Belinda cherished the letters she had received from Ben. But Naomi had hung onto Gabriel's letters after she had married Mr Reed. Would Mr Reed call it fair enough? Did he even know of the letters? Were they the deepest secret of Naomi's heart?

If only her letter had said, *These mean nothing to me now. I love my husband.* If only she had fed them into the fire.

Did she still love Gabriel? Had she returned his letters to reignite his old love? Tormented lovers, doomed to live their lives apart, yet joined for ever in spirit.

She pushed back her chair. 'That tea will be stewed by now.'

'Wait.'

His hand was on her arm, but she didn't turn round. Then she thought better of it and faced him.

'It's a shock for me to receive them,' he said softly, 'and it's upset you too.'

'I'm fine, honestly. I've been engaged before as well, remember. I'm fine.'

Her heart counted the moments while he looked at her. He nodded. 'If you say so.'

She did say so. She didn't believe it, but she did say so.

She headed upstairs. Halfway up, she swung round and came down again. Gabriel looked up from the letters.

'Auntie Enid and Grandma Beattie tried to make me say you're second-best. Oh, they've accepted that we're a couple and our future lies with one another, and they said all sorts of kind things, but they tried to make me say you're second-best to Ben and he was my real love. They weren't as blunt as that, but I could tell. They wanted Ben to be more important than you and they wanted to hear me say it, but I wouldn't. Even though I love them both to bits and I'm grateful for everything they've done for me, I wouldn't say it. Even though it would have given them something unspeakably precious to cling to, I still wouldn't say it – because it's not true.'

'Belinda—'

'When I was young, when I met Ben, at that time in my life, he was all the world to me. If he'd lived, we'd have spent our lives together; but he didn't. He's gone and I'm still here. Now, at this time in my life, I have you and you are my world; and no matter how much I loved Ben, you are not second-best.'

A frown clouded his hazel eyes. 'I never imagined I was.'

'I don't want to be second-best either. I know I've got no business getting in a frap about your old engagement, but I have, and there it is. My old engagement is over and done with, because Ben died, but yours...'

'Naomi is married to another man. That's just as over and done with, in its own way.'

She caught her breath. It was the worst thing he could have said. Her hand went to the base of her throat, where a pulse beat wildly.

'You still love her. You've remembered your feelings for her.'

'What? No. Why would you think that?'

Panic stilled, replaced by a horrible calm. 'Ben died and I was heartbroken, but I learned to live with it and in the end, I recovered. I lived through all that – but you haven't lived through it. You didn't even remember she existed before that day in the magistrate's room.'

'It was the weirdest thing, meeting her and having no memory of her. Seeing her didn't stir up old feelings.'

'But you must remember those feelings now.'

'Yes, I do. I was deeply in love with her, but it's just a memory, the way your love for Ben is a memory.'

How could she make him understand? 'My memories are from all that time ago and they've been part of me ever since. Your memories have suddenly been dumped on you; they're vivid and brand new.'

'Yes, they are – don't turn away.' He seized her hands. 'Remembering everything – and I mean, everything, not just Naomi – is extraordinary. Dr Jennings told me that if my memory returned, it could be an overwhelming experience, but do you know what has stopped its being overwhelming? You have; you and this shop. You and my inheritance made me feel I have a place in the world. You made it possible for me to see a future for myself, even though I didn't have a past.'

He raised one of her hands to his lips, his eyes on hers as he brushed a kiss against her knuckles.

'And that was before I knew you cared for me. Now that I know how you feel, I have everything I need, even though I'm about to lose this shop.'

'What about Naomi?'

'If you're asking, are you second-best, the answer is no, a thousand times no. My feelings for Naomi are remembered feelings, not emotions I'm experiencing now. More than anything, they sadden me, because of what she must have gone through. I ask myself if she loves her husband, but even if she doesn't, even if she had never married him and came to me now as the fiancée I left behind, I wouldn't be able to marry her, because the only girl in the whole world I want to marry is standing here in front of me right now.'

'Do you mean that?' she whispered.

'With all my heart.'

Letting go of her hands, he delved in his pocket and brought out a ring box. Her thoughts scattered, then rushed back and focused on this precious moment.

'Cousin Irene gave me this at the end of the court day. It was my mother's engagement ring.' He opened the box to reveal a gold ring set with a row of five dainty pearls. 'My mother loved pearls. If you'd prefer to have a brand-new ring, I'll understand, but it would mean a lot to me if you would wear this. Will you? Would you mind?'

'I'd be honoured.'

He took the ring, slipping the box into his pocket. He didn't need to reach for her hand, because she gave it to him so quickly. He held the ring at the tip of her wedding finger.

'You may not be my first love, Belinda Layton, but I promise you that you will be my lasting love.'

Her heart swelled with love and confidence as he slid his mother's ring, now her ring, along her finger.

Acknowledgements

I should like to express my thanks to:

My agent, Laura Longrigg, who loved the idea of a story about surplus girls.

The team at Corvus for making me welcome, especially my editors, Susannah Hamilton and Poppy Mostyn-Owen.

Maddie Please and Jane Ayres, for generously taking more photos than you can shake a stick at, when I needed a new author photo.

Jen Gilroy, who is always there when I need it; and Kev, my tech elf, who is always there when my computer needs it.

The LLs, for making the world of writing a better place: Maddie and Jane, Kirsten Hesketh, Karen Coles, Christina Banach, Catherine Boardman, Chris Manby and Vanessa Rigg.